PRAISE FOR
THE INNKEEPER'S DAUGHTER

W9-AWZ-876

"More than a breathless romance, *The Innkeeper's Daughter* is an intriguing mystery that will keep you riveted until the very end. Well-written and well-researched, the plot had more twists and turns than a mouse's maze, but it was the cast of fascinating characters that drew me in, along with a romance that made me sigh and left me wanting more. I can't say enough good things about this book. Read it. You won't be disappointed."

–MaryLu Tyndall, award-winning author of
the Legacy of the King's Pirates series

"Griep creates characters that haunt my dreams, even my waking moments. She is a master craftsman, creating characters that feel like living, breathing beings who deserve a happy ending."

–Elizabeth Ludwig, author of *Tide and Tempest*

"A beautiful tale of God's provision and grace in the middle of dire circumstances, woven through with a ribbon of romance. With the usual Griep mix of quirky characters, lyrical turns of phrase, heart-stopping adventure, and soul-gripping insight, this story will not disappoint!"

–Shannon McNear, author of RITA® nominee *Defending Truth*,
a novella from *A Pioneer Christmas Collection*

"Michelle Griep populates her books with enticing characters, and *The Innkeeper's Daughter* has some of her best. Johanna, beleaguered by debts and deadbeat lodgers like Nutbrown. Alex, an undercover Bow Street Runner, who is hunky and swoon-worthy. Throw them together with smugglers and you have the perfect read that should come with a warning: Will keep you up turning pages!"

–Ane Mulligan, award-winning author of
the Chapel Springs series

"Once again Michelle Griep brings us a stirring Regency novel with just the right blend of suspense, romance, and redemption. Johanna's desperate situation captured me from the opening scene, and I was equally intrigued by Alex's mission to go undercover and capture a traitor to the Crown. Readers who are looking for an English historical romance with page-turning intrigue will enjoy *The Innkeeper's Daughter*."

—Carrie Turansky, award-winning author of
Across the Blue and *Shine Like the Dawn*

"Every character in this romantic Regency suspense comes alive immediately upon introduction, drawing us into nineteenth-century England from the very first page. The well-crafted writing is a repast for the mind and spirit with sweet and savory turns of plot and phrases. *The Innkeeper's Daughter* confirms what other history-loving readers and I already knew: Michelle Griep is a master of the ensemble cast."

—Sandra Byrd, author of *A Lady in Disguise*

"*The Innkeeper's Daughter* is a meticulously researched, can't-turn-the-pages-fast-enough tale of well-written intrigue—and the love story. . .ah, the love story! You won't want to miss Johanna and Alex's complicated road to happiness, and revisiting the wonderful characters of *Brentwood's Ward* is a delightful bonus. Michelle Griep is a gifted force in the world of cloak-and-dagger Regency romance."

—Erica Vetsch, award-winning author of
My Heart Belongs in Fort Bliss, Texas

"Full of intrigue and romance, *The Innkeeper's Daughter* is a fresh and captivating Regency novel. With witty dialogue, colorful characters, and pulse-hammering suspense, Michelle Griep keeps the reader guessing until the very end."

—Sarah E. Ladd, bestselling author of *A Stranger at Fellsworth*

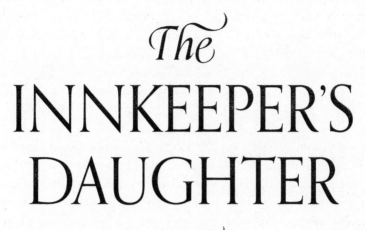

The
INNKEEPER'S
DAUGHTER

a novel

MICHELLE GRIEP

SHILOH RUN PRESS
An Imprint of Barbour Publishing, Inc.

© 2018 by Michelle Griep

Print ISBN 978-1-68322-435-8

eBook Editions:
Adobe Digital Edition (.epub) 978-1-68322-437-2
Kindle and MobiPocket Edition (.prc) 978-1-68322-436-5

All rights reserved. No part of this publication may be reproduced or transmitted for commercial purposes, except for brief quotations in printed reviews, without written permission of the publisher.

This book is a work of fiction. Names, characters, places, and incidents are either products of the author's imagination or used fictitiously. Any similarity to actual people, organizations, and/or events is purely coincidental.

Cover Design: Kirk DouPonce, DogEared Design

Published by Shiloh Run Press, an imprint of Barbour Publishing, Inc., 1810 Barbour Drive, Uhrichsville, Ohio 44683, www.shilohrunpress.com

Our mission is to inspire the world with the life-changing message of the Bible.

ecpa Member of the
Evangelical Christian
Publishers Association

Printed in the United States of America.

DEDICATION

Jennifer Pérez Díaz, a beautiful friend and aspiring writer,
and to all the other hopeful novelists out there
yearning to be published.
Keep writing—your day will come.

And as always, to the Keeper of my soul.
I shall keep believing—for my day will come, as it will for us all.

CHAPTER ONE

Dover, England, 1808

Numbers would be the death of Johanna Langley.

Three hours of sleep after a night of endless—or more like hopeless—bookkeeping. Two days to pay the miller before he cut off their flour supply. And only one week remained until the Blue Hedge Inn would be forced to close its doors forever.

Numbers, indeed. Horrid little things.

A frown etched deep into Johanna's face as she descended the last stair into the taproom. Stifling a yawn, she scanned the inn's public room, counting on collaring their lone boarder, Lucius Nutbrown. His payment would at least stave off the miller. Six empty tables and twelve unoccupied benches stared back. Must all the odds be stacked against her?

To her right, through the kitchen door, an ear-shattering crash assaulted the silence, followed by a mournful "Oh no!"

Johanna dashed toward the sound, heart pounding. *Dear God, not another accident!*

She sailed through the door and skidded to a stop just before her skirt hem swished into a pool of navy beans and water. Across from her, Mam eyed the flagstone floor, one hand pressed against her mouth, the other holding the table edge.

Johanna sidestepped the mess. "You all right, Mam?"

Smoothing her palms along her apron, her mother nodded. "Aye. That crock were a mite heavier than I credited."

"As long as you're not hurt. You're not, are you?" She studied her mother's face for a giveaway twitch in her poor eye. Unlike her father—God rest his soul—her mother would make a lacking card shark.

"I'm fine. Truly." A weak smile lifted the right side of Mam's mouth.

With no accompanying twitch.

Johanna let out a breath and grabbed a broom from the corner. First, she'd tackle scooping up the beans and earthenware shards, then mop the water.

"Where is Cook?" Johanna asked while she worked. "Why did you not let her carry such a load?"

"Ana's gone, child. I let her go this morning."

The words were as vexing a sound as the bits of stoneware scraping across the floor. Though her mother's declaration was not a surprise, that didn't make it any easier to accept. A sigh welled in her throat. She swept it down with as much force as she wielded on the broom. Sighing, wishing, hoping. . . none of it would bring Ana back.

She reached for the dustpan. "I suppose we'll have to forego the plum pudding this year then, too, eh?"

"Pish! Oak Apple Day without plum pudding?" Mam snatched the dustpan from her hands, then bent in front of the crockery pile. "You might as well hang a CLOSED shingle on the front door right now. What's next. . .leaving off the garland and missing the prayer service as well?"

"Of course not." Setting the broom aside, Johanna grabbed Mam's hands in both of hers and pulled her to her feet. "God's seen us through worse, has He not?"

"Aye, child. That He has." For an instant, the lines on her mother's face softened, then just as quickly, reknit themselves into knots. "Still—"

"No still about it. If we fail to trust in His provision, what kind of faith is that?"

"Aah, my sweet girl. . .you are a rare one, you are."

The look of love shining in Mam's good eye squeezed Jo's heart. She'd smile, if she could remember how, but she didn't have to. Boyish laughter from outside the kitchen window cut into the tender moment.

Thomas!

Johanna flew out the back door and raced around the corner of the inn. Boys scattered like startled chickens, leaving only one to face her in the settling dust.

Folding her arms, she tried to remember that Thomas's wide eyes and spray of freckles made him appear more innocent than he really was.

"What are you doing here?" she asked. "You should've been down to the docks long ago. If Mr. Baggett or the Peacock's Inn boy beat you to it, and we miss out on new guests—"

"Aww, Jo." His toe scuffed a circle in the dirt. "You know I'm faster 'an them. 'Sides, the ferry's not due in for at least another hour."

"Even so, if you're not the first to persuade those arrivals to stay at our inn, I fear we won't..." She paused and craned her neck one way then another to see behind the boy's back. Her brother shifted with her movement—a crazy dance, and a guilty one at that. "What are you hiding? Let's see those hands."

His shoulders stiffened. Times like this broke her heart afresh with longing for her father. As much as she needed him, how much more did the young boy in front of her?

She popped her hands onto her hips and stared him down. "Now, young man."

A sigh lifted his chest. Slowly—any slower and she'd wonder if it physically pained him—one arm stretched out, then the other. When his fingers unfolded, crude wooden dice and several coins sat atop his palms.

"Thomas Elliot Langley!"

"Well I won, din't I?" He cocked his head at a rakish angle, his freckles riding the crest of a wicked smirk. "And against Wiley Hawk and his band, no less. Pretty good, eh Sis?"

"You were gambling?" The word filled her mouth like a rancid bit of meat. Sickened, she pressed a hand to her stomach. "Oh, Thomas, how could you? You, of all people, know the evils of such a pastime."

"We were just playing. That's not gambling." A scowl darkened his face, matching the low-lying blanket of grey clouds overhead. "It's fun. Something you wouldn't know anything about."

"What I know is that gamblers are never to be trusted. And worse, you lied about it. Is that the sort of reputation you want spread from one end of Dover to the other? Thomas Langley, the liar? What will Mam say? What do you think this will do to her?"

His toe scrubbed the dirt once again. What had been a scowl morphed into a grimace. "Don't tell Mam, Jo. Please don't."

Was that glistening in his eyes authentic? Hard to say—and even harder to remain cross with his quivering lip and thin shoulders slumping like an old man's.

"Very well." She stretched out her palm. "Hand over that ill-gotten gain, and we'll keep this between ourselves."

With a sly grin, he sprinted off, bits of gravel spraying up from his feet.

As he raced, he yelled over his shoulder, "Sorry, Jo! I've a ferry to meet."

Picking up her skirts, she dashed after him, then lessened her pace as she neared the main road. What would people think of her, chasing her scamp of a brother? She'd never catch him anyway. Oh, what a day this was turning out to be.

She slowed, then stopped, her eyes narrowing. Was that a flash of yellow-stockinged legs dangling over the inn's front-door awning? She flattened against the wall and watched.

A loosened shingle smacked onto the ground ahead of her, followed by the thunk of two feet. So that's how Lucius Nutbrown snuck in and out without her knowing.

Girding herself mentally for a conversation that was sure to be ridiculous, Johanna pushed from the wall. "Mr. Nutbrown, a word, if you please."

For an instant, his body stiffened into a ramrod. Then he turned, the creases around his mouth settling into a smug line. For a man so lean, how he managed to gather such extra skin on his face was a wonder. When he reached into an inner pocket of his dress coat, Johanna rolled her eyes. Indeed. This would be ridiculous.

Nutbrown's hand emerged, covered with a raggedy court-jester puppet, which he promptly held out front and center. "Sorry, Miss Langley." The puppet's head bobbed side to side, the man's falsetto voice as crazed as the movement. "Mr. Nutbrown is late to an appointment. He shall attend you later this evening. Good day."

Nutbrown pivoted, the tails of his coat swinging wide. Did he seriously think she'd let him off that easily?

Heedless of who might be watching, she darted ahead and stopped directly in his path. "I'm afraid not, sir. This cannot wait."

His brows pulled together, drawing a dark streak above his eyes, yet he shoved the jester forward. "Very well, miss. But make it quick."

"Please, put away your puppet, sir. It gains you nothing." She extended her hand. "Pay up your room and board for the past fortnight, and I shall have nothing more to say."

The jester's head plummeted, his plaster nose pecking her palm.

She yanked back her hand. "Mr. Nutbrown! Really! I should hate to bring the magistrate in on this, but if I must—"

"No." Nutbrown's hands shot up as if she'd aimed a Brown Bess at his chest, the crazy puppet waving like a banner overhead. In three long-legged strides, he sidestepped her, lowering the puppet out at arm's length. "By week's end, Miss Langley, you shall be paid in full. You have Mr. Nutbrown's word on it."

The puppet disappeared into his coat, and Nutbrown scurried down the street.

Wonderful. The word of a jester made of cloth and papier-mâché, and the clown who wore it upon his hand. Yet he was their sole source of income unless she could pry those coins from Thomas's fingers, which wasn't likely. Bending, she gathered up the dry-rotted chunks of broken shingle and frowned. Her world was falling apart as tangibly as the inn—the place she loved most. The home she and Thomas and Mam must leave if they didn't come up with the rent payment by the end of next month.

Holding tightly to the shingle remnant, she closed her eyes. At the moment, her faith felt as crumbly as the wood—which was always the best time to pray.

"Please God, provide a way. Fill the inn. . .and soon."

∞

London

Knuckles hovering to strike, Officer Alexander Moore slid his gaze once more to the left. It paid to think before pounding away, be it in a street brawl or—as in this case—on a door. A tarnished brass relief of the number seven hung at an angle, as if no one had given the slightest thought before nailing up the house number. Considering the man who supposedly lived here, the haphazard detail stayed his hand a second more. Had he written down the magistrate's address incorrectly?

Only one way to find out.

He pounded thrice, then stepped back, ready for anything. Behind him, hackney wheels ground over cobbles, grating a layer off his already thin nerves. Magistrate Ford never—*ever*—invited guests over for dinner. So why him? Why now?

Hinges screeched an angry welcome as the door opened. Lantern light spilled over the pinched face of a tall man shrouded in a dark dress coat, dark waistcoat, and darker pants. Rounding out the theme was a single-looped cravat, black as a crypt, choking the fellow's neck. A ghoul could not have been garbed more effectively. The man didn't say a thing, but even without words, Alex got the distinct impression he read, condensed, and filed away every possible facet of him in a glance—from shoe size to propensity for warmed sherry.

And Alex didn't like it one bit. That kind of intelligence gathering was supposed to be his specialty.

"My apologies. I must have the wrong address." Alex nodded a valediction, careful to keep a wary eye on the figure from the dead. "Good evening."

"Step this way, Officer Moore." The fellow set off without looking to see that Alex complied, nor even that the door was shut or locked. The magistrate would never abide such ineptitude down at Bow Street. Surely this was a ploy, or perhaps some kind of test of his wit.

Aah. A test? A slow smile lifted half his mouth.

With a grip on the hilt of his dagger, he unsheathed the blade and withdrew it from inside his great coat. Crossing the threshold, he left the door wide should a quick escape become necessary and trailed the disappearing lantern down a hall as lean as the man he followed.

At the end of the corridor, the grim reaper tapped twice on a closed door, then pushed it open without waiting for a response. The brilliance of the room reached out and pulled Alex forward. He entered a grand dining hall, incongruous in size and opulence with the street view of the ramshackle building. Crystal wall sconces and an overhead chandelier glittered light from one mirrored panel to another. A thick Turkish rug sank beneath his steps. The place was fit to house a peer of the realm, not a law keeper who served out gritty justice to the malefactors of London.

Directly across from him stood Bow Street Magistrate, Sir Richard Ford, stationed at the farther end of a polished table. Ford snapped shut a pocket watch and tucked it inside his waistcoat, then skewered him with a piercing gaze. "Prompt as always, eh Moore?"

"I try, sir."

Flipping out his coattails, Ford sat, then shook out a folded linen napkin and covered his lap. "Put that weapon away and have a seat. I invited you to dinner, not a skirmish."

The butler stepped forward, offering his arm to collect Alex's coat.

Alex sheathed his knife, then shrugged out of his woolen cloak and handed it over with a whispered warning. "You might want to shut that front door."

Across the long table, Ford chuckled. "Your concern for Underhill is admirable, but quite unnecessary. Though my butler's appearance leaves much to be desired, his service is impeccable. As for the door, by now it's not only sealed but would take a two-ton battering ram to break it in."

Sinking into the chair, Alex cocked a brow.

"You doubt me?" Ford's question dangled like a noose.

"Never, sir. Just curious, is all. Seemed a simple enough slab of oak."

"Oak, yes. Well, mostly. As for simple?" Ford shook his head. "Pulleys, gears, a generous portion of iron reinforcement. Try putting in a monstrosity like that without attracting attention from one end of the neighborhood to the other."

The magistrate paused to ring a small silver bell sitting next to his plate. Before the last of the short chime cleared the air, a housemaid entered with a tray.

Ford ignored her as she set a steaming bowl in front him. "I suppose you're wondering why I asked you here."

Only a thousand times. The retort lay dormant on his tongue. To admit he'd anguished over this meeting would show weakness—a trait he'd vowed never again to embrace. He followed the sleek movement of the girl as she placed his bouillon on the table, then returned his gaze to the magistrate. "The thought crossed my mind that, perhaps, I was to be the main course."

A thin smile stretched the magistrate's lips. "Not that you don't deserve to be after your unorthodox capture of Ned Dooley."

And there it was. What this entire charade was about. Alex leaned forward, bumping the table and rippling the wine in his glass. "Regardless of how it was accomplished, sir, Dooley's conviction ended that smuggling ring, saving countless lives, not to mention the expense spared to the Crown. How you can possibly say—"

Ford's hand shot up, cutting off further comment. "You already know my thoughts on the matter. I daresay neither of us will sway the other's opinion, so let us officially consider this topic closed to discussion. There is a much larger scheme prompting this meeting."

"Must be spectacular." Alex sank back in his chair. "Inviting me here is a singular event. As far as I know, not a runner has ever uncovered where you live, and though I begged you time and again as a lad, you never relented."

"Indeed. Sometimes extreme measures are necessary." Ford shooed away the serving girl with a flick of his fingers, then sat motionless until she disappeared through a hidden panel in the wall. He took a moment to sample his soup. "I would like you to go incognito for a while."

Taking the magistrate's lead, Alex picked up his spoon and downed several mouthfuls of his broth, tasting nothing. Something was not right about the magistrate's request. Ford could've asked him the same thing in his office without the pretense of dinner. In fact, he could've asked any number of other officers or—suddenly understanding dawned bright and clear.

He shoved back his chair. "With all due respect, I've hardly forgotten the assignment you handed Brentwood last year. Am I the only available officer for you to proposition?"

The more he thought of Nicholas Brentwood's previous mission, the hotter his blood ran. He'd sooner quit than be saddled with the care of a spoiled rich girl, as had his friend—even though it turned out well in the end.

Rising, he frowned at the napkin as it fell to the carpet. Let the impeccable butler pick it up. In fact, let Underhill have the assignment. "My thanks for your hospitality, sir, but if that is the case, my answer is no. A firm and emphatic no."

"Alexander, wait."

Ford's tone—or was it the use of his Christian name?—slid over his shoulders like a straight-coat, pinning him in place. Suddenly he was ten years old again, compelled to do his guardian's bidding.

"You," the magistrate continued, "are my first and only choice for this position. This assignment is nothing like Brentwood's. Anyone can be a guardian, but only someone with specialized training may fill the role I'm looking for. All I ask is that you hear me out. You owe me at least that after keeping your hind end out of trouble the past decade and a half."

The few sips of soup, the glittery sparkle of the room, the pleading in Ford's voice combined into a wave of nausea that sank to the pit of his gut. He was indebted to Ford, more than he could ever pay back. Had not the man taken him in as a ten-year-old orphan, he'd have perished on the streets. . .or become like the criminals he hauled in. He sagged into the chair like a rheumy old man and locked eyes with his benefactor and superior. "All right. Let's hear it then."

Sconce light glimmered in Ford's eyes. "You will pose as a gambling rogue to ferret out a suspected traitor. A dangerous, highly connected traitor."

"Traitors instead of smugglers, eh?" He chewed on that for a moment.

"Might be a nice change of pace."

"Nice? Hardly." Ford downed another mouthful of soup, then pushed the bowl away and stood, his gaze unwavering. "You should know that once I've told you the details of this particular mission, I will deny ever having said anything about it. And if this operation fails, I shall refute any knowledge of this conversation, to the point of watching you swing from a gibbet if necessary."

Denial? This was new. The danger in the magistrate's proposal crept down Alex's backbone. He straightened his shoulders, counteracting the eerie feeling. "Then, as always, I shall make it a point not to fail. Go on."

Ford grunted as he strolled to a narrow trestle table. He pounded twice on the top then twisted a knob on the middle drawer. Below the table, about knee height, a hidden panel in the wall slid open. Bending, the magistrate retrieved a leather pouch. By the time he crossed over to Alex, the wall looked as solid as ever.

The bag thwunked onto the table with a crashing jingle. By the sound, he didn't have to open the drawstring to know it wasn't a bag of measly farthings sitting next to his plate.

"As you can see, you are now a wealthy man, Mr. Morton."

Alex's gaze shot from the bag to the magistrate. "Mor. . .ton?"

"You heard correctly. From now on, you are no longer a Moore, but a Morton, less chance of a slip up if your alias is a close cousin to your true surname. You are a dealer in fine wines, a buyer and seller for your father." Ford reached inside his waistcoat and withdrew a sealed envelope, the new pseudonym engraved in gold on the front. "This coming Saturday, you shall attend the finest Oak Apple Day soiree Dover has to offer."

"Dover? I can't possibly go back there. My face is known."

"True. A detriment, that. Yet you shall travel in a higher echelon of society this time. This invitation"—he handed over the envelope—"is your ticket into the estate of the Viscount Lord Coburn. How you maintain connection afterwards is your affair, which I am sure will be no problem for you. Nor do I want to know how you operate. In truth, until you discover who is involved in this mess, I give you full and free rein."

Alex's brows lifted. Free rein? This *was* some scheme, and an enticing one at that, even though he'd left behind a few enemies in that part of the country—enemies whose anger likely still festered. Returning to Dover now might be a death warrant.

He slugged back a drink of claret, the challenge of it all leaving a bitter-sweet aftertaste. Setting down the glass, he gazed at the magistrate. "What exactly is this mess, sir?"

Ford's mouth hardened into a grim line. "Someone's been communicating with the French. I'm not at liberty to say how I know. Merely that I know is enough. To what extent military intelligence has been shared, and for what purpose, is up to you to find out. There is a traitor in our midst, and I want him brought to me at any cost. The MP funding this mission has deep pockets. Survive this assignment and you'll be able to retire from the force—in style."

Alex blew out a long, low breath. He'd purposely distanced himself from anything smacking of French intrigue or the military. The London streets were what he knew best.

But how could he refuse Ford's earnest gaze bearing down on him? If it weren't for the magistrate, he'd most likely be moldering in a pauper's grave by now. And retirement at his age? Other than his life, what did he have to lose? He raked a hand through his hair. "Very well, but what if I should need backup?"

"Officer Thatcher will be your only means of communication with me, though he, too, will be under strict instruction to deny you should your true identity become discovered. You'll both be under a vow of secrecy, sharing information between yourselves and me alone. No one else. Do you swear it?"

A queer chill shivered across his shoulders. This was quite an affair, for he'd never been asked to pledge such a vow before. He shoved down the foreboding quaver and lifted his chin. "Yes, I swear it."

"Good. Then Thatcher will check in with you regularly."

"What does that mean?"

"Whatever you want it to." Ford walked the length of the table and reclaimed his seat, leaving his cryptic answer floating on the air.

But gnawing upon a bone was a trait Alex had perfected. "Where shall I connect with Thatcher, or rather, he with me?"

Amusement lifted one side of Ford's mouth. "You will station yourself at the Blue Hedge Inn."

A groan ripped from his throat. "You're jesting."

Ford quirked a brow. "I take it you are familiar with the establishment?"

Alex pressed his lips tight before harsh words escaped. No longer hungry, he pushed away his bowl of soup. The Blue Hedge Inn.

He'd rather sleep in a pig wallow than that dilapidated hovel.

CHAPTER TWO

The driver tossed down Alexander's bag from the roof of the coach. With a grunt, Alex caught it before the canvas hit the cobblestones, then turned to face the Rose Inn—the last stop on the London-to-Dover run. Sunlight glinted off two banks of windows draped with oak leaf bunting. Deep red bricks, too new to be coated over with soot, contrasted with the green foliage. The building stood like a proud soldier, pinned with honorary banners for the upcoming Oak Apple festivities. A patron exited the front door, patting his belly with a smile and a sigh, the aroma of freshly baked bread and sweet cider wafting out with him.

Alex's mouth pulled into a scowl. Was it too much to ask for lodging such as this if his life was to be on the line? Apparently, yes, though he'd done his best to talk Ford into changing his mind through the remainder of last Monday's dinner.

Turning, he stalked down New Street, then headed south on Canon. As he travelled from city center toward the outskirts, buildings cowered in the shadow of the old castle on Tower Hill. But even here, sporadic vendors had already set up their wares for the upcoming holiday. Across the road, one hawker claimed his oils and tinctures cured everything from gout to gluttony. To his side, cinnamon-spiced nuts roasted over an open fire. Ahead, a gamer ran a coconut shell scam, promising a cash prize for anyone who could pick out the shell with a pea hidden beneath.

In front of that booth, a scrawny-limbed lad jammed his hands into his pockets, then turned and began shuffling away. Behind the boy, a wicked grin slashed the face of the gamer. Alex clenched his jaw. It didn't take a Bow Street officer to figure out the low-life had stolen the boy's last farthing.

"You, boy!" Alex waited until the lad cast a glance over his shoulder. "I'm looking for a strong arm to carry my bag."

The boy's steps slowed, not completely, but enough that he turned and faced him, walking backward. "Ye willing to pay?"

Alex paused in front of the gamer's booth. "Aye."

The boy stopped. The gamer leaned forward. Alex smirked. With one word, he'd purchased their attention. A few more, and he'd own them. "I've a coin or two I can part with."

Immediately, the gamer threw his shells into the air, juggling them into a merry circle. "Step right up! Try yer luck! Are you smarter than a coconut?"

It was hard not to groan at the poor verse, nor smile at the boy as he ran back and tugged his sleeve. "I'm your lad, sir. Thomas is me name. Where we going?"

The gamer shouted louder, adding the pea into his juggling mix.

Shrugging the bag off his shoulder, Alex handed it to Thomas, then nodded sideways toward the gamer. "First stop is right here."

The boy's face paled. "I don't recommend that, sir."

"While I appreciate your advice, the truth is," he squatted nose-to-nose with the lad, "I *am* smarter than a coconut."

Thomas shook his head, the gravity of his puckered brow adding years to his youth. "That's what I thought, too, sir. But I were sure wrong."

Righteous anger curled Alex's fingers into a tight fist. *Vengeance is the Lord's* he reminded himself, but it still took a conscious effort to keep the grin fixed to his face. "Perhaps, boy, it wasn't the coconut you were competing against."

The lad's nose scrunched, bunching his spray of freckles into a clump.

Resisting the urge to laugh, Alex rose and stepped up to the booth. He reached into his pocket, pulled out a penny, and slapped it down on the plank separating him from the gamer. "I'll give it a go."

"Very good, sir. Very good." One by one the coconuts collected onto the gamer's open palms, the pea being the last to land. Above his bony wrists, the hems of the man's sleeves were threadbare, more so than the rest of his dress coat. If nothing else, the gamer knew his trade. Given the chance, Alex had no doubt the fellow could hide an entire pianoforte up that sleeve, and by the appearance of it, perhaps he had a time or two.

"Let's see if ol' fate smiles on you, eh sir?" With much swirling and swooping, the man made a great show of arranging the shells into a neat row in front of Alex. He lifted the middle coconut, then set the pea beneath it. "All ye gots to do, sir, is watch carefully."

Thomas planted his feet beside him, pleading with wide eyes. "Ye won't win, sir. He's good, he is. It's not too late to take yer coin back."

Before Alex could yield to the boy's warning, the gamer snapped into action, sliding shells one way and another, even tapping and clacking their edges now and then. Thomas leaned closer, his gaze fixed on the man's hands. Alex ignored the showman's flourishing fingers and instead studied his eyes. The content of a man's soul could be summed up in a blink—or lack of one. Snakes never blinked.

Neither did the gamer.

"There you have it." The man swept one hand back and forth over the top of the shells. "Which one hides the pea? Say the word, and if ye're right, you'll walk away with a jingle in yer pocket."

Alex looked down at Thomas and cocked a brow. The boy bit his lip then edged one finger up to point at the farthest coconut.

"Are you certain?" he asked.

"Aye, sir. This time I know I'm right."

"Well then, I choose. . ." Alex slanted his gaze back to the gamer, whose hand hovered over the far shell.

"This one." He shot his arm across the plank and grabbed the gamer's other wrist. The man screeched like a little girl, but to his credit, he didn't open his hand. Alex squeezed harder, grinding the man's bones to within a hair's breadth of snapping. Tears leaked out the gamer's eyes, and finally, his fingers sprung wide.

There sat the pea.

Thomas flipped open each of the shells. All were empty. "Dash it! You're a flamin' cheater! Gimme back my money!"

"It's the way of the game, that's all." The gamer plied and pried and tried to wriggle free of Alex's death grip. "Let me go!"

"Be a shame to break these delicate bones. Why, you'd be out of commission for all of the Oak Apple Day festivities. Yes, sir"—Alex dug his fingers in deeper and leaned closer—"a shame too, if we spread word about how your little game is played, hmm?"

The gamer's face turned an ugly shade of purple. "All right! All right! I'll give the street-rat back his money."

Alex let go. The gamer recoiled, rubbing his wrist and whimpering on the exhale. Alex folded his arms, waiting until the fellow handed over not only Thomas's farthing, but his own coin as well.

Snubbing the man behind the booth, Thomas flashed Alex a smile, wide with teeth he'd not yet grown into. "Thank ye, sir."

Alex couldn't help but mirror the boy's grin. "My pleasure, lad. Shall we?" He nodded down Canon Street, then waited for Thomas to tuck away his money and heft the canvas bag over his shoulder.

The boy fell into step beside him, two paces to his one. His words flew just as fast as his legs. "That were something. That's what. Why, ye needn't pay me nothin' fer carryin' yer bag, sir. Ye got me my coin back and all. Oh, and you must stay at the inn my family runs. Ye'll be treated like a king. Leastwise by me. Don't know 'bout my sister. I stay out of her way, mostly."

"Oh?" Alex continued at the intersection, though his feet itched to turn southward. The Maiden's Head was halfway down that street—the last of the reputable inns on this side of town. Blowing out a long breath, he glanced down at the boy. "Why is that, I wonder? Is your sister such a shrew?"

"She's all right, I guess. It's just that, well. . ." The boy's toe hit a rock and sent it skipping ahead. "She's such a girl, sir. Makes big to-do's outta nothin'. It's no wonder she's not married."

An undertaker's tone couldn't have been more solemn. Alex bit back a laugh. "Can your father not manage her?"

"Father's dead and gone, sir."

"Sorry to hear that." He studied the boy out of the corner of his eye. Honest emotion rarely met a full-faced stare.

"It's not bad as all that, sir. Never knowed him. He died a'fore I was born." Catching up to the rock, the boy kicked it again, displaying no grief whatsoever.

"About this sister of yours," Alex paused as the boy veered around a corner. How on earth could the lad know he'd wanted to turn here? "She runs the inn herself?"

"Nah." Thomas shook his head and skipped ahead of him—quite the feat for lugging a bag Alex knew weighed at least a stone. Why would the boy speed up when he didn't know how much farther would be required of him?

"She and Mam run the inn. Well, and me too," the boy continued. "Mam can't get along without us, with her bad eye and all. Oh, this way, sir. Shortcut."

Thomas cut into an alley carved into the space between two warehouses. Looking past the lad, Alex squinted. At the far end, the shortcut spilled out onto Blue Lane. "Hold up a minute, Thomas. How is it you know exactly where I'm going?"

The boy pivoted, facing him. "Why I told ye, sir. You must stay with us. Ye'll be treated like a—"

"Yes, I know. A king. Let me venture a guess, hmm?" He closed the distance between them and once again squatted nose-to-nose with the boy. "Are you taking me to the Blue Hedge Inn?"

Thomas's mouth dropped. Awe sparked in the depths of his dark blue eyes. "How'd ye know, sir? I ne'er said the name."

An easy enough guess when that was the only remaining lodging this far from the center of town, but if the lad wanted to credit him with hero status, who was he to deny him? Reaching out a hand, Alex tussled the boy's hair and stood. "Let's be about it, then, aye?"

"Aye, sir. Only. . ." Thomas's mouth scrunched one way then the other, as if the words on his tongue tasted sour.

"Only what?" Alex prodded.

"Just that we do have one other boarder ye should know about."

"Why's that?"

Thomas kicked his toe in the dirt, averting his gaze. "Ye'll be sharing a bed with him."

Sharing a—blast! Alex's toe itched to kick more than the dirt. A dilapidated inn. A shrewish spinster running it. And now he'd be rooming with a stranger. Could anything else possibly go wrong with his stay in Dover?

Setting his boots into motion, he headed down the alley and considered pulling his knife as he turned the corner. The way this mission was beginning, who knew what he'd encounter next?

∞

Johanna frowned at the pathetic green-and-brown pile that was supposed to be a garland. It looked like a heap of ratty leaves raked atop a mound of twine scraps. Bending, she picked up one end of the garland, then stood, pressing her lips tight to keep from mumbling about her brother. If she hadn't had to do that rascal's chores, she could've created a proper swag, every bit as stunning as the one on the Hound's Tooth Inn. Yet there was nothing more to be done for the sorry-leafed trimming draped over her fingers. With the parade scheduled for tomorrow, she could ill afford to wait any longer to adorn the Blue

Hedge's facade—leastwise not if she hoped to attract holiday lodgers.

Casting a last glance up one side of Blue Lane and down the other, she gave up expecting Thomas to climb the ladder and hang the bunting. No smudge-faced boy darted about anywhere.

But neither did anyone else. The street was empty, save for a horse hitched to a cart halfway down the lane. If she acted quickly, she wouldn't be caught mounting a ladder like a hired man.

Grabbing the rail in one hand and holding tight to the garland with the other, she worked her way upward, rung to rung, then stopped at eye-level with the shingled overhang. No sense going all the way up to the roof. The awning would do just as well.

She poked the end of the bunting into a gap between the wooden shingles, then tugged it a bit to make sure it was caught snugly. Satisfied a good wind wouldn't coax it loose—though there was no telling if Lucius Nutbrown's foot might not snag it if he made another escape through the front window—she pulled up slack from the coil on the ground, then searched for another gap, and. . .there. To her right. A bit farther than she'd like, still, she might be able to reach it if she leaned far enough.

Or she might fall and crack her skull.

Narrowing her eyes, she gauged the distance. Moving the ladder each time she wanted to secure the garland would only add extra effort and take more time. The lane was empty now, but that didn't mean it would stay that way. Nothing to be done for it, then.

Wrapping her fingers tight around the ladder, she stretched her arm toward the crevice. So close! But not enough to wedge the garland into the crack.

She sucked in a breath, held it, and leaned a little farther. Her fingertips brushed the breach this time. Barely. Perhaps if she stretched just a hair closer, like so, and shifted her weight the tiniest bit, then—

Wood cracked. The world tipped. Johanna flailed, fingers seeking something—anything—to grab on to. A splinter pierced her skin as wood scraped her palms. She tumbled headlong, a scream to wake the dead ripping out of her throat.

She squeezed her eyes shut, tightening every muscle for impact, and—

Landed on a pair of outstretched arms that scooped her up against a solid chest.

"Careful there, missy."

A deep voice rumbled against her ear, reminding her of an autumn day, all golden and warm. Her eyes flew open. The man holding her matched the voice perfectly. Shoulder-length hair, the color of spent leaves fallen to the ground, framed a face kissed by the sun, browned yet fair. His coat, rough against her cheek, smelled of bergamot and wood smoke, spicy but sweet. If September were flesh and blood, it would look exactly like the man holding her.

She blinked, speechless, breathless—and totally drawn in by his brilliant blue gaze.

"Miss? Are you all right?" he asked.

"I. . ." Her voice squeaked, stuck somewhere between mortified and mesmerized. She swallowed, then tried again. "I am fine. Thank you."

"Well then, let's see if your legs work better than that ladder." He bent and set her down.

Released from the safety of his arms, she wobbled, and he grabbed her elbow. La! She must look like a newborn foal.

Behind her, laughter rang out. "What a catch! You should've seen the look on your face, Jo."

A slow burn started somewhere low, her toes maybe, or her tummy, melting her embarrassment and stoking up a hot rage. She reeled about and planted her fists on her hips. "This was your chore to finish, Brother. Had you been here, I'd not have fallen."

The man stepped between them. "Don't be too hard on him, miss. The boy had his own fall from grace."

"Really?" She took the time to fold her arms and dissected her brother's wide eyes. He directed a don't-say-it sort of gaze at the man. "What have you been up to this time, Brother?"

"Filling the inn, that's what." Thomas's chest puffed out a full inch as he lifted his chin. "I got us another guest, and good thing too, or you'd have smashed your head like a—"

"Alexander Morton, at your service, miss." The man cut Thomas off with a bow, chivalrous to a degree that nearly made her smile. Her brother could learn a thing or two from this fellow.

Stuffing down her irritation, she dipped her head toward Mr. Morton. "Thank you, sir, for indeed, your service was welcome. I am grateful you stopped me from breaking any bones, though I own my pride is a little scuffed." She straightened her shoulders, physically relegating the humiliating incident to the past and resuming her role as hostess. "Welcome to the Blue Hedge Inn. My name is Johanna Langley, one of the proprietors."

"I grant this was an unconventional meeting, Miss Langley, but pleasurable, nonetheless." A rogue wink accompanied his words. "I am happy to make your acquaintance."

His smile scorched through her. Truly, she ought to be offended. So why the sudden heat warming her cheeks? She turned her face to her brother, hoping the fellow hadn't noticed. "See Mr. Morton to the south-side room, would you, Thomas?"

Her brother shook his head. "Can't."

"Why not?"

"Got us some more boarders too."

How had the boy managed to attract more lodgers in one morning than she had in a month? And why was he scrubbing his toe in the dirt? Something smelled more putrid in this than a leftover bit of limburger.

She narrowed her eyes. "How many more? When do they arrive?"

Craning his neck, he looked past her. "Right about now."

She and Mr. Morton turned in unison. He snorted. She sighed.

Coming up Blue Lane was a rickety wagon, painted red and gold, with tassels and banners and more riders than could fit inside. Two dogs played chase around the horses, and even from where she stood, Johanna cringed at the ribald singing and bawdy laughter traveling along with them.

"Oh, Thomas." She shook her head.

Desperate times called for desperate measures. . .but gypsies?

CHAPTER THREE

The closer the gaudy wagon drew to the Blue Hedge, the deeper Johanna's heart sank. From where she stood, she counted at least five adults and three children, and who knew how many more were in back. Unless this ragtag bunch of travellers paid up front, Mam would never be able to feed so many with Cook gone. What had Thomas been thinking? Filling the inn was one thing. Making it the laughingstock of Dover, quite another—and with boarders such as these, they'd scare off any prospect of respectable lodgers.

"No, not them." Her brother stepped past Mr. Morton and stretched out his arm, pointing beyond the monstrosity on wheels. "Behind 'em."

As the wagon closed in, more of the street came into view. Her gaze skimmed past the brilliant colors and landed on black and white. Beyond, six men travelled on foot, garbed in varying shades of dirt and producing the racket she'd accredited the gypsies. The scruffy fellows possessed instruments, haversacks, and—judging by the lyrics of their songs—no morals whatsoever.

Her gaze shot back to the gypsy wagon rolling by. Except for the rattle of tack and harness, and the cry of a babe from within, it was quiet. The driver tipped his head toward her then snapped the reins, moving their cart along without pretense. As it passed, a dark-haired pixy popped her head out the back, merry curtains framing the little girl's face. When her gaze met Johanna's, the girl smiled.

Johanna suppressed a frown and forced a polite nod. Compared to the ragged men behind them, singing of ale and women and something about a dog, the gypsies didn't seem so bad.

The wagon lumbered off, replaced by the six itinerant musicians. One fellow took the lead. Striding away from the group with a jaunty step, he planted himself in front of her brother, overshadowing him but not Mr.

Morton. Both men were of equal height, but this fellow was night to Mr. Morton's day. His hair was dark while Mr. Morton's was fair. His deep olive skin contrasted with Mr. Morton's golden tan. And he was lean and wiry, like an alley cat about to spring, compared to Mr. Morton's thick shoulders and broad stance.

Johanna's frown fought to surface again. What business of hers was it to notice the men's differences in the first place?

The man bowed with a flourish. "Greetings my fine, young friend, Master Thomas." He straightened then pumped the boy's hand. "You drive a hard bargain, m'boy. Yet we acquiesce to your business savvy, happy to serve and be served, aye lads?" He glanced over his shoulder and cocked a brow at the fellows behind him. All five lifted their fists into the air, hooting their agreement.

Johanna smoothed her hands along her skirt, fighting the desire to plug up her ears.

Before the whoops died down, the man slid in front of her. How could he do that? She hadn't even noticed his feet move.

His hat, and the dark curls escaping the brim, were coated with a fine layer of dust, the same color as his grey eyes. He smelled of a long day's worth of travel, meat cooked over a spit, and something more musky. Exotic. And altogether dangerous. His gaze glimmered with the knowledge of what lay beyond her world of inns and family and all that was good. The urge to turn heel and run tingled in her legs.

But his eyes held her in place. "And you must be the lovely Johanna. Your brother speaks highly of you."

The man's breach of etiquette was stunning, though expecting a travelling musician to display proper manners was just as outlandish. Still, to use her Christian name, to look her full in the face as if he'd claimed her for his own, made her feel as if she stood before all the world wearing nothing but a shift.

Next to her, Mr. Morton stepped nearer and cleared his throat. So, he'd noticed as well.

"I am Gabriel Quail, milady." The man reached for her hand and bowed over it, resting his lips atop her skin like a benediction. As he rose, he gazed at her through dark lashes, speaking something in French. His index finger rubbed little circles on the inside of her wrist.

She yanked back her hand, ashamed at the warmth where his mouth had touched.

"I don't believe Miss Langley asked for your name, sir." Mr. Morton closed the rest of the distance between them, standing so close, she remembered the feel of his arms when he'd held her. If Mr. Quail took one more liberty, she got the distinct impression Mr. Morton would pop the man in the nose.

Her own hands fisted with rising frustration toward them both. She'd avoided compromise for five and twenty years without anyone's help. She certainly knew how to handle a forward wayfarer without the assistance of a man's muscle.

"Thank you, Mr. Morton, for your concern." She shot him a sideways glance before angling her head at Quail. "You are correct, sir, that I am Thomas's sister. You may address me as Miss Langley. I am pleased to meet you, Mr. Quail, yet I advise you and your companions"—she lifted her chin and speared each man in turn with an evil eye—"that the Blue Hedge Inn is a reputable establishment. We strive to maintain a certain decorum."

Mr. Quail pressed both his hands to his heart and sank to one knee. "Be still, my heart. Be still! She's beautiful, therefore to be woo'd. She is woman, therefore to be won."

Startled, she opened her mouth, but no words came out. What could she possibly say to that?

Next to her, Mr. Morton folded his arms. "Perhaps, sir, you ought save your Shakespeare for a larger audience."

Mr. Quail's gaze lingered on hers a moment longer before he faced Mr. Morton. "And you are?"

"Not that it signifies, but I am Alexander Morton, purchaser of fine wines, and a guest here at the Blue Hedge."

"Wine, you say?" A smile slid across Mr. Quail's face. "We shall get along famously, my friend."

"I doubt it." Mr. Morton's words travelled on an exhale, too quiet for Mr. Quail to hear, but Johanna didn't miss them.

Turning to the group behind him, Mr. Quail swung up both arms as if he offered the inn for sale to a massive crowd. "Lads, we have found ourselves a home for the Oak Apple holiday. Let the revelry begin!"

More hoots and hollers filled the air as the men passed in front of her and entered the taproom. Mr. Quail followed them in, slapping Mr. Morton on the back as he strode by, leaving her and Thomas with mouths agape, and Mr. Morton with an unreadable expression.

"Well, that was. . ." Johanna nibbled her lower lip. "Interesting."

"Indeed." Mr. Morton snatched up his canvas bag where it sat forgotten near Thomas's feet. "I'll stow this and then—" He nodded toward the heap of garland hanging by one end from the awning. "We'll see about getting that bunting up for you, Miss Langley. Right, Thomas?"

Without waiting for an answer, Mr. Morton disappeared through the door, Thomas quick on his heels. Oh, no. The little urchin wouldn't get off that easily. Johanna dashed ahead and snagged the boy's collar. "Hold on, Brother. A word, if you please."

He turned, shrugging off her hand. "Aye?"

"Mr. Quail said you drove a hard bargain. What bargain did you make?"

"Just a trade. That's all."

Sighing, she bent face-to-face with him, trying to decide if he was purposely being obstinate or if his lack of elaboration was simply a bad case of ten-year-old naïveté. "Thomas, this could take us all afternoon if I must pull every bit of information out of you like a plum from a pie. But if that's what it takes, I shall."

He rolled his eyes. "You said yourself that if the Blue Hedge could only have music, a real rig-jigger of a dandy band to play for Oak Apple Eve, why, we'd have customers coming from miles around." He stood a little taller. "That's what I traded for. I got me some business savvy. Mr. Quail said so himself."

Johanna narrowed her eyes. "Please don't tell me those men in there are expecting room and board for nothing but music and merriment."

"All right." He spun toward the door.

With a long swipe of her arm, she snagged his shirttail, thankful for the first time in her life for his sloppy appearance. "All right what?"

He stalled for a moment, casting her a sly glance over his shoulder. "All right, I won't tell you." With a jerk, he pulled from her grasp and bolted through the front door of the inn. Laughter and the drone of men's voices rolled out, quieting only when the door slapped shut.

She'd sigh, but what good would it do? Just last week, she *had* wished aloud for a band to attract customers. Why did her brother have to choose that one instant to listen to her? And if he'd made such a deal with Mr. Quail, what kind of a pact had he made with Mr. Morton?

Her gaze slid upward, past the ramshackle awning with the ratty strand of oak-leaf garland hanging from one end, beyond the top window that wouldn't shut all the way and over the roof, sagging like the shoulders of an old woman. Not a cloud dotted the afternoon sky. Endless blue stretched clear up to heaven—straight to God's ear. Apparently, He'd heard her speak as clearly as Thomas had.

A slow smile moved across her lips, though she had no idea how she and Mam would provide for so many guests. "This wasn't exactly what I had in mind when I asked You to fill the inn, Lord, but thank You for listening."

∽

Descending the last step into the taproom, Alex winced at the noise, hard-pressed to decide which was worse—remaining upstairs in a room the size of a wardrobe that smelled of mushrooms, or taking his dinner amidst an off-key violin, a bodhran that could use a good tightening, and two mandolins dueling to the death. To make it worse, Gabriel Quail belted out a ballad with a voice jagged enough to weather the whitewash on the plaster.

A muscle in his neck tightened. How was it possible he missed the din of London?

To his right, a checkered blue skirt hem peeked out a door, and for a moment, his spirits lifted. Resting his eyes upon sweet Johanna Langley would take the edge off Quail's singing. His arms warmed with the memory of holding her. And when he remembered the way she'd stood up to Quail, unflinching and unapologetic, a grin lifted his lips. Had he known such a beauty was part and parcel of the Blue Hedge, he wouldn't have given Ford such a hard time.

As the rest of the skirt came into view, his grin faded. It would take two Johanna's to fill that dress. A hefty woman emerged back end first. When she turned and met his gaze, the tray in her hands teetered, and her face paled to the shade of fine parchment. Odd. He often elicited a response from the ladies—even white-haired ones such as this—but it usually involved blushing cheeks or fluttering eyelashes.

He tipped his head toward her. "Good evening, ma'am."

"Evening, sir. I'll see ye have a bowl and a mug straightaway." Above a spray of faded freckles, the woman's brown eyes—the same shade as Johanna's—brushed over him like an artist studying a model to be painted. One eye, however, lagged behind the other. Could she even see out of it?

She turned and crossed the floor to Quail's band of merrymakers. A hitch in her step caused her skirt to ride askew on her left hip—same side as the bad eye. Grey hair made a run for it out the back of her cap, right side, this time. She had trouble reaching with her left arm as well. Johanna's mother obviously had suffered an injury years ago. Perhaps it had something to do with the death of Mr. Langley. Perhaps not. Alex filed the information into a storage bin in his mind to sort through later.

In the meantime, he sank onto a bench in the corner with his back against the wall, giving him a wide-angle view of the room. It might've been a cozy inn at some point, but now the walls leaned in toward the soot-blackened ceiling, giving the impression the entire building wanted to lie down and rest.

His table was one of six and closest to the door. On the other side of the scarred oak, the wall gave way to two paneled windows. Thomas could shimmy through them, but his own shoulders would never fit. The door he'd seen the woman carry the tray through likely led to a back door. As he compiled the list of alternative exits, he traced his fingertip along a set of initials scored into the tabletop. LL. What had possessed LL to pull out a knife and leave the engraved legacy? Drunkenness? Pride? And where was LL nowadays? Behind bars, dead, or reformed?

His finger stopped. So did his breath. Those initials didn't represent one man, but many. *La ligue la liberté*, a growing group of French rebels. He'd bet his soul on it. Casting a glance about the shadowy room, he assessed for possible Leaguers in attendance, though if any were here, their backsides would most likely be warming this bench. Was that why Ford had ordered him to board at this inn?

Johanna's mother reappeared from the kitchen, striding toward him like a hunter to the prey, her dress swishing off rhythm. "Here ye be, sir."

The bowl she set before him wafted a parsnippy aroma, though considering the minute bits of vegetables floating atop the thin potage, it was surprising he smelled anything other than salty hot water. "Thank you," he said, hoping the words themselves would conjure up genuine gratitude for the lackluster meal.

A mug landed next to his bowl. Were it full, a foamy head of ale would've sloshed over the rim. As it was, he could play kick-a-pin with the wooden tankard and spill nary a drop.

"I understand you're a new arrival here at the Blue Hedge. I am Mrs. Langley, proprietor." She cocked her head to the same rakish angle he'd seen Thomas employ. "And you are?"

"Alexander Morton."

"Mor. . .ton, eh?" Her tongue lingered over his surname, her good eye narrowing. Again with the studying gaze? He'd pay a king's ransom to know what this old woman's fixation was about. Had Ford put her up to this?

She leaned closer, though she needn't have. The music had ceased. Quail and his musicians were too busy slugging back their drinks.

"I'm sorry, but from where did you say you hail?" she asked.

Shrewd. Very shrewd. A smirk begged to lift one side of his mouth. He pressed his lips tight. Was she the plant or was he? Had the magistrate ordered him to stay at this establishment in an effort to toy with him, and in the process, sharpen his vigilance?

He doled out a tidbit from his carefully constructed background. "I didn't say, but I was born and bred a Sheffield boy and am on my way home from Porto Moniz."

"Sheffield?" Her mouth folded into a frown. "Humph."

He smiled. "Is there a problem?"

Her lips parted, but it took a moment before any words came out. "None at all, sir. Forgive an old woman." She tapped a finger against her cap, easing her frown into a half-smile. "The mind is one of the first things to go, you know."

She turned, and he watched her weave her way through the taproom. Her body might be hindered, but her mind was as dodgy as a pickpocket's fingers. Maybe it would be better to avoid the woman altogether.

The front door opened silently, and a dark figure slid in on a draft of night air. Dressed head to toe in black, the man wasn't a mammoth, yet that didn't make him any less dangerous. He was solid, compact, and entirely hidden in shadow. Stealth graced his every movement. Quail and his fellows didn't turn a head amongst them as he eased the door shut behind him, but Alex instinctively reached for the blade at his side.

The cloaked figure stalked toward him. Alex wrapped his fingers around the hilt of his knife and pulled it loose. Lantern light dared an advance beneath the man's hat brim, revealing a stubbled jawline and a gaze that could make a saint flinch.

Alex slipped his blade back into the sheath. "Evening, Thatcher." He waited until the man sat opposite him. "You don't waste any time. I arrived just this afternoon."

"I know." Officer Samuel Thatcher's voice was low timbred and smooth, the kind of tone one heard while wondering why the fellow's lips had not moved.

Alex leaned back in his seat. "You always were a ghost in the shadows."

Thatcher merely stared, his dark eyes hinting at neither pleasure nor irritation.

"And a quiet ghost at that." Alex lifted his hand, hailing Mrs. Langley for a drink for his friend. Who knew how long—or hard—the man had ridden.

Thatcher pulled off his hat and pushed back the damp, dark hair on his brow, which answered that speculation. Why the breakneck pace?

Taking a mouthful of ale, Alex mulled over a few possibilities, coming up short-ended on each. "I am surprised to see you so soon. Which leads me to wonder, how often am I to expect you?"

Shrugging out of his riding cloak, Thatcher took the time to lay the garment beside him on the bench before he answered. "Depends."

"On what?"

"On when Ford has a message for you." Thatcher wrapped both hands around the mug Mrs. Langley held out for him and took a long draw before he set the cup down. "Or you have a message for Ford."

He snorted. "So tell me, how exactly does one conjure a spirit?"

While Quail's discordant music wailed, Thatcher stared at him, the kind of gaze that might raise the fine hairs at the nape of a stranger. The fellow had no idea of social norms, or polite and pleasing manners. This was simply the way he was. Inward. Intense. And altogether unnerving.

Finally Thatcher spoke. "You know the trees behind the rocks at Foxend Corner?"

Alex nodded.

"There's a hole in the base of a dead ash, east of center. Smaller of the two. I'll check it as I'm able." Thatcher drained his mug, yet he did not reach for his great coat. Clearly the man had more on his mind.

Alex folded his arms. "Ford isn't seriously expecting me to have a report for him already, is he?"

"On the contrary." Reaching into an inside pocket of his waistcoat, Thatcher pulled out an envelope and slid it across the tabletop. "He's sent a missive."

"So soon?" Strange. Ford had briefed him long into the night and well into the morning before Alex had packed his bag and set foot on the coach. Reaching for the letter, he studied the wax seal on the back. Not that he didn't trust Thatcher, and in fact would with his life, but some habits refused to die no matter the absurdity.

He scanned the first few words, his mouth slowly dropping. Pausing to blink, he reread the immaculate penmanship, then continued on. Surely not. He shifted, tilting the paper to the best advantage in the dim light. Each word sliced into his soul like an assassin's rapier. "Dash it!" He growled under his breath, anger building with each beat of his heart. "Dash it! Dash it! Dash it!"

Thatcher's dark eyes widened. "Is that your official response?"

"No. This is." He shot to his feet, balled up the paper, and lobbed it across the room into the hearth. Quail and his band turned as one in his direction, but Alex didn't sit until flames engulfed the magistrate's note.

Then he leveled a granite stare at Thatcher. "This time Ford's asked too much."

CHAPTER FOUR

Retrieving his hat from a peg on the wall, Alex clapped it atop his head, then straightened his collar. Good enough, for now. He'd fret over his appearance later this eve, when it really mattered.

Happy to leave behind the tiny bed of torture he'd shared with Lucius Nutbrown, he crossed the small chamber in three strides. Nutbrown. Gads! What a bizarre fellow. Spare of mind and fat as well. Reaching for the door, Alex bit back a wince and pressed a hand against the sore spot below his ribs. Nutbrown's elbows and knees had battered him more thoroughly than the time he'd lost a bare-knuckled brawl to Tom Cribb. Aah, but that fight with Cribb had taught him a trick or two—and so had his evening with Nutbrown.

Tonight he'd bed down on the floor.

He pulled shut the door and headed downstairs, the snores of Quail and his band distinguishable in the empty taproom. Sweet heavens! The ragtag fellows made as much racket asleep as with instruments in hand.

Stifling a yawn, he silently cursed Nutbrown and Quail for the fatigue weighing his steps—but he'd likely have laid awake the entire night anyway. He scowled as he passed by the hearth. Ford's directive taunted him from the ashes. Not that he'd never been asked to put his life on the line before, but this? He'd rather face a hundred musket barrels at point-blank range than even consider marrying a woman he'd never met. Why on earth would the magistrate order him to offer for the viscount's daughter? Thatcher better return with some good answers—or this game was over before it even began.

"Excuse me, Mr. Morton, but have you seen my brother this morning?"

The sweet voice of Johanna Langley turned him around, and all thoughts of Ford and weddings evaporated. She stood six paces from him, fresh as the late spring morning, in a blue dress that had no right to brush over her curves so mercilessly. Wisps of dark hair escaped her hairpins, sweeping across her brow in such an innocent fashion, his fingers itched to smooth it back. How soft would it feel against his skin? Like the down of a gosling or the silk of a—

"Mr. Morton?"

A slow burn worked its way up from his gut. Had she noticed his stare? Giving himself a mental shake, he replayed her original question then shot her one of his own. "The lad's slipped you again, has he?"

"Afraid so." When she frowned, a crescent-shaped dimple in her chin appeared, quite beguiling and—

Oh, no. He'd not be caught twice at the same crime. He purposely focused instead on a point just beyond her ear, giving the impression he looked at her but without the temptation to ogle her like a love-struck schoolboy. What was going on with him to skew his thinking so? Lack of breakfast, perhaps. Or lack of sleep?

That was it.

Relieved to have solved the mystery, he rolled his shoulders and returned his gaze to hers. "I am surprised to find you still here. Are you not attending the parade?"

Johanna retrieved a tipped-over mug lying forgotten on the floor. After setting it in the dish bin near the kitchen door, she turned to him. "The running of an inn does not cease for a holiday."

"Right." He swiveled his head, taking in the taproom from one corner to the other. "Quite the bustle in here, I'd say."

She scowled, or perhaps not. Honestly, how did one tell if an angel grimaced?

The thought made him smirk. "Come now, do you never have any fun, Miss Langley?"

"Not if I can help it."

"Then I shall make it my personal quest to remedy that ailment and see you to the parade myself." He angled his arm in invitation.

Johanna's eyes skimmed over his sleeve, but nothing more. Apparently, she'd have none of his offer.

Well then, if entertainment weren't a draw, he'd use another tactic—something he was never short of supplying. "We might find your brother amongst the merrymakers." He added a wink.

For the first time that morning, a smile dawned on her face, bright enough to shame the sun. "You are very persuasive, Mr. Morton."

"You have no idea." He matched her grin.

"Humph." The sound was an exact replication of her mother's. "Give me a moment to grab a bonnet, then."

"Oh, and don't forget." He pointed to a ragged bit of oak leaf pinned to his lapel. He supposed he ought to feel guilty for ripping the snippet of greenery from the gnarly garland he'd hung yesterday—but he didn't. "You should be thankful it was I who came upon you this morn and not Mr. Quail. When he does finally surface, I've no doubt he'll keep a keen eye out for forgetful misses who've neglected to sport a leaf this Oak Apple Day. . .unless you're intending to solicit pinches?"

Her eyes widened into brown pools, complimented by a deep flush spreading over her cheeks. She spun and stalked off, her skirt swishing fiercely enough to stir the ashes in the hearth.

He suppressed a laugh. Making the prim Johanna Langley blush was good sport, but not his purpose here in Dover. While he waited for her return, he devised his plan for the morning. With the town gathered for the parade, he'd have the best opportunity to study people. Though Ford suspected a traitor amongst Dover's elite, a conspirator rarely acted alone. Most likely there was a disgruntled lackey or two among the common folk who carried out the less desirable tasks associated with intrigue.

"All right, I am ready, sir, though I warn you I shan't stay long." Johanna's voice preceded her as she swept into the room. Her dark hair was tucked beneath a straw bonnet, a brown shawl caressed her shoulders, and yes. . .a sprig of oak leaf was pinned to her collar like a warrior's shield. "My mother will need me to prepare for this evening when the inn shall be"—she mimicked his earlier gaze about the taproom—"*quite the bustle*."

He smiled. Prim, yet saucy. . .traits far more alluring than the usual flattering and fawning.

Crossing to the door, he held it wide for her. When she passed, he gained her side, and they proceeded onto an empty street. The low drone of a crowd carried from blocks away, where the parade would begin.

"Tell me, Miss Langley." He glanced at her sideways. "Have you lived in Dover all your life?"

She nodded. "And Mam tells me you're from Sheffield."

He was glad she stared straight ahead, her face half-hidden by her bonnet's brim. The lying part of his job usually flowed smoothly, but this time, with this woman, a queer ripple of conscience came out of nowhere, cutting off his carefully prepared answer. Were she an officer or a scalawag, she'd have caught his hesitation. "Yes, Sheffield it is."

At the corner, they turned right. Latecomers like themselves dotted this street. The distinct tattoo of a drum corps chastened them to up the tempo of their pace.

"How long do you plan to stay here, Mr. Morton?"

"Depends." His answer was as evasive as Thatcher's the night before.

"On?"

He cut her yet another glance, and still she did not meet his eyes. Was she purposely hiding her face? Interesting method. Bow Street could use an interrogator like this woman. "Business."

He expected more inquiry, even formulated a few semi-truths that wouldn't be outright falsehoods, yet she surprised him once again by holding her tongue.

The closer they drew to the festivities, the more they zigzagged around a gauntlet of vendors selling parade whistles and all sorts of sweet treats. A thick hedge of people gathered two blocks ahead along the High Street, where an effigy of King Charles would be borne upon a flower-strewn cart. Alex veered to the left, hoping to avoid the crush of revelers and instead perch upon a stack of crates near the mouth of an alley for a bird's-eye view—though how he'd persuade Johanna to such heights was a mystery.

Good thing he had his tactics.

"Oh, Johanna!" Across the street, a female voice rang above the crowd. "Over here!"

Johanna waved then faced him. "Do you mind, Mr. Morton? I'd like to say hello, if only for a moment."

"After you." He swept out his hand.

The woman they approached was of a slighter build than Johanna. In truth, he feared a stout wind might tip her over—a very real danger this close to the Channel with the breeze gusting in from the southeast. She held a babe, bundled in a thick blanket as if the late spring sunshine were a foe.

"Good day to you, Maggie." Johanna smiled at her friend then fixed her gaze on the child. "And how is little Charlotte?"

"See for yourself." The woman, Maggie, handed the bundle to Johanna. You'd have thought she'd been given the crown jewels. Her face beamed.

*Coo*s and *oh*s and, "Who's a sweet baby?" bubbled from her mouth.

Maggie looked from Johanna to him, then back again. Johanna kept on murmuring endearments to the wee one, oblivious to the awkward situation. If she loved children so much, why was she not married with babes of her own?

Alex stepped forward. "With Miss Langley preoccupied, allow me to introduce myself. I am Mr. Morton."

Maggie dipped her head. "Pleased to meet you, sir. I am Jo's longtime friend, Mrs. Scott. At least we used to be friends, until I had Charlotte. Now I'm not so sure she even knows I exist." She nudged Johanna with her elbow. "Right, Jo?"

"Hmm?" Johanna looked up, then adjusted her voice down a notch from baby talk. "Oh, sorry. May I introduce Mr. Mor—"

"No need, Jo." Maggie slid a grin from her to Alex. "We've already met."

Beneath her bonnet brim, Johanna's brow scrunched, but only for a moment. She turned her face and went right back to gooing and gawing at the babe.

"Mags! Come along, Wife. I've a place for us up front." A shorn-headed man, as excessively stout as Maggie was thin, beckoned from the crowd ahead.

"Sorry, Jo." Maggie held out her arms. "You'll have to play with Lottie another time."

Johanna handed back the babe with a sigh. "I'll hold you to that."

"I have no doubt. I'll stop over in a few days. Good day Johanna, Mr. Morton." The woman nodded toward them both, then scurried after her husband.

By now the drums had passed and trumpeters blasted away. The parade would be over before he could assess the gathering. "If you're up for a little unconventionality, Miss Langley, I've spotted just the place to watch the parade." He pointed toward the passageway across the street.

She frowned, the dimple reappearing in all its glory. "All I see are a pile of boxes."

"Exactly."

Lifting her face to his, she narrowed her eyes. "What have you in mind, sir?"

"There's no time to explain if you want to be able to see the parade—and possibly your brother."

Her brow lifted.

Enough of a consent for him. He grabbed her gloved hand and led her across the road, ignoring another *humph* from her.

Stacking one crate atop another, he assembled a small platform, but with no easy way for a lady to ascend—and he'd used up all the boxes. "Wait here."

He trudged farther down the narrow passageway, scanning the shadows created by the two tall buildings. There ought to be another crate or at least a rock to use as a step. Midway down, a dark figure entered from the other end. With each step, the man grew larger—and each step was unmistakable. One of the man's legs was wooden.

For a second, Alex froze. The village of Deal wasn't that far from Dover, where a peg-legged smuggler had escaped the reach of the law—*his* reach—in the Dooley Affair. A free trader who knew his face.

One who could easily reveal his true identity.

"Aye there, matey," the man called out. "Can ye spare a swig o' the nipper with someone in need?"

The voice was bass, carrying a slight lisp, spoken like someone who'd had half his teeth knocked out. Alex flexed his fists, the scars on his knuckles tightening. No doubt about it. Blackjack Cooper.

Alex wheeled about—

To face Johanna, who'd followed him. "Mr. Morton, are we to see this parade or not?"

Behind her, swinging around the corner of the building and into the alley, came a short fellow with a crop of red hair too wiry to fit completely beneath his hat. "Ay Blackie! Been lookin' for ye."

Alex bit down hard on a curse. Blackjack's accomplice, Charlie Pickens, known as the Axe. Not that he should be surprised. The two were close as scabs on a pox victim.

Sinking a bit, Alex leaned toward the wall, using Johanna as cover. A few more paces and Charlie would gain a full view of his face. But if Alex turned away, he'd expose himself to Blackjack.

His heart pounded hard in his ears. He didn't have any tactics left—save one. Gathering Johanna in his arms, he pressed her against the brick wall.

And kissed her.

Heat spread through Johanna. Feelings she'd never before experienced—let alone would be able to name—made her dizzy and breathless and horrifyingly wanting more. For the second time in as many days, the arms of Alexander Morton held her in a tight embrace. Only this time his mouth burned a fire against hers. Maddening enough, but worse, her body—the traitor—leaned into it, enjoying the swirly-headed sensation of freefalling.

Well, then. There were no other options. She jabbed her knee upward, connecting quite sharply with his most vulnerable area.

He released her at once, doubling over with a groan.

"How dare you!" She spoke as much to herself as to him, hating the way she already missed his warmth.

"Please. . .I can"—he gasped, his voice straining on the sharp inhale—"explain."

She turned on her heel and darted ahead. The explanations of men were never to be trusted, a hard truth she'd learned well from her father.

"Miss Langley, wait!"

It would be satisfying to turn and watch him hobbling behind, but not very effective if she wanted to evade the grasping liar. Had compromising her been his plan all along? If so, she much preferred the libertine Mr. Quail. At least he didn't pretend.

Bypassing two men, one short and one peg-legged, she dove into the crowd, earning herself a few, "I beg your pardon's," and some outright curses. Holding her loosened bonnet atop her head with one hand, she used the other like a plow, turning rows of people and clearing space enough to wriggle through. She dodged a group of schoolboys, skirted an overturned barrel of pickles and an angry vendor, then darted across the street behind a row of redcoats on horseback. The view was not pleasant, neither the odor, but she made it to the other side without slipping in a pile of manure.

The crowd was thinner here, and she soon discovered why. Her dress clung to her moist skin, the sun having full rein to beat down upon the spectators without hindrance. After a glance over her shoulder, she slowed her pace, both from necessity and relief. No broad-shouldered man with hair the color of ripened wheat followed her. For a moment, she considered stopping and watching the last of the parade—until a freckle-faced boy crossed her path.

She snatched Thomas's collar an instant before he could dash off. "How providential, Brother. I've been looking for you. There's an inn full of musicians for you to attend, and they're likely waking just about now. It's chamber pot duty for you, my boy."

"Aww, Jo!" Thomas squirmed in her grip.

"Come along." She tugged him out of the press of the crowd and onto a side street. He rattled off excuse after excuse about why he shouldn't have to work, ranging from an old hoop rolling injury in his knee that he claimed pained him to no end, to pleading he was only a child.

She bit back a smile as she yanked him around the corner of St. James—then froze. Two paces in front of her stood Mr. Spurge, the man she'd been trying to avoid for the past two weeks.

The lien holder of the Blue Hedge Inn.

"Miss Langley." His dark eyes narrowed as he drawled out her name. He towered above her, his height emphasized by a tall, black hat. "How fortunate to cross paths."

Thomas scooted behind her, the coward. Was this how Lucius Nutbrown felt when she confronted him for rent? "Mr. Spurge." She bobbed her head. "G-good to see you."

"I wonder." He stared down his nose as if he were a king. His white hair and beard were as colorless as his voice. "I've stopped off several times to collect what's owed me. I daresay, judging by the frequent absence of you and your mother, that it's a wonder the Blue Hedge Inn operates at all."

"Yes, well. . .I can explain." Wonderful. She sounded exactly like Mr. Morton. For a moment, she considered shoving Thomas to the front and letting his wily tongue spin a whale of a tale.

Spurge held up a gloved hand. "No explanation required. Simply provide what's owed me by next Friday."

She licked her lips. With any luck, sweet words would flow, giving him reason to put off what she prayed wasn't the inevitable. "Perhaps you ought make that the week after, sir. With all the busyness of the holiday, I'm sure you can understand—"

"What I understand, Miss Langley, is that you and your mother need to face facts. The Blue Hedge Inn is going under. I suggest you bail out as soon as possible."

His prophecy hung in the air, as unpleasant as the stink of the soldiers and their horses. Fighting the urge to run away, she planted her feet a little wider apart and lifted her chin. "We've been in dire straits before, Mr. Spurge. God always provides a way out."

"Funny. I've heard that sentiment many times." The lines of his face hardened into angry tracks. "Until a stint in the workhouse changes that philosophy. One week, Miss Langley. Twenty-five pounds. Nothing less."

"Very well." She lifted her chin higher. "You shall have it."

"Yes, I shall." A sneer slid across his face. "One way or another." Without waiting for her reply, he tipped his hat, then sidestepped them both.

She watched his camel-colored dress coat disappear into the crowd, her confidence vanishing along with him.

Thomas tugged her sleeve. "Where you gonna get twenty-five pounds by next Friday, Jo?"

She blew out a long, low breath. Miracles still happened.

Didn't they?

CHAPTER FIVE

Alex handed over his invitation to a footman, who was more primped and tailored than some of the guests. If the viscount's servants were this ostentatious, what would the man himself be like? And worse... what of his daughter?

He swallowed back a bitter taste and forced a pleasant curve to his lips. Better to shove aside all thought of Ford's ludicrous directive for now, tuck it away into a back corner of his mind. Given enough time, surely he could come up with some plan that would release him from obeying such an outrageous command—and perhaps he worried for nothing. He could've misunderstood. Thatcher had yet to return with clarification. Or maybe Ford had changed his mind.

Oh God, make it so.

The footman placed the invitation into a basket stationed next to him. "Welcome, Mr. Morton."

Alex strode into Lord Coburn's mansion as if he owned the place, confidence his best ally for the moment. He grabbed a glass from a passing silver tray and drained the contents before crossing the front atrium. The drink was not overly sweet and left a dry aftertaste. No bubbles tickled the back of his throat, but even so, he had no doubt about the origin of the viscount's wine. Sparkling or not, champagne always made him—

He turned aside and gave in to the inevitable sneeze.

Pinching the bridge of his nose to ward off a repeat performance, he entered a wide corridor and headed toward the open doors of a ballroom. With each step, he collected curious glances from strangers. He knew no one, but could name them just the same. The fat merchant hoping to sell his soul to gain a contract with the viscount was Greed. The servant sneaking off for a tryst in an unused closet, Lust. And the pair of matrons whose plan was to allow their charges enough slack to hog-tie a bachelor? Self-serving

Languor. Here in a manor home or down at a quayside bawdy house, people were people the world 'round.

The first notes of a quadrille welcomed him into the ballroom, and once past the threshold, he fought the urge to cover his eyes from the brilliance of chandeliers, jewels, and hopeful gazes noting his entrance. To his right, a line of dancers bowed in front of their partners, one dark head and slender figure almost familiar. From this distance, however, he couldn't be certain.

Quickening his pace, he skirted the gathering, hoping to gain a closer look. The woman was petite, shapely, and then completely blocked by an ape-shouldered monster of a fellow. Alex angled for a better view and. . . there. Was it? Could that be Johanna Langley?

But when the woman looked up and bright light bathed her face, blue eyes stared back at him, not brown.

And not angry.

He averted his gaze and moved on. Surely one glass of champagne couldn't have skewed his vision already—but yes. Better to blame the fruit of the vine than a truth he dare not admit.

He could not get the woman out of his thoughts.

Aah, but Johanna Langley was a fiery one when roused. He'd spent the better part of the afternoon trying to chase her down and apologize for the kiss. Every time he drew near, she shot off like a fox from a hound. Not that he blamed her. His behavior had been abominable.

But it had worked. By the time Johanna had stomped out of the alley, Blackjack and Charlie had disappeared down the street.

Unfortunately, the ground he stood on now wasn't much safer. How the deuce had he strayed so close to the punch table? Females of all shapes and sizes eyed him over the rims of their cups. He suddenly understood why a stag froze. The slightest twitch would be conveyed as an invitation, drawing a rush of taffeta and ambition.

Slowly, he shifted his weight, prepared for a quick about-face. Handker-chiefs dropped like a cloudburst. If he picked up one, a frenzy would break loose. There was nothing to be done for it, then. Sometimes the best way out was to simply barrel through. So he did—

And came face-to-face with three matriarchs, cocking their heads in unison, eyeing him like a vulture over a laid-out carcass. He swallowed.

They advanced.

He'd rather take on Blackjack and Charlie's swinging axe than this.

"There you are! Come along, ol' scuffer. We've been waiting on you." A deep voice reached his ear an instant before an arm draped around his shoulder and towed him sideways.

The fellow who led him through the crowd was short, the top of his slicked-back hair even with Alex's nose. He smelled of pomade and cherry tobacco—and *strongly*, to be distinguishable in the midst of ladies who'd bathed in rose water and lavender. He was also no stranger to the viscount's mansion. Instead of crossing the length of the ballroom, he darted behind a three-paned partition near the wall, used to disguise the comings and goings of servants. Behind the panel, the man paused in front of a closed door and turned. "That was close. What were you thinking?"

"I . . ." Exactly. *Think*. Should he know this fellow? Had he overlooked any passwords or codes given him during the magistrate's briefing?

Swerving away from a passing servant, Alex summed up his options, the best being to play along with this charade—but charades was his least favorite party game. He looked the man square in the eyes. "Do I know you?"

"Likely not." Stubby, yellowed teeth peeked out of a grin that lifted clear to the man's brow. He'd only seen that once before—on a goat. "You're new here, are you not, Mr. Morton? Oh, hang it all. That's much too formal. I shall call you Alex, if you don't mind, or even if you do."

Alex rubbed the back of his neck, stalling for time. Was this man a threat or as big a ninny as Nutbrown? Either way, the fellow knew his name, a distinct disadvantage for him since Alex couldn't credit who he might be.

"Don't think too hard on it, old man. I had the footman alert me should we have the good fortune of the arrival of a new player. You didn't really want to dance, did you?" The man's gaze flickered over him from head to toe. "You don't strike me as a fleet-footed dandy."

"You might be surprised."

"Pah!" He landed a playful punch on Alex's upper arm. "If we're to be gaming partners, I suppose I should introduce myself. I'm Robert Coburn, but call me Robbie. Quite got used to it over there." His head angled toward the west.

"Bristol?"

"Boston. Served some time as a lieutenant. And now that the formalities are over. . ." He turned and shoved open the door. "Shall we?"

"What have you in mind?"

Robbie glanced over his shoulder before entering a dimly lit stairwell. "You can thank me for this later."

Flexing the fingers of his right hand should he need to draw the knife hidden inside his waistcoat, Alex followed Robert—*Robbie*—up the stairwell. The man's surname was the same as the viscount's, but the spring in his step, lack of polished manners, and careless demeanor labeled him anything but. Probably. Not that he hadn't encountered stranger things.

Alex blinked in the dimmer lighting. Were shadows and confined spaces among his fears, he'd likely be sweating. The higher they climbed, the more the music and laughter of the ballroom faded. With this many stairs, he suspected they'd bypassed the first floor and gone directly to the second.

At the top step, for there was no landing, Robbie knocked on a panel with no knob. Two sharp raps, a pause, then five successive taps. The door opened inward. Cigar smoke wafted out. Before Robbie passed through, he glanced back. "You do play faro, don't you, Alex?"

The muscles in his gut tightened. This had been far too easy. Almost like a gambling rogue had been expected to walk through the viscount's door this night. He wrapped his fingers around the hilt of his knife, taking care to keep the blade concealed.

"Alex?"

He forced a half smile. "Sorry. Just trying to recall the rules of the game. Now that I think on it, I believe I have played a time or two."

"Excellent!" Robbie strode through the door.

Alex stopped on the threshold, ready to sprint back down the stairwell if necessary. A few paces away, a manservant near a sideboard appeared innocuous enough. Hard to tell about the three men seated at a round table halfway across the room, especially since a fair amount of ivory betting chips at center indicated a small fortune was currently at stake.

"Look what I found." Robbie beamed a smile and swept a hand toward him. "Fresh meat."

The thinnest of the men, seated nearest the hearth, flicked an ash from his cheroot onto a crystal saucer. He studied Alex as he might a new card, then refocused on his own hand, discarding the new arrival as a non-trump.

The fellow sitting opposite him stuck out his lower lip, considering Alex as if he were a tray of sliced beef or carved guinea fowl. In truth, the man would likely pass up neither. Gaps stretching between the double buttons on his red coat—the pairs of them giving away his rank as major general—attested to his love affair with food.

The third man, seated with his back to them, didn't move. Not at first. Then a slight ripple whispered across the fabric between his shoulder blades, barely perceptible.

Alex shifted his weight, poised to flee.

The man shot to his feet, turned, and fired a black powder pistol.

A scream gushed from Robbie's mouth. Blood streamed from his hand. He dropped to his knees, clutching the injury to his chest. The bullet had passed through Robbie's hand and lodged into the mahogany paneling dangerously close to Alex. It wasn't a killing shot. It was a warning.

Alex clenched his dagger tighter, ready for anything.

The man holding the gun flicked his gaze toward Alex, summing him up with a sweep of his eyes. Alex returned the favor. The fellow was neither large nor gaunt. His dress coat was well tailored in an understated fashion. The cut of his trousers labeled him neither a trendsetter nor outmoded. His hair, greying at the temples and thinning on top, was brushed back into a nondescript style, his face clean-shaven and without blemish. Truly, he was no more interesting or intimidating than a dish of jellied pigeon livers. Yet with a single nod toward the servant, the man commanded immediate action.

The manservant rushed to Robbie's side and helped him to stand. With an arm around his shoulder, he escorted Robbie out of the room, leaving a trail of stains in the carpet and the remnants of Robbie's whimpering.

"Well, I suppose we'll give you a try, being that you're already here." The man tucked away his pistol and locked stares with Alex. "Are you going to stand there or play cards? Oh, and grab yourself a drink first. Drake will likely be busy with Robert for a while."

Sheathing his knife, Alex closed the door behind him, sealing off the ghostly chords from the ball far below. He counted his steps—twelve—over to the sideboard laden with bottles, glasses, and an intricately carved cigar box. Then he estimated the remaining steps—six—to the only other exit from the room, the door Robbie had been ushered through. Sometimes the difference between life and death was a number. Alex added the information to his arsenal, for he might well need it. The only available seat would leave him facing away from the main door. He'd known one too many officers who'd taken a lead ball to the back of the skull from a situation such as this.

Bypassing a crystal decanter of brandy, he grabbed a green bottle of wine and a glass, then seated himself. He poured only enough to leave the bottle mostly full, then positioned it to his right, two hand spans from the table's edge. It made for a poor mirror, but from that angle, he'd at least see should the door open.

"Two-fisted drinker, eh?" The fat major general spoke, his voice distinctive—like the bark of a dog that'd been at it for too long. Though with the thick folds around the man's neck, it was a wonder words came out at all. "My kind of fellow, but let's be about it, hmm? I assume you have the money to front your bets?"

Alex nodded. "If I didn't, I'd have made a dash for it down the stairs by now."

Without another word, the man shoved five chips toward him, and the game was on. These fellows were serious. Conversation was not only an unnecessary interruption, but clearly an unwelcome one as well. A tip of the head. The blink of an eye. Even the lifting of a finger communicated far more loudly than a roomful of sailors embroiled in a round of hazard.

The first card dealt didn't interest Alex so much as the second, and neither of those as much as the cards toward the end of the deck. He had no clue how much a chip was worth, but no matter. The magistrate had endowed him with a sizable sum, and Thatcher could always retrieve more funds for him. He slid his entire stack of chips onto the nine of spades printed on the felt in front of the dealer—the man he assumed to be the viscount. Coburn flipped over the last card.

Alex smiled, then scooped up his winnings.

As the game wore on, he continued his devil-take-all strategy. At first, the others split their bets between cards, but as his stack grew and theirs diminished, their patterns changed. All of them placed the sum of their chips on what they felt would be the winning card. Alex suppressed a smirk. Monkeys, even well-dressed ones, were known to mimic.

And that didn't slow his winning streak. Though the men looked the part of well-versed gamblers, they weren't. Oh, they'd employed a few winning strategies early on in the game, but nothing he hadn't already encountered during his darker, cardsharp days.

When Alex's chips outnumbered everyone's, the dealer threw down the deck of cards and leaned back in his chair. For a tense few moments, nothing but the ticking of the ornately inlaid longcase clock in the corner broke the silence. That and the loud grumble of the big man's belly.

Finally, the dealer leaned forward, skewering Alex with an intense gaze. "Where did Robert find you?"

Alex smiled, offsetting his jaw slightly, the same grin that'd saved his behind more than a time or two. "He rescued me from a rabid pack of debutantes."

The silence stretched once again, but this time only as far as it took for his words to sink in. Laughter, starting with the fat major general, spread around the table.

"I suppose I ought not have reprimanded him so harshly, then. But you must understand, my nephew has been warned on previous occasions to stop bringing uninvited players to my table. He needs to learn I mean what I say. I am Viscount Edward Coburn, the lord of this manor, or what's left of it after your significant fleecing." The viscount lifted a brow at the winnings heaped atop the last bet Alex had placed. After a sigh, he swept out his hand—a large, gold signet ring flashing with the movement—and indicated each man in turn. "And you've also lightened the pockets of Mr. James Conroy and Major General William Overtun."

"Gentlemen, pleased to make your acquaintances, and especially pleased to take your money." He scooped the chips toward his side of the table. It was a hefty sum. Perhaps he ought be more thankful that Ford had given him this assignment. "I am Alexander Morton—"

A sharp rapping at the door cut him off.

Lord Coburn raised halfway, a distinct growl rising from his throat as well. "I said I was not to be disturbed until—"

The door flew open. Every nerve on edge, Alex reached for his knife, then slowly regained his lost breath when he saw the swirl of a skirt reflected on the bottle in front of him.

"I can hold off dinner no longer." The woman's voice, while cultured and resonant, was harsher than a fishwife's. "Either you come down—now—or I shall lead every last guest up here to your little sanctuary, Father."

Father? A cold sweat shivered through Alex. Slowly, he stood and turned. And looked full into the face of the woman he'd been ordered to marry.

"Will you marry me?"

If her hands weren't full, Johanna would slap the silly, lopsided grin off Mr. Quail's face as soundly as she'd clouted Mr. Morton earlier in the day. She didn't have time for this lunacy, not with a full taproom. Taking care to keep the dishes from toppling, she pulled from Mr. Quail's touch on her arm and turned slightly, wielding her tray of dirty soup bowls like a shield. "How many cups of ale have you downed tonight, sir?"

He clapped a hand over his heart and staggered back, earning himself a tart reply from the redhead behind him. Ignoring her, he kept his gaze pinned on Jo. "You wound me, my fairest, to imply my wits have been compromised."

"Better your wits than me," she shot back.

With a laugh, the redhead craned her neck over Mr. Quail's shoulder. "She's got ye there, she does. Yer better at singin' than courtin'."

"Really?" Mr. Quail shifted his eyes sideways, a tic running along his jaw. "And what would you know about music, except for bawdy house ditties and—"

"Mr. Quail," Johanna breathed out his name as a warning. There was no way he could see the big man approaching to his left, though he might have felt the floor rumble with each of the fellow's giant steps. A brawl now would break more than all the mugs Thomas had dropped this evening.

"There a problem, Lovey?" The man draped his arm around the redhead's shoulder, pulling her toward him.

Johanna forced a smile. "I'd say the only problem is the music has stopped. Should you not be about it, Mr. Quail?"

"That I should." Sneaking in a quick wink, he darted off in the opposite direction of Lovey and her man.

Thomas didn't see him coming. He was too busy weaving in and out of people at top speed with an armful of mugs.

Quail swerved an instant before impact, leaning hard on one foot while swooping his arms to keep him upright.

Thomas teetered like a wobbly top, far to one side, then the other, until there was nothing to be done for it but to throw out his hands like Quail had done.

Six earthenware tankards shattered on the floor. Johanna frowned at them. She ought be glad it wasn't her brother's head hitting the planks—which truly she was. But such an event might knock some sense into the boy. A wicked thought, but one that could not be helped. Had she not told him thrice in the past hour to slow down?

He scooped up the pieces with a laugh, as if the world were nothing but a riddle and he the jester.

"Oh, Thomas." She groaned and her shoulders slumped, rattling the bowls on her tray. Where would they find the extra funds to replace all he'd broken?

"Don't be hard on him, Jo. He's but a boy."

She turned toward her mother's voice. Creases fanned out at the sides of Mam's eyes. Shadows smudged half-circles underneath. Had she ever seen her mother look quite so tired? A woman her age ought to be dandling a grandchild on her knee, not running foamy heads of ale to and fro like a common bar wench.

But at least they had customers to serve. Last Johanna had checked, the coin jar was nearly half full—not enough to stave off Mr. Spurge, but at least the miller would be paid. Blowing out a sigh and a prayer, she repented of her foul attitude.

"You're right." She smiled at Mam. "Thomas is young. I should be thankful he's working and—"

A scream ripped out the kitchen door. Mam's hands flew to her heart. The music stopped as quickly as it began.

Dropping the tray of bowls, Johanna broke into a dead run toward the howling, heedless of who she shoved aside. "Thomas!"

Her brother tore into the taproom, the hem of his trousers aflame. The faster he ran, the higher the fire climbed.

Jo launched forward, tackling him to the ground. She wrapped her arms about him and rolled. Over and over. Smothering the flames between her and the floor. The stench of burnt fabric and flesh was sickening. The heat of his clothes singed her own skin, but she wouldn't quit. She'd roll back and forth until the flames of hell were quenched if that's what it took.

"Lassie, lassie! It's done. It's over."

The deep voice of a Scotsman cut into her nightmare. Breathing hard, she rolled to a stop and pushed up slightly.

Beneath her, Thomas lay still. Eyes shut. Mouth slack.

"No!" She wailed. "God, please. Not Thomas!"

CHAPTER SIX

Alex studied the woman standing in the doorway. Only one word came to mind. Green. Yet color had nothing to do with it. Her off-white gown was embellished with golden embroidery, all loopy and feminine. If he squinted, the design took on a fleur-de-lis pattern—strange icon for an English woman these days. Her hair was dark, her eyes darker. She didn't appear to be ill or jealous, yet all the same she was green. Straight and willowy as a field of grass, lithe as a fern frond, all delicate and wispy. A pleasing sight, one that might turn a man's head—but not his.

She directed a cancerous gaze at her father. "Why will Robbie not be joining us?"

"He is detained." The viscount ground out his cheroot onto an already overloaded salver, creating a small cloud of ash. Then he nodded toward Alex. "I am sure Mr. Morton here will be happy to fill your cousin's seat so that you should not lack for a dinner companion. You will find him a refreshing diversion. Mr. Morton, meet my daughter, Miss Louisa Coburn. Louisa, Mr. Alexander Morton."

Alex kept his gaming face intact, though not without struggle. What an irregular breach of protocol. Why would the viscount seat him, having no knowledge of his heritage or credentials, above known guests who surely bore higher social rank? Clearly the man had no qualms about making enemies or choosing his allies on a whim. Nothing about this evening made sense. What nest of hornets had Ford sent him into?

A scowl marred Louisa's pretty face. "You cannot be serious, Father."

Still, this was an opportunity he shouldn't pass up. Alex advanced, leaving behind the three men at the table. "Your father speaks truth, Miss Coburn." He flourished a bow and finished with a rogue grin. "Not only will I take pleasure in dining next to you, but it is my deepest desire."

Her lips parted, closed, then parted once again.

Lord Coburn snorted. "Flit, girl! Don't stand there gaping like a codfish."

A small dimple—not nearly as charming as Johanna's—indented her chin, deepening when she clamped her lips shut.

Alex crooked his arm. "I should be delighted to escort you."

"Very well." At last she rested her fingertips atop his arm, allowing him to lead her out the door.

He paused. "Left or right?"

Her fingers twitched, the movement frustrating the fabric of his sleeve. "Don't tell me you are too far into your cups to remember which way you came, Mr. Morton."

He glanced sideways. "Not at all, Miss Coburn, though the way I came is a bit narrow for such a wide hem as yours."

"Oh, you are one of those. I expected as much." Her voice held all the warmth of a baited bear. Removing her hand from his arm, she turned left and set off at a surprisingly brisk pace.

He caught up in four long strides. "I am curious about the category you've filed me under. Should I be flattered or affronted that I'm one of *those*?"

"That depends if you consider it a badge of honor to be a member of my father's cronies."

He smiled. Ford would be proud of the progress he'd made in only two days.

Pieces of gilded-framed artwork blurred as they sped down the corridor. When this woman was on a mission, she obviously would not be stopped, a hallmark of determination and danger. He tucked the trait away for later use.

"So tell me, Miss Coburn. Do you fancy him?"

She angled her face, a fine line following the curve of her brow. "Whom?"

"Robbie, of course."

Her step hitched at the top of a grand stairway, and he offered his arm. She ignored it, but the fingers of her other hand gripped the banister tightly. "What a strange question, Mr. Morton. Why ever would you ask it?"

"I noted it was an unwelcome surprise when you discovered Robbie would not be present."

"Which merely indicates I dislike change."

"Aah, but combined with the flare of your nostrils and the heightened color in your cheeks, I wondered if there were something more?"

She descended the stairway without an answer, then stopped at the bottom and faced him. "You are quite observant, sir."

As was she. Her gaze pinged from his left eye to his right and back again, as if he hid truth behind one or the other like the shell game Thomas had tried to master. Her father and his friends bypassed them into the milling guests, heralding the beginning of dinner, but Louisa did not move. Apparently infringing upon etiquette ran in the family, for she ought be leading the other women into the dining room at this moment.

Alex pulled his attention from the daughter to the father, just before Lord Coburn disappeared into the dining room. The man's left foot lingered behind the right, slightly dragging to catch up with each step. Quite the distinctive limp. An old war injury, perhaps? A defect from birth? Or was some disease even now leaching life in increments from the man?

Louisa followed his gaze, her eyes narrowing. "How does Father know you?"

"I am a recent acquaintance."

Her lips puckered like a tot trying to figure out by what means rain fell from the sky. "By what connection?"

"Commerce."

"La, sir! Are you nothing but a merchant?"

He leaned in, close enough to inhale a whiff of civet musk—a scent all the rage in France. "I am a man with many skills, Miss Coburn." He allowed just the right amount of huskiness to his voice, intimating at promises he never intended to make, Ford's directive or otherwise. "The question is what would you like me to be?"

Her pupils widened. The rise and fall of a Cross of Lorraine pendant resting between her collarbones increased. Again, a very curious choice of accoutrement. Surely the traitor Ford sought wasn't this woman.

Or was it? Lord knows he'd collared his fair share of female criminals on London's streets. Perhaps Dover's were no different.

"The hour is late, Mr. Morton, and I have put off dinner long enough." She turned and dashed ahead of him toward the dining room, then slowed her pace to a more regal gait as she entered.

He followed, as did the eyes of every guest awaiting her arrival. Whispers travelled the length of the long table, from powdered women to clean-shaven men, and a fair amount of officers in their regimentals. Louisa sat at her father's right, and Alex sank into the empty seat next to her.

Lord Coburn snapped open his napkin, placing it on his lap while addressing her under his breath. "Must you insist on dramatics, Louisa?"

"I've learned from the best, Father." She mimicked his napkin fanfare.

Alex bit back a smirk. They both belonged on a Theater Royal stage.

Coburn nodded toward the footmen, lining the walls like soldiers. They stepped forward in one movement and opened the tureens of soup. Alex inhaled. Turtle, he'd bet on it.

The viscount sipped an obligatory spoonful before cocking his head at Alex. "I hope you'll give me the chance to win back some of my fortune, Mr. Morton."

"You have but to say when and where, sir."

"Tomorrow evening. Eight, sharp."

Louisa leaned forward. "I was not aware you'd taken to adding common merchants to your circle, Father."

Alex choked back the broth, mind whizzing to line up a plausible rejoinder. Little troublemaker! A common merchant was *not* the professional spin he'd intended to present to the man.

Lord Coburn lowered his brows toward his daughter. "Better a merchant than a slacker, and a dishonorable one at that."

The cut spread a flush over Louisa's cheeks, and she suddenly took a great interest in her soup. Hard to tell if the blush was inspired by shame—or anger.

Alex set down his spoon. "The lady speaks the truth somewhat, sir. I am a connoisseur of wines, travelling the continent to keep my father's vast collection in stock. You may have heard of him, Mr. Jonathan Morton, esquire? Up near Sheffield."

"Don't believe so, no. Unless. . .any military connections?"

"None whatsoever."

"Then it is a definite no." The viscount mouthed another bite of soup, then put down his spoon as well and eyed him. "But what brings you to Dover? Unless I am mistaken, which I hardly ever am, there are no exotic stores of wine to be had in this part of the country."

Alex paused to allow the footman to remove his dish. "I am on my way home from Porto Moniz, escorting a shipment of a fine Madeira vintage."

The viscount lifted one brow toward Louisa. "Hardly a *common* merchant, I'd say."

Her jaw set into a rigid—albeit pretty—line, though she made no further response.

A butler, austere in his black suit and cravat, handed Lord Coburn a folded slip of paper. Turbulence darkened the viscount's gaze as his eyes roved over the words. He balled the note, palmed it, then stood.

"Excuse me." He bypassed the butler and strode from the room.

Another round of whispers ringed the table, making Alex wonder if the guests attended the viscount's soiree for the opulence of the mansion and the richness of the food—or the intrigue that accompanied the event. Surprising, yet fortunate, for now he had Louisa relatively to himself.

He glanced back at her. A half smile softened her lips. Was she glad for her father's departure or the anguish the missive had caused? Whatever, theirs was no simple relationship.

Alex offered her a slice of beef from the platter in front of them and waited for the nod of her head before continuing. "Now that you know what I do, how is it you occupy yourself?"

"Orchids."

Returning the serving fork to the plate, he chewed on her answer before sampling a bite of his roast. Orchids? What the devil could one do with those? Paint them? Sell them on a street corner? Gather them in bunches and decorate the lounges of all the fine women in Dover? "I was not aware that flowers could be so amusing," he admitted.

Either the beef disgusted her, or he did, for she pushed away her plate.

This would never do. Inducing scorn was a far cry from wooing her. He poured all the charm he owned into an earnest tone of voice. "Miss Coburn, I realize I am a poor replacement for Robbie, but truly, I am applying my best effort. It is not my intention to spar with you, for I should no doubt be the one bleeding on the floor."

She frowned. "You are very odd, Mr. Morton."

"And you are very beautiful." The words came out easily enough, but they left a traitorous aftertaste in his mouth. He didn't mean them—leastwise not in the way he would speak them to Johanna.

Johanna? What the deuce? He reached for his glass and drained it. Why in the world think of her now?

"All right, Mr. Morton. I shall be candid as well." She faced him, quirking her brow. "Father wishes me to be on the hunt for a husband, but I fancy working in the garden, hence my orchid preoccupation."

Interesting. Most females relished husband wrangling as a favorable pastime.

"I wonder if gardening is your true love, Miss Coburn, or rather your passion for rebelling against your father?"

"I assure you, sir, I am nothing but obedient."

She turned back to her meal. Providential, for she missed the roll of his eyes. Obedient, no doubt, but not to her father. To herself.

"I think I can help you, Miss Coburn," he drawled.

She didn't look at him, but he'd snagged her attention all the same, for her brow wrinkled. "With what, sir?"

"Hunting."

⏤⏤

Dawn was a heartbeat away, but Johanna couldn't sleep. She wandered the empty taproom, righting benches, straightening tables. She wasn't alone, though. Mr. Quail's snores from upstairs kept her company. The single lantern yet burning cast a blend of shadows and light. Fitting, she mused as she knelt to pick up shards of earthenware. Darkness always found a way to encroach into the brightest parts of her life.

"Oh, Thomas," she whispered. "Why you? Why now?"

The slow shush of the front door answered her. In stepped Mr. Morton, cravat askew, hair loosened and sweeping his collar. Not the polished figure she'd seen leave earlier in the evening, and certainly not a man to be trusted. Even so, for one traitorous moment, she remembered how he'd held her, and the thought of running into his arms and weeping away her heartache swept through her.

"You're still awake?" He spoke soft enough that sleeping ears would not stir.

"That's debatable."

His gaze scanned the room as he crossed the floor on silent feet. If she weren't so tired, she'd marvel at his ability. As he drew near and focused on her, he sucked in an audible breath.

Not that she faulted him. She must look a wreck. Dress ruined with char marks. Hair unpinned and fallen down her back. Her cheeks stung, chapped from tears, and her eyes must surely be swollen. If he cared to sniff, he might think he stood in front of the kiln master on Brickyard Lane instead of a woman.

"Looks like you had quite the evening." Though the comment was light-hearted, concern thickened his voice.

"Quite."

He likely expected her to say more, but one word would have to suffice. Hers was a raw wound, too fresh to consider. She went back to picking up broken tankard pieces and stacking them in a pile. It was a mindless task—and for that she was grateful.

The toes of Mr. Morton's shoes entered her field of vision, but she refused to look up. His clothes rustled as he squatted in front of her.

"Care to tell me what happened?"

Her hands didn't slow. She stacked one piece atop another, and when the pile towered too high and wobbly, she started a new mound.

"Miss Langley, I clearly see you are troubled. Though my behavior of yesterday morning suggests otherwise, I am not a beast of opportunity. I am sorry about that kiss, but believe me, it was necessary at the time."

Stack. Stack. Just like his words. She probably ought to care. She had once. What did a stolen kiss matter now? Tragedy had a blunt way of rear-ranging offenses, or rather, defining them.

She glanced up, surprised to see a bit of color rising on his neck. So, this *was* difficult for him. Perhaps he wasn't as big a scoundrel as she'd pegged him. "Let us forget that incident and move on."

He cocked his head, studying her like a foreign species. "Do you always forgive so freely?"

"It's not my forgiveness that matters. You should have a care for what you'll say to your Maker, for you never know how soon that day will be." Her breath caught as the truth of her own words hit home.

Mr. Morton's clear, blue gaze burned into hers. "Tell me what's happened."

Oh, no. If she answered that, she'd be undone. She snatched the last pottery fragment and set it atop the heap. The pile tipped and crashed into the other. Pieces scattered everywhere, the sound making her flinch. Now she'd have to start over. She reached to begin again.

Mr. Morton's hand wrapped around hers, solid and warm, and entirely too supportive. "You're trembling."

Fresh tears blurred her vision. She blinked, forcing them back, and looked anywhere except at his face—or at the strong fingers entwining with hers.

"Come." He pulled her to her feet.

She allowed him to lead her to a bench near the hearth, in the corner where Mr. Quail and his band had played. Why would this night not end? If she listened hard enough, would she still hear leftover strains of music—or worse, her brother's screams?

A shiver rippled across her shoulders as she sank to the seat.

Shrugging out of his dress coat, Mr. Morton bent and wrapped it around her. Still warm from his body, the fabric carried his scent—bergamot and strength. She shivered again.

Without a word, he grabbed a poker and stirred the banked fire. Ashes knocked back, air breathing life, a flame burst out. Red and deadly.

"Don't!" she cried, then immediately wished she'd said nothing.

He jerked his gaze toward her.

She bit her lip. What must he think?

Without a word, he walked away—and she didn't blame him. If she could, she'd walk away from herself as well. Away from this night. This inn. This life. Closing her eyes, she shut out the evil hearth fire. Where was her faith?

Footsteps returned. The bench jiggled. A cup was placed into her hands. "Here. Drink."

She shook her head then lifted her face to Mr. Morton's. "No, thank you."

"Do it."

It wasn't a harsh command, but a command nevertheless, and one she suspected would take less effort to obey than to argue. When the first sip met her tongue, thirst took over. She drained the mug dry. How could this man know her better than herself?

"There. That wasn't so hard, hmm?" He took the cup from her hands and set it on the bench next to him. "Now then, close your eyes."

Accepting a drink was one thing. What he might have in mind, quite another. "Mr. Morton, I hardly think—"

"Ah, ah." He wagged his finger at her. "Trust me, Miss Langley. Close your eyes." The determined set of his jaw left no room for debate.

Eyelids heavy, she gave in, but not without tensing for a quick exit should he make an untoward move.

The bench jiggled again. A few light steps. Not far. The scrape of one of the instruments left on the table from Quail's band.

And then a single, haunting note on a violin. Followed by another. It was a sweet sound, in an eerie sort of way. The kind of tune that reached in and struck chords in her soul. One she'd hear in dreams to come.

Deep down, a sob began. At first she fought it, scrunching her eyes tighter to keep the tears inside. But the music was merciless, coaxing her to let go.

The next thing she knew, the song was over. Arms wrapped around her. She wept into Mr. Morton's fine waistcoat until it was soaked through.

Finally catching her breath, she pushed away.

He studied her for a moment. The room was no longer dark. The grey light of dawn crawled in through the front window, highlighting myriad questions in his gaze. "Now, would you care to tell me what happened that brought you to such depths?"

"You are very persistent, sir."

He merely cocked a brow.

"I see I have no choice." She sucked in a shaky breath. Could she do this? "It was a busy night. Good business, but as you know, we are short on help. Thomas, bless his heart—" Her voice cracked, and she cleared her throat twice over before beginning again. "He was rushing about. I warned him, but. . ."

Glancing around the taproom, she collected what was left of her bravery. "I'm sure you've noticed our inn is mostly held together by baling twine. We've needed to replace the spit hook in the kitchen hearth for years now, but a smithy is expensive, and the hearth itself took priority. We replaced that and made do with the rest. The hook is yet functional somewhat, *if* one is careful. Thomas wasn't."

She shuddered.

"Go on," he coaxed.

If not for Mr. Morton's fingers on her jaw, turning her face toward his, she'd not have had the courage to speak another word. "My brother leaned over the hearth to scoop a ladle of stew from the pot. He moved too fast, with too much force. The hook broke. The pot fell into the flames. Coals shot out, one catching in the folded hem of his trousers. He tried to smother it, brave boy, but ended up fanning the flames larger. In a panic, he ran. I stopped him. I thought he was"—she gulped back the lump in her throat—"dead."

All expression drained from Mr. Morton's face. This close, she could feel each of his muscles tensing rock hard.

"Is he?"

"No. I did not mean to imply. . ." Words failed her. Some fates were worse than death, and unless God acted in mercy, Thomas might very well find that out.

Mr. Morton breathed out, "Thank God," then pushed to his feet. "Where is the boy now?"

"Upstairs. Mam attends him. He will live."

"That's a relief—"

"But"—she cut him off lest she mislead him yet again—"the doctor won't say if he'll ever walk again."

CHAPTER SEVEN

After two nights of listening to Quail's off-tune fiddling, Alex purposely left his gun up in his chamber. If he carried it to the taproom, he'd shoot the man to put him and everyone else out of their misery. Was it too much to ask that a musician actually play music?

He swigged back the rest of his drink and frowned at the kitchen door, willing a blue skirt to appear. He'd had precious few moments to query Johanna on how Thomas or she fared, and he was beginning to think she and Mrs. Langley were avoiding him.

"Looking for someone?"

Alex tensed. The question struck him from the side, flanking him like a well-planned skirmish. He jerked his gaze to the shadow slipping onto the bench beside him. Only Thatcher could steal inside a sparsely populated taproom without being noticed.

Alex scowled at the man. "Must you always sneak up on a body?"

"No, but that would steal the enjoyment of it." Thatcher reached for the mug, then glowered when he found nothing but drops remaining.

"What are you doing here?" Alex leaned against the wall and eyed the man. "You couldn't possibly have met with Ford this quickly."

"I didn't. I met with Flannery on the road."

"Flannery?" Alex winced, both from the screech of what should've been a C-sharp and the mention of fellow officer Killian Flannery. He'd never worked with the man directly, but after the hair-raising tales he'd heard about him from fellow officer Brentwood, neither did he want to. "Please tell me he's not in on this."

"Only as a pack mule. He brought a message from Ford."

Thunder and turf! This assignment was turning into far more than he'd bargained for. One by one, Alex cracked his knuckles, a vain effort at releasing the tension. "What does Ford want now? Am I to dress as a tart and swing my hips in hopes of luring out the traitor?"

Thatcher's lips quirked—the closest he ever came to smiling. "I'd like to see that."

"No doubt." He held out his hand. "Let's have it."

Thatcher handed over a small paper. Once opened, the scrap was hardly bigger than a playing card. Only five words graced the center.

Clarification: ingratiate, eliminate, then extricate.

Alex blew out a long breath. Refolding the note, he shifted his gaze to his friend. "I'm assuming you've read this."

Thatcher nodded.

"Then let me see if I've got this straight." He angled on the bench, facing the man head-on. "I am to ingratiate myself with the Coburn family by making an offer for Louisa. By doing so, Ford assumes I will be able to identify the traitor—which I'm guessing he expects to be either the viscount himself, Robbie, or Louisa. I arrest said traitor, thus eliminating the threat. At that point, I extricate myself from any betrothal ties before the marriage deed can be carried out. Is that your understanding?"

Thatcher nodded again, his dark eyes giving no hint as to what he thought of the matter.

Which only served to kindle the rising irritation burning in Alex's gut. He purposely lowered his voice, denying a strong urge to shout. "Why the deuce would the viscount or his daughter even consider me as marriage material? I'm a stranger. An unknown."

Thatcher merely shrugged. "You've talked your way in and out of impossible situations before, and it's no secret your. . .*skills* with women are unmatched."

"This is different. Coburn's a peer of the realm. He's not going to let honeyed words alone persuade him."

"Of course not. He'll do a thorough background check."

"For Alexander Morton, a nonentity." He grit his teeth. "Ford better be doing some fantastic slight-of-hand work on my behalf."

"He's sparing no expense on this and is keeping close watch on all that happens." Thatcher leaned forward and lowered his voice. "Though it may seem so, you are not alone."

Alex pressed the heel of his hand to the bridge of his nose, fighting off an ache starting at the back of his eyes. The duplicity of the plan was stunning. So many things could go wrong, the legality of it, the unpredictability of toying with people's lives—the possibility that he wouldn't find the traitor in time to extract himself. It was a dangerous line to walk, but if the scheme worked as Ford hoped, it was likely the fastest way to discover the needed information.

He pinched his nose harder. For the first time in his life, he suddenly regretted his fame for going beyond the rules to bring in a criminal.

"I don't like it," he said at last.

"Because it wasn't your idea?"

He dropped his hand and glowered at the man. "Your job suits you, you know."

Though spare lantern light filled the room, the questioning rise of Thatcher's brow was unmistakable.

"Diplomacy is hardly your strong point," Alex explained. "It's a blessing that riding the countryside gives you little interaction with people."

Thatcher's lips quirked again. Twice in one night? A regular belly-buster of an evening for him.

"Well, I suppose it's not like I've never stretched the limits of how to bring in a suspect." Alex sighed. "But I still need you to meet with Ford."

Thatcher reached for the empty cup and tipped his head back, draining what few drops could be found since neither Mrs. Langley nor Johanna had yet appeared to offer him a drink. He set the mug down and frowned. "I think we both grasp the situation clearly."

"It's not about that. I need more money."

"Gaming skills a bit rusty?"

"No." He laughed. "I suspect I shall have to pay a fine price if I'm to become more enticing than orchids."

"Orchids? Is that a new cipher I need to know?"

Alex clapped his friend on the back and stood, snatching up the empty cup. "Thatcher, I doubt you'll ever need to know about flowers."

∽

Whimpering leached out Thomas's closed door, and Johanna winced. This was her fault. All of it. If only she'd better managed their meager funds, made wiser decisions about what to fix and what not, this whole tragedy wouldn't have happened.

Next to her, Mam frowned, face drawn. "You're doing it again, aren't you?"

"Doing what?"

"Blaming yourself. Stuff and nonsense!" Mam shoved the bucket of soiled dressings into her hands. "Go on down to the taproom and put your mind on other things. I'll sit with Thomas."

"But I—"

"Shush!" Mam shooed her away with a flick of her fingers. "I'll have none of that. Off with you."

Truly, her mother should've been in the military, for there'd be no putting her off. Johanna forced a half smile. "Very well. Come get me if you need me."

Mam nodded and ducked back into Thomas's room. Johanna waited until her mother disappeared, then let her smile fall to the floor. Too bad she couldn't lie there as well. Had she ever been this weary?

Treading down the hall, she descended the stairs and entered the kitchen—where a broad-shouldered man stood slicing cheese. "Oh! Mr. Morton. What a surprise."

"You've caught me red-handed, I'm afraid." He smiled up at her—the warmth of which did strange things to her empty tummy. "Just gathering a plate of cheese and bread for my friend."

"Here, let me do that." She set down the bucket and doused her hands in some water. Mr. Morton's stare burned through the back of her gown. Was he reliving the way he'd held her those few nights ago as vividly as she was?

Shoving down the rising heat of embarrassment, she rehung the drying cloth, then herded Mr. Morton aside by reaching for the loaf of bread on the table. "I apologize for our lack of service the past few days."

"You have been tending Thomas, no doubt. How is he?"

She paused before setting knife to bread, and met his gaze. "Tired of the pain and tired of his room, tired of Mam and tired of me."

Mr. Morton chuckled. A delightful sound. Low and soothing.

"I'd expect no less from a caged boy—and a wounded one at that. I would be happy to sit with him and—"

"No, thank you." She sawed through the thick loaf, using more force than necessary. It was churlish of her to cut him off so, but it couldn't be helped. Tending Thomas was her cross to bear. "Mam and I are managing."

"Johanna."

She jerked her face up, annoyed that he dared to use her Christian name—but more irritated that she wished he'd say it again, for her name on his lips was a curious balm.

He studied her with an unwavering stare. "Let me help."

The knife in her hand weighed heavy. No, her whole soul did. Emotions she ought not be feeling right now swirled overhead and pressed down. He stood on the other side of the table, but the way his blue eyes caressed her, he might as well be holding her in his arms. She frowned. She'd been wise to avoid him the past two days. She bent, sawing off another slab of bread. "You are a guest here, sir. Not the hired help."

"There's only one person I know more stubborn than you."

Finished, she set the knife down. "Yourself?"

He smirked. "You take on too much, you know."

"I must. This inn is our livelihood." She handed over the plate of bread and cheese.

He took it, yet he did not leave. Instead, a great sorrow furrowed his brow. "I am sorry your father is no longer here to help you. This is too much of a burden for you and your mother to shoulder alone."

"While I appreciate the sentiment, the truth is we shouldered the burden long before my father died." She pressed her lips shut. Why had she shared that? How did he manage to pull things from her she didn't even know were buried deep in her heart?

"I am sorry to hear it. Did he suffer long?"

Suffer? The word circled like a vulture, ready to swoop and stab the barely healed scars left behind by her father. "The only thing my father suffered from was too much drink and a lying tongue. I abhor both!"

"So should we all." His tone was soft, low, almost as if he spoke to himself.

"Well," she lifted her chin, "I suppose what does not drive us into the ground only serves to make us stronger, hmm? Now if you'll excuse me, I have a taproom to tend."

She grabbed a cloth and whisked past him, wondering all the while how much stronger God thought she needed to be.

CHAPTER EIGHT

The next day, Alex waited for the light footsteps of Johanna and the bass thwunks of the doctor to pass his door before he cracked it open. Peering out, he paused a moment longer until the fat doctor disappeared down the stairway and his wheezing faded. Ought not a man interested in health take better care of his own?

Easing his door shut, Alex stole down the hallway to Thomas's chamber. He'd tried asking for permission to see the boy, but to no avail.

This time he wouldn't ask.

He rapped once on Thomas's door before entering. It was a small room, walls weeping brown streaks from years of leakage. A single window cast sunlight upon the boy's thin body, lying like a piece of flotsam upon a sea of pain. His eyes were red-rimmed, cheeks pale, and his burnt leg was bolstered up and useless. This was wrong. Unjust in every possible respect. A boy shouldn't be laid out in bed like an old man. He ought to be running, climbing trees, chasing after girls and teasing them.

Aah, Lord, grant Your mercy.

Alex choked down rising emotion with a gruff throat clearing. "Good day, Master Thomas. Did you know you're guarded more heavily than a transfer of gold bullion? Perhaps your mother and sister should give up inn-keeping and join a regiment of dragoons." He winked, hoping the effect would lighten the load weighing heavy on the boy's brow.

"They're more like dragons, if you ask me." A smile curved Thomas's lips, then flattened into a wince as he propped his elbows behind him and pushed upward.

Alex grabbed a chair and pulled it to the lad's bedside, straddling it backward. The sudden movement rattled a bottle of amber liquid on the nightstand. Straight brandy or laudanum? He studied the boy's glassy gaze. Could be either.

"How goes it? Have the past three days been non-stop pain?"

"Aye, sir."

Alex flexed his fingers and leaned forward against the chair's back, resisting the urge to reach out and tussle the lad's hair. Regardless of the injury, the boy had already been coddled far too much. "Sir is for fathers and old people. I am neither. You may call me Alex, for are we not friends?"

"Aye, sir—Alex."

"You're a quick study." His gaze strayed to the boy's leg, covered from the knee down with a cloth saturated in some kind of golden syrup. Maybe honey. Maybe not. The skin peeking out above the poultice burned an angry scarlet. He could only imagine what damage lay beneath the wrap. "What did the doctor have to say? Shall you live?"

"Pah! Mam and Jo would kill me if I didn't."

He glanced sideways at the twist of the boy's mouth. True, Johanna and her mother had turned into squawking, overprotective hens, but agreement would only fan the flames of the lad's discontent.

"You know your sister and mother want the best for you. Their concern is very real."

Thomas blew out a harsh sigh, then grimaced when his dramatics jostled his leg.

Alex smiled. Apparently passion ran in the family. "Give it time, Thomas. You'll soon be back on both feet."

"But…" Tears filled the boy's eyes. "What if I never walk properly again?"

Alex scooted his chair closer. "I've a story for you."

The boy's gaze shot to his. Just the effect he'd hoped for.

"When I was a lad, 'round about ten years old—"

The boy's pupils widened, and Alex knew he'd nailed the boy's age, reeling in his full attention. "I had a bit of a mishap myself. Father told me never—*ever*—to handle his pistol when he wasn't around. Easy enough, since he carried it with him wherever he went."

"Everywhere?"

Alex shrugged. "London streets are not as safe as Dover's."

Thomas nodded as if he'd lived a hundred years roaming Cheapside or Spitalfields.

Scrubbing a hand across his chin, Alex hid his smile. "One day, my father was home after an all-nighter, sleeping. I knew better than to wake him.

Mother was gone. But I was curious. You know that feeling, that need to know how something works? It fairly crawls under your skin, and you have to act on it, for there's no sitting still."

A small "aah" rode the crest of Thomas's exhale. Good, this was working.

"Well, that's exactly how it was for me on that day. Not that Father hadn't shown me his pistol many a time. I could sketch the bronze muzzle and carved handle from memory. The curve of the steel trigger. The sharp angles of the flintlock. Such a beauty." He paused, gauging the time for the gun's image to spring to life in the boy's mind.

"The thing is, Father had never yet allowed me to shoot it. How would it feel? Was there a mighty kickback? I was certain I was old enough, strong enough to handle it, for is ten years of age not nearly a grown man?"

Thomas's face snapped to his. "I tell that to Mam all the time!"

"Well, it's not." He edged closer, whispering the rest. "And I've the scar to prove it. Would you like to see?"

Thomas's head bobbed in a single, solemn nod.

Alex stood, turned the chair around, and pulled off his left boot. His toe snagged for a moment on a hole in his sock, long past the need for darning, but he finally freed his foot and lifted it for Thomas's inspection. There, at center, just above his toes, rose a bubble of marred skin the size of a farthing and the color of an overripe peach even to this day. A tangible reminder of transgression's cost.

"What happened?" Thomas's voice was reverent.

"As I said, I wanted to try out the pistol, but I also wanted to obey my father. I figured him being in the other room fully met the requirements of having him present. So, I gave it a try."

He tugged his sock back on, followed by his boot, then met Thomas's gaze. "Which do you suppose was louder, the firing of the gun, or my screams when the shot tore through my foot?"

"Caw, sir!" The boy's face paled.

"Laid me up for more than a fortnight, I tell you. Got middling good with a cloth-molded crutch. Shall I make one for you?"

Thomas shifted on his elbows, propping himself up farther. This time, though a very real tremor of pain wrinkled across his brow, his smile belied it. "I'd like that. Oh, I would!"

"Good. We'll have you up and about in no time, giving your mother and sister something to really cluck about, eh?" Hooking his thumbs beneath his armpits, he flapped like an overgrown chicken and squawked.

Laughter shook the boy's shoulders.

Mission accomplished. Alex stood and replaced the chair.

"Thomas? Are you all right?" The door swung open, and Johanna's skirts swept in. She summed up Alex with a mighty scowl, the harbinger of a sound scolding.

"Mr. Morton! Have I not asked you to allow Thomas his rest? I insist you leave at once." She stepped aside from the doorway, as if the action, combined with her command, might usher him out as effectively as a gun to the head.

He planted his feet. "It's been three full days, Miss Langley. The boy needed a diversion."

"The boy needs to rest, sir."

"Aw, but Jo." Thomas's thin voice cracked. "Alex was only—"

"It's Mr. Morton, and furthermore"—Johanna looked past Alex to her brother. "Thomas! What are you doing sitting up? You know your leg must remain elevated. The doctor said—"

"It's still on the cushion," the boy shot back.

"Thomas, this is not to be borne. You will not walk again if you do not listen to the doctor's instruction. Is that what you want?"

Her curt question sagged the boy's shoulders. He deflated onto the mattress, pain seeping out in a groan.

Alex frowned. Her careless words had undone in seconds the small amount of good he'd built in the past twenty minutes. He'd hauled in many a brothel madam who'd not be as callous.

Silently, he studied her. A strand of dark hair escaped one of her pins, drooping over her brow. Shadows darkened half-circles beneath her eyes. And was that. . .yes, the wrinkles in her gown were imbedded deep enough that she must've slept in it. This was not the same woman he'd come to know in the past week. Something more was at work here than simply distress about her brother.

"I would have a word with you, outside, if you please, Miss Langley." In two steps, he clasped her arm and led her out the door, shutting it behind them.

"Mr. Morton, really!" She faced him with a scowl.

"Exactly, Miss Langley. What is this *really* all about?"

Johanna clenched her hands so tight, her nails dug into her palms. Was it Mr. Morton's piercing blue gaze or his inquiry that made her feel so exposed? Either way, she didn't like it. Containing her problems was hard enough without him poking holes into her facade.

She lifted her chin. "You had no right to sneak into my brother's room and excite him in such a fashion."

He drew in a long breath and slowly released it. A curious reaction. She'd expected something a bit more defensive. Even a simple raised brow would've done the trick, but the strong cut of Mr. Morton's face was entirely indecipherable. Even with years of experience reading patrons and guests, this man was an enigma at best.

"I admit it was underhanded to wait to visit your brother until you were occupied elsewhere. For that I apologize. But"—he wagged his finger—"that is the sum of my crime. I took the boy's mind off his pain and fear, and you brought it all back with a few thoughtless words."

She stiffened, his accusation chilling her to the core. Is that what she'd done? Slowly, she lowered her head, preferring to study the hem of her skirt instead of the indictment in Mr. Morton's frown.

"As I suspected." His tone softened. "And so I repeat, what is this really about?"

Clasping her hands in front of her, she debated what, if anything, to tell him. Oh, how she missed sharing her burdens with her friend Maggie, but since the baby had arrived, time was a scarce commodity from her. And she couldn't turn to Mam, for her mother was as overwrought as she. That left no other close confidant save God upon whom to unload her troubles, and the skirt fabric at her knees was already worn thin.

She dared a peek up at Mr. Morton. The hard lines of his face had smoothed into genuine compassion—the same look as when he'd held her in his arms and allowed her to make a sopping mess of his shirt.

She sucked in a breath for courage. "Truly, I appreciate your candor, yet I have already overstepped the bounds of propriety. Haven't you heard enough of my troubles? Should you not be out acquiring some fine wines, or whatever it is that you do, instead of counseling my woes?"

"Aah, still a bit of spunk in you. Good." One corner of his mouth turned upward. "Even so, sometimes it helps to get an outsider's perspective."

Was that what he was? An outsider? Then why did she feel as if she ought put on a pot of tea and pour out her cares to this man? She searched his gaze, her problems rising to her tongue. Clearly his mesmerizing blue stare muddled her thinking. Good heavens. What *was* she thinking?

She turned. "I appreciate your concern, but perhaps you ought leave now, Mr. Morton. I'm sure you've bigger matters to attend, and so I bid you a good day."

"That's the easy way out, Johanna."

Her name from his lips shot straight to her heart and tripped an extra beat. Annoyed at the base response, she whirled. "Why must you insist on calling me by my Christian name?"

"Because it never fails to get your attention." His smile dazzled. "And I find that when I anger you, you're more likely to tell me what's really on your mind."

"You are exasperating." As was this conversation. She sidestepped him.

He blocked her path. "And you're avoiding the question."

Faith! What a bully. She folded her arms and for a moment considered how strong of a battering ram she could make herself if she bent forward and charged. There'd be no other way to put him off—but she wouldn't make a dent in that broad chest.

"Very well." She sighed, resignation both acrid and sweet. "If you must know, I am short on the rent payment and the next hearth installment is due in a few days. Now with Thomas's doctor bills. . .well, unless God acts, you may have to find yourself different lodging soon."

"How soon?" he asked.

"Friday."

"How much?"

"Twenty-five pounds."

"How much do you have?"

"Ten."

His nostrils flared, and she got the distinct impression he sucked in more than air. Her own head spun from the swiftness of his interrogation. If this was how he conducted business, no doubt merchants quaked in their boots to cut a deal with him.

"That's quite a shortfall to gather in three days." His tone was even, placid almost, but his conclusion was deadly accurate.

"Oh, what you must think, Mr. Morton." She retreated to the corridor's wall and leaned against it for support. "Had providence not brought you here, we'd not even have that much. It's not like Mam and I haven't minded our accounts. In truth, there are hardly any to mind. Mr. Quail and his band play nightly, which draws in some patrons, but pays only enough to cover the musicians' room and board." She shrugged. "And I've yet to see a coin from Mr. Nutbrown, despite his puppet's excessive promises. Perhaps the Blue Hedge Inn really is cursed."

"On the contrary. I'd say the inn is blessed, Miss Langley, with your fair presence."

The intensity of his gaze heated her cheeks. "If having no rent money is a blessing, then I'd hate to hear your description of mishap, sir."

"Have we not moved beyond sir and mister? The name is Alex. And as I said, all you need is a different perspective."

She threw out her hands. "From where, the workhouse window?"

"Now there is the quick-witted spunk I admire." He smiled. "I see exactly what must be done to cure your monetary ills. Leastwise, for the time being."

"Do tell."

Advancing toward her, he reached inside his greatcoat and pulled out a small pouch. With a touch as light as a whisper, he grabbed her fingers and deposited the bag in her palm, the leather still warm from his body heat.

Without a word, he wheeled about and stalked down the hall.

She stepped away from the wall. "Where are you going, Mr. Morton?"

He kept walking.

"Alex!"

He turned back. "You see? Christian names work for me as well. Now then, there's a certain patron I shall be happy to evict for you."

Her lips parted. Surely he wasn't hinting at collaring Mr. Nutbrown?

"You can thank me later. Now, go tend your brother. He's got an ear for stories, so if nothing else, make one up." He pivoted and disappeared down the stairway.

She gaped. How long she stood there, she could only guess, but slowly, as one surfaces from a deep slumber, she realized her fingers had gone to sleep from grasping the pouch so tightly. Loosening the drawstring, she poked about at the coins, calculating their worth.

Sweet mercy! She must be dreaming. Twenty golden guineas. . .more than enough to pay Mr. Spurge when he came to call on Friday.

The few bites of porridge she'd managed this morning slowly rose from her stomach, and she swallowed. Nothing good ever came of taking money from a man. Absently, she rubbed the small scar behind her ear. That was a lesson she learned early on. This was more than just rent, and while Spurge may be staved off for yet another month, what compensation would Mr. Morton expect for giving her such a sum?

CHAPTER NINE

Darkness had never been a friend to Lucius Nutbrown. An acquaintance, yes, and a familiar one at that, but not a jolly, hobnobbing comrade. No, not a bit of it. Still, he scrunched his eyes shut, closing out the taproom's meager light—and the lurid image of the meat-cleaver-sized hands reaching for him. Maybe this time his frail childhood belief that if you could not see danger, then danger could not see you would prove true.

Come, darkness, hide me now.

Fingers bit into his shoulders. So much for childish convictions.

"Out! And don't come back, ye barmy beggar!" The words flew out the door along with him. Tuck and roll time. Even with a full afternoon of practice, his elbow caught in a pothole, ripping yet another gash into his greatcoat. Gads! Could not a town the size of Dover pay to even out the ruts in the road?

He bumped to a stop and opened his eyes—then wished he hadn't.

A beast of a horse reared over him, the silhouette ghoulish with the sun behind it. Front hooves hovered above his head, about to spear his skull to the ground like a harpoon through an eel.

Lucius jerked sideways. Gravel shards stung his neck when a hoof dug into the lane, but better bits of rock than bits of brain being splattered about.

The stallion screamed, as did the man atop it. "Mind the horse!"

Lucius staggered to his feet, shooting out his puppet-clad hand. "Mind Mr. Nutbrown's head!"

The man atop the horse gave him nary a look as he retreated down the road. Lucius flipped his hand around so the jester's painted face looked into his own. "I get no respect, aye Nixie? None a'tall."

"None a'tall," he repeated in Nixie's voice. "Speeding devils ought to look where they're going, Mr. Nutbrown."

"Right as always, my friend." He slipped Nixie into an inside pocket and bent to retrieve his hat, where it lay crushed on the ground. As he punched the shape back into the felt, a quiver ran down his spine. This could've easily been his head.

Two pair of footsteps, one of them kind of thumpy, drew up along either side of him. A low whistle blew from the short man on the left. He smelled like overcooked peas. "That were a sorry pass, squire. Ye might've been flattened."

The other man slung his arm around Lucius's shoulder, maybe for balance, as one of his legs was wooden. "What's this world coming to when a squire such as yerself can't peacefully cross the street?"

Hmm. All day long he'd been shunned. Why the sudden attention? Shrugging away from the taller man's embrace, Lucius put on his hat and pulled out Nixie. The little puppet's head bobbed though he tried to keep it still, the effects of the near-trampling still jittering his nerves. "Mr. Nutbrown is no squire, sirs, but a true and bona fide businessman."

"Why, I said such a thing when we see'd what'd happened, right, Blackie?" The shorter of the two squinted up at the other. "I says, 'There's a businessman, a right true one.' Din't I?"

"That ye did." The big one bent and shoved his face into Nixie's. "Well, well, little man. Ye're shaking like a maiden on her wedding night. Can we buy you and your partner a drink? If you've the time, that is."

Lucius froze. No one *ever* addressed Nixie except for himself, and he wasn't sure how to feel about that. This would take some sorting through. . .and a mug of ale was just the thing for sorting. He splayed his pinkie and thumb, causing Nixie to spread wide his arms. "Yes, sirs. Mr. Nutbrown is finished with his appointments for the day, so he believes he could fit that into his schedule."

The big man straightened, his smile as irregular as a carved squash. "A right proper businessman, you are, Mr. Nutbrown. We can tell, aye, Charlie?"

"Exactly what I was thinking." The other fellow—Mr. Charlie—lifted the brim of his hat to scratch a patch of shockingly red hair. "It'll be an honor to share a pint with the likes o' you both." He nodded at Nixie and him in turn.

Lucius sucked in a breath. Each of these strangers acknowledged Nixie for what he'd always believed him to be—alive. Which, of course, moved them from the category of strangers to beloved friends.

"Right, let's be about it, then." The big man turned toward the door of the inn from which Lucius had recently flown.

"No!" Lucius swallowed, hating that he'd caused a wrinkle on the brows of his new friends, but mostly hating that he'd slipped and used his real voice.

He kicked his tone up a few notches and held Nixie higher. "That establishment would hardly do for men of our caliber. Mr. Nutbrown suggests the Drunken Duck."

Lucius held his breath, waiting for the questioning lines to smooth on his friends' faces. *Please. Please.* The Drunken Duck was the only establishment he'd not been thrown out of yet, ever since Mr. Morton began the awful trend earlier this morning. Dirty scoundrel, usurping him like that.

Mr. Charlie cuffed him on the back with a firm pat. "The Drunken Duck it is, squire."

His lungs released, as did the tension in his jaw. They fell into step three abreast—four, if he counted Nixie—with him in the middle.

The big fellow talked over his head to Mr. Charlie, his words keeping time with the thump of his peg leg. "I told you from the looks of him, he'd be too far above our station."

Mr. Charlie shrugged. "I says we ask anyway. All he can do is say no."

Lucius glanced sideways at the other fellow, his palm feeling sticky and hot beneath Nixie's cover.

"He don't need our money." The man's words hung suspended for a moment.

Until Lucius grabbed them. Money? There was an opportunity here. He could smell it—fresh and green and more pleasant than overcooked peas. He turned Nixie to face them all. "Do you fellows have a proposition for Mr. Nutbrown? He is a man of business, after all."

Mr. Charlie leaned forward, grinning past him toward the other fellow. "We could sure use a businessman, right Blackie?"

The big one—Mr. Blackie, apparently—rubbed a hand over his stubbly skull, his step not missing a thumpy beat as he kept walking. "Well, we do got a regular transaction coming up. One with ledgers and numbers and all kinds o' business type stuff we can hardly understand. We know, though, that it promises to pay real well."

"*Real* well," Charlie echoed.

Nixie stared at him from an arm's length away, bobbing up and down with each step. One of his papier-mâché cheeks bent inward, dented from a piece of gravel. With his free hand, Lucius rubbed his own cheek, then winced. His was scraped as well. That settled it. He brought his little friend closer to his face. "We ought help out our new friends, hmm?"

Mr. Charlie elbowed him. "We'd be mighty obliged."

Mr. Blackie repeated the action on the other side. "What do you say, Mr. Nutbrown?"

A slow smile crawled over his lips. If he looked close enough, Nixie grinned too. In fact, Nixie perked up so much, his little jester head waggled. "Mr. Nutbrown says yes, gentlemen. We'd be happy to lend our business finesse."

Alex strode down the street, wishing for the hundredth time he could ease the ugly questions he'd created in Johanna's eyes. Not that he blamed her. Men didn't usually hand over coins without the tether of expectations. Side-stepping a mound of refuse swept up by a closing shopkeeper, he huffed out a breath. Money was nothing to him. He'd already put out a word for Thatcher to bring him more. It was the woman distracting his thoughts he couldn't afford. He reseated his hat and strode on.

Ahead, a shop matron grunted as she backed through a doorway, each of her hands loaded with a bucket of flowers left unsold for the day.

Flowers? His steps slowed. A seed of an idea sprouted. Might be a bit forward, but sometimes it paid to take a risk.

He upped his pace. Ignoring the CLOSED shingle hanging in the window, he pushed through the florist's door, setting off a jingling bell.

"We're done for the day." The woman's voice travelled from a back entryway.

"Yet you've flowers left. I'll take them."

The woman poked her head out the doorway, wearing a mobcap so tight, it puckered the skin of her brow. "I said we're done. Closed. Finished for the day. Buy your flower on the morrow."

"I don't want *a* flower." He grinned. "I want them all."

"All the. . .you mean. . .*all* what I got left?" Her gaze shot to his hands, her words wadding up as tightly as the roll of bills he pulled from an inside pocket of his greatcoat.

"All. And may I have use of a pen and a slip of paper?"

"You can have use of the flamin' best stationery in the shop!" She dashed from the back room and swiped aside scraps of twine and stem cuttings littering the counter. After a quick wipe down with her sleeve, she pulled out a tray from beneath, containing his requested items plus a few envelopes.

"Here ye are, sir. I'll wrap those flowers up straightaway."

As she bustled over to the buckets, Alex uncorked the ink and dipped the pen. Now, what to say to a woman who looked at him with eyes of mistrust?

I can help you. Let me.
~ A. Morton

He blotted the note dry and folded it into an envelope, then turned to the woman. "I should like those delivered to Miss Louisa Coburn."

Her eyebrows rose, the mobcap pinching in a whole new way. "You mean the viscount's daughter?"

"Unless you know another Louisa Coburn. Good day." He stalked out, the jingling bell competing with the woman's *ne'er-would-have-guessed* and *didn't-see-that-coming* mumbles. No doubt Miss Coburn would mutter the same when she received the flowers. He blew out a sigh. As of yet, he'd still not figured out how to accomplish Ford's directive without actually marrying the woman, but he'd come up with something. He would. There was simply no other option.

Glancing at the sky, he calculated daylight. An hour remained, give or take. Was he too late? He lengthened his strides, bypassing those headed home for a warm bowl of stew. Shops thinned out the closer he drew to the beachhead. To his left, white cliffs stood like stark sentinels, watching over the harbor. The castle on top loomed over all, a dark reminder that war had been—and always would be—a present danger from offshore. Ahead, earthen batteries rose along the seafront, providing a small measure of protection should the French decide on a bold affront.

He crested the line of defense and trotted down the other side, his boots grinding into the sand, shells, and rocks of low tide. For now, foreign invaders didn't concern him. The smugglers off to his right were a bigger threat. One he could manage, though.

Lifting a hand, he hailed the three men with a loud voice. "Done for the day, Slingsby?"

The two men with their backs to him turned immediately, hands covering pistol hilts belted at their waist. Dark gazes searched the length of him. He returned the favor. Neither were familiar. Judging by the set of their jaws and shoulders, he'd have two bullets to dodge if Slingsby's memory slipped.

Slowly, the old smuggler stood, leaving the fish he'd been tending over an open fire. His eyes squinted nearly shut, then popped wide. "Well, I'll be a toady-headed cully! That you, Ratter?"

"In the flesh." He drew near and offered his hand. Three shakes, a draw-back, then a touch of thumbs, the local code. Leaning closer, he breathed into Slingsby's ear. "But it's Mr. Morton, this time."

"Oh? Morton, is it? A regular gent, are ye now?" Slingsby reared back with a hearty laugh, the cries of overhead gulls squawking along with him. Alex stood and waited. He'd learned long ago the best course of action with the fellow was to let him ride out the wave of whatever emotion swelled inside. The other two men hunkered back down and snatched blackened sticks of skewered fish off the fire.

Slingsby leaned aside and spit out the rest of his laughter along with a stream of tobacco, then lowered his voice. "I'll call ye whate'er ye like, long as yer tipstaff don't bear a warrant with my name on it."

Alex slapped a hand to his chest and staggered back a step. "You really think I'd turn on you?"

"Pah! Save yer playacting." The old fellow dropped to a rock draped with a bit of sailcloth. "Sit yerself down, man."

Alex chose his spot carefully, positioning himself so that his back was to the water and the vista of Dover in front. Napoleon may be an enemy in the rear, but that tyrant was farther away than the thugs before him.

"Thrush, Bane." Slingsby nodded at each of his henchmen in turn. "This here's Morton. I trust him with my life—mostly."

The other men slipped him a slanted glance, then went back to silently chewing their fish. It would take more than an old smuggler's word of endorsement to gain their trust.

Slingsby grabbed a skewer and offered it to him over the small fire.

"Still sore about Ned Dooley?" Alex bit into the fish, chewing slowly to allow Slingsby time to digest his question.

"I admit Ned were a cocklebur of a man." Slingsby shook his head, his dirty neckcloth hanging so loose that it remained motionless with the move-ment. "Still, Dooley were one of the brethren." He leaned forward, the glint in his eye hardening to flint. "None of us take losin' a brother lightly."

"Dooley was a maggot, and well you know it. Smuggling tea is one thing. Slitting throats quite another. I will not abide violence on these shores." He speared Slingsby with a glower of his own. "Do we have an understanding?"

Thrush and Bane quit chewing. All it would take was one word from Slingsby, and they'd turn on him. He shifted his left foot slightly, just enough to yank out his boot-knife if need be.

"Ye hurt me. Hurt me cruel, ye do." The setting sun cast an eerie glow on Slingsby's face, setting the tips of his grey whiskers on fire. Finally, he sat back, taking the tension along with him. "I've harmed nary a fly."

Alex snorted. "You don't need to." His gaze slid from Thrush to Bane, making his point clear.

"Why, these are naught but honest fishermen. Just finished putting away the nets and boat to prove it. Right boys?"

Bane grunted.

Thrush said nothing.

Slingsby hitched a thumb over his shoulder, indicating a ramshackle wooden vessel pulled inland not far down the beach. "Yessir. Fishing. Wenching. Drinking. Other than that, things been real quiet since you were last here. What's yer game this time, Rat—er, Morton?"

Alex pulled off the last morsel of fish from the stick and popped it into his mouth. Sometimes silence accomplished more than words.

"Holding yer hand close, eh? I respects that, I do." Tossing his fish bones aside, Slingsby dragged his hand across his mouth before he continued. "But I'm guessing this here ain't no social call."

"Just keeping a running account, Slingsby. I like to keep an eye on things." He reached into an inside pocket and pulled out a small leather bag, making sure to jingle a few of the coins inside. Three sets of eyeballs followed the movement. "Any new brothers in the fold?"

The brute to his right stiffened. "Why you askin'?"

"Like I said—" He tossed the bag from one hand to the other. "Just keeping accounts. I hear there's some Leaguers hereabouts. I'd like to have a little conversation with them."

Bane eyed him. "Snitches don't live long enough to enjoy any gain."

"No, no. Nothing like that." A slow smile curved his lips. "I'm a collector. I deal in the trade of black market information. Buying. Selling. Sharing the wealth. Ain't that right, Slingsby?"

"All I know is you ain't ne'er one to play by the rules. Still, my pockets are always padded a little thicker whenever yer in town. Must say, ye always done me right." Slingsby folded his arms. "All right. There's a few new faces that joined the ranks since last you were here. None of 'em Leaguers, though, least-wise not that I know of. I can give you names, but they're as real as Morton or Ratter, Bane or Thrush—"

Thrush jumped to his feet, hauling Slingsby up by the collar. "Watch it, old man! I warned you not to bandy my name about."

Slingsby grinned. "Ye ought be worried more about crossing Morton than me."

By the time Bane turned to face him, Alex had knocked Thrush out cold and gripped his blade, ready to slash Bane if challenged.

Bane hacked out a curse and stalked off.

Slingsby chuckled, shaking out his rumpled coat. "There's always action when yer around." Reseating himself, the old man lifted his face. "I'll only say this once, so listen up. Besides those two ye just met, the new brethren are Beak and Sniper. Oh yeah, and a new fish that showed up just a week ago. Goes by the name o' Que."

"Que?" Alex scrubbed a hand across his face, stalling for time. Short for Quail, perhaps? Blowing out a long breath, he swallowed the idea, leaving behind a salty aftertaste.

Slingsby eyed him. "Bludgeoned you, did I?"

Alex rubbed his stomach, hopefully masking his previous hesitation. "Your cooking did. Thanks, Slingsby." He took a few steps, then turned. "Oh, and watch your back. Blackjack and Charlie are hereabouts."

The old man's face drained of color, as bleached as the bones dotting the sand. "Blast! If they're tangled up with guinea boats again, it'll be the devil to pay for all of us."

"Knowing those two, it's likely that and more."

Alex strode away, then stopped at the crest of the earthen mound ringing the bay. A movement near the cliffs caught his eye. Maybe. Maybe not.

Squinting in the last of the sun's rays, he shaded his eyes with a hand to his forehead. A dark silhouette nearly blended in with the rocks, but not quite. The attempt at stealth was valiant enough, just not successful. The shape wasn't necessarily familiar—but the slight limp was. By the time the figure ducked between two rocks, Alex had no doubt about the man's identity. But what interest did Lord Coburn have in smuggler's hideouts?

Hopefully Slingsby had an extra torch on that derelict he called a fishing boat, for Alex intended to find out.

CHAPTER TEN

Darkness rushed in. Nothing more. Johanna craned her neck to look down one length of Blue Lane, then the other. Not a patron in sight. Stooping, she propped open the front door with a brick. Maybe the enticement of the band making merry inside would call to those outside. The music was certainly loud enough. Still, it was a shame Mr. Morton didn't lead the musicians instead of Mr. Quail, for though the man played with enthusiasm, his notes were just enough short of key to set her teeth on edge.

She braved one more glance down the road, conjuring customers with full pockets scrambling toward the Blue Hedge. A week's worth, no, more like a fortnight's worth of ale-drinkers might give her enough money to pay back Mr. Morton, but the only movement was the streak of a cat darting into an alley.

Rubbing her arms against the chill of the early evening air, she turned and strode through the taproom, trying to ignore the fact that there was only one patron nursing a mug in a corner seat. Perhaps a good chat with her mother would set things a'right.

"Mam?" she called as she entered the kitchen, but the room was as barren as Blue Lane. The remnants of a sliced loaf of bread, a few cabbage leaves, and an uncovered jar of applesauce littered the table. Of course. She should've known her mother would've made Thomas a dinner tray and was likely even now serving it.

She reached for the jar lid, but just as her fingers grazed the metal, she was yanked back by the arm and twirled around.

"A dance, milady?" Mr. Quail spun her so fast, she could hardly breathe let alone answer.

He laughed and pulled her against him, waltzing down the length of the small room and back again.

"Mr. Quail!" She wrenched from his grasp and dashed to the other side of the table, putting a stop to the crazy jig and any other inappropriate ideas he might be entertaining. "Really!"

"Of course, really. And actually, and even truly." Laughter rumbled from deep inside his chest. "Oh, Miss Langley, do not look so aghast. Do you never dance? Sing? Laugh out loud?"

"Not if I can help it." She frowned down at the way her skirt hem had hitched itself atop her half-boot and shook it loose, covering her lower leg. Had he seen?

"Life's too short not to enjoy it, especially for a beauty such as yourself."

Insolent man! She stiffened. "Should you not be out in the taproom?"

He shook his head, never once pulling his gaze from her face. "They won't miss me."

She inched closer to the tabletop—and the bread knife. "Was there something you wanted?"

"Just a few words with a pretty lady." In two long strides, he snatched Mam's stool from the corner and perched atop it. Hooking his feet on the lower rung, he settled comfortably. Clearly the man had more than a few words in mind.

Jo folded her arms, scowling. "You can stop the flattery, sir. It doesn't work."

"Can't blame a man for trying, can you?" A rogue grin curved his mouth, which probably worked for other tavern wenches, but not for her.

"What do you want, Mr. Quail?"

"Aah, direct. I like that in a woman." He curled a swath of dark hair behind his ear, then asked, "What do you know about Mr. Morton?"

Her brow tightened. He could've brought up a hundred other topics, but this? "I am not in the habit of conversing about other patrons. If there's something you want to know, why not ask him yourself?"

"I would, were he here." Quail shrugged. "The man is in and out at all hours. It's hard to corner him."

True. She'd not seen Mr. Morton since he'd given her the pouch of money, and that'd been early this morning. She glanced at the mantel clock. It was after seven now. What did he do all day?

"Tell me, Miss Langley," Mr. Quail's grin faded. The tone of his voice flattened into a gravity he'd never before employed. "Mr. Morton's not asked you to pass off any notes or attend any. . .er. . .meetings while he's been here?"

She frowned. Other than the stolen kiss, Mr. Morton had been nothing but kind. "What an odd question. What are you insinuating?"

He leaned forward. "Merely looking out for your interests."

Her interests—she narrowed her eyes—or his? "No, Mr. Morton has asked me nothing untoward. For the most part, he's been a gentleman, even paid up his rent in advance with guineas."

"He paid you in yellow boys?" Quail's eyes widened. "That is interesting. He does seem a bit well to do, hmm? Clothing impeccable. Grooming exquisite."

She pictured Alexander, standing in the hall where she'd last seen him. His brown dress coat rode the crest of his wide shoulders, cut to perfection. An ivory cravat had been knotted and tucked into a collar set just below his strong jawline. Tan trousers of fine wool followed the long lines of his legs and—Johanna tugged at her own collar, suddenly a bit short of breath. Why was it so hot in here?

"Is it not strange that a man of such means chooses to reside here?" Mr. Quail's question was a slap in the face. Heat of a different kind curled her hands into fists, and she popped them onto her hips. "And why not? The Blue Hedge is a respectable establishment. Furthermore—"

"Tut, tut, little miss. No disrespect intended." The man stood and planted his hands on the table, leaning toward her. "All I'm saying is that it's a curiosity when a man who rubs shoulders with the viscount lodges at an inn on the farthest reach of town instead of residing in a more fashionable neighborhood."

"The viscount?" Her fists uncurled, and she smoothed her moist palms against her apron. Mr. Quail was right. As much as she'd love to house a grander clientele, why would a man of social standing stay here? With drafty windows, lumpy mattresses, and meals nothing to boast about?

"I hear Mr. Morton's a new gaming partner at Lord Coburn's table, and apparently is quite a favorite despite the rumors of his nightly wins."

Her breath stuck in her throat. Mr. Morton was a gambler? The thought set her teeth on edge—but so did the way Mr. Quail eyed her. She met the man's stare head-on. "How would you know such information?"

"Oh. . .hearsay."

"From whom?"

"Connections." Quail straightened and sniffed. "It pays to know with whom I share a roof. And so I ask, confidentially, of course, what else do you know of the man?"

"Well, I..."

What did she know? She gazed at the pots hanging from the rack, more sure about them than the lodger who'd managed to crawl into her thoughts day and night. All she knew for certain was that Alexander conducted buying and selling affairs for his father, had recently arrived from Porto Moniz, and was on his way back home, somewhere up near Sheffield. And that he played the violin with so much emotion it made her weep.

She frowned. That was all she knew. Precious little. Much too little for him to have given her a bag of money and a heart full of feelings she'd rather not sort through. If Alexander Morton belonged in society, why had he befriended her rascal of a brother? Or her, for that matter? What could he hope to gain?

Mr. Quail searched her face as she nibbled her lower lip. Drat the man for raising such questions! And what did she know of the rascal in front of her, a flirtatious, itinerant musician—and a bad one at that. "You, sir, take an inordinate interest in Mr. Morton. Why is that, I wonder?"

"Just looking out for you, my little beauty." He angled his head to a rakish angle. "I'd hate to see him pluck such a delicate flower and crush it beneath his heels."

"I am not sure of your meaning, sir, nor do I want to." She snatched the broom by the back door and swooshed it out as if she might scare off a mouse. "What I am sure of is that you ought be out there with your men, playing music as you promised."

Mr. Quail's hands shot up in the air. "I'm going. But, Miss Langley." He lowered his arms, all merriment fleeing from his voice. "Do be careful. Treacherous times are afoot, I fear."

He stalked out, leaving her alone with a room full of doubts.

Who was the real imposter—Mr. Quail or Mr. Morton?

ᗏ

Alex's foot slipped, sending a spray of gravel plummeting into the crashing waves below. Sucking in a breath, he righted himself and breathed out a "Thank God." From the beach, this route hadn't appeared nearly as treacherous. Spare moonlight slid out from the clouds now and again, but not steady enough to grant dependable light.

Balancing one hand against the rock wall, he set off again. The trail was a little more than the width of his foot, forcing him to put one boot in front of the other. Thankfully, the dirt was compacted, flattened by how many men before him? A fair number, apparently.

He inched his way forward, keeping his fingertips against the cliff, and when his hand suddenly gave way into nothing but air, he stopped. The blackened maw of a cave opened to his right.

Cocking his head, he strained to listen above the breakers. No drone of men's voices came from inside. Gravel didn't crunch. Nor did light of any kind exit the cleft. Good signs, unless someone had heard him coming and an ambush awaited.

A smirk lifted one side of his mouth. No risk, no gain.

Edging inside, he entered darkness so alive, it squeezed his chest. He pulled out Slingsby's torch from where he'd tucked it into his waistcoat, the tang of pitch mixing with the earthy air. Mentally, he added a new shirt to his supply list. Ford was going to love this expense tally.

He bent and planted the torch in the gravel, freeing his hands to feel about in his pocket for his flint. With each strike, sparks dazzled a miniature fireworks show, then finally grabbed hold of the pitch and spread into a flame. He blinked and looked away.

Blackness rushed at him, barely stopping at the edge of his circle of illumination. He'd have to examine the area in increments. Starting at the entrance, he hung to the right, scanning the sand and the rock wall with each step.

Twenty paces in, a crate lay on its side. Stooping, he swiped away a layer of grey dust covering some kind of printing. A large *V*, with a small *o* on the descending slope, and a *c* on the ascending. He grunted. East India Company, though their dockyards were miles away in London. A handspan from the crate, two glass balls, smaller than marbles, lay in the sand—spirit beads, used to distill alcohol to the proper concentration. Was this a rum runner's hideout? The disturbed dust tickled his nose, igniting a sneeze—instantly reminding him of the sneeze at the viscount's home. The man's taste ran toward French liqueurs, so maybe not rum after all.

Straightening, he stared down at the display. A slow smile curved his mouth. That was it. This *was* a display. No reputable smuggler would leave behind his spirit beads, and judging by the layer of dust on that crate, it hadn't been used in quite some time.

Hefting the torch, he continued his search. Twenty paces farther in, a black gap punctuated the wall. He ducked, holding the light aloft. The space was as wide as his shoulders, and about as tall, with a tunnel that stretched farther than the flame dared reach. Might be a cramped walk, but the passageway appeared to be stable enough.

He entered, counting every step, memorizing each jut and twist of the trail. By twenty-five paces, he began to wonder if it would ever end. At fifty, he felt sure it soon must. One-hundred erased that certainty.

And at one-twenty-five, his torch started to sputter.

Sweat trickled down Alex's back despite the damp chill. Shadows and earth pressed in, wrapping around him like a casket. What would it be like to be buried alive? Nothing but bones for a smuggler to trip over. His bones. The flesh eaten off by rodents and insects. Breath stuck in his throat, and he swallowed. Was that his heart pounding in his ears—or the foreboding rumble of a cave-in?

Gah! He gave himself a mental shake. He'd heard of men losing their minds in the dark, and he had no desire to find out if that were true.

Turning around took a bit of shimmying and unwedging, at one point almost catching his hair afire from the dimming flame. He snorted, not so desperate for that extreme, but eager enough that he quit counting steps and hastened back the way he'd come.

Naught but an eerie blue light glowed from his torch by the time he unfolded himself from the passageway and reentered the larger cavern. No time to revel in the wide, open space, though. He'd have to finish fast. He scanned what little he could in the poor illumination. Colors were nonexistent. Only greys and lots of blacks.

With his next step, he pitched forward. Curious, when thus far the ground had been flat. He squatted. The dirt and sand compacted into a trail. One direction led to the opening in the cliff. The other revealed a host of boot prints ending at the base of the cave wall.

Why the devil would so many men walk into a wall?

The blue light fizzled dimmer. Even squinting didn't help. Propping up the torch, he yanked off his dress coat, waistcoat, and finally tugged his shirt over his head. Fingers flying, he ripped the fabric into several strips and tied them at the top of the dying flame. Fresh light blazed.

Ford was *really* going to love this expense tally.

The light wouldn't last long, though. Alex shot to his feet and studied the wall. God hadn't created this. That many stacked boulders and rocks smacked of human hands sealing something in—or maybe out.

There, just about shoulder level, a hole. Three feet wide. A handspan tall. Not big enough for a man to crawl through. Why such an odd size?

He shoved in his torch, but that only served to blind him when he looked through the opening. He needed a light on the inside, which is probably where that tunnel he'd followed earlier led. Even if he stripped naked and torched all his clothing, he'd never make it back there and get out before the light was spent.

Working at breakneck speed, he bent and snatched his dropped waistcoat, fastening it into a knot. He took care to leave a piece of the fine silk dangling and touched that corner to the flame. Once it caught, he threw the ruined waistcoat into the hole. It took a moment before growing into a ball of fire.

Alex stared, trying to make sense of the crazy lines and shadows. Hundreds of what appeared to be small wooden ladders filled half of a cave larger than the one he stood in. On the other half were triangle-shaped frames. All uniform, stacked in rows. Why would the viscount feel the need to hide wood? What were the ladders and frames for? Somehow they were connected. *Think. Think.*

The flame flared out.

His torch fizzled to near nothing.

Yet a single, horrid idea burned inside his mind, birthed by the memory of an artillery show he'd recently attended at Woolwich. He stood still, no longer dreading the dark. If he were right, there was a much more ominous threat to not only his life, but also to all those in Dover. He'd have to find Thatcher on the morrow and confirm, for the fellow was better versed in artillery than he.

But as a betting man, he'd stake all he was worth on the wager that those frames were for shooting off some kind of rockets.

CHAPTER ELEVEN

Morning sun slanted through the taproom's window, highlighting a gouge on Alexander's left boot. He frowned. The hike back from the cave last night had proved to be treacherous in more ways than one. Sleep had been a miser during the long hours of the night, doling out scant moments of shuteye. Wooden frames absorbed his thoughts as he tried time and again to figure out what they might be used for other than the destruction of life and limb.

A yawn stretched his jaw, and he rubbed his hand over the stubble on his chin. Snatching a peek at his reflection in the glass as he strode across the empty room, he reconsidered doubling back for a shave. No good, for it looked to be seven already, or maybe half-past.

Behind him, a stair creaked, but not the usual grinding of feet tromping down. The wood groaned on the third step from the top, caused by a loose nail on the right. He'd made that mistake only once, having memorized the quietest route. Whoever descended now was trying to remain undetected—and failing miserably.

He smirked. Five to one it was Quail.

Alex darted into the corner near the hearth. Not the best of hiding places, but one that ought work. Two breaths later, a Quail-sized shape darted through the taproom and out the front door. A bit early in the day for a man who usually snored until noon.

Alex followed, taking care to ease the door shut behind him. Ahead, ragged coattails disappeared into an alley. Should he follow and see what the fellow was about? A glance at the sky supplied an answer. Pah! It was more likely eight, and who knew how long it would take to find Thatcher—if indeed the man were about. If not, Alex had a hard ride ahead of him.

Giving up on Quail, he skirted the perimeter of the Blue Hedge and headed toward the back stable yard. Hopefully the inn maintained a mount or two, or at least should, for it had been a coaching inn at one time. He bypassed a pile of cracked shingles, each step mocking his resolve. Who was he kidding? This place didn't even have a suitable roof. The best he could hope for was a swaybacked mare with the mange.

He pivoted, intent on visiting Farnham's Mount and Tack on the west end of town—until a feminine voice turned him back around.

"Just open up!"

He rounded the corner of the inn, then paused.

Across the yard, Johanna pushed against a half-hung slab of wood until her cheeks flamed a most becoming shade of red. A basket lay forgotten nearby as she put her heart and soul into trying to shove open the stable door.

Alex grinned. He'd wager a guinea in favor of the barn.

Crossing the yard, he stopped a few paces behind her. "It appears to me the door is winning."

She straightened, the fabric of her shawl pulled taut against stiffening shoulders. Was she angry her efforts had failed. . .or that he'd noticed?

Turning, she faced him with a small smile—a practiced one, the kind she likely used on any patron. Which, of course, he was.

Then why the surge of disappointment rising to his throat?

"Good day, Mr. Morton. Can I be of assistance?"

He smirked. "I believe that question ought be mine." Sweeping one hand toward the pathetic door, he asked, "May I?"

"Be my guest. The wretched thing is intent on keeping me out."

"We can't have that now, can we?" He drew nearer, glanced upward, and grasped the edge of the wood. Instead of shoving, he lifted, then coaxed the top wheel into the rail it had slipped from. Two breaths later, he shoved the door open wide. The smell of straw and manure wafted out. A whinny from deep inside raised his hopes. Maybe he'd underestimated the inn's capabilities.

He turned to her, expecting a real smile this time.

She frowned. "You made that look entirely too simple."

"It was. You merely forgot to assess the situation first. The easiest way to manage a difficulty is to think before acting."

Her brows lowered, and though she gazed at him, he suspected she didn't see. Her eyes were too glassy. Her fingers clenched together too tightly. Some kind of sour memory trembled across her lower lip. What tormented her?

Leaving the door behind, he closed the distance between them, alarmed that the proper Miss Langley did not retreat. "Are you all right?"

She blinked up at him, her eyes widening when her senses apparently caught up with the present. "Oh!"

The red on her cheeks spread to her whole face, and she bent to retrieve her basket. "You are out early this morning, sir."

The woman was far more deft at wrangling a conversation than a barn door. "Indeed. Seems a great many people are."

"What do you mean? Please don't tell me my brother is trying to move about."

"No, no. Nothing of the sort. I was speaking of Mr. Quail."

She glanced across the yard to the inn. "Is his whole band awake? Perhaps I ought stay and help Mam."

"No, only him, and he slipped out the front. The rest are yet snoring."

Her "hmm" competed with the song of a morning sparrow, every bit as sweet and pleasing to the ear.

"Then if you'll excuse me, Mr. Morton"—she sidestepped him—"I should be on my way."

He followed her into the barn. Rays of light crawled in through holes in the roof, highlighting her curves as she passed from beam to beam. That he noticed was no surprise, and in fact, could not be helped. What did astonish him was the sudden desire to make those curves his own. Permanently. What would it be like to come home to this woman every evening? To wake to that face every morn?

His steps lagged as an even wilder thought hit him broadside. Once he finished this assignment, he'd have more than enough money to return here and ask for her hand—yet that would require taking her into confidence now for her to even consider him then. And that he couldn't do, not after taking a vow of silence to Ford.

He raked his fingers through his hair. What was he even thinking? Pah! He was becoming as batty as Brentwood. Aah. . .that was it. Naturally his thoughts ran toward matrimony, after having witnessed the happiness of his fellow officer's marriage and with his own dilemma to avoid such with Miss Coburn.

He caught up to Johanna, where she set her basket onto the seat of a pony cart.

"I am in need of a horse, Miss Langley. Is there one I might borrow?"

A shadow crossed her face. "I am afraid our pony would not take you very far, and that is all we have on hand. You might try Farnham's Mount and Tack over on the west side."

"Brilliant idea." He bit back a smirk. "I shall, right after I help you hitch your pony to the cart."

"Really, Mr. Morton, there is no need."

Reaching for her hand, he lifted it, turning her smudged fingertips so that she might see. "Your gloves say otherwise, and I think we both know there's no stable boy to help you."

She pulled back, eyes sparking. "How would you know that?"

A smile stretched his lips. The woman was entirely too easy to fluster. Brave, though, for keeping up a respectable front when everything around her was rotting and raw. He aimed a finger at the harness lying on the floor of the cart. "Your tack is in a heap and dirty, instead of pegged on a wall. It smells like the stalls could use a good mucking. And this floor hasn't been swept in what...two weeks? Or three? From the looks of it, I'm guessing you had to let your stable boy go, and Thomas has been filling in. Though now that he's laid up, this part of the inn is suffering. Am I correct?"

Moments dragged, as did the slope of Johanna's shoulders. Still, her chin refused to lower.

Brave indeed.

"Very well," she said at last. "Posey is over there."

He followed the tilt of her head. Two stalls down, nearly blending in with the shadows, a rough-coated New Forest stood at the stall door—sway-backed, just as he suspected.

Alex blinked to keep from rolling his eyes and strode over to open the stall. The creature twitched an ear, nothing more. At least she was still breathing, he'd give her that, but by faith, he'd seen better horses in queue for the glue factory. Alex coughed to prevent a "Sweet mercy!" from flying out his mouth. No doubt Johanna would be mortified by his thoughts.

"C'mon, girl." He tugged on the head-collar, leading Posey over to the cart where Johanna stood in breath-stealing contrast to her surroundings. For a moment, he paused, impressing her image deep into his mind. It would be a welcome sight to revisit on a cold, dark night. Except for the raven hair pulled up beneath her bonnet, everything about the woman was light and air.

She clasped her hands in front of her, a strange tension lurking behind her beautiful facade. He got the distinct impression that laughter was a friend who rarely came to call on her. What would it take to cause a genuine smile? How would it feel to be the recipient? A foreign urge ran through his veins to be the man—the *only* man—to make her laugh.

"You look at me as though I may disappear at any moment, sir."

He cleared his throat, hoping the action would rid such strange notions. Releasing Posey's head-collar, he reached for the harness. Better to set his mind on something else. "Tell me, what do you know of Mr. Quail?"

"Funny. He asked the same of you last night."

"Did he, now?" He straightened, chewing on that like a tart bite of apple. Why would Quail take notice of him? "And what did you tell him?"

"Nothing much." Her tone rang true, then lowered. "Which is the sum total of what I know of you."

"Would you like to know me better?" The question spilled out from habit. He'd learned long ago that offense with women was sometimes the best defense, but this time the crafty technique sank in his gut, sickening him.

"Yes—no. Of course not." She retreated a step, the pretty glow of her cheeks flaming once again.

Pulling his eyes from her, he threaded the bridle over Posey's head. The pony resisted the bit, but he stuck a thumb in the corner of her mouth to encourage her to open her teeth. "A word of warning, Miss Langley? Be careful around Mr. Quail. He may not be what he seems."

"Are you?" Her voice was soft but the question pricked.

"Sometimes I wonder." His words travelled on an exhale, too low for her to hear, too bitter to remain in his mouth. He settled the back piece over Posey's withers, buckled the bellyband, then slung the breast strap across her chest and buckled that as well.

"What are you doing here, Mr. Morton?"

He made quick work of the breech strap. "Is it not apparent? I'm hitching your pony to the cart." He crossed the reins over the pony's withers, checked all the buckles, then turned to fetch the cart.

"No, I mean why lodge at the Blue Hedge when you might stay at the viscount's estate?"

"Well, well." A slow grin spread across his mouth, and he paused. "It seems you know more about me than you admit."

Her brows lifted, practically disappearing beneath her bonnet. "You don't deny your relationship with Lord Coburn? You make no excuse for warming a seat at his gaming table nightly?"

He shrugged. "Why should I?"

"But"—her head shook slowly, as if she tried to sort out the workings of the universe—"lying and gambling go hand-in-hand."

"Maybe for some, but not for me. I am not a man given to dishonesty. There is no reason for me to cover up either my association with the viscount or how I spend time with him."

"I—I don't understand. Why stay here"—she threw out her hands— "when clearly you can afford better?"

Hah! If only she knew he was on his way to beg more money from Thatcher. Leaving the cart behind, he closed the distance between them, stopping only when the tips of his boots touched her skirt hem. She bowed her head, as was proper for such a bold advance.

But he lifted her chin with the crook of his finger and stared deep into her endless brown eyes. "Why I remain here should be apparent."

She turned so fast, a swirl of dust rose from the barn floor. "I intend to repay you in cash, Mr. Morton. Nothing more."

So, that was the snake that bit. What had happened in her past to cause her such an assumption? His hands coiled into fists at the possibilities, yet he harnessed his rage and lightened his tone. "Johanna."

She whirled, anger etching lines along her jaw, the exact response he expected. But as her mouth opened, a retort about to launch from her tongue, he held up his hands.

"I expect no recompense. Neither in coin nor anything else. Your friendship, your brother's, your mother's. . ." He shook his head, emotion squeezing the air from his lungs. The long dead, little orphan boy within resurrected with a surprising gasp of air, and he staggered back a step, speaking aloud the realization. "Though I am a stranger, I've felt part of your family this past week. That is payment enough. Truly."

Her lips twisted, and it took all his strength not to reach out and smooth them with his finger.

"You don't believe me?" he asked.

"I suppose time will tell. Nevertheless, I shall repay my debt to you."

"Though an admirable trait, determination may be your downfall. Some things are better left in God's hands."

The lines of her face softened, and she murmured, "Thank you for the reminder." Then her shoulders squared, and she blinked up at him. "Are you almost finished? I shouldn't like to hold you up any longer. Where did you say you were off to?"

"I didn't." The answer slid out from an assemblage of evasive responses he'd collected over the years. This time, however, it left a bitter aftertaste. He'd lay bare his life to one of his fellow officers, but never to a woman. Why the sudden guilt for not doing so now?

He bent to work. Lifting one shaft of the cart, he leaned his weight into it, edging it backward, then pulled forward again, threading the shafts through the harness loops at Posey's sides. The poor nag hadn't moved a bit while he'd been distracted with Johanna. Likely it wouldn't go anywhere at her behest, either, but dashed if he'd let her hitch the cart alone.

All secured, he turned to offer her a hand in. "Here you are." Once she settled on the seat, he gave her the reins. To his amazement, as she adjusted her hold and clicked her tongue, the pony's head came up and ears pricked.

"Hopefully you've not far to travel?" he asked.

She quirked a brow. "Surely you don't expect me to own up to my destination when you guard yours like a soldier." The pony stepped out, and the cart slid past him. "Good day, Mr. Morton."

"Touché, Miss Langley."

As she drove off, he stood there. Unmoving. Silent. Counting the beats of his heart to keep from contemplating the desires she created. The more time he spent with Johanna Langley, the more he became a stranger to himself. Who was this man who suddenly envisioned raven-haired children and a wife to warm his bed each night? Family and hearth and home? Blast Ford for bringing up marriage in the first place. He'd managed without a family up to this point in life. He certainly didn't need one now.

He stalked out of the barn with a growl. Better to find Thatcher, finish his mission, and hightail it out of Dover for good—and without a wife.

∽

By the time Johanna reached her friend Maggie's house, a line of foam dripped from poor Posey's mouth. Guilt crawled in, taking root deep in Jo's stomach as she patted the old dear between the ears. "Sorry, girl," she whispered.

Drat that Mr. Morton. She'd pushed Posey harder than she ought, a vain attempt to leave behind his kindness, his curiosity, his rugged good looks.

Why was she enthralled instead of appalled that he'd left the inn with a gruff shadow of stubble darkening his jaw? She should have pulled back immediately when he'd reached for her hand. And what did he mean it ought be apparent why he remained at the inn? Surely it wasn't because of her. But if it were. . .a slow burn spread outward from her heart.

She turned and marched toward Maggie's home, putting an end to such ninny-headed thoughts. Shifting her basket into one hand, she rapped on the front door. Behind the wood, little Charlotte's cry leached out, growing louder with each passing second. Sweet thing, probably frazzling her mother to no end. Good. The tension in Jo's shoulders loosened. This might work.

It had to work.

The door swung open, framing her friend's flushed cheeks and bleary eyes. Her apron hung like an ill-pegged shirt on a clothesline, and stains darkened the fabric of her sleeves. Jo smiled. Margaret Scott was a portrait of desperate motherhood.

Indeed, this *would* work.

"Good morning, Maggie. I've brought you some of Mam's famous baps." She set down the basket of freshly baked rolls and opened her arms. "Let me take little Lottie for you."

"Aah, Jo, you're a Godsend today." Maggie passed off her babe and swooped up the gift, then pushed the door open wider. "Come in, back to the kitchen."

A few coos and baby jiggles later, she followed her friend, nuzzling her cheek against the top of Charlotte's fuzzy head as she went. How good it felt to snuggle a little one in her arms. Charlotte must've agreed, for her crying faded into whimpers and ended in a hiccup.

Jo paused inside the kitchen door. "Oh Maggie, what on earth?"

Pots bubbled over on the hearth, except for one—which had a smear of grey smoke darkening the air above it. Yellow pools of stickiness dotted the floor in splotches. Jars and bowls covered the table, some tipped on their sides, a few broken. An acrid smell of rotted flowers and mouldy lemons hung on the air, competing with the sour odor of soiled cloths heaped in the corner.

Maggie threw out her hands, blowing a piece of hair from her face in the process. "Don't say it. I know this place is a disgrace. I've been trying to finish the last of the elderflower jam for Sam to bring to market, and if I don't get it done today, ach! He'll be very cross. He's already delayed his London trip by a fortnight. Any later and, well. . .I suppose you didn't come to hear me rattle, eh?"

"Actually, your words are exactly what I'd hoped to hear."

Maggie pursed her lips for a moment, tapping them with one finger. "All right, then. Out with it. That twinkle in your eye says you're hatching some kind of scheme, and by the looks of it, you might as well sit yourself down. Seems like it might take some explaining, hmm?"

Jo kissed the top of Charlotte's head, hiding a smile. Her friend knew her entirely too well. Snuggling the babe a little tighter, she sat on the chair nearest the door—the only one not heaped with a basket of elderflowers or lemon rinds. "I'm not scheming anything. I merely had a wonderful idea, a brilliant possibility, really, and here it is. . .let me tend little Lottie every after-noon, or as many as you see fit. That simple. You'd be able to keep up your jam business—strawberries are just around the corner, are they not? Sam would have no more late deliveries, and your customers would be happy. Why, you might even be able to net a larger profit and—"

"Hold on." Maggie stepped over to a bubbling pot and gave it a stir, then turned and folded her arms. "Not that I don't think you charitable, but what's in this for you?"

"Well, with you making more money," she shrugged, hoping Maggie would come to a conclusion without her having to parcel out words she didn't want to say.

Her friend merely narrowed her eyes. Stubborn woman.

"I thought you might pay me a bit to care for Charlotte," Johanna finished.

"I knew it." Snapping into action, Maggie cleared off another chair and scraped it across the floor. She sat toe-to-toe, cornering the truth. "For how much you dote on little Lottie, you'd practically pay me to watch her, so what's happened? What's going on?"

A sigh drained the rest of Johanna's confidence. How to explain?

"See this kitchen, Mags?" She gazed past her friend's shoulder. "The spilled syrup, the burnt pots. . .this kitchen is what my life looks like right now."

"Oh dearest, it can't be all that bad."

She frowned at her friend. How much should she tell her? La, what a thought. Mags would pull every thread of the matter from her no matter how knotted it was.

"There's no secret Mam and I have been struggling. The inn is rundown.

No one wants to stay there, making income scarce. But to attract new customers, we need money for repairs. Money we don't have. I thought that by taking in Charlotte"—she planted one more kiss atop the babe's head—"or any other little ones who might need tending, I could earn the extra capital to make the Blue Hedge into a destination instead of an eyesore."

"Aww, Jo. I'd love to help you. I would, but we're barely getting by as is." A sizzle at the hearth pulled Maggie to her feet. She dashed over and stirred the largest cauldron.

But defeat was not a friend Jo would skip down the street with just yet. Resettling Charlotte on her shoulder, she stood and neared the fire. "What about other mothers who might like such an opportunity?"

"I applaud your determination." Maggie straightened with a sad smile. "But I can think of no one."

Her shoulders sagged. She'd been certain this plan would work. Now what could she do? Charlotte squirmed in her arms, and she didn't blame her. She felt like squirming too, wriggling right out of debt and burdens and hopelessness. A shaky breath escaped her lips before she could stop it.

Maggie pulled the babe from her arms and laid Lottie in a quilt-lined basket, far from popping embers and direct heat. Then she turned and faced Jo. "Are things that bad?"

She bit her lip. "Mr. Spurge will be coming around for the money I borrowed from him to pay the ironmonger for the new hearth. I've got enough to make that payment, but—"

"That's wonderful, Jo! Perhaps things aren't as dire as you're making them out to be. You do tend to look on the dark side of things, you know."

True. She did have the money—but therein grew the seed of her deepest unrest. Despite Mr. Morton's assurances otherwise, surely he expected some kind of reimbursement for such a generous gift. She took to pacing, taking care not to gum up her shoes in the gooey spots. "I am grateful I'll be able to put off Mr. Spurge for another month. The thing is, though, that the money I'm using isn't mine. Not really. Our lodger, Mr. Morton, gave it to me."

Maggie clucked her tongue, tsking as professionally as her own mother. "There's nothing wrong with a lodger paying his rent. I should think you'd be delighted."

"He paid far more than he owes, Maggie. Who knows what compensation he'll require?" With a huff, she halted and absently reached up to rub the scar behind her ear. "I won't be beholden to a man ever again."

"Of course not." Her friend pulled her hand down and squeezed it in her own. "I understand."

"Please, Mags, can't you think of anything? My head hurts with trying to come up with something to gain funding."

A frown weighted her friend's brow, and she sighed. "There is. . .something. But I know you won't want to hear it."

"I am desperate to return Mr. Morton's money. I will entertain any respectable suggestion. Any!" She hated the pleading whine to her voice, but it couldn't be helped.

Maggie's frown deepened. "I am loathe to mention this, but if things are really that bad for you, there's a rumor going around that old Diggery is laid up with the ague. That means Tanny Needler is short-handed with the oakum delivery."

She snatched back her hand. She'd rather owe money to Mr. Morton than do Tanny Needler's dirty work. "Oh Maggie, how could you. . .how could I?"

"Desperate times call for desperate actions." Maggie's eyes searched hers, compassion drawing creases at the edges. "I know it didn't go well with you when you worked for Mr. Needler, but it got you by after your father died. He never failed to pay, and as I recall, was generous at that."

"I can't. I won't." The words oozed out, her voice sounding as ruined as Maggie's kitchen. Maggie didn't know the half of how Tanny had treated her.

Her friend sighed. "If you're intent on returning Mr. Morton's money and paying your rent next month, you just might have to."

She trudged over to the kitchen door, the weight of Maggie's words dragging her feet. It wasn't what she'd wanted to hear—but it did make sense. She paused at the threshold. "Thanks Maggie. I know you're only trying to help. I shall give it some thought. Enjoy the baps, and good luck with the rest of your jam."

Maggie's eyebrows waggled. "If I had to choose between Mr. Morton or old Tanny, I know which one I'd choose."

She turned away from Maggie's knowing look. Of course her friend would choose Mr. Morton. There was no contest between a dashing young man and an angry, pompous wretch—unless Tanny had changed.

Her stomach tightened. God help her if he hadn't.

CHAPTER TWELVE

I n and out at the strangest hours. Dressed and keeping company as a proper gent, yet skilled as a common laborer. No, Mam, there are too many inconsistencies that don't add up." Johanna emphasized each word with a solid punch into the bread dough she worked, relishing every impact. "I don't trust Mr. Morton."

"Your brother does." Across the kitchen, Mam covered a steaming bowl of porridge and set it on a tray. "Implicitly."

Jo opened her mouth. Mam's wagging finger closed it up.

"You can't deny Mr. Morton's been good for the lad, brightening each day with a kind word or a tall tale. Why, yesterday he even brought him a sack of lemon drops. Thomas can't say enough about him, that's a fact."

Johanna smacked the dough with a satisfying whack, trying to decide which annoyed her more—Thomas's incessant hero worship of the man, or the decision she'd made to visit old Tanny Needler on the morrow. "But that's just it, Mam. When Mr. Morton is here, which is precious little, he's entirely too good. Too generous. Why? Why treat us so kindly?"

Mam chuckled as she added a mug of cider to the tray. "Despite my poor eyesight, that's easy enough to see. I've been watching him. There's admiration in the man's eyes when they rest on you—which is more frequent than you realize."

Her tongue—the traitor—ran over her bottom lip, remembering the feel of his mouth on hers when he'd kissed her on Oak Apple Day. An "unfortunate necessity" he'd called it, so why the continued attention? She scrubbed her mouth with the back of her hand, leaving behind a powdering of gritty flour. "That only makes the man's actions all the more suspect. Admiration cannot be bought."

Picking up the tray, Mam eyed her over the top of it. "It may be working, though."

"What are you talking about?"

"Mr. Morton fixed the stable door, broke up a brawl between Mr. Quail's men before they destroyed the taproom, even paid in full for an entire month's residence that he's yet to use. In all the time he's been here, he's shown he's a good man. And deep down, you know that. What's more, I think you admire him."

"Nonsense!" She snatched a dishcloth from a peg on the wall, fighting the urge to snap it in the air. "Why you defend him is beyond me."

"He reminds me of someone. Headstrong. Independent. Kind to a fault, though unwilling to own up to it, and much too good-looking for his own good."

The skin at the nape of her neck bristled. How dare Mam? Choking the life from the cloth, she turned back. "Please don't compare me with—"

"I was going to say your father, Johanna. It's been nice to have a man around here looking out for us. Do not begrudge your brother this time, however short, with a gentleman of good standing. Lord knows Thomas needs it." Mam disappeared out the door with her brother's breakfast tray, leaving behind the scent of oats and apples and disappointment.

Shame sank in Jo's stomach, curdling the milk she'd taken with her tea earlier. The dough in her hands felt heavy and thick. With a little too much strength, she plopped the lump into a large bowl and laid the cloth on top like a death shroud, a fitting end to a grievous conversation.

Hefting the bowl, she crossed to the hearth. Why could she simply not be happy about Mr. Morton? He had been nothing but kind and—except for the kiss—of exemplary conduct. Her mother, Thomas, even Maggie seemed to adore the man. Pish! Who did he think he was? Helping. Providing. Caring. Ever since her father died, those things had been her job. Hers!

The bread bowl slipped from her hands and plummeted to the floor.

Oh, Lord. That was it. She stared, horrified as the bowl landed dough side down—no doubt a punishment for feeling jealous. Shame tasted bitter in her mouth. Should she not be grateful for the kindness of a stranger? Closing her eyes, she begged for forgiveness in the quiet of the kitchen—until a shuffle of feet at the taproom door turned her around.

The day was sunny. The shadow on the threshold was not. She'd seen him before. A man of the night, usually conferring in whispers with Mr. Morton at a corner table in the taproom. His hat was pulled low, the whites of his eyes a stark flash of contrast. Black hair, too long to belong to a person of import, brushed the edge of his raised coat collar. Why did he wear such a heavy mantle on a June morning?

She stepped in front of the fallen bowl, hiding the mess she'd made. "I'm sorry. It's early and we are not yet ready to serve."

"No meal required. I merely ask you deliver this into Mr. Morton's hands." He held out a sealed envelope, gripped loosely in his black-gloved fingers. "He said I could trust you."

Jo advanced a step, then stopped, eyeing the thick packet. The situation smacked too much of intrigue. Did she not have enough drama in her life?

With quick steps, she whisked past the man and his envelope, calling for him to follow. "Have a seat, sir. I shall retrieve Mr. Morton straightaway and you can deliver the missive yourself."

"He's not here."

Stopping at the base of the stairs, she pivoted. "Sorry?"

"I said he's not here."

Tucking a loose strand of hair behind her ear, she re-ran the whole of the morning. She and Mam had been in the kitchen the entire time. They would've heard the departure of any of their guests, so rickety were the stairs.

"How would you know that?" she asked.

The man said nothing, his gaze speaking a language she wasn't sure she wanted to understand.

A shiver crept across her shoulders. Mam's shoes started a rap-tap down the stairway, the familiar groan of the wood complaining beneath her feet.

"Mam," Jo called over her shoulder, "will you knock on Mr. Morton's door and let him know he has a visitor?"

"Aye, child." Her mother's rap-tapping faded back upstairs.

"You're wasting her time, and yours and mine as well." The man's voice was matter-of-fact, but the angle of his chin scolded—or was it the play of light streaming in from the side window, slashing an overlarge glower on his face?

For a moment, she considered running out the front door, away from his stifling presence. This was a man used to being obeyed.

She straightened to her full height. "Who did you say you were?"

"I didn't."

She stifled a gasp. This fellow sounded an awful lot like Mr. Morton.

How were the two related?

Seconds stretched into what seemed hours. The man's gaze never wavered from hers, neither did his resolve, for he said nothing more.

Fine. If she must be the one to take the high road, so be it. She forced her mouth into a smile she stored in her dealing-with-bothersome-customers reserve. "I have some water on to boil. May I get you a cup of tea?"

Mam's voice answered from above. "Mr. Morton's chamber is empty, Jo."

Once again, the man's arm extended, the envelope daring her to move forward and retrieve it. "Now, will you deliver this? I've not the time nor inclination to wait, but if need be, I will."

She didn't doubt him. Those dark eyes would haunt the taproom until Mr. Morton returned, and with his irregular schedule, that might be a long time off.

"Very well." She clipped across the floor, the fabric of her skirt adding a swishing accompaniment, then snatched the missive from his hand. "I'll see that Mr. Morton receives this."

For the space of a breath, one side of his mouth quirked up, almost as if he were pleased. "I thought as much. You'll do."

His words trailed a cold quiver down her spine. "I'll do for what?"

He stared a second longer, then pulled down the brim of his hat and disappeared out the front door, so quickly she wondered if he'd been but a dream to begin with.

But the heavy packet in her hand was real enough. There was no address on the front. No name. No writing at all. She turned over the envelope and studied the wax seal on the other side. Deep burgundy in color, but no identifying insignia. Whoever sent this either didn't own a signet ring or chose not to use it.

A sharp rap on the door stopped her speculations. She shoved the envelope into her apron pocket, then opened the door to a brass-buttoned chest with the Viscount Coburn's monogram embroidered in gold on the lapel. Her eyes followed the line of buttons up to a tall, starched collar and farther to a chiseled chin set as hard as granite. The man neither smiled nor frowned, just observed her as he might some droppings on the bottom of his shoe. Beyond him, four fine horses pawed the ground, attached to a gleaming black carriage, a matching emblem in gold on the door.

A curious urge to curtsy nearly buckled her knees. Nonsense. This was her home. She forced a smile. "May I help you?"

"I should like to see Mr. Morton." The man's tone was as dismissive as his gaze.

"I'm sorry. Apparently he's not here at the moment."

His upper lip curled, not much, hardly at all, but enough to knock her off the social ladder. Her smile faded.

"I suppose I shall have to leave this with you, then." He held up an envelope, the size and shape of an invitation. Swirly embellishments adorned the borders, glinting silver and gold in the morning light. Fine black penmanship in strong lines clearly identified the recipient to be Mr. Alexander Morton of the Blue Hedge Inn. This one was an artist's masterpiece compared to the missive in her pocket.

She reached for it, but his grip didn't lessen.

"First, I must have your solemn word you'll give this to none other than Mr. Morton. We can't have just anyone gracing the viscount's doorstep." He sniffed. "Especially from this part of town."

"Well then, perhaps you ought not trust the word of a girl such as me who is from this part of town." She yanked back her hand and opened the door wider. "Come in and wait for the man yourself."

His mouth slanted into a sneer, yet he extended the envelope farther. "For Mr. Morton. None other."

"As you wish." This time the envelope released and came away light and crisp in her fingers.

The footman pivoted without another word. She immediately shut the door, not wishing to suffer any more indignities should he choose to take off at such a pace as to spray gravel at her.

Crossing to the counter, she paused in front of the shelves and pulled the other envelope from her pocket. The missive in her left hand was elegant. The other plain. One came from wealth and importance. The other from a whisper of a man who smelled of horseflesh and leather. Both as mysterious as the enigma to whom they were addressed.

Why did Mr. Morton keep company with a viscount and a. . .whatever the dark-shrouded fellow was? Why lodge at a ramshackle inn—she cringed at the thought—when he could be lounging in luxury? Why did he evade her questions?

And worse. . .why should she care?

She bent and retrieved the strongbox, then tucked away both envelopes.

A satisfying slam of the lid accompanied the opening of the front door, ending further contemplation on the matter. She stood, prepared to face yet one more courier entering with a missive for Mr. Morton.

But across the counter from her, Mr. Spurge's black eyes pierced her soul. "My wagon stands ready outside, Miss Langley, the paperwork already drawn up for St. Mary's."

"That won't be necessary." How her voice managed to strain through the anger closing her throat was a wonder. She cleared it, then tried again. "My family and I will be staying right here."

"Theatrics, is it?" He chuckled, discordant and altogether unnerving. "Shall I bring in the magistrate and shackles as well?"

"Only if you prefer the weight of irons on your wrists to the greed in your heart." She sucked in a breath. Had those horrid words come from her?

A tic began at the corner of Mr. Spurge's left eye and spread to a vein in his temple. Throbbing, it grew into the size of an angleworm. He leaned over the counter. "Such insolence will gainsay you the darkest of cells at the workhouse." The vein turned purple. "Or worse."

Faith! The mere thought of a damp cell in a workhouse drove a chill into her heart. She forced a calm to her voice that she didn't feel. "I hate to disappoint you, sir, but. . ."

She bent and remained crouched, unwilling to reveal the strongbox to Mr. Spurge. With a quick turn of the lock, she rifled past Alexander's envelopes and snatched the bag of coins he'd given her. She plopped it onto the counter, jingling the coins on purpose.

The sneer slashing across Spurge's face goaded her like a hot iron. Her chin rose. "On second thought, I don't hate to disappoint you at all. There is the hearth payment. Take it and be gone."

He snaked out his hand and untied the pouch. His brows rose, along with a coin. Slowly, he lifted a guinea to his mouth and bit the metal, doubting, testing, frowning. Chucking the coin back into the purse, he turned and gazed about the taproom. "Not a huge increase in patronage, I see." His dark eyes returned to her, pinning her in place. "I wonder if you have taken up a side profession, Miss Langley?"

"I resent your implication, sir." She measured her words, counting the value of each one, praying to God nothing more would slip out her mouth and indebt her to more time on her knees begging for forgiveness.

"You might want to think on it, for I expect fifty pounds next time." The pouch vanished into his pocket. "And no less."

"What? No!" *Fifty?* She staggered back a step. "But the final payment on the hearth plus rent should be only forty pounds."

"Interest, my dear." A slow smile lifted his lips, uncovering the few teeth holding onto his gums for dear life. "You don't think I allow you the liberty of installed payments for nothing, do you? Fifty it is."

She set her jaw, locking it against the rage building inside. "Then you shall have it."

"You're right. I shall. In four weeks' time, Miss Langley." He tipped his hat. "Until then, good day."

With a groan, she bent and slammed the strongbox lid shut.

"Johanna? Was that Mr. Spurge's voice I heard?" Mam's voice called to her from the stairway.

Jo stood, hoping confidence would rise along with the action. "Yes, Mam."

"Is all well?"

She gritted her teeth then forced a smile. "Yes, Mam."

The words tasted metallic. But it wasn't a lie. Not really. For tomorrow she'd visit Tanny Needler and offer herself to do his dirty work. He always paid well.

But could she afford the loss to her dignity?

The smell of rain hung in the afternoon air. Thick and earthy, pressing down on Alex as he stepped from the carriage. He flipped the jarvey a coin and glanced at the sky. When those clouds broke loose and shook out their fury, the whole of Dover would be washed clean—until the resulting mud splattered up against everything.

As he strode to the viscount's front door, he pulled out the invitation that had arrived earlier in the day, when he'd been out. Not that he'd need to hand it over for admittance, still, being that the time of his requested presence was a full two hours earlier than usual, it wouldn't hurt to have it available. Coburn's footman was a puffed-up fellow. Without proof, the man just might make him wait on the stoop until the customary start of gaming.

He lifted the lion-headed knocker. As it fell against the brass plate, he pulled out his pocket watch. The second hand moved on a downward slope.

One. Two. Three. A week of playing cards with the viscount and his cronies had taught him the household ran with military timing—until the cards were pulled out. Then all bets were off, or rather on. Very on tonight, as a matter of fact, since Johanna had handed him an envelope of money from Thatcher.

Four. Five. Six. He snapped shut the watch's lid and tucked it away. The door swung open, as expected. But his eyes widened as a dark-haired beauty greeted him.

"Good evening, Mr. Morton." Louisa's resonant voice poured out like a fine wine.

"Miss Coburn." He doffed his hat and bowed, catching a whiff of civet musk—the same French perfume he'd smelled on her before. As he rose, he captured her gaze with a rogue grin. "A pleasure to see you again."

He'd bet five to one the flash in her eyes was anything but pleasure—nor was the taste of the lie in his mouth.

"Please, come in." She stepped aside.

His footsteps echoed off the marble tile. Crystal lamps already lit the grand foyer, though evening had yet to leave a calling card, such was the greyness of the day. The footman—his usual escort—was nowhere in sight. Alex waited for Louisa to close the door, then asked, "Short staffed?"

"Not at all." She lifted one shoulder, the movement glinting light off the diamonds on her necklace—the pendant she'd worn to the Oak Apple Eve dinner. Did she never take it off?

She swept past him, casting a backward glance. "I simply sent John on an errand."

In three strides, he caught up to her side. "To what end, when you obviously knew I'd be arriving?"

A smile curved her lips, yet she continued to face forward as she led him down the corridor. "To have you all to myself, of course."

He turned her words over in his mind, examining them from every possible angle. She'd had more than enough opportunities to cross his path the past week. Often arriving early, he'd lingered in the sitting room, waiting for the viscount and hoping she might appear. She hadn't. Two days ago, he'd dined here, yet she'd declined the meal. Too fatigued. He'd even taken to riding the surrounding grounds should she venture out for a walk, making sure to pass the windows of the west wing that housed the family's bedchambers. She would have seen him. She could have ventured out. But no. So why the sudden urge to see him now?

He shot her a sideways glance. "I'd say your plan worked, Miss Coburn. I am at your service."

Finally, she faced at him. "Are you always this pliable, Mr. Morton?"

Pliable? He suppressed a snort. If Magistrate Ford heard that one, he'd choke on his own laughter. "I shall have to quote you on that sometime."

Her expression remained placid. Once while on an information reconnaissance in Paris, he'd viewed the famed *Mona Lisa*. Were Louisa's hair let down and straightened, she might have been the model.

She made an abrupt turn into a hallway he'd never seen. Sconces had yet to be lit in this stretch, so shadows escorted them. There were no doors except for one at the very end, making this the perfect corridor should someone wish to entrap him. As they walked, he listened for a floorboard creak from behind, ready for anything. "Where are we going, Miss Coburn?"

"My sanctuary." At the end of the hall, she pulled open the door.

He followed her out into paradise. Palm trees lined a pea gravel pathway. The hydrangea and ivy were easy enough to identify, but Louisa paused to sniff a flower he couldn't name or even guess as to which part of the world it hailed from. The path skirted the garden, close to a high stone wall encircling the area. Bird chatter was as loud as a gathering of washerwomen. The only thing amiss was the pewter sky, clouds bullying down with grey fists. A curious time for a stroll through a garden.

Louisa veered off the gravel onto a worn trail leading into the middle of the plot. The path ended at a fountain, surrounded by four wrought-iron benches painted white. Louisa sat on the nearest. He joined her, leaving enough space for propriety, though he probably needn't have bothered. If the woman had no qualms about asking a man she barely knew to join her in such solitude, she likely wouldn't mind him sitting next to her.

She turned to him. "Do you like riddles, Mr. Morton?"

He bit back a laugh. Did the little vixen not know she was the biggest riddle of all? No, not quite. Even larger was the question as to why Ford would order him to marry the woman—and how he'd get himself out of the situation.

He forced an even tone to his words. "I do. Perhaps you can help me solve one."

A perfectly arched brow rising just slightly was her only answer.

But it was answer enough. He continued, "Why would an English woman wear French perfume, a Cross of Lorraine, and if I am not mistaken, dress in a gown made of silk from Lyon?"

That same brow sank, as did the other. A woman cornered was a dangerous animal. "And why would a man be informed of such things?"

"*Touché*, mademoiselle." He covered his heart with his hand, feigning a direct hit. "Then for the moment, we shall leave my questions tabled. Perhaps it was a riddle of your own you wanted to discuss?"

"Yes, which is why I've brought you here. I've spent many hours thinking on something the past several days, yet can find no answer. What is it exactly, Mr. Morton, that you think you can help me with? And more importantly, why?"

Help? The woman dealt out her conversation like a dropped deck of cards. He scrambled to pick up mental clues for a moment, then remembered the note he'd sent along with the flowers. Draping an arm over the bench's back, he leaned against it. "Apparently you do not recall the conversation we had at the Oak Apple dinner. I offered to help you with your man hunt."

"La, sir." She flicked her fingers in the air as if batting away an offending pest. "If you're speaking of my father's wish to marry me off, you're wasting your time. I have no interest in you."

Half a grin lifted his mouth. What a welcome change from having to fight women off. "That is no surprise, Miss Coburn, for I suspect it's Robbie who's stolen your heart."

A rumble of thunder competed with the cascading water from the fountain. Her face gave no hint as to what went on behind those dark eyes. Were she a man, she'd be fabulous competition at her father's gaming table.

She stood, smoothed out her skirts, and walked over to the fountain.

His grin grew. "Do you deny my premise?"

She traced the rim of the fountain with her fingers. She wouldn't answer the question, of course. Nor did she need to. Her movement revealed more than any false words she might string together.

At last, she turned and faced him, stalking forward on padded feet. A lioness to the kill. "I am an opportunist, Mr. Morton, and I sense an opportunity with you."

Her words were as tempestuous as the coming storm. He kicked out his legs, crossing one over the other. "Now that is a riddle. Do tell."

She stopped directly in front of him. "You're new here. A novelty. One which my father enjoys. I simply ask that you continue the diversion for several weeks more, for I can hardly bear to be in the same room with him after what he did to Robert." The lioness's fangs came out in a small smile. "You will, of course, be well compensated."

"Why several weeks?"

"That's when I plan to leave with Robert. He will pay you well for your distraction."

He smirked. "I was correct, then."

"That's immaterial. Will you do it?"

"I shall, but on one condition."

She angled her chin. A tot couldn't have looked more curious. "What?"

"The diversion is to be of my own making."

She laughed. "Oh, Mr. Morton. I don't care how you manage to keep father's attention, only that you do."

He studied her for a moment. A beauty, but mostly bought, nothing like the natural allure of Johanna Langley. This woman hid her secrets well, all perfumed and tied up with a bow. What was it about her that Ford wanted him to unwrap?

He stood and offered his hand. "Shall we seal the bargain?"

Her fingers were cold against his, clammy and moist. Did his touch unnerve her—or the fact that she'd have no control over his means of distraction?

"You are an enigma, Miss Coburn." He drew back and swept out his arm. "Tell me about this place, your sanctuary."

She eyed him for a moment before answering. "I am in your debt now, I suppose. Come along, and I'll take you the long way back to the house." She turned and bypassed the fountain, choosing the path on the opposite side from the way they'd come.

Thunder rumbled closer, quieting the birds, stilling the insects. Could she not have simply told him about the garden instead of dragging him through it?

When he caught up to her side, she continued, "Perhaps you already know my father's record with the East India Company?"

He nodded.

"That was all before I was born, of course. Such tales, though. So vivid. After Mother died, Father's stories of Punjabis, elephants, and exotic flowers unmatched anywhere in the world, well. . .it was the only thing that quieted me. The only place I could go to escape the pain of losing my mother."

He glanced at her. It was hard to reconcile the steel maiden next to him with a weeping little girl. "You don't seem the sentimental type."

"I am not." The path opened onto a walkway wide enough for a small cart to travel, and she turned left. "Nevertheless, I am human, and as I've said, an opportunist. Father's stories of India filled an empty spot inside me, so much so, that it became difficult to distinguish myself apart from the land. I tried to recreate it in this garden, but the truth is I belong there, Mr. Morton. Nowhere else. Father cannot—will not—understand."

"Aah. . ." He stepped over a small pothole in the trail, all the while looking for holes in her story. Either she was playing him, or telling the truth. But which? "Allow me to hazard a guess. Your father wishes you settled here, firmly planted in English soil. And against those wishes, Robbie's agreed to make your dream come true, hence your little excursion next month. But I wonder, Miss Coburn, what fires you most, becoming a bride to Robbie or to an exotic land?"

She stopped dead in her tracks. As still as the dark air around them. Tension lashed out in her tone, sharp as the crack of thunder overhead. "You are overly perceptive, sir."

For a moment, a very small one, compassion squeezed his heart for the little princess used to getting her own way. Exposure was never a pleasant embrace, as evidenced by the strained lines on her neck.

"Everyone is wild for adventure, Miss Coburn, but forcing one is a dangerous affair. Better you should leave that in the hands of God, hmm?"

Her face cut to his. "I didn't know you were a religious person, Mr. Morton."

"Everyone has faith, Miss Coburn. The question is, Faith in what?"

Storm shadows darkened what daylight remained, hiding her beauty. "I learned long ago that faith in myself is the surest—the *only*—dependable force upon which I may rely."

He smiled. "Then the Indies are the best place for you, and I wish you Godspeed."

"What? No theological debate?" Her voice rose as high as her brows. "No damning of my eternal soul?"

"Not from me." He shrugged. "Your desire will accomplish that, I think. Either that or God intends to grab hold of you as surely as He snatched the fleeing Jonah."

As soon as the prophet's name left his mouth, the heavens let loose. Rain drowned any further conversation. Louisa took off at a sprint down the path. Alex smirked and strolled on. Running wouldn't lessen the drenching of already soaked garments.

"Oh!" A cry competed with the next roll of thunder, just beyond a bend in the path.

He shot ahead. "Miss Coburn?"

Louisa slumped on the gravel, clutching her leg, her skirt pelted with mud. She rocked slightly, moaning with the movement. An embroidered slipper lay upside down behind her, half sunk in a small pool. Pah! Women and their silly shoes.

He dropped to one knee beside her and threaded an arm around her shoulder, the other beneath her knees. Streaks of cosmetics rained down her face as she looked up at him.

"I'm fine. Merely a slip up."

He lifted.

"Mr. Morton!"

"We'll assess inside." He raised his voice, competing with the rage of wind and water. "Hold on."

"Put me down!"

Clutching her against his chest, he dashed forward, dodging falling palm fronds. The flowers around him took a beating, stripping petals, breaking stems. By the time he reached the door of the manor, paradise was battered to death, as was the rest of daylight.

His shoes scritched on the polished floor. He ignored the woman's protests, too busy navigating the inside hallway, for the tiles were more treacherous than the wet gravel outside. Retracing their earlier route, he turned and crossed the grand foyer. The household staff would be up late tonight cleaning his filthy trek onto the carpet in the receiving room.

He bent to set the woman on the sofa near the hearth, but before he loosened his hold of her, a deep voice grumbled from behind.

"Is taking my money at the card table not enough, sir, that you must also take my daughter?"

CHAPTER THIRTEEN

Thunder rattled the windowpanes in the taproom, creating an offbeat rhythm to the music of the band. Jo suppressed a wince at the racket. It was bad enough when Mr. Quail eked out songs on his violin, but at least he had a sense of tempo. Tonight his men were on their own, and judging by the peg-legged sprinting of a folk tune that should ramble, they were quite enjoying his absence.

She handed the customer in front of her a mug, offering him a smile as watered down as the cider.

"Keep 'em coming." His face screwed up like a dishcloth wrung too tightly. "A few more and maybe it won't sound so bad."

"I'll see if they can play something a little less—" *Noxious? Loud? Head-ache inducing?* She swept back a wisp of hair and finally suggested, "lively."

Glancing at several other patrons nursing mugs, she was satisfied when none met her gaze. It was a shame more benches weren't filled, though with the storm, she could hardly expect less. Winding past empty tables, she paused near the band. Their song crashed to a halt at her arrival, the last jarring notes leaving a ringing in her ears that might never go away.

"Did ye like that one, lassie?" Mr. Quail's wooden flute player, Lachlan, leaned over and nudged her with his shoulder, his behaviour as inappropriate as his music.

She retreated a step, dodging his touch and the question. "I'm wondering when Mr. Quail might be down? I've kept your suppers warmed until he arrives."

"Ach, lass. Did I not tell ye?" Retrieving a cloth hanging off the side of his belt, he rubbed down his instrument while he spoke. "Quail's ailin'. Says his throat pains him, so he begged off for the night. Not to worry, though. We won't let you down."

He stuffed the rag away and lifted the flute to his lips. After two notes, the others joined in, and another hair-raising ballad began.

Johanna bolted toward the kitchen, grateful her long skirt hid the flurry of her feet. Mam turned from the hearth, her good eye widening at such an entrance.

Bypassing the larger mugs on the shelves, Johanna settled on a wooden tumbler and faced her mother. "Have we some licorice root left?"

"Aye, there's a bit." Mam squinted and searched her head to toe. "Feeling poorly, Jo?"

"Oh, it's not for me. Thought I'd take some tea up to Mr. Quail. I can't believe I'm saying this, but the sooner he graces the taproom, the better." She ducked into the larder and reached for the small crockery next to the tea caddy. When she removed the cover, she frowned. Mam might need to change her definition of a "bit." Only a few spare nubbins of licorice root remained.

She emptied the contents, replaced the jar, and returned to the kitchen, where Mam stood with a kettle in hand. The hot water barely changed color once in the cup, but at least a faint whiff of spiciness crawled out.

"Mind checking on Thomas while you're up there?" Mam asked as she set the kettle back on the fire.

"Of course." She scurried over to the stairs, trying to shove down the wish for Mr. Morton to arrive and evict Mr. Quail's band as effectively as he had Mr. Nutbrown. No good. With each upward step, the wish grew with intensity, but at least the music lost some of its sting when she entered the hall and turned toward Thomas's chamber.

She pushed open his door with her free hand. "How goes it, Thom— what on earth are you doing?"

On his belly, Thomas sprawled sideways across his bed, injured leg dangling off the edge. The position allowed him to reach the floor, where he'd lined up small soldier figurines in a mock battle. A fake explosion issued from his mouth, and he whaled a clay marble at half the little soldiers before he lifted his face from the skirmish. "Alex told me England expects every man to do his duty. I'm just doing mine."

"And I suppose Mr. Morton felt it his duty to spoil you with a sizable militia. Honestly, Thomas. You should not accept such an offering. We will never be able to pay him back."

"Don't have to. This were a gift."

"Think on it. Why would a man who's known us little more than a week be so generous?"

He stared at her as if she were daft. "Because he likes us."

She frowned. "More likely he expects something in return."

Thomas rolled to his side, propping himself up on one elbow. "Like what?"

"I don't know." She gnawed on her lower lip, trying to work up a more suitable answer. "But I intend to find out."

"Aww, Jo, you make him sound like a no-good, rotten-faced scoundrel. I won these soldiers off him fair and square. He don't expect nothin' for 'em."

Rotten-faced? With that chiseled jaw and eyes the color of an August sky? The way tiny creases highlighted the side of his mouth whenever he smiled. How his gaze made her feel like she was the only one who mattered. Warmth rushed into her cheeks just thinking of his handsome face.

Shaking off the crazy notion, she crossed to the table—when all of Thomas's words hit her. He'd *won* those soldiers off of Alex? She set down Quail's mug and put her hands on her hips. "How exactly does one win a gift?"

"Alex were teaching me a game, and I bested him. Those soldiers were a prize and a gift. He even said so."

"What kind of a game?"

His cheeks puffed out with a huge exhale. "Cards. But don't be angry with him, Jo. He were just helping me pass the time. You wouldn't begrudge me that, would you?"

"Oh, Thomas, don't you understand by now?" She frowned at the way such honeyed words slipped past his lips. The lad was far too much like Father. "If you would but tell me the truth of things up front, I'd not get so cross. Gambling is wrong because it's a poor way to steward our money—but what is worse is that it always leads to lying. Don't you see? You first told me those soldiers were a gift to hide the fact you won them at a game of cards. I cannot tolerate lying, young man. . .*especially* not from those I love."

His head sank face-first onto the mattress. "Sorry, Jo," he mumbled.

With a sigh, she bent and scooped up the soldiers. When would he ever learn? "Very well, now off to sleep with you. Finish your battle in the morning."

Thomas lifted his face. "Don't you *ever* have any fun?"

His question rankled on more levels than one. She'd known frivolity once, years before, so long ago she barely remembered. But over the years, life had leached out her enjoyments one by one, until she'd learned it was better not to enjoy anything—for that delight would surely be taken away.

She shook her head.

Sticking out his tongue, her brother blew an unsavory noise.

Ignoring him—for truly, any response she might give would only encourage the little scoundrel—Johanna collected Mr. Quail's tea and closed the door on the lad. She scurried down the corridor, hoping to arrive before the drink turned completely cold.

She lifted her hand to knock, but before her knuckles met wood, glass crashed on the other side. "Mr. Quail!" Throwing propriety to the floor, she shoved open the door. "Are you all right?"

Nothing but rumpled blankets slept on the bed and the extra pallets on the floor. A gust of wind and rain charged in through a broken pane on the bottom quarter of the window. Why would glass shatter if no one were in here to break it?

Unless someone had been in here until a moment ago.

She dashed over to the window and peered out. Sure enough, below, a dark shape rolled to a standing position. Hard to tell for certain in the stormy darkness, but it might be Mr. Quail. If he'd exited the window and it slammed shut, that would account for the glass and water now on the floor.

But it wouldn't account for a sick man sneaking off into a storm when he ought be downstairs, playing with his band.

∞

"Care to explain?"

Behind Alex, Lord Coburn's words growled a shade darker than the accompanying peal of thunder, both rattling the sitting-room windows. For a moment, Alex tensed, caught between Louisa's mocking gaze in front of him and the angry father at his back.

Slowly, he released her against the couch cushions and stood. Amusement sparkled bright in her brown eyes, chafing as painfully as the newly formed blisters from his wet leather shoes. Spoiled little rich girl. He clenched his jaw. If entertainment was what she wanted, then far be it from him to disappoint.

"An explanation you shall have, sir." He turned and faced the viscount. Sucking in a breath, he steeled himself to bid more than was judicious. Hopefully Robbie and Louisa would make good on their elopement plans. "I ask permission for your daughter's hand in marriage."

Louisa gasped so deeply, she started coughing.

Lord Coburn grunted, but no words followed.

Alex counted every time the yew branch outside smacked against the window glass—better that than count what a high price he was paying to accomplish Ford's intelligence gathering.

"You are full of surprises, Mr. Morton." The viscount bypassed them both, striding over to the mantel. He made quick work of opening and shutting a carved wooden box, then bent, working to light a cheroot from the glowing coals below.

Skirts rustled behind Alex. Breath scented with cloves tickled his ear. "What do you think you are doing?"

He pivoted partway, keeping both the lioness and the king of the jungle within his range of view. "A miraculous recovery, hmm?" he whispered back.

"I told you I wasn't hurt!" Her words picked up speed. "Had you listened, we wouldn't be in this situation. Furthermore, when I asked you to divert my father, I never meant for you to—"

"Save your lover's whispers for another time, Louisa. Leave the room. And for God's sake, change out of those wet garments. I'll not have you taking ill." Lord Coburn straightened, daring her with a widening stance.

She remained silent, but there was no need for verbal rebuttal. Her stilted movements as she left the room said it all. Rebellion lived inside Louisa Coburn—though there was no hiding the way she favored her left foot, whether she owned up to the pain or not.

The viscount tipped the glowing end of his cheroot toward Alex. "I'd offer you one, but I know you'll only turn it down—and that is one of the few things I do know about you." He sank into the chair closest the hearth. "Come. Warm yourself by the fire and tell me why on earth I should give my only daughter to you."

Wet wool, though finely woven and tailored to perfection, stuck to his legs as he took the viscount's suggestion. He stationed himself in front of the coals, warming his backside and facing Lord Coburn. "There is one simple yet compelling reason why you should grant your blessing to me—because you despise Robbie."

"Do be serious." Coburn huffed. "My nephew is not worth that much passion."

"Neither is a bite of rancid meat, yet one forcefully spits such out."

Coburn took a long drag of his tobacco, the end of which glowed like a demon's eye. A curl of smoke piggybacked on his exhale. The tightness in Alex's shoulders relaxed. He'd seen this behavior at the card table, time and again, right before the man made a move.

"Your wit is a fine match for Louisa's, but do not be mistaken. Louisa will not inherit this estate, for it is entailed. In light of that, it is to her benefit to marry well. Tell me, Mr. Morton, what does a wine merchant have to offer a viscount's daughter?"

Without so much as a flinch, Alex stared down the barrel of the loaded question. He would not lie, though he was not averse to stretching the truth into an unrecognizable shape. Calculating the odds of each answer he might deal out, he finally settled on one. "For the past week you have witnessed my skill at the card table. Do you think I will ever lack for money?"

Coburn's face twisted into a sneer. He ground out his cheroot into the ashtray on the side table with more force than necessary, saying nothing.

Alex held his breath. Had he answered incorrectly?

The viscount leaned back in his chair, a faraway glaze in his eyes. "Fortune is a diseased mistress." He spoke so softly that, had not his lips moved, Alex would've doubted he'd spoken at all.

"You speak as one who's had an affair or two."

"Three, to be exact. The pox of such unions still runs through my veins."

Narrowing his eyes, Alex surveyed the man. Skin clear. Nothing sallow in his gaze. Though greying at the temples, the fellow appeared to be in his prime. Still, Alex was no physician. "My Lord, are you unwell?"

"Would to God it were merely that." The viscount pushed from his chair and paced around it, gripping the back with whitened knuckles. "It's the nightmares, my friend. There's no holding back the incubus of past sins."

Coburn's tone bled with a distinct rawness, and Alex bit back a wince. This was an unguarded side of the man he'd not seen before. Did he tip his cards from lack of discretion or on purpose? Regardless, truth was the only salve for such a wounded statement. "If I may be bold, sir, nothing you have done is beyond God's forgiveness."

"Bah! Spoken like a true innocent." The viscount's hands dropped to his side, his shoulders falling with the movement. "Judas paid the price for betrayal, as do I, every day I draw breath, so spare me your platitudes on forgiveness. There is no erasing the terror in a victim's eyes as you watch the lifeblood drain from his throat." He stalked over to a sideboard, where he snatched up a green bottle.

Alex stared, slack-jawed. What kind of devilry had Lord Coburn committed in his past? Worse, what was he capable of in the future?

The viscount slugged back a shot of brandy and turned, still gripping the bottle in one hand, an empty glass in the other. "Care to rescind your offer to unite with such a family?"

Everything within him screamed yes. . .yet he forced out, "No."

"Good." The viscount lifted the bottle. "Join me?"

Alex shook his head.

Coburn poured another drink, then retreated to his seat and deflated. "It is no secret I wish Louisa married by the time she comes of age in a few months, but Robbie is not the man for her, no matter how much she thinks he is."

"You know of her feelings?"

"I am unsure how much emotion plays into the equation. Louisa will not rest until she steps foot in India—and God help her if she does. Robbie is foolish enough to accommodate that whim. So I've been looking for a safer alternative to secure her future. Are you safe, Mr. Morton?"

"That depends upon your definition."

"Wily, as always. Yet. . .oh, do sit down. Surely you've warmed through by now."

Indeed, his backside fairly stung with heat, but standing was a more powerful position. He angled himself so that warmth crawled up the front of his trousers. "I've already ruined your carpet. I shouldn't like to damage the furniture. Furthermore, if I dry out my front, I shall be ready for a long eve of gaming rather than wasting time traveling home to change garments."

"You always have a card to play, and usually one better than my own." The man skewered him with a glower. "Very well. On the matter of my daughter, I don't doubt your ability to provide, and your travels might fill Louisa's need to wander. Still, I must have your word that India is never—*ever*—to be a destination."

The viscount was as determined as Louisa about the continent, though diametrically at odds. Why? Thatcher and Ford might have to do a little digging into the viscount's military past for him. He nodded, satisfied on his course of action and on the freedom to concede without deceit. "Agreed, though it's no difficulty on my part. India is not known for vineyards."

Coburn ran a finger around the rim of his glass, slow and methodical, his gaze never varying from Alex's. "And what of your fine Madeiran vintage to escort back to Sheffield? I should think by now your father would be wondering what the delay is."

"The winnings I've earned at your table provided for a far better escort than I." Or would, if he actually had a precious cargo to transport. "I stayed here because of your daughter."

Setting his glass on a side table, the viscount stood and advanced, slapping Alex on the back. "Then I'd say we have an arrangement, of sorts."

Alex's brow tightened. "What sort?"

"Mere formality. A simple background check. Can't have just anyone finding out my secrets now, can I?" Rounding back to the side table, Coburn snatched up his glass and returned to the brandy decanter. "Nor can I have just anyone joining the family. In that respect, I hope you understand I must be very thorough. Are you willing?"

"Of course." As soon as the words slipped from his tongue, he clenched his jaw. Hopefully Ford had constructed a rock-solid history for Mr. Alexander Morton.

For if the magistrate hadn't, the viscount would put a ball through more than just his hand.

CHAPTER FOURTEEN

F resh. Earthy. Johanna loved mornings like this, the kind that wrapped around her shoulders like a lover's embrace. She inhaled deeply as she crossed the courtyard from inn to stable. Last night's storm had scrubbed the world clean, leaving behind the trill of birds and a peppery scent. This was the type of day in which she could pretend all was right and good in her life—except for the haunting cry of the mourning dove reminding her of her mission. If she listened hard enough, she might almost believe it cooed *poor girl, poor girl, poor girl.*

She upped her pace, grinding the gravel beneath her shoes a little harder than necessary. Surely calling on Tanny Needler was what God wanted her to do. Every other means of raising money had come up dry. She glanced at the sky, blue and innocent.

"That is what you want me to do, is it not?" she whispered.

Poor girl. Poor girl. Poor girl.

A frown folded her lips. If only she could hear God as clearly as the call of the doves.

Reaching out, she grasped the barn door and shoved. The wood didn't budge. Oh, bother! Again? What was it Mr. Morton had—aah, yes. She gripped her fingers tighter and lifted, just as she'd seen him do a few days ago.

Yet the obstinate thing would not be moved. Perhaps if she bent, then heaved with all her might? She crouched and searched for just the right place to plant her fingers, for there was only a thin space between door and wall. When she found it, she wrapped her hands tight and—

A puppet head jutted into her face.

She shot up, barely containing a scream, and slapped a hand to her chest. "Mr. Nutbrown! You scared the breath from me."

The lines of Mr. Nutbrown's face twisted into a question, as if he were the one affronted. "Why, Mr. Nutbrown is exceedingly sorry, miss." His falsetto voice drowned out the sweet morning sounds. "He merely wishes to give you something."

The silly puppet disappeared into the man's dress coat. And my, what a dress coat. Johanna stared. Sunlight glinted off golden embroidery looped along the edges of the lapel, collar, and cuffs. The material was rich green velvet, deep in color and offset by ivory woolen pantaloons. He still wore his ridiculous yellow stockings, but these were of the finest silk. Not a snag or smudge to be found. What on earth had the fellow been up to the past week to affect such a change?

He withdrew his hand and coins emerged, curled into the puppet's body. Mr. Nutbrown shoved the jester and the coins toward her. "For you, Miss Langley."

She turned over her palm. The money landed with a jingle. Fingering through it, she calculated. Six. Seven. Eight. All that he owed for rent. But why now? Why come back to repay her?

Her brows rose. "Well, I'd say your debt is completely paid off. Thank you."

"But there's more where that came from." The puppet bobbed. "Mr. Nutbrown would like you to share in the riches he's found."

She studied his face, wishing she owned the observation skills of Mr. Morton. Whatever Mr. Nutbrown had in mind, it couldn't be good. The man was a consummate slacker. There was no honest way he could've come up with such an amount of money, let alone legitimately offer her a share. She shook her head. "Oh, I really don't think—"

"Ah-ah-ah! One should always listen to the knocking of opportunity." Mr. Nutbrown's arm shot out, and he rapped the jester's head against the barn door.

Johanna frowned, teetering on the fine edge of how to dismiss the fellow without engaging him.

The puppet popped back into her face. "We would like to invite you to a business meeting this afternoon."

Business? Right. Likely some shady affair. And if not, something absurd. She glanced at the sky. Already the sun crept on an upward arc. "I am sorry, sir, but I have my own business to attend. If you'll excuse me."

The puppet thwacked on the door again. Louder. Longer. Was the man not nervous about cracking the head of his precious little jester?

She sighed, fighting the urge to roll her eyes. Clearly, there'd be no putting him off. "Very well, Mr. Nutbrown. Go on."

His puppet jerked away from the door, facing her. "Won't take but an hour of your time later this afternoon, and it pays five guineas."

Five guineas! Combined with what he'd just given her, that would go a long way toward her upcoming rent payment. At that rate, she might even be able to pay back Mr. Morton. Still, this was Mr. Nutbrown. And a puppet. She looked past the jester, into the man's eyes. "That seems an inordinate amount for attending a business meeting for a mere hour. What else is required?"

The puppet's head shot to Mr. Nutbrown's face. "You were right! She is interested." Mr. Nutbrown smiled, broadly, his elastic lips hinting of something more than satisfaction. Pride? Possibly. But with somewhat of a darker shade. Something sinister.

Before she could think more on it, the jester's body waved in front of her. "Here's the long and short of it. You won't actually be attending the meeting. Too boorish for a lady such as yourself. No, no. All you need do is stand outside. Above the meeting, actually. Next to a small hole."

La! And that would pay five guineas? She should've known. Why had she wasted her time? She tucked the money he'd given her into a pocket. "As usual, sir, this conversation is taking a ridiculous turn. I bid you good day."

Mr. Nutbrown planted himself between her and the barn door.

"Oh, very well," she breathed out. "Finish your proposition so that I may be on my way."

"As Mr. Nutbrown has said, miss, all you need do is wait outside for the duration of the meeting. If anyone comes near, you simply drop a pebble down the hole and walk away."

She smirked. Of course. A known smuggling trick. That's where this instant money had come from. Slowly, her lips flattened. It would be easy, though, and paid the same amount she'd likely earn working for Tanny Needler—but without the pain.

Poor girl. Poor girl. Poor girl. The mourning dove's wail crawled into the tiny crack of indecision. Should she? It's not like she'd be committing a crime.

But the smugglers would.

Folding her arms, she set her jaw. "What you choose to do is your own business. I prefer to come by my money honestly, or not at all. Good day to you, sir."

The ludicrous puppet shot toward the barn wall, on his way to what appeared to be a magnificent knocking session.

Johanna flung out her arm, trapping the little jester's head against the wood. Mr. Nutbrown's eyes widened, followed by a sharp intake of breath.

She leaned toward him, emphasizing each word. "I said good day."

Removing her hand, she retreated a step. The puppet dashed for cover inside Mr. Nutbrown's fine coat. The puppeteer straightened his sleeves, his lapel, and finally gave each shoulder a brisk brushing off. A peacock couldn't have looked more ruffled of feather. At last, he pivoted and stalked off.

Johanna watched the silly man until he disappeared through the gate in the side of the wall, her shoulders sinking with each of his steps. That would have been easy money, much easier than what she was about to undertake. But it wouldn't have been honest.

Would it?

She took a step toward the gate. It wasn't like she'd be doing any actual smuggling herself. Besides, she didn't really know if smugglers were involved. Maybe she should have at least checked further into it.

Sweet mercy. What was she thinking?

She turned her back on the temptation and bent to heave the broken barn door. Using every muscle, she lifted. She groaned. She sweated and strained and even jiggled. The door did not budge. Not a smidgeon.

Poor girl. Poor girl. Poor girl.

Frustration nearly choked her. "Be quiet!"

"I've not said anything yet."

A deep voice wrapped around her from behind, and she shot to her feet.

Though she stood at full height, Mr. Morton smiled down into her face, so imposing was his figure—and so near that on the inhale, she smelled his freshly washed scent of sandalwood and strength. His gaze held her, pulling her close without any outward movement. How could the man command such a thing without a word?

"Oh, Mr. Morton, I didn't mean. . .I mean, I didn't. . .I wasn't—" She forced her mouth shut, well aware she sounded more preposterous than Mr. Nutbrown. When Alexander Morton stood this near, combining words was impossible—yet wholly necessary. She'd hoped to corner him this morn for a bit of a chewing out over his teaching Thomas cards the day before.

She lifted her chin. "Actually I was hoping to run into you this morning."

"Are you?" Sunshine sparkled brilliant in the twinkle of his eyes.

Eyes she shouldn't be so admiring of. She frowned. "Yes, I was hoping for a few words with you. I would appreciate it in the future if you would refrain from showing Thomas any more card games. Gambling is not a virtue."

"I beg to differ."

Her jaw dropped, so stunning the conviction of his claim. "But there is nothing honest about it. You may wish to lose your money in such a fashion, but pray do not teach Thomas to do the same."

"While I yield to your point that gaming can and oft' times is dangerous for those lured by money, at the same time, it is valuable in teaching control and self-discipline—something I think we can both agree Thomas would benefit from. As in all of life, Miss Langley, no risk, no gain, right? The key is to never wager something you cannot afford to lose." The blue in his eyes danced a merry jig. "Now then, would you like more help with the barn door?"

Her mouth dried to sawdust, and suddenly she could drink two full mugs of cider. Not only had the man whittled her mountain-sized concerns over gambling to naught but an anthill, he did it all with a grin and a glimmer. The knack he possessed for calming her worries was positively breathtaking.

And so was the man. She clenched her hands to keep from fanning herself as she stared at him. No one should look this fine so early in the day. How could she help but notice the slope of his nose, the shape of his lips? His clean-shaven jaw was a contradiction of smoothness and hard lines. His shoulders were wide enough to block out the sun. He gazed at her as if she were the only one in the world that mattered. Her. Johanna Langley. She no longer heard the keening of the mourning dove, only the thrumming of her pulse in her ears.

"—the door?"

A jolt shot through her, and she licked her lips. How long had he been speaking? "I'm sorry. What did you say?"

"I said"—he cocked his head, his eyes looking into hers—"did you want to continue your hand-to-hand combat, or shall I assist you with the door?"

"Oh, I. . ." She swallowed. What was wrong with her this morning? This man was a patron. She, an innkeeper. This was business, nothing more. "Yes, truly, I wouldn't mind your help. I tried to lift it exactly as you did last time, but apparently I'm doing something wrong."

"Indeed." He laughed. "Remember what I said?"

Faith! She could barely remember to breathe. Retreating a few steps from his invisible pull, she scoured every memory she owned. Aah, yes. She smiled up into his face, satisfied that her faulty senses had returned to normal. "Assess the situation first. The easiest way to manage a difficulty is to think before acting."

His grin widened. "I am pleased you remembered, but did you understand?"

"Of course, I—"

He stalked away before she finished speaking.

"Where are you going?" she asked.

He held up a hand as he bypassed the stuck door and strode beyond, to the smaller side door at the other end of the barn. Shoving it open with his shoulder, he vanished for a moment. A few scrapes and a knocking noise later, he shoved open the bay door from the inside, grasping a hay rake in one hand.

Johanna frowned. How had he known to do that?

His laughter once again rang out, warm as the early summer morn. "Don't look so vexed. You merely forgot to assess. The wheels hadn't fallen from the track this time. This rake had toppled over on the inside, keeping the door from opening. Tell me, Miss Langley, what will you do when I am no longer here to save you in such situations?"

A sudden sadness tightened her throat. Of course the man would leave when he concluded his business in Dover, but a dark knowledge that the Blue Hedge Inn would no longer be as merry settled deep in her chest. She forced a pleasant tone to her voice, but even in the trying, it came out as soulful as the mourning dove's cry. "I suppose I shall continue the battle of the barn door on my own, yet I thank you for helping me today."

He shrugged. "My pleasure."

"But why? Why take such pleasure in helping my family and me so often?" The questions flew out before she could snatch them back, and she slapped her fingers against her lips. For shame. No wonder he spent his time at the viscount's, surrounded by ladies who likely weren't as bold.

Alex eased the rake against the outside of the barn wall, well away from the door. Sunlight pooled on his shoulders as he strode to stand in front of her, making him appear a being of light. "As I've said, you're good people.

Is that so hard to believe?"

She lowered her hand from her mouth. Mam and Thomas—mostly—were good, but herself? No, she'd never believe that. Lifting her face, she met his stare. "Surely there's more to it. There are plenty of good people in the world. Why us in particular?"

"Your brother reminds me of myself when I was a lad. Your mother, well, my own would be about her age now, had she lived. And as for you. . ." He leaned toward her, his hand reaching toward her cheek. The air between them charged like the sizzle before a lightning strike.

If she moved, just a little, she'd feel the strength of this man against her skin. His warmth. His touch. Is that what she wanted? Her breath hitched with a sudden realization. She did. More than anything. To lean into his embrace and forget debt and want and loneliness.

A whinny carried from inside the barn, pulling her back to the stark reality of an aging mare, a rickety pony cart, and the upcoming trek to Tanny Needler's—a fate the perfectly tailored Mr. Morton would have no experience with. Of course he wasn't interested in her. Not like that. He was a gentleman—and she was as outlandish as Mr. Nutbrown.

She retreated a step. "Let me guess, I remind you of your sister."

He shook his head. "I don't have a sister, though I would have liked one as attentive as you. Thomas is fortunate. What you have here, with your mother and brother, your strong ties. . .would that I'd have known such as a lad."

"Surely you and your father share such a bond, else he would not trust you to manage his winery."

"My father?" A shadow darkened his face, though the sun went unchallenged in a cloud-free sky. "Of course."

Aah. Maybe she didn't corner the market on loneliness, for there was a hollow edge to his voice. Clearly the man missed his family. "How long has it been since you've been home?"

"I scarcely know what home is anymore." His voice faded for a moment, then picked up, as intense as the blue in his eyes. "But trust me when I say I am in no hurry to go back."

Her lips parted as she struggled for air. Surely he didn't mean because of her.

But everything in her wished that he did.

The early summer sun burned Alex's back, scorching the fabric of his dress coat. Was it the sun that heated him—or the fire in Johanna's gaze? Grace and mercy! He could get lost in those eyes. Dive in. Swim deep. Never surface for air. Johanna stood so close, so vulnerable, his bones ached to sweep her up in his arms, abandon duty and honor, all that was right and good.

But then he'd be no better than the brigands he brought to justice. And honestly, was he? To have offered for one woman, and fraudulently at that, yet stand here longing for another?

He withdrew a step, yet couldn't resist the temptation to make her cheeks deepen in colour. "Are you warm, Miss Langley? You look a bit flushed."

Her fingertips flew to her face. Too late. Scarlet spread well past what her gloves could cover.

Laughter welled up from his belly. "You are altogether too much fun to tease."

The colour crept down her neck, but in the space of a blink, before mortification gave way to anger, he'd seen it. A flash of desire. For him. What was he to do with that? He didn't have time for a woman, a relationship, a family. Blast! Why did he even entertain such thoughts whenever she was near?

And what would flash in Johanna's eyes when she heard he was betrothed to Louisa Coburn? The urge to tell Johanna the truth here and now welled to his lips, but he pressed them tight. She abhorred liars—and he was the biggest one of all.

He nodded toward the gaping barn door, shaking free of such an unprofitable line of thinking. He could no more marry Johanna Langley than he would Louisa Coburn. "I assume you're in need of a certain pony cart?"

"Please, don't trouble yourself any further." She marched past him.

He followed. "I believe we've had this conversation before. Do we really need to repeat it?"

She stopped at the cart and pivoted, gradations of light accentuating every curve. "You are a most determined man."

And you are most beautiful. He bit back the sentiment before it launched from his tongue. "You make it sound as if that's a crime."

"I can see there'll be no putting you off." She swept a hand toward the little mare. "Be my guest."

He went through the same motions as a few days before, though familiar now with the lay of the stable, his movements were more rote than anything.

Johanna watched, quietly at first, then she finally broke the silence. "Our friend Mr. Nutbrown was here, just a bit ago."

"Was he, now?" Alex looked up from checking Posey's buckles. "For what reason?"

"He paid all his back rent."

Alex straightened. "I wonder who suddenly sprouted morals, him or his puppet?"

A sweet smile lifted Johanna's lips. "Neither. I suspect it was naught but an enticement to ensnare me in his latest wealth-gathering scheme."

Next to him, the horse snorted. Alex stifled one of his own. "Did it work?"

"Really, Mr. Morton, do I look like I'd join a band of smugglers?"

Standing there, caught in a web of sun rays reaching in from all angles, she looked more an angel than a woman. He bent, finishing up the buckles on Posey. Better that than gaping at her like a lovesick sailor. "What makes you think that's his game now?"

"Only smugglers and highwaymen fear gathering together without aid of a lookout."

Satisfied with the tightness of the harness, he faced her. "And when was this gathering to be?"

"This afternoon."

"Do you know where?" Not that he had the time nor inclination to attend, still, intelligence was power—and one never knew when power must be wielded.

An endearing little wrinkle creased her brow. "I did not entertain the idea, and so did not ask questions, unlike you."

"Lives are won and lost in details, Miss Langley. You'd do well to remember that."

Her mouth opened, but the stomp of feet entering the barn cut her off. He wheeled about. Five men—*large* men—blocked the entry.

One stepped forward. "You Morton? Alexander Morton?"

"I am." As he answered, he recalculated the paces it took to reach the side door. Ten. Could he make it before they flanked him?

"What is this about?" Fear wobbled in Johanna's voice.

And stopped him cold. If he made a run for it, would the men give chase—or leave one behind to torment her?

Two of the brutes stalked forward, one pulling out a pair of wrist shackles from inside his great coat. Alex's muscles tensed. Flight having been abandoned, he was left with but two choices. Fight or submit.

Johanna stepped next to him, the fabric of her skirt shivering around her. "Mr. Morton?"

His name from her lips sounded jagged. He glanced down at her and—bah! A fight with these men, with her standing so close, would put her in danger.

There was nothing to be done for it, then. He advanced, guiding her behind him with one arm, hopefully to safety. "The lady asked you a question, gentlemen. What is this all about?"

The man on his left swung behind him, wrenching his arms behind his back. Shackles bit into the bones of his wrists. Johanna's cry stabbed his heart.

"Stop it!" She skirted them all then whirled to face them, the silhouette of an avenging angel the way the sun blazed in from outside.

A shove to the small of his back pushed him forward. "Move along!"

"Step aside, miss." One of the men by the door reached toward her.

A roar ripped from his throat. "Leave her! You asked for me, and so you've found me."

Johanna arched away from the man's grasp. "Mr. Morton is a guest here. You have no right! Where are you taking him?"

The man swiped for her again. "As I said, miss, step aside, or we'll take you in as an accomplice."

She dashed just beyond his fingers, a cloud of dirt and questions in her wake. "For what?"

"Treason."

Alex's heart quit beating. It was bad enough that Ford wouldn't be able to get him out of this.

But worse was the disillusion bleeding from Johanna's gaze as he was led off.

CHAPTER FIFTEEN

S un burned Johanna's cheeks as she set the pony cart's brake and alighted in front of Tanny Needler's shack. Even so, she shivered from a cold gust driving in from the Channel behind it. Must the weather be as contradictory as she felt, as what she was about to do? As the hundred swirling thoughts about Alexander Morton that wouldn't leave her alone? Clearly the man was capable of many things. Compassion. Strength. Looking entirely too handsome in a tailored suit. But treason?

She could not reconcile the indictment with the man, no matter how hard she tried—and she'd tried the entire journey out to Tanny Needler's Hemp and Oakum.

She reset her skewed bonnet, tired of the mystery and exhausted from the swing of emotions Alexander created in her. For a moment, her gaze followed the circling route of a seagull, screeching overhead. Her own collection of screeches welled in her throat. She hated what was to come, hated even more that there was no escaping it. Were she to look in a mirror, surely she'd see the same wild blaze she'd seen in Alexander's eyes as he'd been led off in shackles.

The gull dove, disappearing behind the carcass of wood and nail that made up Tanny's shack. So be it. She shoved down all her misgivings and advanced on a path of gravel and broken shells. Coils of rope, barrels, pallets—some whole, others in pieces—littered the yard. The closer she drew, the stronger the stink of tar and washed-up seaweed. She tried not to breathe, not to think, to simply do what must be done. With a whispered prayer for forgiveness, she rested her palm on a door she vowed she'd never again touch, then shoved it open. She crossed the threshold before she could change her mind.

"Awk! Hands on deck! Hands on deck!" A birdcage swayed in the front window, the hook-nosed parrot inside hopping from one branch to another as he squawked.

Ahead, a grey shape turned from behind a counter. How could a man she'd not seen in half a decade look exactly the same? Though truly, she should not expect any different. Other than the covering of skin upon bone, Tanny Needler's appearance would not change were his corpse uncovered ten years after his death.

She shuddered. What a horrid thought.

Deep-set eyes stared her down, nearly lost in the shadows of the sockets were it not for a wet glisten at the corner of each.

"Well, well." Tanny's voice crawled up his Adam's apple, over his teeth and past his lips, all the gruffer for the effort. "Look what the tide washed in. Haven't seen the likes of you for what. . .five? Six years now? Din't think I'd live to see this day." He nodded, a colorless cap atop his skull sliding back and forth with the movement. "Missed ol' Tanny, have ye? They always do. They always come back."

She stopped midcenter of the small room, clutching her hands in front of her. "I am not sure of whom you speak, sir."

"Oh? It's sir, now, is it? I likes that. I likes that real well. Learned you some manners, eh?" He slipped out from behind the counter and circled her, his joints cracking with each step. "Filled out a bit too, I'd say."

"Awk! Filled out!" the wretched parrot repeated. "Filled out!"

Johanna stiffened, enduring the observation. Barely.

Tanny stopped in front of her, close enough that the odor of the fish he'd eaten for breakfast fouled the air she breathed.

"You know the routine, girl." The widening of his stance was a mandate.

She bit the inside of her cheek so hard, the salty taste of blood filled her mouth. That pain was nothing, however, compared to the full weight of understanding beating her down.

Tanny hadn't changed at all.

Slowly, she lowered to her knees in front of him. He held out his hand. Beneath translucent skin, veins crisscrossed like worms unearthed by a spring rain, the gangling mess looking as if that was all that held his bones together. Not that she didn't know this was coming, but still. . .she'd rather kiss a thousand worms than rest her lips on that cold flesh.

"I'm waiting." A sneer coloured his voice.

She bent and touched her mouth to the back of his hand.

"Oh, that's good. That's very good." Tanny's laughter filled the room, violating her in ways that ached in her teeth.

Recoiling, she fisted her hands at her side to keep from wiping her lips. She'd done that once. The scar behind her ear burned white hot with the memory.

Tanny laughed all the way back to the counter, taking his creaking skeleton with him. "What is it you want, girl?"

"Your Grace." She clipped out the words in even measure. Better to focus on steadying her voice than on the anger throbbing in her temples. She lifted her face, but not her body. To stand before he allowed would merely earn her another scar. "I have come here to do business. I heard Diggery is laid up and perchance you might need a replacement."

"That's right." He paged through an overlarge ledger while she waited. And waited. Outside, waves crashed. Inside, the parrot's claws scratched. Johanna held her position, regardless of the way the hard floorboards ground into her knees. This was a power game, nothing more.

But this time she'd win.

Eventually, Tanny slammed shut the book and looked up. "I might be able to take you on, depending."

"Dependent upon what?"

Leaning sideways, he reached for a switch of briars hanging from a hook.

"Your Grace," she amended quickly. "Dependent upon what, Your Grace?"

"Awk! Your Grace! King of the land! King of the land!"

Tanny tapped the switch on the countertop in time to the parrot's squawks. "Things didn't go so well last time you were under my employ."

She clenched her hands in front of her. "No, Your Grace. They did not."

"You can't expect to frequent a gaol yard, girl, and not take on a pinch or two."

The unfairness of it all stole her breath, leaving behind a sore throat. "About that. . .I was wondering, Your Grace, if you might have a different task for me this time. I've become proficient in figures. I thought maybe I might help you with your ledgers? That would free you to make the delivery."

The switch slapped the countertop, loud and sharp. "No one looks at my ledgers, especially not a snippet of a surly wench like you."

She shrank as he rounded the counter, switch in hand. *Oh, God. Oh, please.* Why had she come here? Stupid, stupid idea. She averted her gaze to the warped floorboards. Hopefully a bowed head might appease him until she could escape.

His scuffed boots stopped in her circle of vision, the switch dangling next to them. She held her breath. Surely he would've struck by now if he were going to. Maybe he had softened, leastwise a little. Slowly, her muscles started to unclench.

"Awk! Surly! Awk! Wench!"

The parrot's voice struck at the same time the switch stung the tender skin between bonnet and collar. Once. Twice. She held back a whimper. To do so would only encourage a frenzy of strikes.

Thrice.

She gritted her teeth. She'd been wrong. Terribly wrong. Tanny had changed—and in the worst possible way.

"Aah. I've missed this, I have. Flogging's been a might scarce since you left." The switch lowered to the side of his boots once again, where she was forced to look upon the wicked barbs up close.

But better that than to gaze up into the black pits of his eyes.

Tanny spit again, the splotch landing next to her skirt and splashing up a dark spray. "It's delivery or nothing, girl, for three weeks. Be here at sunup. Bring a load of tarred oakum to the gaol, reload with the cleaned, then bring it back here, same as always. Pays a penny pound. Take it or leave it."

"Awk! Take it! Awk! Leave it!" The parrot's voice pecked at her back.

She stared at the switch. Three weeks. Only three. Her shoulders drooped, along with her spirit. Three would feel an eternity. She'd hoped for a larger wage, but what choice did she have? If they lost the inn—if *she* lost the inn— what of Mam and Thomas? The workhouse was worse than delivering oakum.

She drew in a deep breath. "I'll take it, Your Grace."

"Knew you would. Like I said, they always do." His empty hand shot out.

This time she barely felt his skin beneath her lips, for it was nothing compared to the chill settling in her soul.

⟶

The wagon lurched to a stop, the movement snapping Alex's head and releasing a fresh, warm trickle down his temple. He bit back a wince—and a smirk. Fitting that they'd pulled up in front of the black bones of a scaffold. Ford's words replayed with stark clarity. . .

"If this operation fails, I shall refute any knowledge of this conversation, to the point of watching you swing from a gibbet."

His throat tightened. Perhaps instead of the mantle of the law, the magistrate ought don the robes of a prophet.

"Move!"

A boot to his back jerked him forward. Flanked by two men, Alex edged himself toward the open gate at the back of the wagon, where two more men stood, all wearing scowls and angry, red bruises—except for the fellow on the right. A deep gash bloodied his lip, and the lump on his nose promised to grow into magnificent proportion.

Alex glowered at the men, but inside his heart, he smiled. Truly, he ought not take such satisfaction in the ripped fabric and flesh he'd caused. Wicked? Likely. But not as wicked as the sharp pain cutting from foot to knee when his feet hit the ground. Aah, but that had been some escape attempt. Five to one normally wasn't a problem, but with his arms shackled behind him, it had been an unfair disadvantage. Still, he'd given it a champion try.

Too bad he'd failed.

Standing this close to the Market Place Gaol, he recanted of ever having thought the Blue Hedge Inn a run-down hovel. Sunshine soaked the building's bricks, but the life had been drained from them long ago. If not for the blanket of soot wrapped tightly around the place, the walls would lie down and die, buried beneath the weight of guilt and age. Windows were barred in uneven rows, and the roof curved earthward, like an eyelid shutting for eternity. This was no gaol. It was a pox. A leper's spot. A gangrenous limb of justice that should have been cut off long ago.

"I said move!"

A shove between his shoulder blades thrust him forward. Each step up to the scarred front door shot a new agony through his ribs. One was broken for sure. Hopefully, only one. But that wasn't the only thing cracked. For the entire ride, he'd tried to piece together the fragmented logic of hauling a supposed traitor away from Dover castle—where one accused of sedition would face a military tribunal—and instead depositing him here, at a municipal gaol. Clearly, someone wanted him out of the way for a while. But who?

And why?

The prison swallowed them all in a gulp—him, the four men, light, air, all that was good and true. The stench of death and despair punched him in the gut. In truth, though, losing his breakfast on the shoes of the brutes beside him would be gratifying. Aah, yes. He was wicked, indeed.

Lord, forgive me.

They entered a vestibule the size of a large crypt, which opened into a small, circular room. Farthest from them stood a tall desk, marred with nicks and blackened in splotches by the blood of frantic prisoners. It sat like a sentinel in front of a stairwell leading up into darkness. At either side were two doors. One would be the home of hapless debtors or vagrants, snared into working their way to freedom. The other—oh, that it may be so—the one he'd go through. The door to a holding room for prisoners able to pay their way out of humiliation.

"This the man?" The turnkey's voice boomed from behind the desk. He was perched on a stool, unless the man was of freakish stature. Surely the fellow had been born with a nose, but only two slits remained. His left eye slid halfway down his cheek, and no wonder his voice boomed. He could not close his mouth, for one lip was gone. Completely. Either the fellow had taken a devastating fall from a horse and landed on his face, or he'd been shot in the head with a blunderbuss at close range.

The brute to Alex's right answered the man. "Aye. He's the one."

The turnkey's gaze studied one guard after another, his good eye widening as it travelled from bruise to cut. Finally, it rested on Alex. "Bit of a troubler, are ye?"

Alex's lips parted, but a strike from behind drove him to his knees, knocking the air from his lungs. Sucking in a sharp breath, he fought against pain and doubled vision.

"Not anymore." The brute chuckled at his own joke.

"Right, then take him up."

A yank to his collar nearly choked him. Half-stumbling, half-dragged, he was propelled forward, bypassing the door of hope. Before he fully rounded the backside of the desk, he twisted and launched forward, planting his body against the blemished mahogany. His blood added to the stains left behind by countless men before him. "Wait! Who brings charges against me, and what of the registry? Or the garnish? I can pay, and pay well."

"Oh? Regular jailbait, are ye?" The turnkey leaned sideways, tipping his stool onto two legs. From this angle, his body appeared whole—and wholly knotted with muscles. "But there ain't nothin' regular 'bout this, guvnor. Take him up, boys."

"No! I demand a—"

A cuff to his head knocked him away from the desk, and he staggered like a sailor on leave.

The turnkey laughed, long and throaty. "Save yer demands for yer new play-mates. Like as not they'll be interested. Real interested, and that's a promise."

The men closed in on him, herding him around the desk and up into the blackness of the stairwell. Nothing was right about this. No writ served. No documentation of his stay. Only a verbal charge, but from whom? He could rot here, die here, and the only one who would know would be his nameless accuser, the thugs that led him upward, a turnkey who'd never once spoken his name. . .and Johanna.

He gritted his teeth. Merciful heavens. What she must think of him.

There were eighteen treads up. Add that to the twenty from front door to desk, and give or take nine from desk to stairwell. Fifty. Just fifty paces to freedom. He'd hold on to that number like a beacon, lighting some kind of scheme to break free.

The stairs opened into an antechamber hardly bigger than a wardrobe. Again, two doors punctuated the walls on either side. Thick ones. Pocked with nail-heads and reinforced with iron bands. Women's weeping and hys-terical cries leached out from the door on the left. The man with a ring of keys opened the one on the right. The stink of sweat and urine poured out, barely doused by an afterthought of vinegar.

"In you go." Another jab to the back hurled him forward.

He wedged himself against the doorjamb. "For God's sake, take off the shackles."

"God don't live here."

He landed flat on his face, pain riding roughshod along every nerve. The lock clicked behind him. Darkness extended a calling card, one he pushed away. He staggered to his feet and retreated toward a wall, refusing to be circled like a carcass on the side of the road. Near the ceiling, sickly light crept down from barred windows, so thin and ruined, they reminded him of the turnkey's nose. In the shadows, ten pairs of eyes raked him over, mea-suring, judging, cataloging his weaknesses, assessing his strengths. Some of the prisoners were gaunt, marking them as longtime residents. Others were wiry, built of sinew and possibly madness, for their breathing sounded beast-like. And one of them truly was a beast. All thick and hairy. Only half the men posed any real threat—but a very real one at that. These were convicted felons.

What was one more murder to their credit?

CHAPTER SIXTEEN

S top! You're killing me!"

Lucius Nutbrown cried out as he flailed for a moment, taking his puppet on a wild ride, then righted himself from a near-slip on the gravel. He jerked his puppet to within inches of his face and eyed the little whiner.

"I've had enough of your grumbling, sir," he shouted at Nixie. As much as he hated to stifle his friend, he really *had* had enough. He opened his great coat and stuffed him inside. "You'll ride it out there, my friend."

He'd also had enough of this horrendous trek up a barely discernable path in the darkness before dawn. Even so, he continued to pick his way, step by step, along the crushed rock trail, glad it was fashioned from the white stone of the cliffs and not the darker flint of the shoreline. Curious choice of venue. Strange time for a business meeting as well. Mr. Charlie and Mr. Blackjack certainly conducted an interesting operation. Their last meeting, two days ago, had taken place on a Saturday afternoon up near Deal, and he still wore the blisters on the back of his heel to prove it. Maybe it was a good thing Miss Langley had declined that one.

Twenty paces to his right, far below, surf crashed against rock, covering up the sound of his footsteps. The path was narrow, but at least it wasn't on the edge of the drop-off. Small miracles did happen sometimes—leastwise that's what his mother had always said. But not big ones. Never big ones. He knew that for a fact.

Ahead, briars congregated like a horde of fat, black monsters against the backdrop of a rising wall of a hill. Good thing Nixie was safe inside his coat. Things were about to get rough.

He slowed as he neared the hedge, then bent, looking beneath the thorny verge. Oh, for a lantern. Though there might be some truth to Mr. Charlie's insistence that he not bring one along. Just like the man predicted, his eyes had grown accustomed to the dark. But these briars weren't merely dark—they were the gaping jaws of hell itself. He padded along, half-bent, looking, searching, squinting until finally. . .was it?

He smiled. A crawlspace punctuated the bottom of the hedge. For a moment, his hand hesitated over his breast. If he pulled Nixie out, his friend would surely crow some praises for this victory. But he'd need that hand—and his knees—to clear the thorny tunnel in one piece. Hopefully this wouldn't snag his stockings too horribly. Taking great care, he shuffled ahead on all fours.

The bristly hedge-tunnel was short and opened up to the mouth of a cave, wherein a lantern glowed sun bright. Voices increased in volume. "Coburn's not going to be happy. This fool can't even pull off the few tasks we've given him. I say we kill him."

Egad! Someone was in for trouble. Lucius rose to his feet and duck-walked through the cave's opening and into a carved-out cavern. Stretching to full height, he dusted himself off—then immediately bent once more, examining his legs. Oh figgity! Flesh peeked out from a tear on his hose, dousing some of the yellow glory from his stockings. His lower lip quivered, then he sucked it in between his teeth. Nothing to be done for the mishap now.

"'Bout time you showed, Nutbrown. We were about to give up on you." A gravelly voice interrupted his inspection.

Lucius met the gazes of Mr. Blackjack and Mr. Charlie, who both sat near the light. They scowled almost in unison, their brows drawn into a V. If he didn't know better, he might almost think they were cross with him—but of course it was only the play of shadows from the inconsistent lantern light.

Mr. Charlie shook his head, red hair the colour of spilled wine in the dim illumination. "So far your performance hasn't met with our expectations. And here we thought you was a businessman."

This would never do. He had a reputation to uphold. He yanked Nixie from his coat and popped him onto his hand, shoving the puppet out to take care of this potential disaster. "Mr. Nutbrown assures you, gentlemen, that you'll find none more businesslike than himself. None at all."

Mr. Blackjack scratched the scruff on his chin, the sound rasping overloud in the contained space. "Let's see. . .you failed to get us a lookout for our last meeting. This time you're late. We've already spotted you enough money to dandy up an entire gentleman's club, but other than promises, you've given nothing in return." He swung his shaggy head toward Mr. Charlie. "What kind of business you suppose that is, Charlie?"

"Bad, I'd say. Maybe the worst kind of bad. Disappoints me, it does." He reached for the straps on his back, biceps bulging like a butcher's, and slowly pulled out an axe. He tapped the flat of the blade against his palm, the thwapping noise a crazed heartbeat bouncing from wall to wall.

Or was that mad pounding his own heart? Lucius swallowed a sour taste in his mouth and bobbed Nixie's head from Mr. Blackjack to Mr. Charlie. "Mr. Nutbrown is your man, sirs! Don't doubt it for a minute. He'll do anything for his friends. And we are friends, are we not? Friends and businessmen, one and the same."

"A'right. We don't have time for this. We're on a tight schedule, and the gears are clicking into motion." Mr. Blackjack shifted, his wooden leg scraping the ground as he moved, the sound eerily like bone on bone. With a thick hand, he patted the dirt next to him. "Sit yourself down and listen up."

In a trice, Lucius dashed over to the spot and sat, cross-legged, making sure to keep Nixie's head at a pert angle.

Mr. Charlie didn't say a word, but he stopped thwacking the axe against his palm.

"There's a shipment coming in, about three weeks from now," said Mr. Blackjack. "All our groundwork must be in place. Preparation is key. As is secrecy. Wouldn't want word to get out to smugglers now, would we?"

"Smugglers?" Beneath the cloth and plaster of the little puppet, beads of sweat popped out on Lucius's skin. "Horrid creatures."

"Right." Mr. Charlie lifted his gaze from his axe blade to stare at Lucius, bypassing a glance at Nixie. "Which is why we hire only respectable businessmen, such as yerself. But yer not going to be enough. We need a woman to work along with you, just for a small task. Someone who's familiar to the town, of good standing and that sort. We need you to find one of those for us. Think you can do that?"

Mr. Charlie slapped the axe blade against his palm so sharply, Lucius and Nixie jumped.

"Why, of course Mr. Nutbrown can." His voice came out squeaky without even trying—maybe a little too squeaky, judging by the knowing look passed from Mr. Blackjack to Mr. Charlie. Lucius cleared his throat and tried again. "But you gentlemen had no trouble acquiring me. Why don't you find a woman yourself? Ought not Mr. Nutbrown's talents be put to more use like ciphering or scribing?"

"Do we look as proper as you?" Mr. Blackjack shrugged one shoulder, the ripple of muscle as fluid as the swipe of a dragon's tail. "Why do you think we gave you new garments in the first place?"

His eyes dropped to the awful snag in his stocking, and it took all his reserve to keep Nixie atop his hand instead of tucking away his friend and attempting to mend the tear. "Of course. Mr. Nutbrown sees." He whipped his puppet's face to his as if to confer, then held Nixie back out into the fray of conversation. "It will take a gentleman—such as Mr. Nutbrown—to solicit the service of a reputable lady."

"Right. That's your next assignment." Mr. Blackjack leaned toward him, his tone lowering to a near-growl. "And if you fail again, you're out."

Nixie trembled, his little cape shivering against Lucius's shirtsleeve. "Umm, a little clarification, if you don't mind. Out? As in. . .?"

Mr. Blackjack and Mr. Charlie laughed loud and long. Nixie looked from one to the other, trying to understand the joke. Poor puppet. Too bad Nix was of limited intelligence. Lucius reached and straightened the jester's tiny collar with his free hand, trying to impart some sort of dignity to his companion.

Mr. Blackjack slapped Lucius on the back, the movement knocking Nixie's head askew. "We'll see you *and* the lady tomorrow. Five sharp at the Pickle and Pine."

Lucius's eyes widened. Gah! The only woman he could think of—who would even consent to a conversation with him—was Johanna Langley, and she'd never leave her precious inn near dinnertime. "If discretion is of the utmost, sirs—" he yanked Nixie's head upright— "the Pickle and Pine won't do. Too many patrons. Too many ears. Mr. Nutbrown suggests you consider the Blue Hedge Inn."

Mr. Charlie snorted. "That rat hovel on the edge of town?"

Lucius bobbed Nixie's little chin up and down.

"Fair enough. Five tomorrow. Blue Hedge. But don't disappoint us." Mr. Blackjack aimed a pointed stare at the sharp axe blade lying in Mr. Charlie's lap.

Mr. Charlie ran his thumb along the blade, opening a line of flesh, bloodying both skin and steel.

Lucius flinched. So did Nixie.

Mr. Blackjack leaned back and looked down his nose at both of them. "There's no holding Charlie back when he's disappointed."

Lucius's throat tightened, and for a moment, he wished Nixie could speak on his own. "N-not to worry, friends. Mr. Nutbrown will be there. On time. Early, even."

He shot to his feet and darted to the door, forgetting to duck and smacking his forehead in the process. Naturally he'd be there, but how to get Miss Langley to agree to sit and listen?

∽

Johanna clamped her jaw to keep her teeth from rattling. The wagon she drove juddered from every rock, dip, or uneven groove on Dolphin Lane, the ride as merciless as Tanny's switch. Resettling her backside on the unforgiving seat, she flicked the reins, urging the horse forward. The animal was hardly more animated than Posey. Not that she blamed the poor bay. Scars crisscrossed his rump from Tanny's wrath. Though she hated inflicting more pain on the horse, it was a must. She was late.

Passing by the Magpie Inn, she glanced at the pots of roses, periwinkles, and pert little candytufts. Now there was a good idea. She could paint an old barrel in the barn and transplant some wildflowers for the front of the Blue Hedge. It wouldn't cost anything and it couldn't help but perk up the facade.

Farther down the lane, she bumped past the White Horse and admired the green- and yellow-striped awning over the door. A sigh deflated her. New awnings were out of the question for now.

The sun grew brighter on the horizon with every turn of the wheels. She'd already passed a few drays loaded with crates for an early delivery. Pedestrians ventured out. Johanna snapped the reins a little harder and ducked her head when Mrs. Dogflacks emerged out a door, shaking dirt from a rug. If the woman saw her driving Tanny's wagon, she'd spread Johanna's shame from one end of town to the other.

At last the Market Place Gaol loomed ahead, hunched on a foundation of crumbling stone. Five years ago, Johanna had held her breath when driving beneath the archway leading around to the exercise yard. This time she stopped the wagon and eyed the disaster before daring a pass.

The first set of gates stood open, one bent and hanging by a single hinge. The other was completely missing. Light gaped through the ragged openings of the overhead archway, where stones finally gave up their ghost and fell to their death. Maybe if she hugged the right side, she'd make it through without a rock to her skull. Why they'd not torn down this ruin long ago baffled her—and the entire town. Money, likely. It always came back to pounds and guineas.

With a "walk on" to the horse and a prayer heavenward, she rolled onward, not breathing until she cleared the arch and entered the narrow road between two walls. Spiked iron rods jutted from the top of the barrier closest to the gaol. Sharpened flint grinned like jagged fangs atop the other. Lot of good that would do them should an inmate clear the first wall and walk free out the broken gate.

The air was close here. Pressing in. Pressing down. It stank of waste and hopelessness, followed by a pungent waft of vinegar. Her stomach lurched. The stench was even more unpleasant than she remembered—and she was on the outside of the walls. Poor Mr. Morton was locked up inside. Often he'd invaded her thoughts the past two days. How was he holding up? Would she see him today? Did she want to?

She rolled to a stop at the back of the building, then set the brake and climbed down. The bay complained with a snort as she rang a bell next to the rear entrance of the yard. A metal slidey-door shot open on a thin slot. Eyes the color of a great, grey rat stared out.

"Oakum delivery and pickup." Her mouth formed the words from memory, the phrase rising from a graveyard where she'd thought them buried long ago.

Behind the slot, the eyes widened. "Yer not Diggery. Not Tanny, neither."

Retrieving the invoice from a pocket of her work apron, she held it up. "Diggery has been given leave for the next three weeks."

"Has he now? Well, well. I don't mind that."

The slot closed, and before the wide doors opened, she pulled herself back up to the wagon seat and released the brake.

The guard's gaze followed as she guided the wagon through the gate and along the edge of the wall. He relocked the doors and rang for an inmate to unload her noisome cargo. The gravel yard was empty, but not for much longer. Soon the gaol would spit out criminals of all sorts, doomed to spend endless hours picking tar from the used hemp she brought.

Setting the brake once again, she parked the wagon next to a gleaming pile of cleaned oakum—yesterday's work—then frowned at the small size of it. Half a wagonload, at best. And next to that, a gnarly pile yet remained to be cleaned. They'd not even finished it? This wouldn't go over well with Tanny.

Across the yard, the gaol door opened, which prodded her to climb down. Sometimes the rear wagon gate stuck, and it wouldn't do for her to still be fiddling with the latch when the guards brought the prisoner on work duty to unload her delivery. She'd made that mistake once, and discovered Tanny was a sweet-spirited altar boy in comparison to a convict.

She hastened to release both pins—thankfully only one needed coaxing—and lowered the gate. Now to return to her perch of safety in the front. She scooted around the side of the wagon, neared the iron step up to her seat, and—

A grasp on her shoulder spun her back. Rat-grey eyes coated her with an oily gaze. "How 'bout I show you the guardhouse while you wait?"

"No, thank you." She ducked from his hold and turned, reaching for the seat to hoist herself up.

Fingers dug into her arm, yanking her around so quickly, the world blurred for a moment.

"Isn't safe for a skirt hereabouts." His words carried more than a warning, the bass rumble of it weighted with an insidious promise.

She jutted her jaw, well aware the move was less than ladylike, and not caring a bit about it. "Safer than a guardhouse, I'd say."

"Oh, a bit salty, are ye?" A feral smile lifted his thin lips, all sharpness and edges. He leaned closer, reaching with his free hand to fondle the hair fallen loose at her temple. "I like a bit o' salt."

"Leave off!"

It was her thought exactly, but not her voice. It came from behind—and stiffened her shoulders. Unsure if she should be mortified or relieved, she froze. Of all the prisoners to be assigned to unloading duty, it had to be Mr. Morton?

The guard in front of her lowered his free hand—still not releasing her with the other—and looked over her shoulder. "You again? Might've known. Why'd you bring that one, Billy?"

"Bagsley's orders. This 'un needs a good breaking."

He laughed, returning his soulless gaze to her. "As I said, won't be safe for you here. Not with this one nearby. Come with me—"

"No!" She wrenched from his grasp and ducked around him, not wishing to be caught in the coming storm.

As she suspected, a wave of toast-colored hair bobbed amidst a flurry of fists. Three guards. One Alex. Unfair. She raced to the back of the wagon and retrieved the pitchfork used for unloading. Profanity polluted the air, accompanied by grunts, and—oh, sweet heavens! Not the click of a gun. Should she hide or try to be of help to Alex?

A shot exploded.

Then silence—except for heavy breathing.

Time stopped. A host of emotions attacked her from every conceivable angle, pinning her in place.

"Johanna?" Her name was a ragged whisper.

Dropping the pitchfork, she dashed around to the front. Three bodies lay on the ground. All clad in blue wool. Alex bent, head down, hands on thighs, shoulders heaving.

"Mr. Morton?" She stopped in front of him, suddenly unsure of what to do. "Are you all right?"

Slowly, he straightened, and as he ran his fingers through his hair, brushing it back, her heart quit beating. The right side of his mouth was swollen, red and angry. His left eye was purpled and but a slit. One cheek sported a fresh welt, and blood trickled from his nose. His fine clothes were ripped and ruined, a taunting reminder of his fall from grace. All this could not possibly be from a tussle with three guards. What sort of anguish had he suffered the past two days?

Tears burned the backs of her eyes, and her throat tightened. "Oh, Alex . . .what have they done to you?"

CHAPTER SEVENTEEN

Alex's lungs heaved, and he flexed his hands, releasing the leftover energy from the fight—but all the while memorizing the sight of Johanna, the way the morning sun painted her in golden light, the brightness of her blue skirts against the backdrop of ugly grey. Pink brushed along the curves of her cheeks. She was an ethereal contrast to the netherworld of this gaol yard. He'd frown, if his lip weren't so swollen. "What on earth are you doing here, Miss Langley?"

Behind him, across the gravel expanse, shouts issued from the prison's door, a discordant harmony to the moan of the guard laid out on the ground beside him. "And be quick about it, we haven't much time."

"Oh, Alex!" His Christian name came out shivery—

And sent a pang straight into his heart.

"I am sorry for your suffering." Johanna's eyes brimmed with tears, authentic and altogether too alluring.

He drew in a ragged breath. How could she show such compassion when she had no idea the validity of his supposed crime? "Why are you here?"

"I have taken on a side job, oakum delivery." Johanna leaned sideways, glancing past him, then drew near, bringing the fresh scent of lavender with her. "Are you *really* a traitor?"

Fat lip or not, this time he did arch his lips, upwards, into a smile. The woman could make a statue grin simply by the command of her presence. "I am a man of many talents, but not sedition. Never sedition."

Her eyes searched his, and the uncertainty there pained him more than his cracked rib. Much as he'd like to grab her hand and run free, defend his innocence and honor, reality pounded the gravel at his back, kicked up by approaching guards.

He closed in on her, bending to whisper into her ear. "Listen. Write a note. One word. Sackett. Put it in the base of the dead ash, east of center, in a stand of trees behind the rocks at Foxend Corner." Pulling away, he flashed her a last smile. "Oh, and find yourself a different occupation. This is not the place for you. Now, stand back."

He pivoted and strode forward three paces, then dropped to his knees, hands up and behind his head. If he had a white flag, he'd wave that too. Anything to spare Johanna from viewing another brawl.

Four guards surrounded him, all training pistol barrels at his skull. Alex tensed, not from the guns, but from the beast in a grey woolen uniform directly in front, one he'd grown to know intimately well the past few days—leastwise the man's knuckles. *Lord, did he have to be on duty today? Truly?*

"Getting handy with the delivery girl, are ye? We'll have none of that." The fellow to his left flipped his gun around, preparing for a sound pistol whip.

Alex hesitated, one, two, then leaned away at the last instant before the strike, avoiding the whack to the head but not the incoming boot to his belly. Air rushed out in a groan as he doubled over. Agony radiated from gut to ribs. How much beating could a body take before breaking beyond repair?

Johanna's "No!" rode the crest of the brute's "Move him out of here."

Hands gripped him under each arm, hefting him up, dragging him forward, pulling him from Johanna's protests and toward the snickers and slurs of fellow prisoners coming out to the yard. By the time he gained his breath, the gaol swallowed him into a narrow throat of a corridor.

The guards prodded him onward, two beside, one behind, and deposited him where he'd begun two days ago—in front of the slip-faced turnkey behind the scarred desk.

"What's this?" The man scowled down at them all, and Alex tried hard not to give in to the horrid fascination of staring at the ruined flesh that should have been a nose.

Beside him, the biggest man growled out a profanity. "He took out Briggs and Grimley, sir."

"That so?" The turnkey's gazed fixed on him. The man blinked, an odd effect from the offset eyes, like the half-flicker of a dying candle. "Didn't fancy picking oakum today, hmm? And here I thought the honest work would make a new man of ye. Aah, well. We gots other methods."

Though it ripped a fresh wave of torment through his bones, Alex straightened and threw back his shoulders. "You have no right to hold me here. By who's order am I detained?"

"Rights?" A croak of a laugh issued from the turnkey's mouth. "You sound like a flamin' American."

"You have no idea who I am." His swollen lips once again lifted into a smile. "Pity. You ought choose your enemies more wisely."

Purple crept up the warden's neck, crawled over his chin, and bloomed upon his cheeks like a bruise. "What's that? A threat from a scarpin' piece of jailbait?"

"A promise."

The turnkey reared back on his stool. "That's it! Take him down, boys. We've wasted enough time on this one. He can rot."

Fingers bit into the soft flesh beneath his arms, yanking him back into the corridor. The biggest fellow led them on a return path to the yard. At least he wasn't going toward the gibbet. A small mercy, that.

As they neared the door, he considered an elbow jab to the fellow on the right, just for spite, but that would be the best he could manage. Trapped between two guards and spent beyond exhaustion, any resistance he might give would cost more strength than he owned.

The big man opened the door, holding it wide, then swiveled his head to the guards. "Let him go."

The fellow gripping his arm on the left dug his fingers in deeper. "But warden said—"

"I'll do as warden asks—and more." A wicked grin exposed the brute's mustard-coloured teeth. "Just go open the hole for me. That's all."

Alex stumbled, though he was hard pressed to decide if it was from the sudden freedom of being released or the revelation of his new home. The hole? That couldn't be good.

"Go on." The beast at the door glowered at him. "Move it."

Fine. With a defiant lift of his head, Alex strode out—and a boot to his back sent him sprawling down the stairs. He landed chin first in the gravel, the sting against flesh hardly a comparison to the humiliation of knowing Johanna likely saw from across the yard—if she were looking. For a moment, he lay, stunned. *Oh God, please don't let her see this.*

A yank on his collar lifted him from behind. Airborne, he was driven around to the side of the staircase, where a cellar door gaped into blackness.

"Kneel."

Hardly a command, for the man's fists drove him to his knees.

"Hands behind your head."

A sigh emptied his lungs. Fight or flight? What choice did he have? It was eight stairs up to the gaol door, but then the impossible odds of making it through the corridor, past the turnkey, and out the front. Or, had he enough stamina in store, he could take out the brute behind him and dash across the yard, disable the guards by the gate, and flee in Johanna's wagon. He grimaced. The way his muscles quivered, he'd be lucky to crawl the distance, let alone dash. Blast it!

Slowly, he lifted his arms.

"Yer nothin' but jailbait. Rat bait. Hell bait. Any way you look at it, bait's what you are, and you ought not forget it." Behind him, the man leaned closer, his breath fouling the skin on the back of Alex's hands. "If you move, if you flinch, if you so much as make a noise, that hole in front of you will be your grave. Understand?"

Alex sucked in air and held it, steeling his body for whatever torment the brute had in mind.

Without warning, the sharp point of a knife cut into the flesh at the nape of his neck. Alex bit his tongue, trapping a cry. The blade dug a long line, from hairline to shirt, not deep, not to kill. Just to mark. He bit harder when the point struck again, slicing two curves attached to the line. Warm wetness drained out, soaking into his shirt, sticking the fabric to his back. Sweat dotted his forehead, but still he did not move.

"There's a *B* for you to remember what you are, Bait. Think on that. Think real well. I'll give you all the time you need—and then some."

While the man chuckled, Alex dove, unwilling to suffer one more kick in the back. He somersaulted down moist rocks, each bump jolting pain deep enough to uproot the marrow in his bones. He landed on muck and rolled over, fighting to breathe.

"That's right, scurry off, vermin." Above him, the man's silhouette was a demon against the sky, but only for a moment. The door slammed.

Blackness attacked, and he blinked as he rose to sit. But no. This was not a blinding dark. It was worse. A crack of light reached down from a weathered scar in the hole's door, taunting him.

Oh, God. Please. Not this.

Rage shook along every muscle, masking the pain of cut and bruise and brokenness, and he pounded his fists onto the mucky earth. Over and over. Not this! Who'd put him here? And why?

Finally spent, he leaned back, ignoring the fire on his neck from the torn flesh. *Don't look. Don't do it.* He repeated the words, shoring up against a coming attack that would leave him more ruined than a knife point.

Just. Don't. Look.

Too late.

His gaze shot upward, and as he stared at the crack in the door over his head, suddenly he was ten years old again. Alone. Isolated. Utterly, completely helpless. As powerless as the day his parents were gunned down.

When he'd watched from the darkness of a closet through a crack in the door.

⌒⌒

Johanna pulled back on the reins, halting the old nag. She needn't have. The horse had stopped more often than not on the entire plodding route up to Foxend Corner. Perhaps it was a small mercy the oakum load hadn't been overlarge today, or the animal would've keeled over long ago.

To her left, a margin of swaying grass dropped off to the crash of wave and wind below. She set the brake and climbed down, rounding the wagon in the opposite direction, then hesitated before a pile of leftover boulders. Should she climb over the rocks, or skirt them and fight with waist-high brush and scrub? She sighed and lifted her gaze skyward. *Is this a fool's errand, Lord?*

The trek up here supplied ample time to sort through her thoughts, so why were they still such a tangle? On the one hand, her heart broke afresh each time she replayed the blows Alex had suffered in her sight. On the other, why would he have been arrested in the first place were he not suspect?

She searched the sky for answers. Hoping for. . .what? Direction clearly written on the parchment of a cloud? Maybe she really was a fool after all.

Setting her sights on the stand of trees beyond the rocks, she hoisted her skirts and began picking her way from stone to stone. Were Thomas up and about, this adventure would've suited him. The sun, high now in the sky, was a ruthless taskmaster, as was the gusty wind vying for her bonnet. Perspiration dampened her shift. Her toe caught on her underskirt, ripping the hem and teetering her off balance. Was Mr. Morton worth this much effort?

She paused, her vision suddenly watery. Her last glimpse of the man, bloodied, beaten, and plummeting into some kind of cellar was answer enough. Traitor or not, no one deserved such violence—and he'd taken the brunt of it on her behalf simply by fighting off that ill-mannered guard.

For a moment, she lifted her face to the sky, and prayed for the man who was a strange mix of honor and secrets. A man who took big risks but paid his debts, never seeming to wager what he could not afford to lose. She sucked in a breath as a stunning realization hit her for the first time.

Maybe—just maybe—there was such a thing as an honorable gambler.

The thought was so preposterous and alluring, that she hopped down from the last boulder, landing in weeds up to her knees. This close to the trees, beneath a leafy canopy, the wind took on a chillier note. She'd have to think on such disconcerting ideas later.

Now then, which tree? She scanned the branches and found the leafless limbs, east of center. Swishing through the vegetation, she neared the dead ash and bent.

Just as Mr. Morton had described, she spied a hollowed opening at the base of the trunk. She retrieved the small note from her pocket and poked it into the hole. Hopefully an animal or the wind wouldn't steal it. Ought she put a rock or something in front of it? Well, that would be easy enough to find. Rising, she turned.

Then screamed.

A pace away, dark eyes stared down into hers, what she could see of them, anyway. The man wore his hat brim low, his black hair framing a face better suited to night and shadows. He was a ghost, this one. A spectre. A spirit.

And entirely familiar.

"La, sir!" She slapped a hand to her heaving chest. Had Mr. Morton known his friend would be here? Why had he not warned her? "You scared the breath from me, Mr. . .who *are* you?"

His mouth, set in a flat line, didn't move. Nothing about him did. The man was as hard and unyielding as the boulder pile. Even the blessed wind hardly riffled the tails of his riding cloak.

"Who I am is of no consequence." His gaze flicked past her shoulder and landed at the base of the ash. "More important is what's on that piece of paper."

The next slap of breeze snagged a piece of her hair loose, a usable excuse to stall as she tucked it beneath her bonnet. Should she give him the note? Was this who Alex hoped would receive it? Clearly he had some sort of relationship with this man. Besides, if she didn't give the paper to him, he'd simply take it when she left or maybe even shove past her to grab it.

Bending, she fished the missive out and handed it over.

He unfolded the message, his hat sitting so low it was impossible to read a response in his eyes. But she didn't have to. His jaw clenched, and the muscles on his neck stood out like iron rods. The note disappeared in his fist as he shoved it into his pocket. "Blast!"

She flinched. Not that she hadn't heard coarser language in the taproom. No, it was the roar behind it, the man's guttural, livid tone. She'd heard once that a tiger's growl could kill a wildebeest just from the fright of the sound. She hadn't believed such a fairy tale—until now.

"What does it mean?" Her voice squeaked in comparison.

Taking the hat from his head, he ran a hand through the tangle of black hair beneath and looked up at the sky. A sigh, long and low, slipped past his lips like a prayer. Finally, he reseated the hat and stared at her. "Better not to know."

She fought her own tigerish growl. Frustrating man. She stared right back. "You are a friend of Mr. Morton, are you not?"

His head dipped, a clipped sort of nod yet fully believable.

"He is in trouble, sir. I think you know that, though I cannot fathom how the single word *Sackett* penned on a slip of paper conveys such a message." She stepped toward him, stopping an arm's length away, willing him to see the desperation that surely must be written in the lines on her face. "Mr. Morton needs your help. He is in gaol, for what I suspect is a wrongful accusation. You must go speak for him."

A shadow crossed his face. What went on behind those dark eyes? Was he devising a plan? Composing a note for her to return to Alex? Deciding which official to speak to first?

Without a word, he turned and walked away.

Johanna's jaw dropped. What? Why would a man turn his back on a friend?

Clutching handfuls of her skirts, she ran after him. "Stop! You owe me an explanation. Both you and Mr. Morton." She grabbed his sleeve, trying to turn him back around. "The least you can do is tell me what I'm involved in."

"I said it's better not to know." He shrugged from her grasp and continued his long-legged pace to where a horse waited near the edge of the trees.

In the few moments it took him to untie his mount, she caught up to him. "Listen, Mr. Whatever-your-name-is, I could barely stand to look upon Alex—I mean, Mr. Morton, without weeping. He is a beaten man, sir. What I know is that he suffers. What I do not know is if he really is a traitor, as accused." She lifted her chin, daring him with a direct gaze. "Nor if you are."

"You would not be here if you truly believed him a traitor."

His words were a blow to her heart. How could he know what she barely acknowledged? Slowly, she nodded. "True, I believe Mr. Morton is a good man. You, I'm not so sure about."

It started small, a tiny twitch, hardly more than a whisper really. Then slowly, methodically, his mouth curved into a full-blossomed smile, his face years younger. Boyish, almost. The look captured her by surprise, for she never imagined this dour enigma could transform into such a dashing figure.

"As I've said before, Miss Langley, you will do, and quite well." Humor softened the edges of his words.

"I can do naught. Will you help him, sir? Will you ride into town and speak to the magistrate?"

Quick as a late spring tempest, his grin disappeared. His eyes sparked gunmetal grey, cold and unrelenting. "I cannot."

"What is wrong with you? You're his friend. You coward!" Her fingers flew to her mouth. What had gotten into her? She'd done what she'd been asked. Delivered the note. End of deed. Why provoke for a cause she owed no further allegiance to?

The wind lifted his collar. Beside him, his horse stamped a snort, and still he did not move. Had she pushed him too far? She retreated a step.

But his quiet words pulled her back. "That word, Sackett. It's a code. Long ago, Giles Sackett was a man imprisoned at Newgate. An innocent, chained for a trumped-up accusation of debt by a vengeful duke. Word got out to his family, his friends, and though they played by the rules, seeking justice in court, they were denied. Treachery begets treachery, and so they devised a plot to rescue him through bribery and violence, stealing him away by dead of night."

He stopped, abruptly, his story like a wagon gone off one of Dover's cliffs.

"What happened?" she asked. "Surely there's more."

Turning his back to her, he swung one long leg up and over the saddle, then looked down at her. "They were all killed, Miss Langley. Every last one. The word Sackett means back away, leave off, which is what I intend to do."

He reached for the reins—as did she. "No! If Mr. Morton is innocent, you can't leave him undefended and alone."

"He is not. He has you." He yanked the leather from her hands and heeled his horse onward, into the tall grass, toward the road leading to London.

Johanna growled at the sky, as deeply primal as the man's earlier roar. What else was there to do?

CHAPTER EIGHTEEN

Johanna opened the door to chaos, then stood there, jaw agape. Nary a space remained on any of the benches in the taproom. Around every table in the Blue Hedge Inn, women chattered, men wiped foam from their upper lips, and off in the corner, four children squatted on the floor, playing a game of pick-up-sticks. All looked to be fed, happy and in no hurry to leave. What in the world?

Across the room, Mr. Quail bounded down the stairway and entered the throng, a smile on his lips and bounce to his step. Clearly the man was not as ill as his friends had claimed him to be the previous evening, nor did he appear any worse for the wear from having fled into a rainstorm.

Johanna loosened her bonnet and tugged it off, then worked her way toward him. "I see you've made a quick recovery, sir."

"Hmm?" He turned at her voice, and a grin spread as his gaze landed on her. "Aah, yes. I am blessed with a strong physique." His chest puffed out, and had he the space for it, no doubt he'd make a show of flexing his muscles. "Nothing keeps me down for long," he drawled.

She clenched her bonnet brim to keep from smacking the leer off his face. "You don't fool me, Mr. Quail."

"The beautiful Johanna can hardly be called a fool. But tell me." He reached out and fingered a loose curl of her hair. "What is it you think you know of me, kitten?"

She batted his hand away. "I know you are responsible for breaking a window last night, and I expect full reimbursement."

"All right."

She froze. That had been entirely too easy. What was his game now? "All right what?"

"You shall have it." He shrugged.

"Good." She sounded like a sulky child.

Yet the smoldering flash in his eyes labeled her anything but.

If Alex had looked at her that way, her heart would beat with warmth. Coming from this man, fury fired in her stomach. "And use the front door next time! The folk around here turn a blind eye to smuggling. There's no need to sneak out."

She fled before he could reply and wound her way past milling customers, frustration upping her pace. Darting into the kitchen, she slung her bonnet on a hook.

Mam looked up from behind the worktable. A streak of mustard was smeared on one cheek, and her cap hung at half-mast.

Anger seeped away at the sight. Johanna reached for her apron. "What's going on? Why this many patrons on a Monday afternoon?"

"About time you return, Daughter. You're becoming a regular scamp like your brother." Mam shoved her cap aright with the back of her hand. "Seems there's a ship not yet in, supposed to pick up that lot early this morn." The tilt of her head toward the taproom undid her previous nudge to her cap, and the white fabric fell askew once again. "I hear tell all the taprooms of Dover are filled. Give that pot a stir, would you?"

Johanna crossed to the hearth and grabbed the long-handled spoon off a hook. "Well, that's a blessing for our strongbox, but I'm sorry I wasn't here to help you."

"About that, I thought you agreed to a morning run only, and here it is afternoon. Did everything go well for you?"

She scowled. Well? Sure, if you counted a whipping from Tanny for being late, an unfruitful conversation with an obstinate man who refused to help Mr. Morton, and the awful violence she'd witnessed against Alexander. Unbidden images of his face came to mind, beaten and battered, bloody and pained. How to explain what she'd seen, and especially how she felt, when she wasn't even sure herself? She scraped the stuck bits from the bottom of the pot and set the spoon aside. If only it were as easy to loosen the conflicting emotions caught on her heart.

Straightening, she faced Mam. "The run for Tanny took longer than I expected. I'd forgotten how much work pickup and delivery can be."

Her mother's good eye narrowed. "There's more to it, I think."

"There's no hiding anything from you, is there?" Jo shook her head and bypassed her mother, grabbing an empty pitcher off a shelf. "Remember when I tried to keep that stray kitten a secret out in the barn?"

Her mother laughed. "For a girl not partial to drinking milk, your sudden thirst was a giveaway. And though you're putting a valiant effort into swaying this conversation, I'll not have you dodging the subject. Tell me, child."

Johanna paused, feeling the weight of the pitcher in her hands and the gravity of what she'd seen. Ought she tell Mam? Her mother had fed the crew of customers single-handedly. No sense adding burden to fatigue. "We'll talk later, I promise. Go put your feet up, and I'll tend the patrons."

"They've been fed and mugs recently filled. They'll hold for a few minutes. You've seen Mr. Morton, and I would hear of it."

The pitcher slipped from her hands, but she snatched it up before it hit ground. "How do you know—?"

"Pish! It doesn't take a barrister's mind to figure that out. You ran a load of oakum to the gaol where Mr. Morton is currently housed. And from your hesitation to speak of it, I'd bet my grandmother's teapot you saw him."

A fierce frown pulled her lips. "Mam!"

Her mother chuckled. "Sometimes you're as dour as old Mrs. Stickleby. Life's not always as tragic as you make it out to be. So, how is Mr. Morton faring?"

Exhaling long and low, she set down the pitcher and leaned back against the tabletop. There was no escaping a mother on an information-gathering mission. "I hardly recognized him. They've beaten him. One eye is so swollen, I doubt he can see from it. There are welts and bruises, and worst of all, a guard pulled a knife on him, cutting the back of his neck. His neck, Mam!" Hot tears burned in her eyes. With effort, she blinked them away. "How can men be that cruel?"

Her mother's mouth pinched. "You, of all people, know how harsh the world can be, Jo. How is he taking it?"

She swallowed as a memory welled of how he'd shoved her back to safety and stepped forward himself, taking on the guards' brutality singlehandedly. "Bravely." The word came out as a whisper. "He fought only when he thought I was in trouble."

"Were you?" Mam dashed over to her and grabbed both her hands. "I'll not have you going back there if you are in danger, whether we need the money or not."

Her mother peered into her face, driving home her point. New worry lines creased the sides of her mouth, and when had her skin become so transparent? This inn, this life, was too hard on her. On them both.

Lifting one of Mam's hands, Johanna pressed a kiss onto the back of it. "Don't fret. It's nothing I can't handle. Do not fear for me, but rather for Alex—Mr. Morton." Mam's brows rose, as did her own irritation. Why did his Christian name fall so easily from her lips? "Keep Mr. Morton in your prayers, for he needs them more than I. They put him in a cellar. I saw him tumble in. Lord knows if they'll let him up for air or even feed him. I don't know how long he'll be able to last in such conditions. I wish there were something we could do to ease his suffering. Who is to help him, if not us? Even his friend has run off to London."

"The man with the hat?" Mam pulled her hands away and retreated a step. Her gaze travelled every inch of Johanna's face. "When did you see him?"

"That's why I was late. Mr. Morton asked me to deliver a message, up near Foxend Corner. By the time I made it back to Tanny's, he was none too pleased." She tugged on her sleeves, making sure the hems hadn't slipped upward. Though probably less swollen, the welts on her arms from Tanny's switch would be quite the shade of ugly purple. "I'll see to the patrons now. You ought put your feet up for a few minutes."

She turned and reached for the pitcher. A grip on her forearm spun her back around, and she barely stifled a cry.

Mam's eyes burned into hers. "This message, what did it say?"

"Just a name, apparently. I'm not sure I believe the tale behind it. Regardless, Mr. Morton's friend is of a cowardly nature, for he refused to go help—"

"The word, Johanna." Mam's grip tightened. "What was the word?"

"Sackett."

Mam's fingers fell away. So did the pain, thankfully.

Her mother staggered sideways and lowered onto a barrel. "You're right. I ought put my feet up."

"Oh dear! I knew it. This has been too much for you." Alarmed at the grey shade of Mam's face, Jo dashed to the corner and grabbed an empty crate, then returned and set it in front of her mother. Stooping, she helped set Mam's feet on the wood, one leg at a time. "We'll hire back Ana to cook. We will. As soon as we pay off the final debt on the hearth, that's what we'll do next. And with today's extra earnings, we just might have enough."

Mam shook her head. "Don't be so sure of it."

"If we fail to trust in God's provision, what kind of faith is that?"

Her mother's gaze locked onto hers. "Just make sure it's Him you're trusting, not yourself."

The words washed over her like a bucket of cold water, and she turned away with a shiver. Mam *always* knew too much.

⌒⌒

Water. Alex would trade his life for just a sip, for he was surely about to die without a drink, anyway. Throat raw, strength spent, he sat motionless in the darkness, hugging his knees for warmth and finding none. Judging by the angle of light breaching the tiny crack in the overhead door, and from the grumble of prisoners in the yard, picking their fingers to nubs with the oakum, he figured it must be morning, day two of confinement. Or was it three? All he knew for sure was dampness, pain, hunger, and worst of all thirst, for he'd had nothing to eat or drink since he'd landed in this godforsaken pit. A small blessing, he supposed, for truly where would the waste have gone except that he should wallow in it?

He dropped his forehead to his knees. By now the magistrate would've learned of his fate, for none exceeded Thatcher's horsemanship, assuming Johanna delivered his message, of course. Mouth dry, he tried to swallow, but he couldn't even accomplish that. Failure tasted burnt and bitter, as agonizing as the torn flesh on his hands from searching every inch of this pit, clawing, pounding, scratching for a way out. Nothing remained but to wait and see how quickly death paid a visit—and wonder whom he had to thank for his ticket to heaven.

A groan rumbled deep in his chest, but stayed there, too weak to rise out his mouth. What a way to die. He'd always dreamed his demise would be in a blaze of glory, guns afire, upholding justice as Bow Street's finest officer, celebrated and revered. . .not wasting away in a hole in the ground, helpless and hopeless.

Is this it then, God? Will Yours be the next face I see?

Who would even know he was gone? Who would mourn? Ford, maybe. He'd watched out for him since his parents' deaths. Thatcher? Not likely. The man was all rock and iron. Brentwood? Too busy with his new wife and son. And that was it. The sum of his friends. He'd spent a lifetime holding everyone at arm's length, and apparently, he was a champion of it.

But what of Johanna?

He winced at the thought of her. She knew he was here. He leaned his head back against the dirt wall, unable to even sob. *Oh, God.* He had caused the confusion he'd seen in her eyes. She probably yet believed him a traitor and was likely regretting his acquaintance in the first place. Ironic, really. The whole situation. Sent to find a traitor and now wearing the placard himself. Locked in solitary, just when he was ready to open his heart.

His fingers raked into the muck where he sat. It would have been better if years ago he had raced out of that closet, shouted in the face of the murderers, and taken the knife as a ten-year-old.

"Why? Why! Why spare me for such an end as this?" The words spewed past his lips, taking the rest of his voice with them. All that remained were ragged breaths, broken dreams, and the vague urge to whisper what might be his last prayer. "Yet even in this, Lord, I suppose I must trust You, for there is nothing else."

The dirt walls muffled his prayer, but the words circled back and slapped him sober. *There is nothing else. There is nothing else.*

Stunned, he blinked. Why hadn't he realized such a truth before? There was nothing else to be done but trust alone. Maybe—just maybe—he'd taken on too much, more than a lad should way back when, more than a man could even now.

"Oh God," he gasped. "There never was anything else, was there? Only You, not me. *I've* been standing in the way."

More than a decade of pride and presumption bled out with the realization. He'd been so busy keeping everything under control, managing all the aspects of his life, he'd missed out on the peace that now slowly wrapped around his soul. Light. Air. Freedom. Everything changed. Oh, the damp darkness of the pit lingered, and maybe even death was near, but had he known such contentment was possible, he'd have given up long ago.

Without warning, boot steps thumped overhead. A key clicked into a lock and snapped it open. Interesting timing. An angel, perhaps? He'd smile, if it wouldn't hurt.

The rattle of a chain scraped against the wooden door. Hinges rasped, and finally, white light, glorious and stabbing, filled the enclosure. He jerked his forearm to his eyes.

"Move it out!" The harsh command came from a devil.

Like an old man, he braced his free hand against the wall and pushed himself upward. His legs shook—and down he went.

"I said move it! Haven't got all day. Unless you want to stay in there, all cozy like."

Alex drew on every remaining morsel of strength left to him. This chance might not come again. "God, please," he groaned as he fought his way up.

Hands reached down and grabbed on to his, wrenching him upward. He landed outside, face-first on the gravel of the courtyard, not caring that it ground into his cheek. Air, fresh and precious, filled his nostrils, and he lay there, reveling in the act of breathing.

Until a boot to his ribs made him curl up with a grunt.

"On yer feet. You've a visitor."

A yank on the back of his collar lifted him. He half-choked and half-gagged as two guards lugged him up the stairs and into the guts of the gaol. His mind raced faster than his feet. A visitor could only be Johanna—or the person who'd put him here. His heart hoped for one, his fists, the other.

The guards led him to a door in the main hall—one he'd not noticed before, hidden in the dark paneling. There, the turnkey stood, tapping his foot. "We'll be waiting out here. Don't try anything, or it'll be the worse for you. Understood?"

Sweet, blessed mercy. He could barely walk and the man was worried about him busting out?

"Please." The word clawed out his throat. "Water?"

A sneer twisted the man's face into a macabre sight, as if his features were made of wax and he stood too near a flame. He said nothing, just nodded at the guards and opened the door.

Jabbed between his shoulder blades, Alex stumbled past the threshold and barely caught himself from tumbling headfirst onto the floor. Behind him, the door slammed shut. In front, two wonders. No, three.

One, Johanna's mother sat at a table, the only furniture in the room besides an empty chair. Two, a plate of meat and a crust of bread sat on a plate. And three—

He lurched forward and snatched a green bottle, not caring if it contained water or cider or arsenic, for it was liquid and he was a desert. With each gulp, life seeped back into him.

"Go easy or you'll regret it." Mrs. Langley's admonition, while good advice, was impossible to follow.

He drained the bottle and collapsed into the chair with a moan. His stomach heaved, and he doubled over. For a horrible eternity, he feared he just might lose what he'd gained.

"Tut, tut." Mrs. Langley clucked her tongue. "You look a sight."

When the wave of nausea passed, he straightened and wiped his mouth with the back of his hand. He worked his jaw for a moment, until he was sure words would come out. "Not to be disrespectful, madam, but what are you doing here?"

"I couldn't very well leave you to suffer in solitary." She pushed the plate of food toward him.

This time he paced himself, starting with a small bite of bread. "So, Johanna told you."

"Aye."

"But how did you do it? Get me out, I mean. You're hardly a magistrate." He chewed on a few possibilities, none of which made sense, unless. . .no. The thought was too horrible. Surely his instincts couldn't be that far off. He stared at her, slack-jawed. "Of all the unholy justice—did you accuse me of treason?"

She laughed, crinkling her nose the same way Johanna did. "I'm many things, but not the bearer of false witness. And I'm afraid you're not free. I merely bribed you out of solitary for a visit, a plate of food, and some water. That was the best I could manage with what we had."

His mouthful of meat turned foul, and he shoved the plate away. "Please don't say you used the rent money on me."

"All right. I won't." Leaning across the table, she nudged the food closer to him. "Now, don't waste my coins."

For one with so many years tucked beneath her bonnet, she still had a lot of kick in her. With a grin, he picked up the bread. "Thomas takes after you."

"And you take after your father."

The bread turned to wood shavings in his mouth. Either she thought she knew Ford's creation of a father up in Sheffield, or. . .once again, the thought was too horrible. Too wonderfully horrible. He sat back in his chair, food forgotten, and tilted his head, prepared to listen with his whole body. "What would you know of my father?"

Her eyes twinkled with knowledge and what? Pity? Grief? No. Neither.

A tremor moved deep in his bones, rippling outward, like standing next to a reverberating gong.

She gazed at him with compassion. "What I know is that you're no wine merchant, are you, Mr. Moore?"

He sucked in a breath. If she knew the truth, then how many others. . . wait a minute. . .*had* she been the one to put him in here? If so, the woman belonged on a Royal Theater's stage, so good was her act. But why? Every muscle in his body clenched. Was Mrs. Langley the true traitor? Did she know who murdered his parents? Were the two somehow related?

"Breathe, son. Just breathe. You look as if you may give way at any moment." She glanced at the door then back at him. "And I doubt we have much time left."

He set his jaw, then winced at the pain of it. "Perhaps you ought explain yourself."

"It took me a while to figure things out. The old cogs don't turn as quickly anymore." She tapped a finger to her temple, then aimed it at him. "But it's plain as the nose on your face and the striking blue of your eyes. The hair, that threw me, for Charles Moore's mane was dark, as could be his mood at times. I assume 'twas your mother who gave you the fair streak, in hair and character, hmm?"

He'd been speechless once. Shortly after Ford had taken him in, the magistrate had discovered him playing on a fine piece of evidence—a Stradivarius—down in the courtroom's cellar. Of course he'd been reprimanded, but eventually Ford had awarded him the violin and the continuation of his lessons.

He gaped. This didn't even begin to compare.

"Oh, I suspected," Mrs. Langley continued, "but I couldn't be sure until Johanna told me the contents of the note you asked her to deliver."

He shook his head, but the movement did no good. "How on God's green earth would you know the meaning of *Sackett*?"

She lifted her chin. "I believe the real question is why would Ford place an officer at my inn? What is the old fool up to?"

The room began to spin. Or maybe the entire world did. Pain or not, he scrubbed his face with his hand. "I assure you, madam, I am as baffled about that as you. How do you know Ford?"

She pushed back from the table and stood. "I'll not question you further, nor will I answer any of yours. No one can know we had this conversation. Ever. Now eat and drink as much as you can hold, for I won't be able to do this again."

He shot to his feet. "But—"

"Keep your trust in God, son. It is the best any of us can do. And remember, your present situation is not your final destination." She strode to the door and rapped. "Ready."

The little lady disappeared, leaving him with a full belly, renewed hope, and more questions than ever.

CHAPTER NINETEEN

Dumping the contents of the strongbox onto the counter, Johanna shook it for good measure. No more coins joined the small piles already counted and recounted. Horrid, horrid numbers! They wouldn't just be the death of her, but of them all. One by one, she picked up each pence and shilling, recalculating carefully as she put them back into the box.

Her heart sank. The exact same total—and far smaller than what it should've been.

She slammed the lid shut, relocked it, and set it beneath the counter. *Think the best,* she scolded herself. *Wait expectantly. Hope continually.* Had she not read that this very morning?

Marching toward the kitchen, she prayed with each step. Maybe Mam had simply tucked the money away elsewhere for safekeeping. Of course. That was it. It *had* to be it.

"Mam?"

Her mother whisked about from a basin full of dishes, hands flying to her chest and water droplets spraying everywhere. "My stars, girl! What's going on? Is it Thomas? He's not trying to get out of bed again, is he?"

The bloom on Mam's cheeks kindled guilt in Johanna's stomach, and she pressed her fingers against her middle. "No, nothing so dire. I am sorry to have frightened you. I was just putting away my first payment from Mr. Needler and I noticed a fair amount of money missing from the strongbox. Where did you put it?"

"Me?"

"Surely it must have been you."

Mam turned back to the dishes. "Must it?"

Her fingers pressed deeper, as if she might hold in the dread that bubbled to come out with her last cup of tea. If Mam hadn't moved it, then. . .

"Oh, no. No, no. We've been robbed, Mam! And with only three weeks before Mr. Spurge comes looking for his payment. Now even with my extra work, we won't be able to pay him." She leaned against the doorjamb, shoring herself up. "We are ruined."

Leaving the sink behind, Mam wiped her hands on her apron and crossed over to her. "Such dramatics." She reached up and tweaked Johanna's nose. "A wise woman once asked me if we fail to trust in God's provision, what kind of faith is that, hmm?"

She sighed, her own words boxing her ears—no doubt what Mam intended. "Feeble, I suppose."

"And there's nothing feeble about the Johanna Elizabeth Langley I know. Come on, chin up." Mam cocked her head, looking out with love from her good eye—her bad eye weak and squinty—

And a tangible reminder to Jo that she must remain strong, for Mam's sake, as well as her own. She forced a smile. "You're right, of course. We shall wait and see what God does."

"There's my girl." Her mother returned her grin. "Now off with you. I hear patrons in the taproom, and I've not yet brought Thomas his lunch tray."

Grabbing an apron off a peg, Johanna slipped it over her head and worked the ties behind her back while she swept out of the kitchen. At a table near the door was a big man with eyes so cavernous, she wondered if such depth darkened his view. He sat at an angle, one of his legs jutting into the aisle. Across from him, a crazed mop of red hair topped a shorter man. Both their shirts strained against muscles. These were obviously working men. Dockhands, perhaps, judging by the deep color of their skin and huge biceps. Her step hitched. Something wasn't right about this. At this time of day, they ought be heaving crates, not swilling ale. Good thing she'd thought to hide the strongbox.

She neared them with a professional smile—one that froze on her lips when a pair of yellow stockings slid in the front door. No, there wasn't anything at all right about this.

"Not late. Not late! Mr. Nutbrown is on time, sirs." Lucius and his clown puppet raced to a chair between the two men and sat so forcefully, it suspended precariously on two legs for a moment before thudding back down on all fours. Without missing a beat, Mr. Nutbrown shoved his jester toward her. "Afternoon, Miss Langley. My, but you're looking fine today."

Her mouth flattened. "Mr. Nutbrown. Gentlemen. What can I do for you?"

"Ale for the three of us, miss." The big man jerked out a hand the size of a small frying pan and slapped a coin on the table.

The flash of the golden guinea drew her a step forward. Why would a dockhand flaunt such an amount here? And where had he gotten it in the first place? "I am sorry, sir, but I won't be able to make change for that. Have you anything smaller?"

"Not to worry." He eyed her with a grin shy of several teeth. "No change required."

La! They'd be passed out on the floor before that much ale was consumed. Still, a drunkard's coin was no less valuable than a rich man's. Maybe this was how God was providing? She considered the possibility all the way to the counter, where she filled three mugs.

"Here you are, sirs." She set down their drinks and stepped back, not liking the way the red-headed one kept his gaze pinned on her every movement. "Let me know if you require anything else."

She turned, but a puppet pecking on her arm pulled her back around. She narrowed her eyes and glared. "Mr. Nutbrown! I'll thank you to stop—"

"Mr. Nutbrown has another business opportunity for you, miss."

The beginnings of a headache pounded in her left temple, and from the beat, it promised to be quite a superb one. What a day. First taking Tanny's abuse, then discovering missing money, now this. "I told you before that I will not serve as a lookout for underhanded or illegal activities. I have not changed my mind."

"You'll have to excuse Mr. Nutbrown." The big man leaned toward her, bidding her closer with a crook of his finger and lowering his voice so that only she might hear. "He's a few cards short of a deck, you know."

Across from him, the red-headed man shoved one of the mugs toward Nutbrown. "Put Nixie away now. There's a good fellow. Here, have your drink."

With Mr. Nutbrown occupied, the other men faced her. The big one spoke first. "I'm Mr. Cooper and this is Mr. Pickens." He indicated the redhead with a nod. "As Mr. Nutbrown was about to say, we have an opportunity for a young lady of upstanding character and connections. He vouches for your integrity on both accounts."

Danger throbbed inside her skull. Or was that just the headache? She should turn right around and escape into the kitchen, send Mam out here, anything but consider whatever these men were offering. But the flash of the golden coin on the table held her in place. It wouldn't hurt to listen, and ought she not judge according to looks?

She crossed her arms and nodded at the big man. "What is your offer, Mr. Cooper?"

"Mr. Nutbrown has been doing some paperwork for us. Reading and ciphering aren't our strong points, eh Charlie?" Mr. Cooper lifted a brow at Mr. Pickens.

The redhead slowly brought up his fist, flexing his arm. "No, sir."

She frowned. If the man thought muscles impressed her, he could think again, though she doubted very much he thought deeply about anything at all. The bump of a nose broken too many times showed he used his brawn more than his brain.

Mr. Cooper continued, "Still, we've a business to run, and we're stretched thin at the moment. Mr. Nutbrown suggested you might be able to help. He's doing a little task for us tomorrow down at the harbourmaster's, but, well. . ." He leaned toward her once again. "I'm not completely confident he can do it on his own."

"What has that to do with me?" she asked.

"There's a particular shipment we're expecting, a profitable one. Coming in from Woolwich. We just need to know the name of the ship and the time of arrival."

Reaching up, she massaged her temple with two fingers. This wasn't making sense, no matter how hard she tried to unravel it. "Seems that wouldn't take any reading or writing. Why don't you go and ask yourselves?"

"That's just it, miss. Mr. Pickens and I are expected elsewhere. Were it only reading and writing, why Mr. Nutbrown would do just fine. Champion, he is."

Mr. Nutbrown perked up at the mention of his name. He set down his mug and rummaged in his waistcoat. Surely a ridiculous puppet conversation would follow.

But the big man pivoted on the bench, turning his back to Mr. Nutbrown. "This task requires conversation, miss. As you can understand, the harbourmaster won't likely give out information to a puppet."

While true, the explanation hardly clarified. She folded her arms. "Then why send him at all?"

"Why, to save you a trip, miss." Mr. Cooper smiled, and she wished he hadn't. It was like watching a coach crash, so disturbing was his grin. "You give the information to Mr. Nutbrown, and he'll deliver it to us. Shouldn't take but an hour of your time."

She shook her head. Right now, a cool cloth in a darkened room sounded much better than this offer. "I don't know, Mr. Cooper. I have my own business to run."

"Did I mention it pays five guineas?"

"Five!" She choked, then narrowed her eyes. "Why so much? Are you certain this is not illegal?"

The big man laughed. "Nothing illegal about asking for information, is there? And as I said, this shipment will be very profitable for us. Five's a pittance. What say you?"

She lowered her arms, smoothing her hands along her apron. There was nothing wrong with what he asked, yet it didn't seem right. Still, maybe this was God's provision. And if it did turn into something underhanded, in even the slightest fashion, she'd walk away—or run, if need be.

"Very well," she agreed, but the words tasted sour in her mouth. "Tomorrow afternoon, then."

∽

Once again Alex trod down the gaol's corridor, a guard on either side in the usual fashion. This time, though, no one dragged or shoved him. In truth, the men hardly even looked at him, as if they didn't care whether he tried to escape. That could only mean one thing, possibly two. Either the charges had been dropped, or the gallows in front was rigged out and ringed by a crowd, waiting to watch his demise. A smirk twitched half his mouth. Either way, he would be free.

As they swung around a corner and cleared the entrance hall, he still wasn't sure what to expect. The master turnkey was not at his station behind the tall desk. In the shadows near the main doors stood a short man in a dark greatcoat, back toward him, hat set low. He turned at the sound of their footsteps, and his lips curled up, revealing short, yellowed teeth.

The guards dropped back as Robbie Coburn advanced. Whatever the arrangement had been, or might be, Alex kept his feet moving toward freedom. There'd been no paperwork, no final admonitions, not even a word that his time was up. Quite the irregular release. Then again, his arrival had been anything but conventional. He apparently had Robbie to thank for that—and he would with a sound thrashing.

"Thanks, fellows." Robbie gave the guards a smart salute, then drew up alongside Alex, slapping him on the back. "My, but you're looking a little rugged. Had quite the stay, did you?"

Alex winced, the clap of Robbie's hand managing to whap against one of his more recent bruises. "Quite." His hands curled into fists at his side. Once they were outside, he'd give Robbie a little taste of his stay for putting him here. He glanced at the man sideways. "Am I to thank you for my holiday?"

Robbie laughed, the sound incongruous inside these walls of guilt and desperation. He shoved open the front door with one arm. "No, not me. I'll explain on the way."

Slowly, Alex's fists unfurled, and he strode out into freedom, then paused on the top step and breathed in until it hurt. Early evening air, moist with saltiness, fragrant with honeysuckle, filled his lungs. He allowed the sweetness to wash over him. Dried blood, sweat, and grime remained, but even so, he felt cleaner. He probably ought wonder where Robbie was taking him, but truly, as long as it was away from here, he found it hard to care.

"Not having second thoughts about leaving, are you?"

When he opened his eyes, Robbie was already down to the curb, one foot up on the carriage step. Seated atop, a driver in gold-and-navy livery held the reins to a smart set of bays. Alex descended, straightening what remained of his dress coat. Hopefully the viscount would be in a charitable mood, for if he didn't miss his guess, that's exactly where they were headed.

With a grunt, he hoisted himself upward and sat opposite Robbie. The thick scent of cherry tobacco and leather chased away the fresh evening air. As he sank into the cushions, he wondered for the hundredth time in the past few days if he weren't getting a mite old for this lifestyle.

Robbie retrieved a pocket watch, then snapped shut the lid with a curse. "Bah! Shouldn't have stopped off for that pint, I suppose." He rapped on the ceiling and the coach lurched into action. "The old man won't be happy"—he tucked away the watch with a grin—"but then, he's never happy with me now, is he?"

"Lord Coburn?"

"The very same. You can thank him in person for your recent *holiday*."

The viscount had put him in gaol? Anger shook through him as the coach rattled over gravel. He speared Robbie with a frown. "That explains the anonymity, but why the accusation?"

"Oh, nothing personal, I assure you. My uncle's methods are rarely orthodox." He held up his hand, a thick white bandage yet wrapped around the middle where the bullet had taken one of his fingers that first fateful night they'd met. Robbie let it fall back to his lap without a wince. Apparently the wound was healing well. "My uncle merely needed the time to check on your background. Can't marry his daughter off to just anybody, you know."

His gut clenched. That's what this whole thing had been about? He'd anguished and suffered and nearly given in to failure and doubt, all for the whim of a rich man who needed assurance? Rage prickled along every nerve, too spiky and abrasive for the coach cushions to soften. "He couldn't have done that without locking me up?"

Robbie's shoulders shook with a good chuckle. "Anger will gain you nothing, friend, leastwise not with the old man. Trust me. I've learned that one the hard way." His tone took on a biting edge, belying the remnant of a smile yet on his lips. "Hence the need for my secrecy with Louisa. He'd never give her to me willingly. Oh, and thank you for your rather timely diversion on the matter. You will be well paid."

Gloaming crept in the open window shades, hiding Robbie's face in shadow. Alex leaned forward, hoping to catch some kind of facial tip off. "Cousins marry every day. Why not you?"

He turned his face, a pretense of staring out at the night, for there was nothing to see outside. Even so, there was no hiding the stiffness of his shoulders. "Let's just say that Uncle and I disagree over politics."

Robbie? Political? He stifled a snort.

"But enough of that morose topic, hmm?" Quick as a summer storm, Robbie pulled out a flask. The silver flashed in the darkness as he held it out.

Alex shook his head. "I think some food would be in order, first."

"Aah, sorry. Didn't think." He swigged back a drink and tucked it away, breathing out the tang of bourbon. "In a fortnight, give or take, Louisa and I will sail away on our adventure, but what of you? What will you do with the tidy sum I intend to pay you? Live large? Chase a few skirts or—no. I know. You'll take it to the table, won't you? Will it be Brook's or White's? Or maybe someplace a little more risqué? St. James's, if I don't miss my guess."

Outside the windows, torchlight flashed bright then dark, bright then dark, indicating they'd pulled onto the viscount's estate. He met Robbie's gaze, slipping into his gambling mask. "I've never been one to turn down a game."

"Thought as much." When the carriage pulled to a stop, Robbie didn't wait for the door to open. He worked the latch himself and jumped down.

Relieved that the elopement plans were still moving ahead, Alex exited and joined him on the drive.

Robbie nudged him with an elbow. "Why don't you see the old man alone. I'm a little gun shy. And with my uncle engaged, there's a certain lady I'd like to entertain."

Without waiting for an answer, Robbie dashed up the front stairs and through the door. By the time Alex gained the entry, the footman stood scowling. His upper lip curled higher when the stench of the gaol, woven into the fiber of Alex's clothing and grease of his hair, met the man's nose. To his credit, the footman said nothing.

But the fat man striding down the hall did. "Egad!" Major General Overtun clapped his hat atop his head then lifted a gloved finger to block his nose. "You smell like a gang of *Coolies* come in from a day beneath the Indian sun."

"Trust me," he smiled, "I feel as beat. Are you not staying for tonight's game?"

"No, not tonight. Duty calls, I'm afraid." The general gave him a wide berth as he edged past. "Good evening, Mr. Morton."

"Good evening, General." He saluted his goodbye.

As soon as the footman shut the door behind the man, he turned and led the way to the viscount's drawing room. Though Alex kept downwind of him, he doubted the servant breathed the whole way. For a moment, Alex toyed with the idea of pausing on the threshold as he passed the man, seeing just how long he could hold his breath.

Setting down a pen, Lord Coburn looked up from where he sat behind a burled oak desk, polished to a glassy finish. "Well, a new suit is in order, I think." He wrinkled his nose. "And a bath."

Alex eyed one of the leather library chairs in front of the bureau. Better to sit and cool down than dash across the room and give Coburn a taste of the violence he'd endured the past week. "Mind if I sit?"

"By all means." Coburn leaned back, steepling his fingers. "Your father speaks well of you."

Taking his time to settle in the chair, Alex wondered what actor Ford had paid to play that part. Whoever, the fellow ought to receive a bonus for pulling it off. He frowned, mixing just the right amount of ire and resignation to the bend of his brow. "I would expect nothing less. I hope you are satisfied."

"And I hope you understand it was necessary. A man in my position cannot be too careful."

"What is that position?"

Pushing back his chair, the viscount stood and stalked to the mantel like a panther on the prowl. He opened the lid of his precious cheroot box and proceeded with the ceremony of lighting and puffing before he strolled back and reseated himself. "It was curious, you showing up here, at such a time. I have many enemies and thought perhaps you might be one."

The viscount took a drag on his tobacco, his gaze skewering him. For a few loud ticks of the corner clock, the man said nothing, then slowly, a stream of smoke curled out of his nostrils like a great dragon. "Of course, I know differently, now. I think, instead, that you were a godsend."

Were he a horse, he'd have reared. There were many things the viscount might've labeled him. A godsend never crossed his mind. "Pardon me," Alex said, "but I didn't take you for a religious man."

"Nor did I peg you for a man of violence." The red tip of the viscount's cheroot glowed, as murderous as his statement.

Alex ran a hand through his hair, giving ample alibi for the flinch he couldn't deny. What had Ford's man told the viscount?

"Yet I am glad of it." Coburn ground out the rest of his tobacco and laid the stub to rest on a silver platter. "Your sharpshooting skills might come in handy. Your father is quite proud of your talent with a gun. Though I suppose that's to be expected in your line of work."

Sweet, merciful heavens. What story had the viscount been fed? Sure, he could manage a muzzle, but put to the test, he was no crack shot. He cleared his throat, unsure how to respond, hoping—desperately—that words would magically appear.

Coburn held up a hand. "No need for false pride. I didn't believe for a moment that you were a simple wine merchant. Your military service is exemplary for one so young. A sorry shame that friendly fire took you out of commission. Had I known of your injury, I'd have paid for better accommodations in the gaol."

Alex grit his teeth to trap a grimace. Not only was he a sharpshooter but an injured one? Well, thanks to this man, at least he had plenty of aches and pains to make that believable—but if Ford were here, he'd get an earful of censure.

"Good thing your daughter is worth it," he ground out.

The gleam in the viscount's eyes hinted at approval. "All water under the bridge, eh? Good. We move forward from here. I'm expecting a shipment in a fortnight that I could use some help with."

Alex shifted in his seat. Though he'd love to throttle the viscount for having him arrested, at least the gaol time had garnered him some capital with the man. "I know very little of shipping, other than the transport of fine wines. What kind of help is it you want?"

"In times like these, I find it best to compartmentalize information. It's safer that way. You'll be given information as needed." Once again, leaving his desk behind, Coburn crossed to the mantel and tugged on the bell pull. "In the meantime, you've a week to clean yourself up. Are you sure you prefer to remain at The Blue Hedge? I can accommodate you here."

Alex ran a finger along his bottom lip, thinking. The man was very cagey, very shrewd. Was Robbie in on this? The timeframe he planned to run off with Louisa matched up. If so, how much did he know? What kind of family secrets mouldered beneath the wealth of the viscount's roof?

"Alexander?"

He startled at Coburn's use of his Christian name, and slowly pushed himself up, using his battered appearance to his advantage. "Er. . .yes, sir. Forgive me. Afraid the past week has taken a toll on me physically and mentally. The Blue Hedge is fine for now, but tell me. . .what exactly is it I'm cleaning myself up for?"

"The betrothal dinner, of course. Get yourself a new suit of clothing down at Featherstones on the High Street, and spare no expense. I'll give word you're coming and that it's to be put on my account. Can't present you looking like a beaten thug dragged from a rookery, can I?"

Alex pressed his lips together. Why not? That's exactly how he felt, though he suspected he'd feel worse when his engagement went public and word spread that he was to wed a woman he didn't intend to actually marry.

CHAPTER TWENTY

Johanna wrung out a cloth so frayed and thin, even a ragpicker would turn it down. Cool evening air stole in from the taproom door, propped open to encourage customers. She frowned at the darkness outside. Closing time already and she'd served only two dray drivers nothing but a mug apiece. Pursing her lips, she set about scrubbing off tables that were hardly dirty. Surely she'd made the right decision to visit the harbourmaster on the morrow.

Behind her, the last strain of a violin chord screeched into oblivion, taking some of the tension in her shoulders along with it. At least one tribulation was drawing to a close. That would be Mr. Quail's last song under this roof if she had anything to say about—and she did. Plenty.

Weaving around tables, she crossed the room to where he packed up his violin. "Excuse me, Mr. Quail, but I must speak with you."

He snapped shut the lid and grinned down at her. "Delighted."

The man was relentless. If he practiced his music with as much dogged pursuit as he did his flirtations, he'd be a virtuoso. "You might not be once you've heard me out."

"Oh? Intriguing." He leaned close, his grin widening. "And I love a good intrigue."

With a sigh, she retreated a step. "Nothing of the sort. I merely wish to inform you that your services here are no longer required. You and your band may pack up and leave in the morning."

He staggered back, slapping a hand to his heart as if shot through the chest with an arrow. "You wound me!"

It took all her willpower to keep from rolling her eyes. "Really, Mr. Quail. Such dramatics. This is a business matter, nothing more. Your expenses far outweigh your benefits, Oak Apple Day is long gone, and so you must leave."

"Ah-ah-ah." He wagged a finger at her. "My band has brought in customers. You can't deny that."

"Not enough to cover food and drink. And let's not forget that broken window for which you still haven't paid me, hmm?"

Like a dropped cannonball, he plummeted to his knees and hung his head. His hands folded in prayer as if she were a goddess to be offered devotion. "Have I not begged sufficient forgiveness for that unfortunate incident, my queen?"

She tried, valiantly, but this time there was no stopping the roll of her eyes. "Yes, of course you're forgiven, but that does not fix the glass. Now get up, please. You have some packing to do."

He rose, snatching one of her hands on the uptake and kissing two of her knuckles before she could yank them away.

"Two weeks, my sweet Miss Langley. Just a fortnight more, and my band and I will gladly move on."

"I am sorry." She shook her head. "There are simply not enough funds to keep housing and feeding you for free."

His face darkened like a quick-rising storm at sea, then evaporated with the snap of his fingers. "I know! Yes! Why, I should have thought of this before." He laughed and snatched up his violin case, waving it over his head like a lunatic. *"I'll have grounds more relative than this—the play's the thing!"*

Though she ran the words through her head several times, he might as well have been speaking Portuguese. Perhaps he truly had become mad. Had she caused him to snap by asking him to leave? She leveled a firm glare at him. "What are you talking about?"

"A play, Miss Langley. Who doesn't love theatrics?" He swung about, taking his violin case for a merry ride.

She opened her mouth, a hearty reprimand on her tongue, when he silenced her with a finger to her lips.

"Tut, tut. Other than you, I mean."

Pulling from his touch, she swept out her arm. "Look at the size of this taproom, sir. We haven't the space to put on a play. By the time you clear an area for a performance, you'll have no room for patrons. A play would not be profitable."

"I see." He rubbed the back of his neck, his gaze darting about. "Something of a smaller scale, then."

"Something of *no* scale." She sighed. "It is time for you to move on. Are you not travelling musicians? I should think you would be happy to get on the road."

She might as well have been speaking to a deaf man. He pivoted, continuing his search for who-knew-what around the room. One brow rose, then the other, and eventually his whole head bobbed. "I've got it."

"Mr. Quail, are you even listening to me? I said it is time to move on—"

"Here." He strode past her and stopped at the counter, littered with her wash bucket and leftover serving dishes. Shoving a tray aside so that the mugs atop it rattled, he bent and eyed the area. "Looks to be maybe two feet wide, seven or eight in length. Some wood, nails, a simple modification is all, and...yes. This will be perfect."

She scowled, gaining his side. "Perfect for what?"

"A *Punch and Judy Show*, of course. A few boards, some drapery, and *voilà*. A puppet stage that will take up no more additional space in this room."

La! The man *was* daft. Curling her hands into fists, she planted them on her hips. "And how am I to operate without use of the counter? No. Absolutely not. I have a special abhorrence of puppets."

"We can be ready in a week. I'll make up some handbills and begin spreading them around on the morrow." He flashed her a smile and dashed toward the stairs. "Good night, Miss Langley. Big day tomorrow."

"Mr. Quail, I insist you come back here right now. This discussion isn't over."

But his footsteps didn't slow.

"Mr. Quail!" She growled. Infuriating, pig-headed—

"Angry at Quail again, eh? Apparently things haven't changed much."

She spun at the deep voice behind her. Her jaw dropped, unladylike yet completely unstoppable. Alex stood framed in the front doorway, like a macabre painting of a war scene. The longer she gaped, the more her heart broke into piece after piece, until it was a wonder the thing could beat at all. As a young girl, she'd come across a crushed robin, wings broken by a wagon wheel, flying a thing of its past. She'd run home to Mam, horrified, weeping.

But this time, there was nowhere for her to turn.

She sucked in a breath, frantic for air. The gentleman she knew was gone. His dress coat was ripped and dirty. He wore no cravat. His pristine white shirt was torn and bloodied beneath what remained of his waistcoat, both gaping at the chest. An ugly gash cut across his cheek, disappearing into a growth of beard, matted with more blood. Even his gaze was a bruise. No one deserved that much brutality, especially not a man who'd been nothing but selfless and compassionate toward others. Toward her.

"Oh Alex," she sighed, her voice as derelict as his face.

∽

It took him a moment to understand the emotion in the sag of Johanna's shoulders and that the crackle in her words belonged to him, like a gift from a secret admirer, given without a tag. And he wasn't sure what to do about that. Wrap his arms around her—or run out the door? He settled for shoring his shoulder against the door frame.

Tears shimmered in her eyes, caught by lantern light. She cared. About him. Not that in the past other women hadn't, but this? This was entirely different. His heart pounded hard against his ribs. He harbored such affection for this woman that it cut into his soul she would hurt for his sake.

What kind of man loved one woman yet let everyone believe he'd marry another?

He ran a hand through his hair and winced when his fingers grazed a gouge behind his ear. Good. He welcomed the pain, for only a scoundrel would carry out such a vile act.

"You're back," she whispered.

The quiver on her lips and in her voice, the charged tension between them, was too much to bear. Either he ought kiss away every worry she'd suffered on his behalf—or completely change the subject. The latter was honorable, of course, but the first? Aah. . .desire rippled through him from head to toe.

He settled for clearing his throat. "Still have a room available?"

A smile broke, then. One to shame the brightest star in the heavens. "Of course."

She snapped into action, apron strings flying as she pivoted. "But first come to the kitchen, and I'll fill a basin of warm water. Those wounds need a good cleaning."

He followed, his step hitching halfway across the taproom. The crooked floorboards. The beat-up tables and rugged chairs. The way the roof sloped at the corner near the hearth, debating whether to cave in or not. Alex's gut twisted, but wonder of wonders, not from scorn. This place felt like home. Comfortable. Familiar. Worn by decades of life and love, not tatty by sinister neglect.

He upped his pace. Clearly several nights in a gaol had affected him deeply.

Johanna pulled a stool away from the worktable, and he sank onto it. One of his eyes was squinty from a leftover right hook, so he angled his head and watched her gather a bowl and some cloths with his good eye. "What's Quail done this time that's got you agitated?"

She slammed the bowl onto the table, rattling a wooden mug, then retrieved a teapot from the hearth. "He and his band have overstayed their welcome."

"Sounds like your earlier problem with Nutbrown. Shall I evict them for you as well?"

"No." She dipped a rag into the basin and wrung it out. "I suppose I can put up with them for two more weeks if I must, but you can be certain—"

"Two weeks?" he thought aloud. Itinerant musicians didn't usually operate on such a strict schedule. "Did he say why?"

"He did not. I suppose it's anybody's guess with that lot. I'll just be glad to see them go. Now then, let's get you taken care of." She stood so near, he inhaled her sweet scent of rosewater and heat, alluring as a dusky summer day. Her fingers guided his chin sideways, and she dabbed at the slash on his cheek.

"You have suffered much," she murmured. "Too much, I think."

Despite the sting of it, he leaned into her ministrations. He could get used to this attention. "The suffering is over now. I am free."

She pulled the cloth away, her brown gaze smiling into his. "You are not a traitor after all?"

"Did you not believe me?"

She dipped the rag again. The water in the basin turned pink. "One doesn't usually get thrown into gaol for no reason."

Hah! He could think of at least twelve men currently gracing the cells of Millbank and Newgate prisons whose only crime was being in the wrong place at the worst possible time. "You'd be surprised," he said, and left it at that.

An easy silence fell, as soothing and healing as Johanna's deft touch. She worked with a gentleness that tightened his throat. Each time her cloth plunged into the water, the basin deepened into a murkier red.

Eventually, she stepped back and examined her work. Satisfied, she quirked a brow. "There. Your face is nearly as good as new."

Right. He still couldn't see out of his left eye. "You are a poor liar."

She flashed a smile. "I shall take that as a compliment, sir."

But just as quickly, her smile evaporated. She clenched the rag until her knuckles whitened. "I—I saw what they did to you. That day I was there, when they...when you... Well, I should tend that wound on the back of your neck, but I suspect you shall have to remove your shirt. Shall I call Mam?"

"No need. While I have no doubt of your virtue, I suspect you've seen more than the average young lady who's not tended an inn—especially with no father to take care of the, er, dirtier business of maintaining a taproom. Am I correct?"

Pink blossomed on her cheeks, but to her credit, she did not shrink from his assessment. "As usual, a sharp observation on your part."

While she busied herself emptying the basin and replacing it with fresh water, he slipped his arms out of what remained of his waistcoat, then shrugged out of his shirt, biting back a cry as the fabric stuck to the dried blood on his back. To save her the embarrassment of having to look him in the eye while he sat bare-chested, he turned on the stool, facing the kitchen door instead of her.

But he almost turned back when she lifted his ragged hair aside and sucked in a sharp gasp.

"That can't be good," he said.

"It's not." She blew out a long breath, warming the skin on his back. "But I suppose in time, and with some of Mam's famous salve, it will clear up. The wound is quite infected. I'll have to trim your hair so it's not in the way."

"Doctor, innkeeper, cook, and now a barber as well? You are a woman of many talents."

While locks of his hair fell to the floor, he pondered what she'd mentioned about Quail. Why would the man want to stay a fortnight more? Did this tie in somehow with Robbie and Louisa's planned elopement in two weeks? And what of the viscount's shipment arriving in that very same time period? Some thread knotted them all together.

"What does it mean?"

Johanna's question mirrored his thoughts—but she could have no way of knowing. Could she? "What does what mean?"

"This mark on your neck." She laid the scissors on the table next to his elbow, then leaned closer, her warmth heating his exposed flesh. "It almost looks like the letter *B*. Why would someone cut you like that?"

He gritted his teeth, shoving away the painful memory when knife met flesh. "Despite God's edicts, man is not always kind."

"True." The weight of the world hung in her single, exhaled word. She knew exactly what he was talking about—and the knowledge kindled a rage deep in his belly. It was one thing for him to experience the depravity of man, but she ought not. Ever.

Her skirts rustled. A jar lid opened. The acrid scent of liniment—a strange mix of turpentine and vinegar—filled the room.

"I am sorry," she said, "but this may sting a bit."

Fire followed her warning, burning to the bone, and spread from his neck down his spine. "Grace and mercy! You trying to kill me?"

"No need. You've been doing a good enough job of that yourself. Now, mind your tone. You'll wake Mam."

He steeled himself and straightened. "Please don't tell me you put this on Thomas's leg."

"Of course not. We used something much stronger. Bear up. I'll work quickly."

Darkness crept in on the corners of his vision, but he kept his breathing steady and forced himself upright. Eventually, a cool cloth pressed against the base of his neck.

"There. All finished. You'll survive, I suppose."

"I usually do." He turned then, catching both her hands in his before she could bustle away. "But this time I have you to thank. You are a rare gem, Johanna. I wonder if you know that."

A cloud darkened her face, like a shadow on the sun, then just as quickly vanished. "Off with you, sir. It is late, and you need rest, but first a good scrubbing is in order, I think. I shall fill a hip bath in your chamber. Wait here. I shan't take long."

She disappeared out of the kitchen, taking along with her the whole of his heart.

He slumped on his chair, weary beyond words. This assignment was wearing on him in more ways than one. Would that Ford had decreed he not only reside at the Blue Hedge Inn, but marry the innkeeper's daughter as well.

CHAPTER TWENTY-ONE

Johanna yawned. Again. Fatigue competed with the refreshing breeze wafting in from the Channel as she paced the boardwalk in front of the harbourmaster's office. The briny droplets in the air ought keep her awake, but she'd spent the night tossing one way then the other, the memory of tending Alex both repellant and attractive. She'd been called many things by past patrons, but never a gem. Not that the compliment meant anything, for flattery was a commodity she was often paid. No, his words were nothing extraordinary. It was the huskiness of his voice, the clench of his jaw, the earnest way he'd stared into her soul when he'd spoken. He meant what he said, but more than that—he wanted her to believe it as well. Why would a man care what she thought of herself?

She spun on her heel and retraced her steps, searching the boardwalk for yellow stockings. If she waited for Mr. Nutbrown any longer, Mam would wonder at her absence. She never should've agreed to work with him in the first place and more than likely would have better luck inquiring at the harbourmaster's without him and his preposterous puppet.

Mind made up, she stopped her pacing and pushed open the office door. The room was small, made even more claustrophobic by stacks of papers piled atop the counter. Good thing the front windows gave a grand view of the harbor, for otherwise the place might as well be a crypt.

"Afternoon, miss. Can I help you?"

Though the man's question and gaze required an answer, her tongue stuck to the roof of her mouth. This was no man. He was an ostrich. La! What a neck. The fellow looked as if someone had grasped the top of his head and pulled until giving up on the endeavor. The length from cravat to chin had to be a good eight inches. Was such a neck a requirement of the job—or an unfortunate result of gawking over stacks of paper?

"Miss?"

"Sorry, yes, of course you can help. Forgive me." She spoke as much to God as to him. "I am here to inquire about a ship's arrival."

"All right. Which one?" He folded his hands atop the papers in front of him, and though she ought not be surprised, the length of his fingers was equally amazing. Another job hazard from paging through documents?

"Er. . ." She bit her lip. Had Mr. Cooper or Mr. Pickens told her the name of the ship? She revisited the conversation in her mind, but honestly, she'd not paid much attention until the payment part. Forcing her gaze to remain on the harbourmaster's spectacles instead of his neck or fingers, she offered him a brilliant smile. "Once again, sir, I apologize. I am not quite sure of the name."

"Very well. We can likely pin it down if you can tell me where the ship is coming from."

Victory! She knew this one. "Woolwich."

"Aah." His brows lifted then his head dipped. Like a lighthouse beam, he surveyed the stacks of documents upon his desk and reached for a binder to his left. "Dock number?"

Her smile faded. So much for victory. Drat that Mr. Nutbrown for his tardiness! Did he know these missing pieces of information? "I am afraid I'm not quite sure of that."

The harbourmaster stopped rifling through the packet, his gaze spearing her like a hook through a codfish. "Well, what type of ship is it? Merchant? Brig? Cutter? Sloop?"

"It is. . ." She licked her lips. How to answer? "Of the floating variety."

His mouth pulled into a frown nearly as long as his neck. "What about the kind of shipment, then? Chartered? Licensed? Packet? Military or civilian?"

Glancing over her shoulder, she longed to see yellow stockings crossing the threshold.

"Allow me to hazard a guess, miss. You're not quite sure of that, either."

She turned back to the man. "You are very perceptive, sir."

He shook his head, and for a moment she worried that the movement might topple the thing from its long perch. He paged through the documents in the binder, then set the folder back down. "Sorry. Don't see anything in the next few days arriving from Woolwich."

"Well, it might not be that soon. Would you mind looking further into the future? Over the next several weeks or so?" She fluttered her eyelashes.

Which worked, somewhat. He flipped through more pages, but the accompanying scowl on his face could not be missed. "No. There is nothing. Are you sure Woolwich is the port of departure? You know that's a military arsenal, not often used for common shipments. Maybe you're mistaken. Was it Weymouth? Worthing? Westham?"

Hmm. Was she sure? Tapping her lip with her finger, she recalled the entire conversation. She could've sworn Mr. Cooper had said Woolwich, but then again. . . "I suppose I might have heard incorrectly. Would you mind checking on those?"

He stood and turned, rifling through pages on another counter against the wall. Hopefully that's all it would take.

The door flung open. A puppet entered, followed by Mr. Nutbrown, his long legs encased in crookedly sewn hose.

Her eyes widened as he opened his mouth. If he spoke now—or rather the jester did—her chances at finding out the information would be lost. She shoved the puppet down and glowered at the man. "No!"

"Sorry?" The harbourmaster turned back.

"Oh, my friend here just arrived, reminding me we are running late." She forced a small giggle. "If you wouldn't mind?" She wiggled her fingers toward the back counter.

She waited until he busied himself with the documents, then scolded on a low breath, "Put that puppet away."

Mr. Nutbrown pursed his lips, then shot out his arm, the absurd puppet front and center over the desk.

"Don't!" She warned, pulling on his sleeve.

He shot her a glance from the corner of his eye, then opened his mouth. She batted his arm, a little too forcefully. The jester bobbed.

So did Mr. Nutbrown. His arms flailed, smacking into the stacks. Papers flew, some behind the desk, some in front. A snowstorm of documents.

The harbourmaster's head swiveled at the noise—a disconcerting sight on such a neck. "What's going on?"

"So sorry! My friend lost his balance. We shall pick these up straight away." She yanked Mr. Nutbrown down to the floor with her.

"Put that puppet away," she whispered. "You're ruining everything!"

For a horrible eternity, he shoved the puppet into her face. If the harbourmaster gawked his long neck over the counter, he'd see the spectacle and kick them both out the door. But thankfully, after a huff and a flare of nostrils, Mr. Nutbrown started picking up papers—the puppet still attached to his hand.

She gathered the documents scattered on her side of the tiny room, then paused as she scooped up the last one. There, written at the top in neat, black letters was the word Wool with a long line after it. Could be Woolwich, or maybe not. Looked like the name of a ship beneath it, and a date. She held it closer—

And Mr. Nutbrown snatched the page away with his free hand.

This was more than anyone should have to bear. "What are you doing? Why—"

"My sentiments exactly." The harbourmaster's head craned over the counter, directing them both an evil eye—which suddenly narrowed. "Get out! Or I shall call the constable immediately."

Johanna shot to her feet, setting the stack of papers atop the counter. "My apologies, sir. My friend here is a little, well, he's—"

The puppet popped up beside her. "Mr. Nutbrown is exceedingly sorry for the commotion. Won't happen again."

"Out!" A squall raged in the thunder of the harbourmaster's voice. "Both of you!"

"But Mr. Nutbrown sincerely—"

Johanna grabbed the silly man's sleeve and tugged him out the door, leading him down the boardwalk while his jester squabbled. When they cleared the warehouse at the side of the office, she stopped. "Really, Mr. Nutbrown! When will you learn that not everyone welcomes your absurd puppet?"

"Not to worry, Miss Langley. Our mission is accomplished, and here you are." He pulled a small pouch out of his pocket.

She shook her head. "How can you say that? All we saw was a slip of paper with part of a departure name, not where the ship is set to dock, or even what kind of ship it is. I don't feel I can take the full amount, for surely Mr. Cooper and Mr. Pickens will not be satisfied."

He shoved the pouch into her hand and bobbed the jester in front of him. "Mr. Nutbrown assures you they will be very satisfied, for he's got the eyes of a snake. All the information is safe and sound." He tapped the puppet against the side of his head. "You may take the payment in good conscience."

A sigh deflated the rest of her fight. She had found the paper, he had read it—and she desperately needed the weighty little pouch in her hand. "Very well," she conceded.

"Many thanks, Miss Langley. Must be off, now. Mr. Nutbrown is late." The puppet disappeared around the corner of the warehouse, along with the man.

Johanna peered into the small pouch, poking through the coins with a gloved finger. All as promised. This was a good start to rebuilding the empty safe box, but not enough to satisfy Mr. Spurge.

And she had only a little over two weeks left to come up with the rest.

$$\infty$$

Whistling a tune to keep Nixie happy, Lucius sped down the High Street, dodging afternoon shoppers. It wouldn't do to be late. Not again. His business partners surely were not the cheeriest of fellows and at their last meeting had been downright abrasive. It was much more pleasant to work with Miss Langley—even if she didn't acknowledge Nixie.

A cramp bit into his calf, and for several steps he hop-skipped on one foot while trying to rub away the pain. It didn't help. Fig-niggity! This would slow him down.

Pausing, he leaned against a brick wall and kneaded out the spasm. Thick stitches of thread marred his hose. New stockings would be his first order of personal business once he received the next payment. He glanced at the sun while working out the knot. Perfect. He ought have enough time to collect his fee and make it to the hosiery store before it closed. Just the thought of luscious, new stockings drove away the remnants of his cramp, and he darted back onto the walkway.

Two blocks down, he turned into Barwick Alley, then took another turn into a gap between two buildings. If he stretched out both hands, he could touch the walls on either side. How cozy. As if each structure were the best of friends with the other, wanting to be so near. He patted the papier-mâché lump in his waistcoat. Just like him and Nixie.

Ahead, two dark shapes took form. Mr. Charlie sat atop a barrel. Mr. Blackie propped himself against the wall on his good leg. They were bosom companions as well, yet they'd taken him and Nixie into their circle. Perhaps he ought not think ill of them.

Mr. Charlie jumped down off his barrel. "You got the information?"

Retrieving Nixie, he held out his partner and cleared his throat. "Mr. Nutbrown sometimes may not run according to schedule, gentlemen, but he always accomplishes his purposes."

Without moving away from the wall, Mr. Blackie held out his hand. "Let's have it, then."

He tapped Nixie to his temple. Twice. "It's all up here."

A shameful word exploded out of Mr. Charlie. Strange. Was he having a cramp as well? Maybe, judging by the way he lunged forward on one leg.

Mr. Blackie left the wall and shot out his arm, holding back his friend. "Not yet." Then he angled his face, ignoring Nixie and drilling a black stare into Lucius's eyes. "You don't have the document, but you know what it said?"

He bobbed his puppet's head. "Of that you can be sure."

"Well what did it say?"

"Confidential."

A worse profanity fouled the air, this time from Mr. Blackie. "Of course it was confidential. Besides that!"

Nixie looked back at him, giving him time to recall everything he read before he turned the jester's little head forward again. "It said there's an East Indiaman due sometime late July third. No actual arrival time listed."

"Cargo?"

"Confidential."

Mr. Charlie strained against Mr. Blackie's arm. My! Despite his wooden leg, Mr. Blackjack was a strong fellow. His muscles bulged beneath his shirtsleeve.

Even his voice was strong as he bellowed out, "I said besides that!"

"No, you don't understand." He shook Nixie's little head back and forth, emphasizing the word. "That's what was written on the line after the word *cargo*."

"Humph." Mr. Blackie lifted a brow at Mr. Charlie. Some kind of conversation went back and forth between them, but a silent one. Finally Mr. Blackie looked back at him—once again ignoring Nixie.

"And the point of departure is Woolwich, you're sure of it?"

"Well. . ." Nixie's voice stalled out.

Mr. Blackie dropped his arm. Mr. Charlie sprung forward and grabbed Lucius by the throat, lifting him to his toes.

Precious little air made it to his lungs. Even less made it to Nixie's, but the brave little fellow managed to choke out, "Mr. Nutbrown. Is as sure. As he can. Be."

"Axe!" Mr. Blackie shouted. "Drop him."

Mr. Charlie let go.

Lucius rocked back on his heels, rubbing his neck with his free hand and coughing. Nixie spluttered too. When they finally caught their breath, he held out Nixie to explain. "Because of the nature of the document, the departure was shortened to Wool with a dash after it."

Mr. Charlie shot a glance at his partner. "Could just be from Wool. We can't afford to make a mistake."

"Could be. But not having the cargo listed, and. . .hmm." A raspy noise bounced from wall to wall as Mr. Blackie scratched his jaw, then he leveled a deadly stare—at Nixie. Lucius shivered.

Mr. Blackie glowered at Nixie. "You're sure there was a dash after Wool?"

Nixie bobbed his head so hard, for a horrid moment Lucius feared it might pop off. "Yes! Yes! No doubt at all."

A low breath grumbled out of Mr. Blackie, but then he pulled his awful gaze from Nixie and faced his friend. "That's got to be it."

Mr. Charlie narrowed his eyes. "For our sakes, I hope so."

"You and me, both." He faced Lucius. "You'll have to write down that information so's we can deliver it."

"But why can't you just say it like Mr. Nutbrown—"

This time Mr. Charlie leapt for Nixie. Lucius snatched him back, horrified. Indeed. He much preferred working with Miss Langley. Despite her sometimes scolding tone, at least she didn't resort to such violence.

"Not yet, Axe." There was no denying the command in Mr. Blackie's voice. Mr. Charlie retreated—but only a step away.

"What do you think we're payin' ye for?" Mr. Blackie pulled out a money pouch, the jingle of the coins inside sounding like new stockings. "Now then, I said write it down."

Confusion bowed Nixie's head. How was he to write here? No proper desk. No ink or parchment. He held Nixie in front of him, lifting his brave little face. "Mr. Nutbrown hasn't pen nor paper."

Mr. Blackie snapped his fingers. Mr. Charlie pulled out a folded scrap tucked inside his belt and held it out.

Lucius retrieved the piece of rag paper. It was small, but with several folds. If he opened it, he could easily fit the information on one side. Nixie flung out his arms. "There's still the issue of a pen, gentlemen."

A growl rumbled in Mr. Blackie's throat—and a knife whipped out from a sheath at his side. Before Lucius could blink, Nixie was plucked from his hand and thrown to the dirt. Pain, worse than the cramp, stabbed his fingertip. Blood swelled. Deep red.

"You better write quickly." Mr. Charlie laughed.

Nixie whimpered from the ground—or was that him? He leapt toward the wall and opened the paper full, glad for the size of it. Flattening the paper against the bricks, he bit his lip as he scrawled words with his fingertip. His letters were thick as he wrote. *July 3. Late. East India* . . . the pain began to ebb. So did the blood. Sweat beads popped on his forehead as he looked up at Mr. Blackie's dark scowl. Oh dear, sweet mother! The man might sever his entire hand if he didn't finish the message. He shoved his finger into his mouth and sucked on it, drawing a fresh flow. Finishing the last letter, he pulled his hand back from the gruesome sight.

This time Mr. Blackie laughed. "Good. Now read the other side."

He hesitated, worried for Nixie. Worried for himself. Worried about what might be written on the flip side.

"Do it!"

Mr. Charlie's harsh bark forced the page over. Lucius's eyes skimmed from word to word.

"Out loud, you idiot."

A lump lodged in his throat. How was he to speak without Nixie? He shot a wild look to where his friend lay facedown in the alley.

Mr. Charlie rolled his eyes, but scooped up Nixie and handed him back.

Aah. Glorious unity. Nixie trembled, and so did he. With his free hand, he gave the paper back as Nixie relayed the message. "The note says, '*Arrange for transport of frames to Ramsgate on a vessel large enough to suit. Hire a minimal crew.*'"

Tucking the paper back into his belt, Mr. Charlie faced Mr. Blackjack. "If the Indiaman's coming here, why we taking the frames to Ramsgate?"

Mr. Blackie shrugged. "Dunno. Not ours to question." Then he shoved a finger into Nixie's chest. "You, lay low and stay put. We'll find you when we next need you. And here." He dropped a bag onto the vacated barrel. "I suppose you've earned this."

Shoving past him and Nixie, they disappeared down the neck of the alley. It took all his power to simply breathe. Nixie too. That had been completely disagreeable in every possible way. Slowly, Nixie turned his little head toward him. "Why do you suppose picture frames require such a covert enterprise?"

"I don't know, friend. But I have a feeling these gentlemen aren't so gentle."

CHAPTER TWENTY-TWO

Alex swiped his hair over his eye, covering the ugly purple and green remnants. Not that Thomas would mind, and in fact might think the bruise a trophy to be admired. But there was a fine balance between concealment and blocking his vision, so it took him several tries. Finally satisfied, he snatched the crutch resting against the wall and yanked open his door.

Out in the hallway, Quail stopped and pivoted at the sound. "Well, well. . ." He dissected him with a smirk. "Look who's returned—and not looking too good at that."

Alex pulled the door shut behind him and faced the man. "You know, for an itinerant musician, I wonder that you're still here."

"And I wonder that a. . .how did you put it? Aah, yes. Why would a *purchaser of fine wines* remain in Dover? Not a hotbed of vineyards."

"Nor is it a sufficient market for entertainers."

"Never at a loss for words, eh Morton?" Quail narrowed his eyes, the squinty effect likely meant to be intimidating. "Neither am I."

Alex stifled a smile. The man posed him no danger whatsoever—physically, at any rate. But if he were somehow tangled up with the traitor, or in fact was the traitor himself, well. . .better to let the man think he held the superior cards. He remained silent.

Quail took a step forward and lowered his voice. "Nor are you at a loss for money, apparently. Miss Langley tells me you pay your rent in guineas. However do you manage that?"

Alex froze. What the deuce? Why would Johanna tell him that? And what other information had she served Quail along with a mug and crust? He took his own step closer, matching the man's accusing tone. "Tell me, how do you manage to survive from that cat screeching racket you call music? But I think we both know you are not a musician."

Quail's nostrils flared. "Nor are you a gentleman."

A clean swipe on Quail's part, but Alex parried with a smile. "You admit it, then."

One by one, Quail's fingers pulled into fists. "As neither of us are who we claim to be, then I'd say this is a draw, Morton. But I suggest you stay out of my way. Who knows? I might even return the favor."

The man stomped down the hall and disappeared into his chamber. Alex hesitated, unsure if he ought file the conversation away under *Curious, Inconsequential*—or *Threatening*. He opted for *Risky* as he strode to Thomas's door.

"Thomas?" He rapped the crutch against the wood. "Feel up to company—"

"Yes!" The answer came before he finished his question.

Tucking his gift behind him, he entered and drew near the boy's bed.

"Caw, sir! What happened to you?" Thomas lifted up on his elbows. "You look worse than the time I took a tumble from Nanny Shuttleworth's apple tree and she chased after me with a switch."

As if making a solemn vow, he held his free hand over his heart. "May you never see the inside of Dover's gaol, young sir."

Wide brown eyes blinked up at him, an interesting mixture of horror and respect shining in them. Alex couldn't stop a smile—nor did he want to. His heart hitched a beat, taking him completely by surprise. How could a scrap of a lad evoke such a strong emotion? He shoved down the feeling and pulled the crutch from behind his back. "Think you could put this to good use?"

Thomas beamed. "Aye, sir!"

"Shall we give it a go?"

"Aye, but. . ." The boy's smile faded, and he looked away.

"But what?"

"Will it. . ." Thomas's lips pressed into a thin line, and he slowly lifted his face. Whatever he had to say would cost him dearly. "Do you think it will hurt awful fierce?"

No wonder the boy's voice quavered. Pride always exacted a price.

"Not if you keep the weight on the crutch instead of your sore leg." Alex crouched, face-to-face. "But if you like, I'll help bear you up for the first try."

At Thomas's nod of approval, he helped the boy to a sitting position, propped the crutch beneath his armpit, and prayed he'd calculated the height correctly. "On three, all right?"

At one, Thomas bit his lip. On two, he paled. But when Alex said, "Three," the lad sucked in a breath and pushed up with all his might. Brave fellow.

After several halting steps from bed to door then back again, he helped Thomas lower onto his mattress. Sweat dotted the boy's brow, and his thin arms shook, but a sweet smile lighted his face.

"There now. That wasn't so hard, was it?" He tussled Thomas's hair, then straightened. "We'll practice a bit each day, and within a week, I wager you'll be getting about all on your own."

Thomas blinked up at him. "I didn't know, I mean. . .well, having a mam and a sister is all right, I guess, but having you here—I. . .I missed you, that's what. And I didn't know I missed having a father either, not till I met you."

Alex stared. The boy's hero worship was a knife to his heart. What a sorry hand life had dealt the lad. Thomas ought have a father to admire—a real father—not a deceiver such as himself. He swallowed the bitter aftertaste of that truth and forced out words he meant more than the boy could possibly know. "I missed you too, Thomas."

Behind him, the door swung open. "What's this?"

He turned at the question.

Johanna glared at the crutch in his hand. "What is that?"

He leaned the boy's gift against the wall—making sure to keep it within arm's reach should Thomas be brave enough to practice without him. "I had some time yesterday. Can't simply lie around, can I? And neither can your brother."

Thomas bounced on his bed. "Alex thinks that if I practice a little bit each day, I'll be able to get about by myself within a week—just in time to see the Punch and Judy show Mr. Quail promised."

"That's a bad idea." She scowled.

"Aw, Jo!" Thomas matched her glower. "You never have any fun, and you never let anyone else have any fun, either."

Alex stepped between them and faced Johanna. Sometimes the best way to squelch a brawler was to block the view of the opponent. "You can't keep the boy in here forever. He's on the mend, and surely you'll want his help again soon."

A sigh bowed her shoulders. "I suppose." She rose to her toes and peeked over his shoulder at Thomas. "But at least wait until the doctor comes in two more days. If he says it's all right, then all right."

Alex gifted her with a grin. "Well done."

She arched a brow, clearly partaking of none of his charm. "But in the meantime, knowing the both of you, I'll hold on to that." Leaning sideways, she reached past him and grabbed the crutch, the effort lifting her sleeve away from her wrist and inching the fabric slightly up her forearm—where three bruises ugly enough to match his own marred her skin.

His smile disappeared. God help the man who'd put them there.

He stepped to the door. "A word with you, Miss Langley. Out in the hall, if you please."

She clutched the crutch to her chest. "You're wasting your time. I'll not change my position until we get the doctor's go-ahead."

He shifted a pointed gaze to her arm. "It's not about the crutch."

∞

Johanna stiffened. Drat! Though she'd tried to keep her sleeve close to her wrist, Alex's face had hardened when it slid upward. Did the man miss nothing? She'd known him for barely a month, yet she knew what that offset angle to his jaw meant. And the rigid line of his shoulders. He'd have his way or die in the trying. He'd evicted Mr. Nutbrown for a simple lack of payment—and quite forcefully, at that. What would he do to Tanny if he found out the man roughed her up now and then? Not that Tanny didn't deserve a good dose of his own medicine, but still. . . Alex yet wore the bruised remains of gaol on his face. Another visit and he might not have a face left at all.

She darted past him and scurried down the hall, calling over her shoulder, "Sorry, no time now."

"I won't be put off so easily." His footsteps kept time with hers, down the stairs, through the taproom, across the kitchen—even out the door and into the back courtyard. Really, the man ought to go into business with Mr. Spurge, so fixated was he.

She dashed toward the stable.

His shoes pounded the gravel, close behind. "Not that I mind the view from back here, but how long will you keep up this merry chase?"

She ignored him, upping her pace. To face him now would only encourage his roguish charm.

"Johanna, for the love of all that's righteous, just stop. I'll not give up. And if you think you can hitch up Posey to outrun me—"

Gritting her teeth, she whirled and planted her fists on her hips, cutting him off. "There is nothing to discuss. Go about your business, and I shall go about mine."

Afternoon sun lit golden strands in his brown hair, highlighted even more as he closed in on her. "Fine, but first roll up your sleeve. I wish to see your arm."

Pah! He was as bullish as Mr. Needler. But as she breathed in his warmth and sandalwood shaving cologne, her knees weakened in a completely different way than when she faced Tanny.

Still, he had no right to be so demanding. She didn't budge.

He reached for her arm.

She retreated a step. The outright boldness! "You may wish all you like, sir, for I will not roll up my sleeve. I am no servant to be ordered about, nor am I a loose skirt."

Instantly, his hand dropped to his side, a grimace pulling at his lips. "My apologies, for you are correct on both accounts. My directness suits for my work, I suppose, but I never should have used such a manner with you. Forgive me?"

He hung his head while peeking up at her through his lashes. A sheep caught in a briar couldn't have looked more contrite. She stifled a growl. Who could stay cross when facing this?

"Yes." She sighed. "I forgive you. Now, if you'll excuse me." She spun, returning to her previous mission—retrieving a big bucket for Mam.

A tug on her shoulder turned her back around. "Even so, I will see your arm, with or without your cooperation."

Once, on the High Street, she'd seen a mule dig in its hooves, refusing to pull a cart one more inch despite the railing of the driver. Curses, blows, even the offering of a carrot would not convince the animal to budge.

Such was the ripple of resolve lining Alexander's brow—right at the point where his discolored bruise faded into tanned skin. Was tenacity the reason he bore such wounds?

She scowled—but slowly pushed up her sleeve, then held out her forearm like a peevish four-year-old.

Stepping near, he cradled her arm in his big hand and bent over it, his breath warmer than the June sunshine against her skin. Her heart beat loud in her ears. Curse the man for making her feel so precious, like a teacup to be mourned for the chip on its rim. She had no right to feel this cherished. His gentle grip cupped her elbow, treating her as if she were delicate and prized and dearly loved.

He studied the marks with a penetrating gaze, then carefully pulled the fabric back down to her wrist. When he let go completely, she nearly wobbled from the loss.

"How did that happen?" His voice was low and dangerous.

She bit the inside of her cheek. What to say? If she named Tanny, surely Alex would seek retribution. But to lie. . .well. . .was that not as ugly in God's eyes as Tanny's brutality? She'd be no better than her father.

Even so, a perfectly plausible falsehood sprang to her lips, and she bit her cheek harder. Suddenly she knew exactly how Thomas felt when she cornered him. . .how her father had when confronted by her mother.

Alex lifted a finger to her lips and tapped lightly. "And do not deign to tell me those marks were somehow caused by accident, for they were not. You are a woman who prizes honesty, as do I."

She swallowed, suddenly overcome. This man was nothing like her father, despite his gaming ways, for he valued truth as much as she. Maybe it was time for her to trust God and take a risk of her own in allowing herself to love Alexander Morton.

"Very well." She lifted her chin. "I was late in my oakum delivery to Mr. Needler."

"Blast!" Anger banked in his eyes, turning the blue to a smoldering ash—and threatening to flare into a red rage. "You are finished there. Do not go back."

She'd laugh if bitterness weren't closing her throat, and it was a fight indeed to force out any words. "That's easy for you to say."

He shook his head. "There are other means of gaining income, if that's what you're about."

"You don't understand. There *is* nothing else." She cast her hands wide, wishing she could as easily cast all her troubles to the wind. "Believe me, I've tried. Needler's oakum and Quail's silly Punch and Judy show are my last hope to pay the rent in two weeks."

There. She'd said it. Aloud. And voicing it made the workhouse all the more real and dreadful and—the world turned blurry. Hot tears burned at the back of her eyes. No. She would not cry, not in front of a bruised man with enough troubles of his own.

She pivoted and fairly ran toward the stable.

"Johanna!" He darted around her, quick as a jackdaw, and stood immovable in her path. "You're right. There is nothing else, but not in the way you mean it. As valiant as your efforts are, all this striving of yours is but a puff of wind. I had a lot of time to think and pray while in solitary, and I learned something that may be of help, for I see some of the same tendencies of mine in you. Would you like to hear it?"

She sucked in a shaky breath, shoving back the good cry that threatened. Not trusting her voice, she gave a stiff nod.

"It's a simple truth. One I've overlooked all my life, and here it is." Running a hand through his hair, he tipped his face up to the sky. "There is nothing more—nor less—than trusting in God. Therein surrender, and you will find rest."

"Rest?" She spit out the word, despite his earnestness. "What kind of rest is there in the workhouse? I can't let that happen."

His face lowered to hers, his stare unrelenting. "It's not up to you, Johanna. It's up to God. Do you believe that?"

"Of course I do."

"Your actions say otherwise, the way you're running yourself ragged, the worry I see in your eyes, the sharpness with your brother."

She shrank back, her gaze driven to the ground. Truly? Was that what she'd been doing for all the world to witness? For Alex and Mam and—she sucked in a breath. For God to see? Shame twisted her stomach.

Oh God, forgive me. He's right. He's so, so right.

Slowly, she lifted her face. As much as this man rankled and shook her world, she ought give him credit for speaking truth. "Thank you."

A grin spread, making little crinkles at the corners of his eyes. "I'm not the one you should be thanking."

He skirted her and strode toward the inn, leaving her alone in the center of the courtyard. Alone with myriad upon myriad of thoughts.

She lifted her face to the same sky he'd faced just moments ago. "Things might not get any easier, Lord, but even so, Mr. Morton is right. It is You I should be thanking *and* trusting. The thanking part I can do, but the trust? Ah, Lord. . . You know me, better than I know myself. I cannot make any promises to trust You like I should, but I shall try—with Your help, that is."

The sun beat down, pure and strong, as hot and real as the new hope springing up inside her—but would hope alone be strong enough to sustain her and Mam and Thomas should the workhouse be their end?

CHAPTER TWENTY-THREE

Dover was a'scream this early in the morning. Literally. From knife-sharpening hawkers to arguing dray drivers, noise boxed Alex's ears more thoroughly than his shouting match with Tanny Needler. The scoundrel. It had taken all of his self-reserve—and an extra measure gained from an on-the-run prayer—to keep from bloodying the man's nose. He flexed his fingers as he dodged a sausage-seller's cart, temptation to turn back still surging. Needler deserved an uppercut and worse for his conduct toward Johanna.

But a croaky voice echoing in an alley slowed his steps. He cocked his head, listening hard, and there, a layer beneath the hum of commerce and life on the High Street, a familiar twang crawled out from the alley. Alex dared a peek around the corner, though he needn't have. Blackjack's toothless dialect was one in a million.

Two shapes, one tall and listing sideways on a single, strong leg, the other short and squat, with a shock of red hair escaping a hat brim, faced a wide-eyed Nutbrown. If Blackie or Axe turned his way, the knuckle-buster he itched for would be satisfied—but also ruin his mission. And on these crowded streets, he'd not only provide entertainment but newspaper headlines as well.

Alex eased back, remaining within hearing range yet out of their sight.

"But gentlemen, Mr. Nutbrown has said he's excessively sorry to be late once again. Business, my fine fellows. Business is a harsh taskmaster and prodigiously time consuming."

Blackie's expletives punctuated the high-pitched voice of Nutbrown, but the man kept right on talking—or rather, his puppet did. Did he seriously have no notion of the danger he faced?

"For the love of women and song, shut up!" Axe's command was followed by the smack of fist against flesh and then a howl.

Alex gritted his teeth. What to do? Save Nutbrown? Walk on? Or—

Blackie's next words made the decision for him, leastwise for the moment.

"Quit yer whining, Nutbrown. We'll give you another chance, for we've one last thing for you to do. Come along."

Boots ground into gravel, growing louder with each step. Alex shoved away from the building and zigzagged across the street, missing—barely—a skull-cracker of a collision with a wagonload of bottles. Losing himself in a swarm of pedestrians, he upped his pace toward Featherstone's. He might yet have to add saving Nutbrown to his list of tasks to accomplish if Blackjack had a *last* thing for the man to do. The simpleton could have no idea what the villain meant. But for now, Alex had an appointment with the tailor and—judging by the slant of shadows—he was late.

Three blocks later, he shoved open a glass-paned door, setting off a jingling bell. The woolsey smell of merino and cheviot gave a cheerful greeting. Behind the counter, the sour pull of the clerk's jowls did not. Nor did the squint of his eyes, amplified into drawn slashes behind his thick spectacles. This was Dover's finest? How could the man possibly see to cut a bolt of fabric let alone thread a needle? A mystery—but not one tantalizing enough to solve.

Alex offered a smile and a greeting. "Good day. I am sorry I am late."

Understanding dawned on the clerk's face, for his eyelids suddenly lifted like the rising of twin suns. "Aah. Of course. You will find Dr. Swallow's office two doors down."

"Oh? Are you feeling ill?" Alex stepped forward. "Shall I escort you?"

The man's eyes narrowed again. "I meant for you."

"Never felt better, thank you."

"Then you've obviously taken a wrong turn." The clerk's voice pinched as he studied the leftover bruises on Alex's face. "Decker's Boxing Club is over on Priory."

"If boxing were what I was about, then I don't think I'd be standing in a tailor shop now, would I?"

Slowly, the man's glower evened. "I see. What you'll need to do then is head south on the High Street and turn left at Snargate. Bagsby's Thread and Needle is the third building past the fishmonger. Good day."

The clerk turned his back and ran a finger along a tower of fabric bolts stacked on a shelf behind him. Whispered numbers filled the room like so many scissor snips.

Alex folded his arms. Was this to be more of a fight than his skirmish with Needler? "While I appreciate your fine embroidery of directions, sir, nevertheless, I am exactly where I want to be."

The clerk cut a glance over his shoulder. "You do realize this is the most exclusive tailor in all of Dover? We don't serve just anyone. For the last time, I bid you good day, sir."

"You serve the viscount, Lord Coburn?"

The man wheeled about so quickly, the flaps of his neck swished against his collar. Truly, if he were such a crack tailor, could he not do something about tightening up those loose folds of skin?

"Of course the viscount is a client—and you are clearly not!" A fine shade of red spread over the man's cheeks. "Now rid yourself from this establishment before I call the constable."

Alex pulled out a small, white paper from inside his pocket and placed it on the counter, shoving it toward the man with one finger. "I believe he sent word I was coming."

With barely a glance at the calling card, the clerk retrieved a wooden box and flipped open the lid. He paged through a row of index cards, snorting a few *humph*s as he worked. Finally, he pulled out a cream-coloured card and held it at arm's length, his pupils roaming behind the glass of his spectacles like two balls rolling across a carpet. The longer he read, the more his jaw dropped, until at last the index card fell too.

"Oh, my. Oh, sir! My apologies." Dashing around the front counter, the clerk dipped his head, giving the impression of a naughty schoolboy caught cheating on a test. "I never meant, I mean, I can surely see that you are a gentleman of quality."

A second ago he was barely above a vagrant and now he was a gentleman? Alex smirked. "No hard feelings. Let's just get on with it, shall we?"

"Yes! Oh, absolutely." The man straightened and swept out his arm, pointing to a velvet-curtained doorway. "If you'll step into the farthest fitting room on the left, just down that corridor, I'll give you a moment to shed your coat and shirt for some measurements."

Shopkeepers. All the same. Once they detected a jingle in your pocket, suddenly you were their bosom friend.

Alex swiped the curtain aside and strode the length of the corridor. He passed several doors, all of which stood open. Only one was shut—on the left, far end. Had he heard incorrectly? He glanced back at the curtain, entertaining the thought of asking the fellow, but after their already strained conversation, decided against it.

He opened the door. A shirtless man stood on a pedestal, back toward him. Nothing surprising, really. This was a tailor's shop. But just above the fellow's shoulder blade, right side, a dark, puckered scar burnt into the skin an indelible letter *D*. Alex stifled a gasp. You didn't see that every day.

In front of him, kneeling with a mouthful of pins and a tape measure running from pedestal to ankle, a tailor jerked his face toward the door. In a competition, Alex would bet a sovereign that this fellow's glower would easily beat out the front clerk's.

"Sorry." Alex grabbed the knob, intending to make a hasty exit. "I must have the wrong room."

"That you, ol' chap?" The man on the pedestal turned, Robbie's ever-present grin a stark contrast to the tailor at his feet. "Thought I recognized the voice. Had I known you were coming, we could've shared a carriage. Here for your engagement suit, hmm?" A knowing gleam lit Robbie's eyes. "Thought I'd get myself one as well."

This time he did gasp. It would not be contained. "Er. . .yes. That I am."

Behind him, hurried footsteps shushed against the carpet's nap. "Mr. Morton, I've made a ghastly mistake! I directed you to the wrong door. Over here, if you please."

Alex tipped his head toward Robbie. "Duty calls, I'm afraid."

He pulled shut the door and crossed over to the clerk, not hearing another one of the man's blustering apologies—nor anything else he said the entire length of the fitting. Who could pay attention to a pandering shop-keeper when—if he were correct—that branded *D* on Robbie's back labeled him a deserter. But from which branch of service?

And why?

∞

Clicking her tongue, Johanna urged her pony with a jiggle of the reins. But Posey continued to plod one hoof in front of the other. A steady clop. *Clip. Clop. Clip.* Until Johanna wanted to scream. It would not go well for her if she were late to Tanny's. She frowned. Then again, it never went well, were she on time or not.

Still, she'd left Mam with a table full of dirty dishes from the breakfast she'd thrown together. Then there was the bread to bake, the stew to make, and the management of a crazed set of musicians trying to build a puppet stage.

"Oh, Posey, please. Move on!"

Clip. Clop. The horse twitched her ears. Nothing more. Johanna resettled on the pony cart's seat, wishing to do something about her ears as well. The noise of the High Street carried on the breeze even to this side road, two blocks over. Behind her, the hooves of more motivated horses pounded on the dirt. She guided Posey closer to the side, allowing room for the other vehicle to pass.

It didn't. A shiny barouche with the top folded back pulled alongside her. The four horses leading the carriage stood nearly twice as tall as hers, spooking Posey. The voice greeting her set her own teeth on edge.

"Good day, Miss Langley." Mr. Spurge leaned back against his red leather cushions as if he owned the world—which he practically did. "You're out early. What, no guests to serve at the inn?"

"Good morning to you, Mr. Spurge." She forced a prim smile then snapped her face forward.

"I suppose it's good practice for you."

His words dangled like bait on a hook, willing her to bite. She fixed her gaze on Posey's rump. Better that than look at Spurge's smug face. "I have no idea what you're talking about, sir, and I've not time for riddles."

"I hear inmates at St. Mary's are up before dawn, so you see, my dear, you'll have to be a bit more industrious than this."

She squeezed the reins until her knuckles cracked beneath her gloves. The gall! Oh, to give him the evil eye, with a hefty serving of what for. But that's exactly what he wanted, like a boy poking a stick at a hedgehog to see him roll up.

Holding steady, she kept her voice even. "The workhouse will not be my end, Mr. Spurge. You shall have your money, and not a moment before it is due."

"Indeed. I shall. One way or another. Drive on!" His matched greys stepped lively, the barouche finally gaining speed. As a parting gift, Spurge leaned over the side of the carriage and tipped his hat. "Enjoy your last days at the Blue Hedge, Miss Langley."

"That's weeks, sir, not days."

"Days, weeks, a trifling matter, for that inn will soon be mine."

She waited until his carriage disappeared around the next corner before she allowed her brow to sink into a scowl. Wicked man. How could he sleep at night?

Posey continued plodding, but Johanna's thoughts chased circles the rest of the way to Tanny's. In a little over two weeks, she'd have to face Spurge again. The money she earned delivering oakum would put a dent in that payment, but she'd still be short. That better be some Punch and Judy show Mr. Quail put on. But what if it wasn't?

"There is nothing more—nor less—than trusting in God. Therein surrender, and you will find rest."

Alexander's words prickled across her cheeks, as twangy as the gust of wind carrying off the Channel. Even so, her stomach cramped as she set the brake on the pony cart in front of Tanny's. Of course she must trust God, but it wasn't as if she could simply say, "Ready, set, go!" and instantly do it.

Could she?

She hopped down from the cart just as the door to Tanny's shack opened. Tanny emerged, a curse on his tongue and a clip to his step.

And a switch clutched in his fist. "Get on with you. You're done here."

Her stomach cinched tighter, and she dropped to her knees on the dirt, his favorite stance. "I am sorry I'm late, Your Grace. It won't happen again, I promise."

He pulled up in front of her. "I know it won't, because I said yer done."

She forced her gaze onto the scuffed tips of his shoes. "You also said you'd employ me for three weeks, yet I've barely served half that."

"Oh? I'm to have a serving of your salty tongue now, am I?" The switch slapped against his leg.

She flinched. To say anything more might land the thing on the tender skin at the base of her neck.

"Your lover didn't pay me enough for that."

She jerked her face upward. "My what?"

A small pouch thwunked onto the dirt between them. Tanny's lips twisted into a sneer. "Count it. It's all there."

"I—I don't understand." Why would he pay her for unfinished work?

"I don't care a Christmas pudding what you understand. Do as you're told." The switch shook in his hand—a snake to be loosened at the slightest provocation.

She retrieved the bag and opened the drawstring. Five guineas jingled against one another as she dumped them into her palm. Dots of perspiration broke out on her brow. Was this a trap? She lifted her gaze to Tanny. "But why?"

"Tell the big oaf I met his price and kept my word, so there's no need for him to come back here with his threats and impudence."

Suspicion rose like a mist on a moor. Better to know for certain, though. "I don't know who you're talking about."

"Oh? You're a prim lady now, are ye? All high and mighty. A lacy little princess, all buttoned up tight with nary a loose moral." His long legs lifted in a jig, his feet kicking sand against her cheeks. Then as suddenly, he stopped and crouched, shoving his long nose into her face. "I know what you are. You're nothing but a tart. Now, go on. And don't come back."

"But—"

"Go!"

A spray of spittle violated her lips, and she recoiled.

Tanny shot to his feet, raising the switch. "Off with ye before I change my mind."

Clutching the pouch, she dashed to the cart. Even without Tanny naming him, she knew exactly who was responsible for this windfall. The big oaf had to be Alexander, for there weren't many shoulders as broad as his. Of course she'd anticipated him to act, maybe confront her more forcefully about such work or go directly to Mam to voice his concern, but this? Must the man always exceed her expectations?

With a "Walk on," she urged Posey to move, but her thoughts wouldn't be prodded off topic as easily. They never were when it came to Alexander Morton. The man consumed her mind by day and dreams by night.

What was she to do about that?

CHAPTER TWENTY-FOUR

A fternoon sun warmed the taproom, and for the space of a few breaths, Johanna paused on the kitchen's threshold and drank it in. Weather such as this was a rare customer. Salty air wafted inside from the propped-open front door, ushering in the sweet scent of wildflowers where she'd planted them in barrels. Why could not all of life smell as fresh?

Balancing a tray of washed mugs, she crossed over to the counter, then frowned. A monstrosity of wood and nails leaned like a drunken dockhand atop it. If Mr. Quail was so fired up to produce a puppet show, why was he not down here constructing a proper stage? She'd seen nary a hair of him or his band since last night. Nor had she seen Alex.

Alex? Must her every thought be waylaid by the man? For the hundredth time, she mulled over why he'd rescued her from Tanny—and came up short once again. Nor had she been able to ask him outright, for she'd scarce seen him to inquire.

She rounded the counter with clipped steps, the tumbledown stage mocking her every movement. Mr. Quail had already plastered the town with handbills advertising the Punch and Judy show. If that scoundrel thought to leave her with a derelict excuse of a stage and no one to operate the puppets—or the puppets themselves, for that matter—then she'd. . .she'd. . .

She'd what?

Helplessness chafed worse than the poorly darned stockings she'd put on this morning. With a growl, she stowed the mugs, then snatched up a hammer and a stick of wood. She could hardly do a shoddier job than Mr. Quail.

Skirting the counter, she faced the front of the eyesore, deeming how and where best to begin. The rickety frame could use some shoring up, especially at the base. That settled, she set to work.

Each pound of the hammer rattled the entire structure, and she feared the whole thing might fall apart. Thankfully, it held. She grabbed another piece of wood and started on the other side. It felt good to strike hard and see progress, to pound away tension.

Whack! That was for Tanny.

Smack! One for Mr. Quail.

She swung back for a mighty strike against Mr. Spurge, put all her weight into the blow, and—

"Ow!"

Sharp pain crushed flesh and bone. She dropped the hammer and popped her thumb into her mouth.

"Still taking on the world by yourself, are you?"

She whipped about at the sound of Alex's deep voice. Pudding and pie! She'd not seen the man in two days and he had to appear at this moment?

With a quirk to his lips, he held out his hand. "Let's see it."

Emotions pecked her like a flock of martins. Frustration, irritation, but mostly embarrassment that she'd once again appeared the inept female. She yanked out her thumb and hid it behind her back. "No need. I am fine."

His outstretched hand didn't waver. Neither did his gaze. She knew that look, for she steeled her jaw to the same angle whenever confronting Thomas.

Slowly, she offered her throbbing thumb.

His touch was an exquisite agony as he lifted her hand to eye level. His own injuries still marred his face. Purple tainted the corner of one eye, but the edges of the bruise faded into greenish-yellow. The cut near his temple sported new, pink skin where it started to grow together. Doubtful, though, that the carving at the nape of his neck was healed.

He turned her hand one way then another, his breath warm against her skin. His manly scent was familiar now, in a way that connected her to him like a cherished memory.

"I don't think anything is broken," he murmured.

Oh, but he was wrong. Her pride lay in hundreds of jagged pieces. Good thing he studied her hand and not the flush spreading to her cheeks. "I find it curious, sir, that whenever I am in some sort of predicament, you appear. I fear you'll put my guardian angel out of work."

"If the position should ever open"—his blue gaze shot to hers—"I wish to be the first, and only, candidate."

Bypassing the offending thumb, he pressed a kiss to her wrist.

Heat shot up her arm, radiating out from where his mouth touched naked skin. She pulled back her hand, heart jolting. Traitorous body!

Would he now expect such liberties in return for freeing her from Tanny Needler? And why did she hope that he would? Breathing hard, she speared him with a glower, unsure if she were angrier with him or herself.

"Please, stop the pretense, Mr. Morton. I know what you've done, and I ask you to answer honestly." She searched the depths of his blue eyes, desperate for truth. "Why would you do such a thing?"

∽

Panic washed over Alex like a dip in a January pond, frigid and unsettling. What did Johanna know? Had she heard of his fitting for a betrothal suit earlier in the week? Was it common knowledge he was expected at his own engagement dinner tomorrow evening? Or was she asking how it could be that a man would so fiercely love one woman yet agree to marry another?

He schooled his face into a frozen mask—matching the state of his heart. Why *would* he do such a thing? Loyalty to Ford was one thing, but this was his life. If Robbie didn't steal away Louisa soon, he'd have to come up with some other plan to escape the noose of matrimony.

"Mr. Morton?"

Burying his feelings deeper than a sexton on a bender, he forced an even tone to his voice. "What have I done to upset you?"

"Did you think I wouldn't guess?"

He dissected every word or action of the past few days that might've tipped her off. But no, he'd taken care to cover his tracks. Kept his mission at the viscount's manor strictly confidential. Yet maybe it hadn't been him at all, but some other source she'd heard from. Her friend Maggie perhaps?

"Why did you pay off Tanny Needler?"

Her question was scissors, snipping away the tension from each muscle in his shoulders. Was that all that bothered her?

A smile curved his mouth, and he shrugged. "I told you that oakum delivery is not a job for a woman such as yourself. You ought to be attending dinners and dances, not gaols."

Bypassing her, he retrieved the hammer from the floorboards and hefted it.

She huffed behind him. "A gentleman's son may have no shortage of invitations to the viscount's manor, but in case you haven't observed, I am an innkeeper's daughter."

"Oh, do not be mistaken." He turned from the sorry excuse of a puppet stage and stared straight into her heart. "I observe everything about you."

Red flamed on her cheeks. It was entirely too easy to make this woman blush—and for that, he thanked God.

"My point is, sir, that dinners and dances are beyond my reach."

"Were there any justice in the world, that would not be so." He clenched his teeth with the truth of that statement. The justice of this world was a cruel jest. Poisonous women like Louisa Coburn lived in luxury while Johanna scraped to keep a roof over her head. There was nothing fair about it.

"You, my sweet Johanna." Her name rolled off his tongue before he thought. Her eyes widened, but this time she did not denounce his use of her name.

Emboldened, he advanced, stopping a breath away from her. "You deserve ribbons and laces and walks through a garden, not ramshackle puppet stages and the leftover stench of ale."

A sad smile wavered on her lips—lips he very much wanted to kiss. And he could, if he bent just a little.

"It is kind of you to say." A curious little quiver, almost too faint to discern, shivered across her chin. "But I am not the angel you make me out to be."

He'd taken kidney punches before. This one stunned him most. Despite his best efforts to retain a poker face, his brows shot upward. "What kinds of mortal sin could you have possibly committed?"

She stood like a soldier before battle, bearing up to fight God knew what army of demons. Tears filled her eyes, shining, glossy, a rainstorm held in check by the thinnest of threads, for they both knew if she spoke, the dam would burst.

Every muscle in him strained at the leash, begging to draw her into his arms and hold her forever. But this time, it would have to be of her own volition to seek his comfort, or better, to seek God's. So he held back, barely, and prayed that his words would suffice. "Are you under the impression that what you have or have not done is what gives you worth? Because that is nothing but a vile lie. God stamps His value on everyone—on you—by virtue of His grace."

The truth of his words hung in the air, ripe for the picking. Would she?

Her trembling spread, the skirts of her gown rippling slightly, but she remained silent.

So he plowed ahead. "Tell me, Johanna, is worth the real crux of why you feel you must be the saviour of this inn? Is working yourself to death some kind of atonement?"

"You don't understand," she wailed. "It's my fault. All of it!"

Her tears broke loose, washing down her cheeks until they dripped from her jaw. Though he wished to wipe them away, he clenched the hammer tighter, unwilling to stop the flow, for clearly this was a needed release.

"What do you think is your fault?" He probed carefully, quietly, not expecting her to answer but hoping she would.

Her gaze lifted to his, but he doubted she saw him. He'd seen that look before, in a criminal facing the gibbet, the ugly moment when past sins paraded and blocked out the last few breaths of life.

"I failed," she whispered. Her throat bobbed with effort as she pushed out further confessions. "I failed to tend the fire beneath the soap, and now my mother is blinded in one eye. I have failed to keep up the inn as my father asked. It's my fault I didn't get the hearth hook fixed and now Thomas is scarred." Her voice ratcheted to a keening cry. "I failed! Don't you see? I am a failure!"

She turned from him.

He reached out, staying her with a touch to her shoulder before she could scurry off. "You're wrong, you know. Just because you fail doesn't mean you are a failure. It simply means you're human."

Her backbone stiffened, as did the muscles beneath his touch. She was nothing but bone and glass. The slightest movement might shatter her to a million pieces. So he stood there, suspended, tethered to her by his fingers and the truth.

"You are too kind," she said at last.

Then grabbing up her skirts, she ran as if chased by the hounds of hell and disappeared up the stairs.

A glower carved heavy into his brow. She couldn't have been more wrong about him. There was nothing kind about loving her so deeply while agreeing to marry another. Would to God that Robbie would steal Louisa away before he was forced to sign a contract. Better yet, would that he might figure out who the wretched traitor was and be done with the whole affair.

He seized a board of lumber from the stack, and his first hammer swing collapsed the whole rickety structure. Good. Building a new puppet stage was a far better venture than cataloguing his iniquities.

He pried out former nails, banged them back into straight lines, then overhauled the whole design with a sturdier construction. At one point, a man stumbled in from the street, looking for someone named Grouper, but other than that, Alex worked alone and unhindered. The stage took on a shape he hoped would please Johanna. The desire to see her smile at his accomplishment drove him on. Just one more board and—

"It's a little crooked."

A deep voice came out of nowhere. The hammer plummeted. His thumb was smashed between wood and iron.

And he knew exactly how Johanna had felt.

"Blast!" Throwing the hammer onto the counter, he veered around and faced a dark spectre. Thatcher. He should've known. "Can you not give some kind of warning when you enter a room, man?"

Eyes black as coals glowed beneath Thatcher's hat brim. "That would defeat the purpose."

Alex threw his hands wide. "What purpose? To startle years off my life?"

"That's merely a side benefit."

"Bah!" His thumb throbbed as he stomped over to a table and sank onto the bench.

Thatcher followed, leaving a cloud of dust particles thick on the air behind him. When he sat across from Alex, a fine sprinkling sifted onto the tabletop as well. The man looked as if he'd ridden through the depths of the earth and came out the other side a piece of dirt himself.

Alex propped his hand on the table, any lower and his thumb pulsed too painfully. "Well, what have you? Surely you didn't come all this way to remark on my carpentry skills."

Thatcher loosened the kerchief at his neck and removed it, then proceeded to rub out a muscle in his shoulder. So, it had been a long ride. "You asked me to check into the viscount's background."

Alex grunted. "That bad, eh?"

"I've heard worse."

"Then why such haste?" Alex leaned across the table, shoring himself up to receive dreadful news.

A narrow flash of white grew as Thatcher smiled in full. "Even a ghost needs a drink now and then."

A drink? Alex threw his head back and laughed. The man toyed with him as surely as a cat with a rat—and he'd fallen for it.

Still chuckling, he launched from the bench and retrieved two mugs from behind the counter, then filled them from a keg already tapped. He slapped one down in front of Thatcher and eased onto his own bench.

"All right. I'm listening."

Thatcher slugged back several swallows and wiped the leftover foam from his mouth.

"Coburn was part of a military force back in the eighties in India. Bengali to be exact."

Alex rifled through all he knew of East Indies intrigue—and came up shorthanded. Not that he'd let Thatcher know of his scant foreign intelligence. He met the man's gaze. "Sent to quell uprisings or some such?"

Thatcher nodded. "Coburn was good. Some say too good. Prestige has a way of going to one's head. Mix that with greed, and the combination is lethal." He paused to down another swig of his drink. "Coburn wasn't content with his conquests or his military pay grade. When a local rajah approached him, promising gold and lots of it, he sold himself to the devil. A regret I suspect he holds to this day."

Alex blew out a long breath. Coburn had hinted at past sins, and awful ones at that. "What happened?"

Thatcher swirled the liquid in his cup as he spoke. "The Rajah assigned Coburn to lead a contingent of Indian nationals and wipe out a neighboring village. Coburn had no love for the native peoples, so he took the job. But he didn't do his homework. That village contained more than Indians. There were British in residence—a fact he didn't discover until he'd already burned and killed half the population."

Alex's heart hitched a beat. If the viscount had no qualms about killing fellow citizens across the Indian Ocean, what about here? Was he the turncoat?

"Are you saying the Viscount Lord Coburn is a traitor?" Alex listened with every nerve standing at attention.

Thatcher shook his head, his dark hair brushing against his collar. "You'll find no truer loyalist. Once Coburn discovered English blood being spilled, he turned on his own contingent. He barely made it out of the village alive, or out of India when the Rajah heard of his duplicity. Your viscount had to flee the country."

He whistled, long and low. "That must've been a powerful man he crossed."

"The Rajah Bulbudder is the lineal descendant of an ancient family in Hindustani. So yes, Coburn couldn't have aligned himself with anyone of more importance."

"I suppose you don't fear the devil if you're holding his hand." Lifting his mug, he washed back Thatcher's information along with a big drink. "No wonder the viscount forbids his daughter a return visit. I hear the Indians carry a grudge as long as an elephant's memory."

"Aye, well don't get too comfortable holding the viscount's hand, either." Thatcher drained his cup and set it back onto the table. "Coburn has murdered countless innocents. He is not to be trusted."

Alex grunted. The pain in his thumb faded, replaced by a new, more urgent ache in his bones. If Coburn weren't the traitor as he'd suspected, that left either Robbie. . .or Louisa.

He was getting closer.

CHAPTER TWENTY-FIVE

Despite the scuff of clouds draping over Dover like a filthy canvas, the afternoon was most definitely yellow. Lucius Nutbrown couldn't pull his gaze off his beautiful new stockings as he strode toward the Blue Hedge Inn. And as he thought on the golden opportunity he and Nixie had dreamed up, his legs pumped faster, creating a vivid shock of colour along the dusty street.

Rounding the corner, he caught sight of a blue skirt. Fancy that! Just the other colour he'd hoped to spy. He upped his pace. "Miss Langley!"

She turned. A great brown sack in her arms sagged her shoulders. Perhaps he ought offer to carry it, but how to manage that while yanking Nixie out of his pocket? No, quite impossible. He held out his tiny friend as he approached the woman.

"My, but you're looking lovely today, Miss Langley. Mr. Nutbrown is wondering if he might have a moment of your time?" Nixie asked.

Pride swelled in Lucius's throat. How polite. How endearing. Good ol' Nix always knew just what to say and how to say it.

Miss Langley shifted her sack, ignoring Nixie and frowning at him. Sorrow panged an arrow through Lucius's heart. Why could she not see his friend? Acknowledge his presence? As much as he disliked the brutish Mr. Blackie and Mr. Charlie, at least they respected Nix.

"Very well." She sighed. "But only a moment. Come in while I drop this off."

He followed her into the taproom, but as she continued into the kitchen, he stopped—as did all his bodily functions. Breathing. Heart. Hearing, sound, feeling. No, not feeling. Tingles ran the length of him, as did a delicious warmth, bathing him from stocking tips to the sweaty part where his hat band pressed against his skull. Had he died? Was this heaven?

There, right in front of him, was the most majestic puppet stage he could ever imagine. Whitewashed wood framed red curtains with three-inch fringe dangling at the hem. Golden whorls and curlicues embellished the sides of the frame, and in a superb hand, the words *Punch and Judy* reigned above all, like a message from God written for mere mortals.

He barely acknowledged the thump-step, thump-step drawing closer to his side, until a tug at his dress coat forced him to look down.

Leaning on a crutch propped beneath his armpit, Thomas Langley grinned up at him. "She's a beauty, aye?"

Nixie whimpered. So did he. Beauty was too minuscule a description.

"Punch and Judy show tomorrow night." Thomas eyed him. "You coming?"

"Oh!" Nixie squeaked. He'd squeak too, but some of his ecstasy might leak out—and that was something he definitely wanted to savor.

He forced Nixie to look away from the glorious stage and face Master Thomas. "Yes, my fine fellow. Mr. Nutbrown wouldn't miss it for anything."

"Cost you a penny jes' to get in the door. You and Nixie." The boy thrust his chin out at Nix.

The acknowledgement vibrated through Lucius, adding pleasure upon pleasure. Indeed, there had never been a more yellow day.

Thomas lifted two fingers. "That'll mean two pennies."

"No!" Nixie shouted, stunning even Lucius. "No, no, no! A puppet show is worth at least a thruppence per head. Mr. Nutbrown shall pay the full value."

The boy's eyes widened, and well they should. It was an insult asking for a mere penny.

"Thomas, Mam needs you in the kitchen." Miss Langley swept into the taproom.

Instantly the boy's face folded into painful lines. His back hunched like a coal miner's who'd spent decades burrowing in tunnels. He gripped his crutch as if he might topple over at any minute.

"There's still a fair amount of peas to be shelled," Miss Langley continued.

"My leg pains me something awful, Jo. I need a rest, I do."

Lucius exchanged a glance with Nixie. Had his friend noticed the boy's sudden deflated tone as well? But the lad had seemed so perky only a moment ago.

"All right. But see to it you return as soon as you're able." Turning her back on the boy, she faced Lucius. "What was it you wanted, Mr. Nutbrown?"

Nixie wavered between him and Miss Langley, silent. Lucius couldn't help but follow the boy's stealthy movements, especially when the lad lifted a finger to his lips. He skirted the wall, staying out of Miss Langley's line of sight as he edged toward the front door. What a curious place to go take a rest when a perfectly good bed was to be had upstairs.

"Mr. Nutbrown, you are wasting my time."

"Hmm?" He snapped his attention back to the lady in front of him, then raised Nixie a little higher, for his poor friend had slid to an unacceptable height. "Oh yes, there is a new business opportunity Mr. Nutbrown would like to share with you."

She shook her head. "I am not interested, sir."

"Please, Miss Langley, just listen. This venture has the potential to be highly profitable." Inside Nixie's hollow head, he crossed his fingers. This had to work. It must.

"Allow me to be plain." Miss Langley stepped closer and lowered her voice. "Those men you're working with are surely smugglers. I will not entangle myself any further, no matter how profitable."

Smugglers? Ghastly wretches! Lucius tugged at his collar with his free hand, the memory of Mr. Charlie gripping his throat still lingering.

Nixie shivered. "Mr. Charlie and Mr. Blackie are a bit rough around the edges, and that is exactly why Mr. Nutbrown intends on breaking company with them."

"A wise move, sir. Now, if you'll excuse me."

Lucius shoved his hand into his pocket and pulled out a pouch of coins, making sure to jiggle it a little so the money clanked together. "Mr. Nutbrown has developed a new business enterprise, and it has nothing whatsoever to do with nefarious lawbreakers."

Miss Langley glanced at the pouch. She didn't say anything, but neither did she shove him out the door—yet. Emboldened, he bounced Nixie, drawing her attention back to his friend.

"Once Mr. Nutbrown wraps up his business with Mr. Charlie and Mr. Blackie, he plans on. . ."

Just to be on the safe side, he swiveled Nixie's head to scan the room, then pushed him closer to Miss Langley. "You will keep this confidential?"

She rolled her eyes. "I doubt anyone will ask me, but yes, I will."

Perfect! He'd clap Nixie's little hands if he didn't still have his fingers crossed. "There's unclaimed cargo down at Blisty's Warehouse, namely a load of hemp rope what would bring a good price from fishermen here-abouts. We buy the rope at a bargain, then sell it at a profit. You shall be the cheerful face of commerce, Miss Langley, selling a needed product to a worthy people. Mr. Nutbrown shall keep the books and work on finding other merchandise to sell."

A crease furrowed into the lady's brow. "Have you seen this cargo?"

"Not actually, but Mr. Nutbrown has it on good word—"

She brushed Nixie aside and jabbed her finger onto his chest. "You, my gullible friend, must learn to discern. Were that rope anything worth having, Tanny Needler would've snatched it up long ago. It's likely rat-chewed by now, and what isn't has rotted. That cargo will not be a good investment. No one will want to buy it."

Nixie pushed away the offending finger, such a true and loyal companion. "Aah, but that is exactly why Mr. Nutbrown deems this an excellent deal. The fishermen need never know the state of the product until money has first been exchanged."

"That is not honest, sir!"

Not honest? The accusation floated around but never landed, like an annoying black fly, just buzzing, buzzing, buzzing. Why would she say such a thing?

"But of course it is." Nixie shook his head, as puzzled as him. "Money is paid for goods, goods are exchanged for that money, and that *is* the heart of business."

"Mr. Nutbrown, I fear you have no heart at all, nor any sense. As much as I could use the funds, I will not take part in this offer. I am done scheming up ways to provide for my needs and instead shall leave it up to God. I suggest you do the same." She jerked her thumb over her shoulder, toward the front door. "Good day, sir."

"But—"

She shoved Nixie down, and quite forcefully, too. "I said good day, sir." Nixie's face turned to his, defeat bowing his little chin.

With a last look at the magnificent puppet stage, Lucius tucked his money back into his pocket and sidestepped the silly woman. Clearly she was the one with no sense.

Outside, the day no longer seemed as yellow. It was dull beige, the glitter gone. The colour drained. A flat, soured buttermilk of an afternoon.

"Well, Nixie." He studied his friend's scuffed-up nose. "We gave it a good try, eh?"

Nixie's black eyes stared into his. "That we did. But without Miss Langley, how will we sell to the fisherfolk? Not many take kindly to me."

He patted his precious friend on the head, careful not to snag any of the threads on Nixie's torn jester cap. "They don't know you as I do." His voice hardened to steel, and before that hardness could work its way to his fingers, he pulled back lest he dent Nixie's skull. "But Miss Langley or not, we will prevail. We shall finish our business with the likes of Mr. Blackie and Mr. Charlie, then strike out on our own."

"Excellent." Nixie drew close, nose to nose, and whispered. "I don't like them anymore."

Lucius shuddered. "Nor do I, Nix. Nor do I."

∞

Why was patience a virtue? Why couldn't sweet-blazing-mercy-hurry-it-up be a virtue? Alex stood at the top of the inn's stairwell, waiting, waiting, waiting. Then waiting some more. And still Johanna's blue skirt flashed at the bottom of the stairs, flitting back and forth as she served customers.

Retrieving his pocket watch, he flipped open the lid. Blast! He should've been at the viscount's half an hour ago. Even so—his lips twitched into a smirk—it would be quite the betrothal dinner without the prospective bridegroom.

He rubbed his thumb over the watch's glass face, debating which evil would be the lesser. Dressed in his new suit, clearly dandied up for a special occasion, ought he risk an inevitable run-in with Johanna down in the taproom? Or should he hazard a slip out the window with the possibility of tearing the new garments? He blew out a disgusted sigh. If Thatcher or Brentwood had a peek into his thoughts right now, the teasing would be merciless.

Behind him, footsteps clipped down the corridor. Not the thump-step of Thomas, yet the sound closed in on him from the direction of the lad's room. He turned.

Mrs. Langley stopped in front of him, cap askew, her good eye leveled straight and true on him. "Well, well. . .look at you. You're a hair overdressed for the Blue Hedge. On your way out?"

"I am." He flipped his watch lid closed but held on to the thing. Why did this old woman always make his inner little boy run off on guilty feet? Was it the directness of her questions? The motherly tone? Or did the young lad inside him instinctively know she'd crush him to her bosom in pity if he'd let her. And if he admitted he craved that pity, he'd no longer be a man but a crying ten-year-old once again.

Facing Johanna was better than facing her mother. He shoved the watch back into his pocket and took the first stair. "If you'll excuse me, I am running late."

"Good. Then you won't mind if I hold you up a minute more."

The statement stopped him cold. Since his release from gaol, the woman had avoided him. *Now* she wanted to talk?

"It won't take long. Just a few questions."

Her hook set deep in his craw. The betrothal dinner be hanged! Questions were exactly what he'd love to ask her. He pivoted and reclaimed the top stair, then followed her down the corridor to an alcove at the end of the hall.

The best defense was always offense, so he spoke first. "I thought questions were off the table, madam. You made that quite clear when you visited me in gaol."

"In your line of *work*," she drawled out the word, once again revealing she knew more of him than he did about her. "You of all people should know how quickly things change."

Hmm. . .what had changed? He rubbed his jaw, ransacking memories of the past few weeks, but nothing came to mind.

"I've heard rumours that, thus far, Johanna has not." The short lady lifted her face and impaled him with a glare. "Tell me, sir, what exactly are your intentions toward my daughter?"

A stone sunk to the bottom of his gut. What did this woman know?

Her good eye narrowed. "Do you deny your feelings for Johanna?"

"Yes. No! I—" Words stumbled like drunken sods past his lips, and he shut his mouth. Suddenly he was a boy again, being interrogated by his own mother for using his father's gun.

Father?

The sickening rock in his gut lightened. He could use this opportunity. "Very well, Mrs. Langley. A question for a question. Fair enough?"

The waning light of day leaked in the corridor's sole window, and while weak, it softened the woman's terrible gaze. "All right, but you'll answer mine first."

He sucked in a breath. Was he ready for this? Were any of them? Once spoken, his sentiment would be run up a flagpole for all to see, for words could never be refolded and shelved once expressed.

Widening his stance, he met the challenge head on. "I do not deny that I love your daughter."

There. He'd said it aloud, and despite the awkwardness of professing such deep emotion about a woman to her mother, it felt right, freeing, and he said it again. "I love Johanna with all my heart."

He studied the woman's face, expecting horror, surprise, something. But. . .nothing. The lady could sit at the viscount's table and hold her own.

"And your intentions, sir?" she pressed.

A slow smile stretched his lips. "That is not our deal, madam. The next question is mine." He lowered his voice. Why, he couldn't say. No one was around. Not up here. But even so, it seemed more respectful, almost sacred, when speaking of the hallowed dead. "What do you know of my father, Mrs. Langley?"

Though her expression didn't change, her fingers gnarled into her apron. "In part, he was my husband's associate."

Alex shook his head, trying to make some sense of the information. "But my father was a Bow Street Runner, not in the business of keeping inns."

"Oh, son, I didn't always live in Dover." The hard lines on her face ebbed away. The gleam in her eyes—even her bad one—spoke of years spent, knowledge hard earned. Love won and lost.

She sniffled, just once, then continued. "My husband, William, and I moved here from London, after a murder took place. William and his partner brought the killer in for justice. During the trial, the villain swore a blood-vengeance against those who'd put him there. The man escaped before his execution, and his threat fair shook my husband to the core every time he looked into his baby daughter's eyes. And so he left the force."

Alex gaped. "Are you saying—?"

"Tut-tut, sir." Mrs. Langley wagged her finger. "I have the next volley."

"But—"

"Mind the rules, Alex, or I shall stop the game."

His name on her lips was a smack to the backside. Once a mother, always a mother, no matter the age. He dipped his head. "After you."

"By your own witness, you love Johanna. That being said, what are your intentions? You should know I will not see the girl hurt. She's suffered enough in her young life."

The thought of Johanna's head bent in grief after her brother's injury, the tears, the cries, cut low and deep. He strained to speak past the lump in his throat. "I would never willingly hurt her. She is far too precious to me for that."

"Will you offer for her then?"

Mrs. Langley's question hit him like a boom gone wild, knocking the air from his lungs. Of course he would, in a heartbeat, were he not even now on his way to his own betrothal dinner.

The woman's good eye narrowed, as if she could read into the darkest recesses of his soul.

"No," he said, "I will not answer that question. With our first round complete, we shall have to continue this game another time, Mrs. Langley. As I've said, I am late."

She was silent for a moment, creases etching the sides of her mouth, making it hard to cipher if she were disappointed, angry, or simply amused.

"Then Godspeed to you, wherever it is you're going. I look forward to another round at your convenience."

He schooled his step to keep from running down the hall. Though the match had clearly been a draw, why did he feel like the loser?

CHAPTER TWENTY-SIX

The taproom was a boil of people, bubbling chatter, men bobbing about, air thick and hot and altogether uncomfortable. But even with so many patrons, not many extra coins for the inn's coffers surfaced. Standing near the side window, where the last flames of sunset cast an orange glow against the glass, Johanna arched her back, then bent to wipe another table. She ought be tapping into another keg by now, but hardly any customers were interested in ale. Most gawked at the finished puppet stage. She should've charged an entrance fee just to look at the thing.

Across the room, a flash of burgundy moved at the corner of her eye, and Johanna turned her face toward the rich colour. Immediately, she straightened and gaped, openly, for her jaw would not shut. The rag slipped from her fingers. Without a word or a glance, Alexander commanded her attention.

He strode the length of the taproom in a tailcoat the hue of fine wine, but it wasn't his suit that attracted. It was him. The man. The way each of his steps pounded with determination on his way toward the door. He didn't have to weave through villagers or skirt past anyone. People simply moved from his path.

Wishing away all the sweaty men who blocked her view, Johanna leaned sideways, unwilling to lose sight of him.

Alexander Morton was a king, so regal his bearing, so powerful his stride. His buff trousers were well tailored, the muscles beneath defining the suit instead of the suit defining the man. His hair was brushed back, and as he passed by a sconce, lantern light gleamed streaks as gold as a crown atop his head. His jaw was clean-shaven, creating a strong line above an ivory cravat. And before he disappeared out the door, he clapped a beaver hat atop his head, adding to his height so that he had to stoop when he crossed the threshold.

Johanna dashed to the window, all but pressing her face to the glass, and strained for a last look at him. Sunset sat upon his shoulders, the breadth of them wide enough to hold up the sky. He hefted himself up into a shiny, black carriage, and when the door shut behind him, she gasped at the sudden loss.

She turned from the sight before the coach rolled off. It was too bittersweet a picture. Of course he must attend to his father's business, and the Blue Hedge was not the place to conduct such commerce. It made perfect sense. But all the same, she wished she might put on a pretty gown and join him.

La! Silly girl.

She snatched up her rag and wound through the tables. Maybe if she fried up a fresh pot of pork cracklings, she could tempt some appetites and put her mind on something other than Alex. Aah, but he had been a glorious sight. The stuff of dreams, and one she hoped would revisit her tonight when her head hit the pillow. Wherever he was going, he would surely be the most striking gentleman of all and—

"Oh!" On reflex, she reached out and grabbed Mam's arm to keep her from toppling to the kitchen floor, for she'd run right into her. "Sorry, Mam! I didn't see you."

"Apparently not." Mam's puckered brow smoothed. "No harm done, though. Better you bumped into me than one of those big men out there." She hitched her thumb over her shoulder.

"Yes, well, it's those men I'm hoping to coax some coins from. Thought I'd fry up some cracklin's."

"Good thought. I'll put on the pot of fat."

Jo strode to the crockery of salted rinds and retrieved a bowl full, then set about cutting the pork into smaller bits. While she worked, Mam hummed a folk tune. The melody soon faded, though, as memories of Alexander in his fine suit reinvaded Jo's thoughts. He was so kind. So thoughtful. She'd never met a man like him before, not one of his standing who'd even deign to give her a second look. For the first time in her life, she wished to be something other than a mere innkeeper's daughter.

The blade slipped. Red bloomed in a thin line on her finger, wider by the moment. Dropping the knife, she huffed her disgust and reached for a cloth.

"Johanna!" Mam scooted over to her. "Here, let me do that. What's got you this addle-brained tonight?"

"I. . ." She stepped aside, allowing Mam to chop the rinds. She couldn't very well tell her mother she wasn't thinking straight because of a well-dressed man.

She sighed—again—afraid to admit out loud that truly it was more than smart clothing that befuddled her. It was Alex. He permeated everything and had since the day she'd fallen into his arms. Whew. She fanned her face. The heat of the taproom must've followed her into the kitchen.

"I can see, girl, there's something—or rather someone—on your mind."

Meeting her mother's gaze, she swallowed. What would Mam think if she told her?

"Oh, Johanna." Mam set down the knife and pulled her into her arms. "You've got it bad, don't you?"

"You were right, Mam. You were right all along." She returned her mother's embrace. The top of Mam's head came just to cheek level, and Jo laid her face against her mother's mobcap. "Mr. Morton is a good man. He's a perfectly wonderful man."

"Humph." Her mother pulled back and returned to chopping the rinds, giving the next piece a great whack. She mumbled while she worked, something that sounded like, "I hope so."

Jo cocked her head. Surely she hadn't heard that right. "What was that?"

Mam paused with the blade in the air. "I said I hope so many patrons won't tire you out. Looks to be a full house tonight."

"It is. Though the puppet show isn't until tomorrow night, word has spread." Unwrapping the cloth, she peered at her injury, still leaking red, then rewrapped it. "Mr. Nutbrown sang the praises of the stage from one end of Dover to the next, and now everyone wants a peek at it. Didn't Mr. Morton do a brilliant job on the construction? He is so handsome—I mean handy. He is so handy." She bit her tongue, hard, to keep the thing from further blunders. Hopefully Mam had missed that one.

"Johanna, please." Mam scooped rinds back into the bowl, then searched Jo's face with her good eye. "Be careful."

Despite the warmth in the room, she shivered at the flatness in Mam's voice. Alarm throbbed through her, settling in the cut on her finger. "About what?"

"Just. . .have a care for your heart, my dear. I wouldn't want to see it broken."

"Why are you telling me this?" Her words came out tied on a frayed thread of a whisper.

"Because I'm your mother." Mam reached up and tweaked her cheek, her good humour clearly returning. "And you will do the same for your daughter when the time comes."

She shook her head. "I am already five and twenty. Marriage isn't likely."

"Don't be too sure about that."

"You are very cryptic tonight." She peered at her mother. Who knew what secrets she kept tucked beneath that mobcap? "Is there something I should know about?"

Mam clicked her tongue. A smile broad as a beam lit her face, before she turned her back and toddled over to the hearth.

But Johanna wasn't fooled. Mam knew more than she let on—and it more than likely involved Alexander.

☙

"Are you finished, sir?"

The question rattled around inside Alex's skull like pebbles in a tin can. He was finished all right—with the cloying odor of too much perfume, the congratulations of Dover's finest society gathered around the table for dinner, and especially done with this whole loathsome marriage charade. Tonight he would gather new information about the traitor, or die in the trying—which was one way out of this whole mess.

He leaned back in his chair and speared the servant with a direct stare. "Yes, I am. Thank you."

His untouched plate of lobster cakes swimming in béchamel sauce vanished from in front of him, and he reached for his glass—which was as empty as his soul. The conversation with Johanna's mother had drained him more than he cared to acknowledge. Despite the beautiful Louisa Coburn seated next to him, every time he looked at her, all he could see was Johanna's face and hear her mother's question.

Will you offer for her?

He held up his glass. "Refill, please."

Across the table, Robbie mimicked his action, then pushed back his chair and stood. "Attention!" He tapped his goblet with the edge of a spoon. "A toast!" Robbie directed his glass toward Louisa. "To the fairest of the fair,

225

the honorable Miss Louisa Coburn. May you bloom radiant in marriage, like one of the many flowers in your garden."

A round of, "Hear, hear!" circled the table like a chant.

"And to you, my fine fellow and soon-to-be cousin-in-law." Robbie angled his cup toward Alex, the flush of his face indicating he'd had more than enough wine already. "May you find satisfaction with the prize that is sure to be yours."

Most guests smiled and tipped back their glasses, but a few brows scrunched at the cryptic tribute, wheels spinning fast to figure it out. Only he and Louisa could possibly know the meaning—and she gave the loudest, "Hear, hear!" of all.

Not to be outdone, the viscount stood. The movement—or perhaps his glower—drove Robbie back to his chair.

Lord Coburn cleared his throat, then bowed to his daughter and Alex in turn. "To the happy couple, despite the turbulence of the times, I wish you a life of peace."

This time there were a few *amens*.

Flipping out his tails, the viscount sat. Heads swiveled toward Alex, closing his throat. He'd have to say something. But what? This was not the right time, the right place, and definitely not the right woman that he wanted to speak highly of.

Slowly, he stood on legs that felt a-sea and forced a smile. "To the beautiful Louisa, a bride any man ought to cherish and dote upon. And"—he turned toward the viscount—"to Lord Coburn, a force to be reckoned with—especially at the card table."

Laughter filled the room. Even the viscount chuckled.

Alex tossed back his drink and sat while everyone went back to chattering. This was supposed to be a happy night, as evidenced by the merriness of those around him. But happiness for him was out of reach, even if he strained to grasp it. He stifled a groan, though he needn't have bothered. No one would've heard him anyway. What a sham. What a sorry, wicked, farce he played out, sitting next to the woman he was to marry while only hours ago professing love for another.

Louisa's fingers appeared on his sleeve, and she gave his arm a little squeeze. "Don't look so glum. This will soon be over."

He grunted. "Sooner than you think."

"Oh?" Her gaze sought his.

Setting down his glass, he absently ran his finger around the rim. "Apparently you're not aware your father has decided to skip the banns and has attained a bishop's license ready for me to sign—tonight."

The whites of Louisa's eyes expanded, much like a horse pushed to extreme excitement. "But you cannot!"

He shrugged. What else was there to do? If he could get Robbie alone, he could plead with the man to elope with Louisa tonight—but the fellow had been as slippery as a cutpurse in a crowd. Alex sank back in his chair. Even if he did persuade Robbie, that would defeat the purpose of Ford's assignment. He couldn't very well let the two he suspected most escape at large. No matter which outcome, none were good.

Louisa pulled back her hand. "Well I certainly will not sign such a thing."

She was a spitfire, he'd give her that. "I'm afraid, sweet Louisa, that you already have."

She frowned, and for a moment her eyes glittered cold and shrewd. "What do you mean?"

"Your father signed it for you."

She tapped her lip with a perfectly manicured nail. "We'll see about that."

"Now, now." A large grey-haired lady—the major general's wife—bustled over, stationing herself between them. She smelled of far too much rose water mixed with the leftover scent of pork. "The time for lovers' whispers is not yet. Come along, Louisa. Take leave of your man."

Louisa smiled at the woman, though she spoke under her breath for him to hear. "There's nothing I'd like better."

Alex watched all the painted ladies with their swishing skirts disappear out the door, leaving the men behind with their port. Some stood and arched their backs. A few immediately broke out large cigars from glass cylinders they'd been pocketing. The viscount and Major General Overtun secreted themselves off to a far corner, backs toward the rest of the company and clearly engrossed in some sort of espionage. Alex smirked at the thought, but then leaned forward. Perhaps he'd not been so far off the mark, judging by the way they bowed their heads together. The two hardly spoke even when given the opportunity at the gaming table and were total opposites in personality and stature. So why the bosom friendship?

Robbie's voice pulled him from his thoughts. At the far end of the table, the man had gathered the rest of the gentlemen, and was currently embellishing a ribald tale of his conquest of Lucy Starr, a known slattern over on Parson Lane.

Despite being in a room full of people, emptiness washed over Alex like a North Sea breaker, drowning the life from him. Air. He needed air and lots of it. Taking great care to edge back his chair without garnering any looks, he stood and skirted the table, sticking close to the wall. He moved on silent feet, and had nearly gained the door when a deep voice stopped him on the threshold.

"No matter how crafty you are, you'll not be able to steal Louisa away from the women."

Blast! He turned to face Lord Coburn.

The viscount clapped him on the back. "But I would steal you away. Won't take long."

The man bypassed him into the hall and led him up to the first floor. Alex followed, knowing the way to the man's study by rote. Each step carried him farther from the party below—and from any chance he might've had with Johanna.

Lord Coburn ushered him into his private quarters, then closed the door and strode over to his desk. "Might as well get this part of the deed done, eh?" He held out a pen like a sword.

A cold sweat broke out on Alex's brow. This was it. The moment he'd either lose or gain all, but this time it wasn't a trifling pot of gaming money on the line. It was his life. He'd never before gambled what he could not afford to lose. Was the gain really worth the risk this time?

"Having second thoughts?"

He met the viscount's gaze. "Yes, actually."

"Excellent." A slow smile curved Lord Coburn's mouth like a scythe. "I'd worry if you didn't."

Sucking in a breath, Alex forced his legs to carry him across the room. The marriage license lay on the desk like a mantrap, ready to snap him in half if he got too close. But what were his options? Renege and lose all the confidence he'd built with the viscount? Sign away the rest of his life? Or pray for a lightning bolt to take him out now? He'd been in hard places before, but never one as deadly as this. Blast Ford for being such a high-handed employer!

He grabbed the pen, his grasp nearly cracking it in two. Signing this document was far more than any occupation ought to require—and therein lie the crux of why he stayed when every muscle in him screamed to run off. He owed Ford more than merely being a dutiful employee. He owed him his life for taking him in after his parents' brutal murder.

Swallowing a bitter taste, he bent and signed his name, then threw the pen down. The only thing to save him now was that hopefully this document wouldn't stand in a court of law with the pseudonym of Morton.

The viscount shoved a glass tumbler into his hand. "Here."

He slugged it back—then immediately coughed. A trail of fire burned from mouth to gut.

Lord Coburn smirked. "I thought you'd appreciate an aged cognac."

Alex thumped his chest with his fist, balancing out the pain. "Indeed."

The viscount sank into one of the chairs near the hearth. "I took the liberty of setting the date for the wedding one week from today. That gives Louisa enough time—and me, for I have some preparations of my own which need tending before that."

"Oh?" Setting his glass on the desk, he took the other chair and was glad for the support. His head was starting to spin, a distinct disadvantage when it appeared the man was finally going to say something of importance.

"I'm expecting a shipment to arrive on July third." Flames from the hearth painted a hellish glow on the viscount's face. "I should like you to join me in seeing that it arrives safely."

"A shipment of what?" It took all his strength not to lean forward. Appearing too eager might shut the man down entirely.

Lord Coburn swirled the brandy around in his glass for a long time— long enough that Alex was glad he hadn't held his breath or he'd be blue in the face.

"Better that you don't know," the viscount said at last. "Just in case."

"In case of what?"

"As I've said. . .I have many enemies about. If you were to be targeted because of me, ignorance could be your best asset."

He grit his teeth. It was far better to see what demon you faced than come up against one blindfolded. "My lord—"

The viscount held up his hand. "Edward."

"Edward, I assure you I am capable of dealing with enemies. If you want my help, then you're going to have to be straightforward."

The swirling stopped. The glass clinked onto the table. The viscount leaned forward, his dark eyes studying every inch of Alex's face. "You're not bluffing."

Alex angled his head. "No, I am not."

"Very well. Your blood be on your own hands then, if it comes to that."

"I would have it no other way."

"Well, then. . ."The viscount deflated back into his seat, the leather shifting beneath his weight. "On the morning of the third, meet me here just after daybreak. We'll ride to Ramsgate to meet a ship arriving from Woolwich. Your job is to keep a sharp eye out and have your gun handy along the way. Not that I'm anticipating trouble, but one never knows with Boney's minions about. Nasty little infiltrators." He clicked his tongue as if expelling a seed from his teeth. "We board the ship to ensure it arrives safely in Dover before sunrise, which gives you plenty of time to freshen up before a ten o'clock wedding ceremony later that morning. Is that straightforward enough?"

Alex mulled over the information. It was the most the viscount had fed him at one time, but a queer aftertaste remained. "Why me?" he asked. "Surely a redcoat accompaniment would provide better protection. Why not have your friend the major general supply you with a few good soldiers?"

"And draw attention?" Lord Coburn shook his head. "No, you and I alone. We'll simply be two dockhands on the road to Ramsgate, looking for employment opportunity. So dress appropriately. No finery."

Risky—yet not surprising. The viscount was particularly dodgy at the gaming table. Why not in life?

"All right," Alex conceded. "I understand. This shipment must be very profitable to assume such great personal risk."

"Oh, I assure you, it's more than personal. It's of national value. So what do you say?" Lord Coburn's gaze burned into his. "Can I count on you?"

Of national import? This was intriguing—and perhaps may be the very reason Ford had sent him here to begin with. Though the viscount still hadn't divulged the cargo, once aboard, Alex could surely slip away and sneak a peek. Bag the traitor. Dodge the marriage.

He quirked a brow at the man. "Absolutely. I'm your man."

CHAPTER TWENTY-SEVEN

B lowing an errant curl from her damp brow, Johanna filled two more pitchers and elbowed her way back into the crowded taproom. Even after a full night's sleep and a busy day preparing for this evening's Punch and Judy performance, she still hadn't been ready for this onslaught. Half of Dover crammed into the public room. The puppet show had yet to begin, and already her feet ached abominably, her apron strings hung half tied, and her hair drifted down her back. From now on she'd take better care of what she wished for.

She topped off half-empty mugs, collected more coins, then retraced her steps to the kegs. As much as she hated to admit it, she had to give Mr. Quail credit. His idea attracted more customers than the Blue Hedge had seen since her father died. But would the profit be enough to pay off Mr. Spurge?

Please, God, make it so.

She prayed silently as she shoved her way through the crowd. Nearest the stage, Mr. Nutbrown sat at attention on a bench, front and center, his little puppet quivering at the end of his arm. Now and then, when the stage curtain rippled from a jostling by Mr. Quail or one of his men behind it, Mr. Nutbrown let out a small cry. A dog with a mutton chop couldn't have been more delighted. Hopefully he'd be able to restrain himself and not join the puppeteers. But who knew? Perhaps that would be as entertaining.

From this angle, she stood on tiptoe and scanned from head to head, looking for two in particular. One golden brown, and the other with a shock of hair above a freckled face. She frowned. No sight of Alex or Thomas. If they didn't hurry, they'd miss the show.

Skirting the room as best she could, she worked her way back and was just even with the front door when it flung wide. A spray of freckles hobbled in on a crutch, accompanied by a golden-topped mountain of a man.

Johanna quirked her brow at them. "I was beginning to worry about you two."

"Aw, Jo." Thomas screwed up his mouth as if he sucked dry a lemon. "Quit bein' such a girl."

"Aah, but she can be no less. She is too beautiful to be otherwise." Alex tussled the boy's hair, then faced her with a slow grin. "My apologies. On our way back from posting the last of the handbills, I stopped off for this."

He held out his hand. A small, wrapped package sat atop his palm.

She looked from the brown wrapper into his brilliant blue eyes. "What is it?"

Alex cocked a brow. "Only one way to find out, hmm?"

Cradling her empty pitcher with one arm, she reached for the gift. A single string held the paper together. She tugged it loose and poked the paper aside with her finger. The scent of roses wafted out, a welcome diversion from the sweaty patrons.

"Rose petal soap," she murmured, then shot her gaze back to Alex. "What's this for?"

"A good soak will be just the thing after this." He swept out his hand, indicating the clamoring customers. "Don't you think?"

She blinked, completely tongue-tied. Had ever a man treated her so kindly? With so much consideration and thoughtfulness? He'd taken his time, his money, to stop at a store with the sole purpose of purchasing her a comfort item, that at the end of the night she might strip off her soiled clothing and—

Fire blazed across her cheeks. Had he thought of her undressed in a tub of water?

He leaned close, the warmth of his breath whispering across her ear lobe. "Exactly the effect I was hoping for."

The rogue! She retreated a step and lifted her chin. "I am sure I don't know what you mean."

"The show's about to start." Thomas tugged at her apron. "Did you save us seats?"

She frowned down at him. "Look about you, Thomas. Do you really think I had the time?"

"Not to worry. You shall have a great view." Alex bent and hoisted Thomas up to his shoulders, then winked at her. "I didn't really want to see it anyway."

Wedging his way past her and the other guests, he gave Thomas the ride of his life.

Johanna couldn't help but smile at the man, the boy, and the soap in her hand.

"Miss!"

A call from a back table turned her around. "Coming."

But her steps slowed as she passed two ladies seated next to one another, deep in conversation, for one of them pointed at Alex.

"That's him. That's the one!"

The woman beside her shook her head, the netting holding up her hair jiggling from the movement. "Can't be. Yer daft."

The first lady leaned forward, squinted, then sat back. "I'm certain of it. He's the man. My sister were in attendance last night and told me all about it. Quite the affair."

Johanna edged closer.

The hair-netted lady reared back her head. "Law! What she doin' rubbing shoulders with the likes o' such?"

"She's one o' the hired help at the manor whene'er a big affair is afoot."

Though empty, the pitcher in Johanna's arms weighed her down heavy with guilt. She ought be serving patrons and collecting coins, not listening to two gossipmongers rattling on.

Laughter rang out from the first lady's mouth. "You know when it comes to men, she's got a keen eye. Take a look for yerself. She told me that the man had eyes the brilliance of a June sky, hair the colour of honey taken fresh off the comb, and he were tall and broad enough to make a brigand think twice before aiming a muzzle his way."

The other lady's eyes widened. "Sure looks like him."

Jo agreed.

"O' course it is." The first lady elbowed her friend. "She got a good gander at him, 'specially when he stood in front of God and man and gave his speech."

"Miss! O'er here!"

Duty called, but so did the lure of these two women speaking about her Alex. She froze. *Her* Alex? Where had that come from?

"They'll make a handsome couple," the hair-net lady said. "But one wonders why he boards here."

Couple? Her stomach clenched. Surely she hadn't heard right. On the pretense of passing the ladies, she circled to the back of them, then leaned close.

"That'll change. The viscount's daughter wouldn't set a slippered toe in this place." The first lady chuckled. "She'll be leading him around on a leash in no time."

Sickened, Johanna darted back to the kegs. Such chinwagging natter! It had to be. Nothing but pure, wicked rumours that couldn't be true. With a huff, she shoved the soap into her pocket.

Though it would explain why Alex had looked so fine when he'd left the inn last night.

∞

Funny how dismantling things always took less time than the building—in puppet stages or in life. Alex smirked at the thought as he pried out nail after nail, demolishing the stage. The leftover stench of so many bodies lingered on the air, but at least it was silent now.

While he worked, Johanna bustled between kitchen and taproom, clearing away the last of the mugs and straightening chairs. It was a companionable rhythm they labored in, and for some reason, it caused an exquisite ache deep in his soul.

The front door swung wide, and in stumbled Quail, breaking the magic of the moment, especially when he lurched over to Alex.

"Ha ha!" He spread his arms wide. "Now here's a man of hidden talents. A wine merchant, a carpenter"—the tang of rum travelled on the man's breath as he leaned closer—"and a soon-to-be bridegroom."

Straightening, Alex shot a glance around the taproom. Thankfully Johanna was in the kitchen for the moment.

He faced Quail. "That was a fine show you put on. Didn't think you had it in you." Shoving a finger into Quail's chest, he pushed him back. "I wonder what other talents you're hiding."

"Nothing for you to worry your pretty head over. And speaking of pretty heads..." Quail's dark eyes brightened as they followed Johanna's reappearance into the taproom. "Have you told her yet?"

Clenching the hammer, he fought to keep from swinging the thing at Quail's head just to shut him up. He narrowed his eyes at the fellow. "Didn't you say you'd be leaving once this puppet show was done?"

"A week more, then I'm gone." He shrugged. "And what of you?"

He glowered at the man. "That's none of your affair."

"Affair? How apropos." Quail shifted a knowing glance from him to Johanna, then staggered back a step and slapped one hand to his chest. The other he held up in the air, a Shakespearean pose—one that crawled under Alex's skin. "Many a true word hath been spoken in jest."

Tossing down the hammer, Alex grabbed the fool by the collar. "I am not jesting. Stay out of my business."

He released him, and an interesting transformation took place. A thunderhead darkened Quail's face, all signs of mirth—and drunkenness—vanished and was replaced with a deadly stare. Quail's voice lowered, his words sharp as a lance. "I haven't the time for the thrashing you deserve, but you'll meet your comeuppance one day. And I shall be glad to hear of it."

He stalked past Alex and disappeared up the stairs, boots pounding the planks.

Setting down her cloth, Johanna strolled over to Alex. Even after an evening of racing about, waiting on customers, she looked lovelier than ever with her skin aglow and hair loosened to fringe her face. Her fresh innocence stabbed him like a knife in the back—for that's exactly what his announcement would do to her when he told her of his engagement. And he'd have to now, before Quail bandied the news about.

"Mr. Quail looks none too pleased." She quirked a brow at him. "What was that about?"

"You know Quail. Nothing but drama. It's in his blood." He tried to turn away from her, to avoid telling her what he must, but heaven help him, he couldn't. He knew that. He just didn't know how. Helplessness spread over him like a rash.

She smiled, brilliant enough to shame an August sun. "But he did do an excellent job. We are well on our way to paying Mr. Spurge."

He couldn't help but smile back. "I am happy for it."

She stepped closer, so near, the heat of her lit a fire in his belly.

"There is...something..." For a moment she looked away, as if she might find the courage to speak from the corner of the room. Maybe if he looked there too, he'd find a store of bravery to tell her about Louisa.

"What I mean to say is..." Straightening her shoulders, she met his gaze head-on. "There's something I must ask you, Alex—"

She clapped a hand to her mouth.

He chuckled. Such a prim little miss. Reaching, he pulled away her hand, and against his better judgment, did not let go. "Don't be so mortified. I rather like hearing my name pass over your lips."

Scarlet blazed a flush on her cheeks, and her hand trembled in his grip. "What you must think of me."

He bent close. "Would you like to know?"

"Yes." Her voice was nothing more than a fairy's breath, altogether too alluring.

War waged in his chest, heart pumping blood and guilt and desire. Wisdom screamed to step away, put space between them, tell her of his duplicity then walk off. He should, and he would, but now? Impossible, not with the way hope and yearning intensified the brown in her eyes.

He lifted her hand to his mouth. "I think you are kind." He kissed her pinky. "You are strong." His lips moved to her ring finger. "None compare to your beauty—"

"Not so," she interrupted. "Especially not now."

He pressed his mouth to her middle finger. "That is exactly what I find most attractive about you." Her index finger melted against his lips. "You do not flaunt your loveliness." He finished by pressing a kiss into the middle of her palm, then lowered her hand, hating himself for what he must say next. "Johanna, there's something I must tell you."

"Oh, Alex." His name was a quiver between them. A promise. A vow.

He had to end this. Now. "You need to know I—"

"I love you." She launched forward and pulled his mouth to hers.

Her body moved against him with the heat of a thousand fires, and he staggered from the force—of the kiss, of his desire, of the knowledge he'd already signed a document pledging himself to another. This was wrong in so many ways, on so many levels, too many to count.

And far too impossible to withstand, especially when she fit herself against him.

"Johanna," he whispered against the lobe of her ear, the bend of her neck, the bare skin at the curve of her collarbone. A groan, primal and hungry, rumbled in his chest. This was the woman he wanted, the one he must have, with a need that would not be mastered. A shudder tore through him from head to toe.

"Johanna—" His voice broke, and he gently set her from him. Everything in him screamed to profess his love to her, as she had for him, but he couldn't. It wasn't fair. It wasn't right.

The passion in her gaze rose bile to his throat. The gleam of her smile, with lips yet swollen from his kiss, punched him in the gut.

She reached, and with a touch so tender it cut him to shreds, she placed her palm on his cheek. "I never thought to be this happy—is this a dream? Are you a dream?"

No. He was a vile, filthy scoundrel of the worst degree.

His fingers shook as he gently pulled her hand from his face. The question in the bend of her brow shattered his heart. He'd never be the same.

And neither would she, not after he crushed her with the words he must speak. Sucking in a breath, he retreated a step. In wagering that he could extract himself from an engagement to Louisa, he knew now—and without doubt—that he'd lose the beauty in front of him. Would to God that he'd never thought otherwise in the first place or things might've been different.

"Alex?"

He memorized her sweet tone, the way her lips moved when his name whispered over them, for it would be the last time she ever spoke his name in love.

"Johanna," his ragged voice violated the sanctity of what had been. "I am engaged to another. We are to marry by week's end."

CHAPTER TWENTY-EIGHT

Dazed, worn, cheeks chapped by tears and throat sore from crying, Johanna sat in the stable yard on an upturned barrel, staring at the sky. The sun had risen not long ago—maybe. Hard to tell with an underbelly of grey clouds dragging low. Had she a pin, she'd poke a hole in them to release a torrent. But would that do any good? She'd sat here crying all night and didn't feel the better for it.

Clenching her shawl tight at the neck, she hung her head, glad the sun didn't gloat on her sorrow. Better if it didn't show its face, for she never wanted to see it—or Alex—again. *Oh, Alex.* What a fool she'd been. Her heart constricted, and she folded deeper and lower, hunched like an elder ready to fall into a grave.

The kitchen door creaked, but it took too much effort to lift her head. So she sat, listening to footsteps grow louder but helpless to acknowledge whoever it was that drew near.

"Johanna?"

Mam's voice wavered—or had her hearing begun to shut down as well? "Oh, my girl."

Arms wrapped around her, tucking her close.

"My precious, only girl." Mam crooked her finger beneath Jo's chin, forcing her to meet her gaze. "What has you in such a state?"

She worked her jaw, but nothing came out.

"Jo?" Her mother peered closer, her good eye searching for truth.

"Alex—" Johanna shuddered. Just saying his name cut sharp. "Alex is to be married." The awful words stabbed so deeply, she winced.

But it was the sagging of Mam's brows, the quivering downturn of her lips that undid her.

She wilted into Mam's arms and buried her face in her mother's shoulder. Grief, sorrow, pain so awful it was not to be borne surged out until her tears waned—and then another, stronger flow convulsed her again.

"I was wrong, Mam," she cried. "I was so wrong about him. I thought he loved me. I truly did. He's nothing but a liar, just like Father."

"In some ways he is—but in many more he is not. Don't be so hasty, my love."

Her tears stopped. The sniffles didn't. Between shaky breaths, she listened hard, waiting for Mam to explain herself, but her mother simply continued to rub a big circle on her back.

Finally, she withdrew and looked at Mam. "What do you mean?"

"Well. . ." Her mouth quirked, not a smile, for that would be irreverent, but a definite movement nonetheless. "He's not married yet, is he?"

Johanna broke away and set her feet in the rut she'd worn in the dirt from pacing the long night away. "You don't understand."

"Then tell me."

She plodded her way to the broken hay rake then back to the barrel. Again and again. Taking up the cadence she'd developed from hours of practice. Perhaps if she focused on her steps, the words would come easier. "I've never loved a man in this way. I never even knew what love was. Last night I. . .I gave my whole heart to Alex, just handed it right over, and he shattered it into a thousand pieces." She stopped and faced Mam. "What kind of man does that?"

"One who is as confused as you."

Her jaw dropped. Surely Mam wasn't suggesting Alex had been less than brutal. A hundred retorts burned on her tongue.

"Tut-tut. Let me speak." Mam wagged a finger at her. "I suspect it was as excruciating for Alex to tell you of his betrothal as it was for you to hear."

Unbelievable! Her mother stood there defending the man who'd caused her such pain? She threw out her arms. "How can you say that to me? I am your daughter! Should you not care about my broken heart? It hurts, Mam!" She clasped her hands and wrung them, scraping flesh upon flesh, bone upon bone. "It hurts so much."

"I know, my sweet. Well do I know." Mam closed in on her, wrapping one arm around her waist and leading her back to the barrel. With gentle pressure, she guided her to sit.

"It is hard to believe now, Johanna, but love gets easier once the heart is broken. It's a casting away of the shell. Of course it hurts. It's meant to. But broken things are always the beginning of better things. A plant could not grow without first the ground being broken. The most plentiful yields come from a field ravaged by a plow."

The anger she'd been simmering all night boiled into a rage. "I don't care! I don't care about fields or plants or anything. I can't. If that's what love is about, I'll have none of it—ever again."

Mam gathered Jo's hands into her work-worn fingers. Veins spidered blue across the backs of them, tracks enlarged by years of hard living and labor. "Take care, my dear, for your words smack of bitterness."

"I am bitter." Her voice sounded as petulant as a toddler—and she didn't care one whit. "I am angry and ragged and torn. How can God stand by and watch this happen to me?"

"Johanna." With a single word, Mam rebuked more soundly than a month's worth of sermons. "God is not sitting about, watching impassive. Our tears are His. You never—ever—cry alone." She reached and tucked a loose coil of hair behind Jo's ear. "You must bring your broken heart to God—or your broken heart will make you leave Him. What will you do?"

A sigh—as sharp as the pinprick she'd wished for earlier to poke the sky with—deflated her shoulders. "I don't know, Mam. I just don't know."

"It's all right, my girl. Sometimes answers don't come easy. But I intend to uncover a few." Mam turned on her heel, her lopsided gait pounding toward the kitchen door.

Jo stood. "Where are you going?"

Mam glanced over her shoulder, her good eye gleaming. "To strike up a little conversation."

❧

Morning light crept in the window on tentative feet. Alex couldn't blame its weak entrance. If given the choice, he wouldn't want to keep company with himself either. He flung the pillow he'd cursed all night across the room and sat up, fully clothed. Why he'd even bothered to try to sleep annoyed him further. Every time he closed his eyes, all he saw was the shattered, horrified pain in Johanna's eyes. Hurt put there by him. In all his years as a Bow Street officer, he'd locked up many a lesser villain than the scoundrel he'd become. This time he'd gambled everything—and lost.

A rap on his door drew him to his feet. He'd not heard heavy footsteps, so it was a woman, most likely. He'd bet five to one it was Johanna, wanting an explanation, or maybe wanting to vent her wrath. His heart plummeted to the floor, and were it visible, he'd stomp on the thing. When he'd told her last night he was to be wed, the blood drained from her face until he feared she might swoon, then without a word, she'd turned and walked away. No screaming. No tears. No anything. Rage of that caliber had to blow sooner or later. It appeared the time was now—and he deserved every bit of it. Steeling himself, he yanked open the door.

Piercing brown eyes sparked up at him beneath a mobcap.

"Mrs. Langley." His head dipped, driven downward by respect and shame and guilt. He'd prepared for battle with the daughter, not the mother. His stomach roiled like the one—and only—time he'd taken too much libations and was sorry for it the morning after.

"I can only assume this is about Johanna," he mumbled. Apparently even his voice wanted nothing to do with him today either.

"No, it is about you." She bustled past him, forcing him to either step back or be flattened, then she shoved the door shut. "Can you think of a more secure place to talk?"

"No." He dragged over the single chair gracing the room and offered it to her, then sat opposite the woman on the corner of his bed. Her all-knowing gaze, the kind only a mother could produce, sagged his shoulders. He looked at the floorboards. "I'll be leaving today, but before I go, you must know I never meant to hurt your daughter. I hate what I've done to her."

"And I hate what Ford is doing to you."

He jerked up his head, the direction of her words nearly whiplashing him. One side of her mouth curved. "I thought as much. If you intend to marry Louisa Coburn for the sake of a directive, then you're stepping beyond the bounds of being a good officer into a foolish one."

Stunned, he worked his jaw, but was hardly able to formulate questions in his mind let alone speak any. He shook his head, completely at a loss. "No more games, Mrs. Langley. Please."

She folded her hands in her lap, calmly, as if she weren't addressing the reprobate who'd broken her daughter's heart. "I was young once, beautiful, like Johanna. And just like her, I fell in love with a Bow Street officer."

"At least you and your husband had a happily ever after."

"I wasn't speaking of my husband."

His eyes shot wide. This lady, who ran an upstanding if not ramshackle inn, had dallied with another man?

She chuckled. "Oh, it's not that I didn't love William, for I did, but in a different way than I loved Richard."

Surely she didn't mean. . .but of course. It made sense, if not in a twisted fashion. He leaned forward, the straw tick crunching beneath him. "Richard Ford?"

She nodded. "Richard was never satisfied with mere officer status. He wanted more, to become a magistrate, which was an impossibility for he held no land. He would need an act of parliament. When a high-paying assignment involving an MP came up, he took it, no questions asked, hoping to garner favor from the man." Her lower lip quivered, and she shut her eyes. "The reckless fool."

They sat in silence, save for the muted snores from down the hall. Mrs. Langley's mouth pinched, little ruffles of skin tightening together in fine pleats. Whatever she remembered couldn't be pleasant.

"And the assignment was?" he prompted.

Her eyes fluttered open, and she smoothed her hands along her apron. "Richard was to deliver the MP's daughter safely to her mother, a colonial who'd returned home months earlier. Shortly after setting sail, Richard took ill. Unattended by necessity, the girl was ravished and left unable to identify the attacker. By the time they landed, she knew she was not only ruined, but with child. Richard blamed himself, of course, for such is his strong call to duty. So, risking his own happiness, he married the girl. When I received his letter, I was devastated."

Alex dug deep into the farthest fields of his memories, a fruitless harvest, for he'd never once heard of the magistrate's wife. "I had no idea Ford was married. I am sorry for your loss."

"Not as sorry as I was, though William Langley was a comfort. And, well, I wouldn't have my sweet Johanna or Thomas were it not for him." For a moment, the lines of her face softened, and it was easy to picture her as she might've looked in younger years, when a fellow named William and one named Richard both loved her.

But the creases reappeared, carving row upon row at the sides of her mouth and corners of her eyes. "Richard Ford threw away what he wanted for what he thought was right—but that didn't make it so." Her voice grew hard as well. "If you lose what you love to gain that which you don't, merely out of a sense of duty, such an action can never be right. Think on that."

The words smacked hard, and he stifled a wince—barely.

She stood and rested her hand atop his head. "Ultimately it is God you're accountable to, Alexander, not to me or Ford, to Johanna, or even to yourself. God alone." Her edict hung on the air as her feet pattered over to the door.

She let herself out and good thing, for he couldn't move. He sat dazed, the same slack-muscled, washed-out feeling as after a good row. She was right, of course. Every word of what she'd said rang so loud and true that his head buzzed.

But when he was this close to discovering a traitor, was it any more honorable to back out of the situation and put the lives of Englishmen at risk by the French?

CHAPTER TWENTY-NINE

tep-glide. Step-glide. Lucius practiced stretching one foot forward then bringing up his lagging leg in a smooth motion as he made his way down Wiggett Lane. This late in the day, not many pedestrians remained out and about. A good thing too. Cross looks or laughter didn't help his concentration. He hadn't quite yet mastered the flowing movement he'd been practicing the past five days. Aah, but Punch had made it look so easy as he'd slid back and forth across that puppet stage. If only he could move with such grace.

The last ray of sun blazed on a flash of red, and he jerked his head to the side. Behind a large glass window was a pyramid of all sorts of folded fabric, stacked to attract the eye. His gaze skimmed past the yellows, despite their magnificence, and went to a bit of red wool at the top. The colour was so pure, a shiver skittered from shoulder to shoulder.

He stopped and faced the window. "Look, Nixie. What a jumper that would make for you."

Nixie's little nose pressed against the glass. "It's the same shade as what Punch wore at the puppet show, Mr. Nutbrown."

"I know." He sighed. "I can't stop thinking on it. Seems like yesterday."

Nixie's dented face turned toward him. "You should buy that fabric. Then you can always remember it."

"Brilliant! I shall." Discarding his step-glide practice, he darted toward the door. Even though the shop was likely closed, sometimes all it took was a little persistent rapping and knob-jiggling to get one to open up.

Nixie bobbed between him and the door. "But are we not late to our business meeting?"

"Indeed." Inches from the knob, he pulled back his free hand. Not that he minded the income, but he was worn weary from always having to meet with Mr. Blackie and Mr. Charlie. It cut into his free time far too much.

He patted Nixie's little head. "What would I do without you to care for me, my friend?"

Nixie leaned into his touch. "I will always take care of you."

"Pray do not be offended, Nix. I know you shall."

He tucked his friend into his pocket and set sail once again down Wiggett Lane, then turned sharply onto Bledsoe. This part of town smelled like milk gone bad. He practiced holding his breath instead of glide-walking.

Halfway down the block, he swung into the Broken Brass pub. The stench in here punched him in the nose worse than on the street. Unwashed bodies filled the room, but that wasn't the worst of it. It was the corners. Those dark shadows hid all manner of waste, for more often than not, the drinkers didn't bother with going all the way outside to do their business. He'd stop breathing altogether if Nixie weren't in such need of him.

He wedged his way through muscles and beards and bones, only once tripping over a fellow who'd not even made it to a corner to double over and retch. Near the back door, at the farthest table from the bar, he stopped.

Mr. Charlie lunged up from his seat and grabbed him by the throat. "Yer late!"

His windpipe folded beneath the man's grip. This method of greeting was becoming increasingly annoying. He tried to yank Nixie out to let the man know, but his fingers were starting to feel tingly.

Mr. Blackie leaned across the table with a growl. "Not yet, Axe."

Splaying his fingers, Mr. Charlie dropped back to his seat.

Lucius coughed, sucking in air the wrong way. He pulled out a chair and sank into it. Slowly, Nixie emerged, a little crooked on his hand, but in better shape than he felt at the moment. "Mr. Nutbrown"—Nixie hacked a bit himself—"is excessively sorry for his tardiness, gentlemen. It's the way of business sometimes."

A sneer slashed across Mr. Blackie's face like a wound. Perhaps he'd had a bad day? His big, sausage finger speared a folded slip of paper and slid it across the table toward Nixie. "Read this. Out loud."

Lucius shook out the paper so both he and Nixie could see it. "Load tomorrow," Nixie read. "Deliver to Ramsgate."

Mr. Blackie and Mr. Charlie exchanged a glance, then Mr. Blackie's sausages reached for the paper.

Nixie darted out, front and center. "But there's more."

"Then read the blasted thing! Ye soft-brained coddle-headed—"

Mr. Charlie continued spouting unkind epithets, and likely would for a very long time, so Nixie slid over to Mr. Blackie's face—almost as smoothly as Punch might've. "This paper says you're to make a list of names of the men who serve so they may receive their reimbursement."

"Re–im–burse–ment?" The word jerked and juddered past Mr. Blackie's thick lips. Picking up his mug, he slugged back a big swallow of ale, then swiped his mouth with the back of his hand. His dark eyes sought Mr. Charlie's. "I don't like the sound o' that."

"Me neither." Lifting his cap, Mr. Charlie scratched a patch of hair on the crown of his head. "Don't seem right killing those what help."

A foul curse ripped out Mr. Blackie's mouth, blending in with a host of other off-colour language from the other patrons. "He better not expect us to do the re–im–burs–ing. Let the little dandy dirty his own fine suit with blood."

Blood? Nixie's head angled from one man to the other. "Excuse me, gentlemen, but are you under the impression that reimbursement involves the spilling of blood?"

Their faces swiveled toward him, bypassing Nixie altogether. "Don't it?"

He squirmed on his chair. This much scrutinizing reminded him far too much of his younger years under Mr. Shrewsby's evil eye, the master of Beetroot Home—a shelter for castoffs and misfits.

Nixie rescued him, rising up like a knight on a white horse. "No, sirs. Reimbursement simply means pecuniary compensation."

Dead fish eyes held more glimmer than that in Mr. Charlie and Mr. Blackie's stares.

"It means they'll be paid," Nixie explained.

Mr. Blackie leaned back and drained his mug dry, slamming it on the table when he finished. "O' course I knew that, ye daft muggle. I was jes' seeing if you knew. You passed the test."

Lucius flipped Nixie around and smiled at his friend. My, but they were a smashing team! Such a pair. The best of the best. A finer duo the world had never—

Mr. Blackie's voice interrupted him. "You remember all those men we talked to?"

With his free hand, Lucius tapped the side of his head, but Nixie spoke.

"Mr. Nutbrown never forgets a face."

"Good. Bring us the list tomorrow afternoon, three o'clock, and we'll give you yer last assignment."

"And don't be late." Mr. Charlie poked Nixie in the chest. "We'll be giving you your re–im–burse–ment."

Lucius stood, snapping a sharp salute to his forehead with his free hand. Nixie tried, too, but his little puppet hand never did quite reach his brow. "Tomorrow, then, gentlemen."

He turned to go, but Mr. Blackie's voice pulled him around. "Oh, and Nutbrown, this time we'll be meeting out back." He hitched his sausage finger toward the door leading out into a slop lane.

Lucius tucked Nixie back into his pocket. It was a rather unconventional choice of meeting venue, but at least with an appointment that early in the day, he'd have time to buy the red wool for his little friend. The thought was so appealing, he nearly laughed along with Mr. Blackie and Mr. Charlie.

But inside his pocket Nixie shivered as Lucius pulled out his hand. What did his business partners find so amusing?

∽

Plink. Plink. And *plink.* Johanna dropped the last coin along with the last of her hopes into the strongbox. Pressing her fingertips to her temples, she rubbed little circles as if the action might magically move the numbers in her head from the negative to the positive. It didn't. And by the sounds of only two customers out in the taproom, neither would enough magical money appear tonight, either.

She slammed the lid shut with more force than necessary, rattling the wooden bowl on the kitchen table. What a horrid week, as nauseating as the leftover stench of the cabbage soup she'd burned at lunch. She'd lost the man she loved, and it appeared she'd also lose the Blue Hedge. Her head sank in defeat and—as Mam might point out were she not abed with a cough—she was now in the perfect position to pray.

Please, God. Provide a way.

A small sound, not a still voice, but more like a slow and quiet creak answered. She lifted her face, listening with her whole body—then she shot up from her chair and darted to the back door. She yanked it open to a smudge-faced, crutch-leaning, wide-eyed boy.

"Evenin' Jo." Thomas grinned. "I were just coming in to help you with the—"

"Stop it." With a yank on his sleeve, she ushered her brother inside and shut the door. "Do not lie to me. If you wanted to be of help, you'd have been here long ago. Where have you been? And no spinning any tales."

He shifted on his crutch, hiking up his injured leg a little higher—no doubt trying to garner her sympathy. "Out with my friends. That's all. Eew! What's that smell?"

"Humph." She grunted with as much force as Mam, ignoring his diversion tactic. Studying the boy from head to toe, her gaze snagged on a bulge in his pocket. "What were you doing with your friends?"

"Oh, you know. Just jawin' a bit, out behind the Broken Brass. Gotta run now, though. Ought keep my leg up, aye?" He tried to squeeze through the open space between her and the table.

She sidestepped and blocked his route. "I would see what's in your pocket before you go, Brother."

"Aww, Jo! You can't—"

She held out her palm.

Scowling, he shoved his hand into his pocket and pulled out a fistful of coins—which he purposely kept just out of her reach.

"Thomas Elliot Langley! I told you not to gamble anymore."

His chin jutted out, so reminiscent of her father that it tightened her throat.

"You told me not to gamble *here* anymore."

"You knew very well what I meant. There is to be no gaming with your friends here or anywhere else. You are finished." She reached for the money.

He swung his hand behind his back, leaning precariously on his crutch. "I can't just up and quit. My friends are expecting me tomorrow. Wouldn't be right not keeping my word, would it? You're the one always harping on being trustworthy"

"Oh, really? Since when do you care about honesty?" She leaned forward, bending nearly nose to nose. "You will go tomorrow and tell those boys you are done—or I will tell Mam what you've been about."

His head hung, and he mumbled something.

She lifted his face. "Thomas, I mean it. This wagering is a sickness. Once it took hold of Father, it led him—and us—into ruin. He couldn't think straight, couldn't eat, couldn't sleep. It was all cards and betting, nothing else.

He lost sight of those he loved until he wasted away. Do you want that to happen to you?"

Thomas's Adam's apple bobbed with a swallow. "I–I'll quit. I promise."

"Good." She straightened, but held out her palm once again. "And I'll take that ill-gotten gain to make sure of it."

His wide eyes narrowed, and she got the distinct impression that had he not a crutch to hold on to as well as a handful of coins, he'd have slapped her hand away.

"You're a shrew!" he shouted. "A rotten, mean, horrible—"

"Enough!" A deep voice with a hard edge made Thomas flinch and her stomach drop.

What was *he* doing here?

She turned, wanting and not wanting to see Alex's blue eyes. Why did he have to come here again?

Thomas used the distraction to hobble past her—but broad shoulders blocked his exit from kitchen to taproom.

Alex stood, arms folded, an impassible, unmovable mountain. "That's no way to speak to a lady, young Thomas. You will apologize. Now."

Slowly, Thomas hobbled back to her. Without making eye contact, he mumbled, "Sorry."

Johanna kept her gaze on her brother. Better that than look at the one she'd been trying to forget.

"You can do better than that," Alex coaxed.

Thomas's freckled cheeks blew out with a puff of wind. "I'm sorry I called you names, Jo."

How could she remain cross with that? Her lips quirked into a half-smile. "You are forgiven."

"There, that's better. Now run along." Alex left his perch on the threshold and strode into the kitchen, giving Thomas enough space to dart as fast as he could with a crutch out the door.

Johanna backed away, putting the table between her and the man she'd sworn to never speak to again. Refusing to meet his gaze, she looked only at his chest, but that was a mistake. All she could think of were the times she'd taken shelter there—and her heart broke afresh. What in all of kingdom come was he doing here again? Walking back into her life and rubbing raw her already ragged emotions?

He stopped on the opposite side of the table. "That was quite a storm from your brother. What is the problem?"

The problem? Did he mean the way her heart twisted and wrenched merely from the sound of his voice? She glowered up at him, breaking her vow of silence. "Nothing you need concern yourself over, Mr. Morton."

Her sharp tone cut the air, and he flinched. Good. She'd like to see him do more than that, to wilt, to droop, to drop to his knees, ruined by a hurt as great as the one that ate her soul. A hundred blistering retorts prickled on the end of her tongue, the urge to see him felled beneath her righteous rage growing stronger with each heartbeat.

But wasn't that just what Thomas had tried to do to her?

She lowered her gaze to the table. "Why are you here? Something wrong at the Rose Inn?"

"No. I came to bring you this."

A pouch landed on the wooden table with a jingle. His big hand shoved it to a stop next to the strongbox.

She retreated as if he'd set down a snake. "Your lodging was already paid. You owe nothing."

"Is your final hearth payment and rent not due soon?"

His words landed like pebbles thrown into a pond, the ripples sending her reeling. All she had to do was reach out and take it. Solve her troubles while maybe putting a dent in his pocket—or at the very least keep him from buying his new bride some baubles or trinkets.

Tempting as it was, she pushed the pouch back to his side of the table. The thought of him with another woman was so abhorrent, not even taking his money would lessen her disgust. "As I've said, sir, it is none of your concern. Now go away."

"Johanna, please." He sighed, the huff of his breath jagged at the edges. "Don't be stubborn and lose all for the sake of your pride. May a friend not do a good turn for another?"

"Is that what you are?" A dark, throaty roar clogged her throat. The audacity of the man! Did he think he could buy his way back into her good graces? She shook her head, again and again. "A friend doesn't inflict a mortal wound, then leave the injured to bleed out alone."

Beneath the tan of his skin, a flush deepened on his face. "If I'd stayed here, would that have not been more cruel?"

She threw out her hands. "Then why come here at all? Go back to the Rose. Go back to your wedding plans. Go back to your happy life and Louisa—"

She spun away. Too many tears threatened to spill. Too much pain twisted her face, far too much to hide—and she wouldn't give him the satisfaction.

Behind her, boot steps pounded on the flagstones, rounding the table.

No! She'd not have it. Darting sideways, she snatched a frying pan from a hook on the wall and hefted it. "If you even think to touch me, I will mark that face of yours worse than any gaol keeper."

He froze. Emotions, too many to count, flashed in his blue gaze. Finally, his shoulders slumped, and he aged a decade in a second. "I am sorry, Johanna. I never meant to hurt you. I. . .I thought I was doing what was right." His jaw clenched, and he looked away. "Yet I hate what I have done."

"That makes two of us." She blew out a long breath and lowered the iron pan. "Go away, Alex. Just go. And don't come back."

CHAPTER THIRTY

Stew bubbled in the pot, and Johanna stirred it absently, watching snippets of potatoes and fine bits of parsnips surface and sink, surface and sink. The sight soothed in a mesmerizing way—the chopped pieces of once-living things now caught in a death spiral at the end of her spoon. Floating and dropping. Just like the last month of her life.

She leaned close and sniffed. At least this stew smelled better than yesterday's failed cabbage soup.

The back door crashed open, but she didn't turn. She simply didn't care. The grim reaper himself could barrel into the kitchen and she'd still stand here, stirring and stirring.

"Jo! You got to see!" Thomas's crutch thudded in time with his words.

"Whatever it is, show it to Mam. I'm busy." The spoon trailed round the edge of the pot, round and round.

He tugged her skirt. "Come on, you got to look."

Blowing a bit of hair out of her eyes, she stared at the stew. Likely he held a toad, or a squirming vole, or some other boyish torture device. "Go away, Thomas."

"Jo, please."

Her spine stiffened. Besides the fact that Thomas never used the word *please*, the panic in his tone alarmed her. Pulling the spoon from the pot, she tapped off the drips and turned.

He held out a dirty scrap of red fabric, all balled up in his hand. "I found this lying next to the rot pile out back o' the Broken Brass."

Frowning, she set down her spoon, then took the soiled lump from him. She poked at it with her finger, and the fabric unfolded, bleeding over the edges of her palm. It appeared to be stained scarlet wool sewn haphazardly in the shape of a little jumper, with one arm torn off. What in the world? She scrunched her nose at Thomas. "What is this?"

He dug into his pocket and pulled out another lump—and when it landed in her hand, a shiver raised gooseflesh on her arms.

Mr. Nutbrown's puppet, leastwise what was left of it, stared up at her, one eye missing. So was half of its head. The other half was flattened. Only a frayed scar of the jester hat remained where glue held the ripped strip in place. What used to be a painted smile now gaped open in a broken hole. Knife marks slashed a jagged line at the neck.

A shiver passed through her. "Where did you say you found this?"

"Behind the Broken Brass. You gotta go get Alex, Jo. You're faster than me. I'm sure Mr. Nutbrown's in trouble."

Crossing to the table, she set down the crushed head and tattered fabric, unwilling to look at either anymore. "I'm sure he's fine," she mumbled. Drawing strength from her words, she turned to Thomas. "Mr. Nutbrown probably just dropped his puppet, that's all."

But the statement branded her a liar even before it finished passing her lips.

Thomas scowled. "That ain't so, and you know it. You gotta get Alex! He's the only one who can help."

Pinching her lips tight, she strode to the door and snatched her hat off a peg. She'd be hanged if she asked Alex for anything. She could take a quick stroll and look for Mr. Nutbrown herself and still be back in time to serve dinner.

She fumbled with the ribbon beneath her chin. Why were her fingers shaking? "I'll go. I'm sure I'll find some ridiculous yellow stockings roaming the town, looking for a lost puppet."

"No!" Thomas hobbled between her and the door. "It's too dangerous. Alex has a gun, and he's from London. If Mr. Nutbrown's in a bad way, he'll know exactly what to do."

The information stunned. Alex was from Sheffield. . .wasn't he?

"How do you know that?" She studied her brother. What other knowledge lurked beneath those freckles?

He shoved her in the arm. "Yer wastin' time, Jo."

The smashed puppet head on the table implored her with its single remaining eye. Nixie's tiny voice cried silently in her mind, *"Mr. Nutbrown would never leave me."*

Whirling, she slipped out the door and entered the stable yard, then shot toward the broken gate. The afternoon sun bowed to the horizon. She'd have to be quick to make it back in time for any patrons looking for a bowl of stew. But where would someone like Nutbrown be?

She mapped out a route in her head as she turned onto the High Street. If Thomas had found the puppet at the Broken Brass, then that would be the most logical place to start. She upped her pace toward Wiggett Lane, when a shiny, black barouche turned the corner. Her blood drained down to her feet. She'd see Mr. Spurge's sneering face next week when he came to collect his due—a due still short a pound. The thought of an encounter with him sickened her more than the ruined puppet head.

Crossing the street, she darted down a narrow path that led to the harbor. If she skirted the waterfront, she could double back and work her way home through town while looking for Mr. Nutbrown. But trekking on the shingle slowed her steps. It would be faster to hike closer to the water where her shoes could grip firm sand. And she'd have the added benefit of the berm to hide her from Mr. Spurge's eyes on the chance his carriage swung down to Harbor Lane. She hiked her skirts, crested the berm, and pattered down the other side.

Across the beach, a line of men hefted something—boards? Flat boxes? She squinted. Hard to tell. Whatever their cargo, they loaded it onto rowboats that skittered over the water toward a ship anchored just off the coast. A strange time to load. They wouldn't get very far before dark, unless they planned to set sail at daybreak. But why then was the ship not moored in the harbor? She bit her lip, puzzling for a moment, but no matter. It was none of her business.

She hurried to the sand as fast as the rocks beneath her feet would let her. Once there, she lowered her skirts and sped along, making up for lost time. She'd turn away from the men before drawing too close, then head back to the city proper.

But just before she could veer off, her steps slowed. Then stopped. A shape emerged from behind a rock, with a peg-legged gait and a gun pointed at her. For a single, awful eternity, she longed for Alex to be at her side.

Glancing at the berm, she calculated the distance. She could easily outpace the man's hitch-stepped run and make it safely to town—but she couldn't outrun a lead ball. What to do?

"This ain't no place for a lady." The big man, Mr. Blackie, if she remembered correctly, stopped in front of her, and thankfully lowered the muzzle of his gun. "Say. . .you be that girl from the Blue Hedge. The one what helped us, aye?" A glower folded his unshaven whiskers into dark lines at the sides of his mouth. "You were paid, and paid right fine far as I remember. If yer lookin' for more, missy—"

"I am not. I am looking for Mr. Nutbrown." She cut the fellow off before he worked himself into a swirl. Men such as this rarely liked to be parted from their coins, a lesson well learned from Tanny Needler.

But instead of relaxing of his shoulders, Mr. Blackie yanked the gun back up, aiming squarely at her chest.

"Now, now. . .what ye be wantin' him for?"

Drat that Mr. Nutbrown! The man had been nothing but trouble since he set foot in the Blue Hedge—and this time it appeared to be the worst trouble of all. Forcing back a lump of panic, she swallowed and retreated a step. "I suppose it can wait. I see that you must be busy with that ship you were expecting, so I'll just be on my way. Please tell Mr. Nutbrown I have something of his when you next see him."

She turned to go.

The click of the gun and Mr. Blackie's growl stopped her cold. "If it's Mr. Nutbrown yer wantin', I can take you to him."

"No, no. I'm sorry to have bothered you." She forced a light lilt to her tone—yet the words came out strained. "Another time, perhaps."

"Now's the time." Cold metal poked her in the back. "This way. And keep yer yap shut or it won't go well for you."

Prodded along by the muzzle of the gun, he nudged her, step by step, over to the men. She desperately tried to make eye contact with those filing past her, headed toward town. None of them glanced at her, all too busy laughing and talking of women and drink. Several other men swung their legs over the gunwales of their rowboats and set off toward the ship. They'd be no help. Only a few yet picked their way down the cliff face, wooden frames hefted over their shoulders.

A short, red-haired man—Mr. Pickens—was the first to set foot from rocks to beach. He passed off his load to another man, then faced his partner. "What you got there, Blackie?"

"Hold up, girl," the voice at her back growled. "This one's sniffin' around for Nutbrown."

A grin rippled across the shorter man's face. "Then let's take her to him."

Her stomach heaved. Clearly wherever Mr. Nutbrown was couldn't be good.

A wad of spit hit the sand behind her. "Pleasant as it would be, the deed would take too much time. I say we tie her up and leave her."

"That eats time as well, and this is the last o' it." Mr. Pickens hitched his thumb over his shoulder at the remaining four men edging down the rock trail. "I say we kill her and be done with it. Dead men—or women—don't talk."

Her heart slammed against her ribs, and she searched desperately for escape.

Behind her, Mr. Blackie laughed, the coarseness shredding away the last of her courage. Would she die on this strip of beach, surrounded by thieves and murderers? What of Mam? Of Thomas? Why hadn't she gone for Alex?

Another gun behind her clicked.

"That be a waste of a pretty face—and an even prettier amount o' gold." The voice was altogether too familiar.

Her gaze snapped to the man whose boots pounded toward them from the rock face. Mr. Quail's eyes peered out from beneath a mop of dark, curly hair. Her mouth hung open. Behind him, the rest of his band dropped to the beach from the rocks like so many beetles falling off a rotted log, each one hefting lumber on their shoulders.

"What ye jawin' about, Que?" Mr. Pickens flicked sweat from his brow—the movement so sudden she flinched.

Mr. Quail flashed her a smile as he answered. "I say we sell her along with this shipment. Those fancy French gents pay a fine price for the novelty of an English maid."

Alex shifted in the saddle. Thatcher would've thrived on this part of his mission, tearing across the countryside like a crazed stallion on a running jag, but not him. He was better at nabbing thieves on foot. At least after the last swap of horses, Coburn had finally relented and slowed their pace, for they'd made good time. They'd be at Ramsgate by nightfall. He shifted back the other way. After a full day of riding, his backside would appreciate it.

The breakneck pace had given them little opportunity for any conversation—which was good and bad. It gave little time for Coburn to speak of tomorrow's wedding, but allowed for way too much rein on his own thoughts. And they always turned to Johanna. To her welling tears. The betrayal sagging her shoulders. The sharp edge of her voice when she'd told him to go away.

Enough! There was nothing to be done for it now. He glanced over at Lord Coburn, riding beside him. Better to poke a bear than wrestle with monstrous memories. "We're nearly to Ramsgate. No one's around. Now's as good a time as any to tell me what this little venture is really about. I'll find out soon enough anyway."

From beneath the brim of a dockhand's flat cap, Coburn's grey eyes studied him. "We aren't there yet."

"If I were going to harm you or your enterprise—whatever it may be—I'd surely have done so by now."

Coburn faced forward again, the late afternoon sun bathing his profile in brilliant light. "It's not you I'm worried about."

"Then who?"

"I don't know." He sighed. "But I have a feeling someone, somewhere, is gunning for us—for me."

Interesting. Was it leftover guilt from his Indian affairs that left the man suspicious, or did he truly have a deadly premonition? Alex tugged down the brim of his own longshoreman cap. "I am not that man."

"No, I don't believe you are."

They rode in silence for a ways, nothing but the River Stour lapping just past the grassy ridge on the other side of the road.

"You will find out sooner rather than later, I suppose." Coburn scratched at his chin. "Several months back I received confidential intelligence from Major General Overtun."

"Our gaming partner."

Coburn grunted. "My relationship with him goes well beyond wagering. We served together, long ago, in India. But that's neither here nor there. The crux of the information is that Napoleon's planning an attack across the Channel on July fourth."

This time Alex shifted in his seat to keep from falling off. "Tomorrow?"

Coburn smiled at him. "A bit poetic, don't you think?"

More than that. Tensing, he thought aloud. "Using the remnants of their revolution to rub our noses in our loss of the Colonial uprising. But did we not fortify a few years ago and make the Channel secure?"

Coburn sucked air in through his teeth. "Of course."

Blowing out a long breath, Alex scoured every bit of information from the sparse news he knew of the situation. "Last I heard the fellow was busy with Prussia, not eyeing us."

"One can never be sure which rock a snake hides beneath, and it never hurts to be prepared. General Overtun charged me with setting up a little surprise welcome for old Boney, should he decide to visit." He tugged the reins, guiding his horse's mouth away from a tasty patch of sweet grass at the side of the road before he continued. "We are accompanying a shipment of Congreve rockets to be set up along the shore. Before the *Devil's Favourite* can attack, we simply blow him out of the water."

"Cutting it a little close, are you not? Should this not have been done yesterday?"

Coburn chuckled. "Didn't want to tip off the Frogs by showing movement too early. It will be a quick setup. Robbie is getting the frames in position now. And there are plenty of men to operate the equipment from the castle."

"But why did Overtun use you? You are no longer military."

"For that very reason. There are spies about. In a hive of men, there's increased likelihood of an informant, whereas by Overtun appointing me, there's less chance of intelligence being leaked."

"Hence your, er, *compartmentalization*, as you called it." Ducking a swarm of gnats, he urged his horse onward. "But why Ramsgate? Why not simply meet the ship in the dark of night at Dover?"

"These are notorious smuggling waters. I will relieve the captain of his duty on this last stretch of the journey, removing any temptation to sell out."

"Quite the elaborate plan."

"It took some arranging but—"

"Sh-sh." He lifted a finger to his lips and reined his horse to a stop.

"What is it?" Coburn whispered.

Narrowing his eyes, Alex studied the surroundings. On one side, the tall grass, some trees, then the river. To the other, nothing but a rolling sward. The rasp of insects started up, but other than that—hold on. There it was again. He listened with his whole body.

Laughter, coarse laughter.

He angled his head for Coburn to follow and led him off road, up to the rise of a small hillock. From that perch, a good view of the road spread out. Not far ahead, two men led two horses. . .or were the horses leading them? Hard to say for the way they staggered. At least they'd had the sense to dismount before they fell off. But were they truly in their cups?

He turned to Coburn. "That drink you offered earlier. I should like it now."

Coburn's mount blew out a snort, apparently as offset as his rider. Coburn said nothing, but slowly reached in his pocket and pulled out a silver flask.

Alex snatched it from him and poured most of it down the inside of his collar, dousing it on like a lady might bathe in rosewater. Then he pointed at the trees opposite them by the riverside. "Take cover down there."

Coburn scowled. "If you're this concerned, simply shoot those villains now and be done with it. It's your duty as a loyalist and why I brought you along."

He gritted his teeth. Sure, a crack sharpshooter could do such a thing. But not him. Persuasion was his best weapon. "You brought me along for protection, not murder. It's likely nothing but a few drunkards got ahold of some nappy ale, but it never hurts to check. Wait down there, and I'll be back."

Coburn locked gazes with him, the steel in his grey eyes sparking, but then he clicked his tongue and rode off.

Alex gripped the flask in one hand and the reins in the other, riding haphazardly as if he were the one who'd swigged one too many bottles. Humming an old bawdy song, he neared the two men, taking stock of their assets. Two horses, strong muscled, far too expensive for the likes of itinerant drinkers, a Brown Bess strapped onto each. Military guns for this ilk? The men dropped their leads and fanned out onto the road, watching his approach. Neither swayed nor laughed—instant sobriety.

He tipped back his head and drained the remaining drops in the flask, taking care they saw the action but not a flash of silver. He made a show of shaking it, then tucked it away and slid from his horse. "Afternoon mates." He drew close, reeling on his feet. "Got a few drops to spare fer a fellow traveller? Appears I'm out."

The shorter man with a broad nose sniffed the air. "Nab off, ye drunken cully."

"Just need me a sip, boys." He stumbled around, reaching out a hand as if to keep him from tipping over, and slapped one of their horse's in the flank. The mount moved ahead, as did the other. He grinned at the men. "I'm powerful thirsty. Just shared my last bit with a gent a ways back."

"A gent you say?" The other man's voice was strangely high pitched, as if he'd been punched in the throat one too many times. "Well, well, we be looking for a particular gentleman. About yea high," the man lifted his hand to Coburn's height, "and walks with a crooked gait. A fancy gent, nice clothes and all. Is that the man you seen?"

Quite an accurate description of the viscount—almost as if they expected Coburn to be travelling this very road. Alex grinned. Judging by the looks of them, that's exactly what they were up to.

"Not a bit of it." He forced a belch then pounded his fist against his chest. "The fellow what I saw were bow-legged and chin high to a grasshopper, so short was he."

"Well then," the fellow lifted the barrel of his gun. "Like my friend said, be on yer way."

He faked a hiccup, then swiped his mouth and held up his hands. "Ay now, no harm. I'm off."

He lurched around, giving the fellow enough time to lower his guard, then swung back around with a kick to the man's arm. Bone cracked. The gun dropped. The bullet went wild. Horses took off, and before the other fellow could draw his pistol, Alex aimed two guns at him. "Disarm. Now!"

The man's eyes turned to slits, but at least he complied. The other man wailed, holding on to his useless arm.

"Turn around, friends. We're going for a little walk—uh-uh! Hands in the air, gentlemen." He waited until three arms reached, for the broken one would never be so flexible. "That's it. Now head to the river."

They set off, the tall grass breaking beneath their boots. Clearing the downward slope, they stopped at a jutting drop where, over time, water had cut a deep gullet into the curve.

"Jump," Alex ordered.

"Ye daft? I can't swim!" the shorter man shouted.

"Then you'll learn. Off you go." He shot one of the guns just over their heads.

Both men jumped.

He retraced his route to the road and collected the dropped weapons, all the while scanning should there be any more assailants about. His mount had taken off, so he'd have to hoof back to where he'd left the viscount.

Keeping to the cover of the tall grass, he dashed ahead, hoping Coburn would be gracious enough to share his mount. But as he approached the stand of trees where he'd ordered the viscount to wait, that hope fizzled and a new fear kindled. There was no horse and no man. Had the villains he'd dispatched been nothing but a ruse to lure him away from Coburn?

He retreated to the road and crouched, examining the ground for clues. Hoof divots headed into the grass, then about five paces over, headed out, along with quite a kicked up bit of gravel. Some kind of skirmish happened here—and just might again, for something thundered up the road.

Straight for him.

CHAPTER THIRTY-ONE

With each pull of the oars, the shore slipped farther away. Once again Johanna considered heaving herself overboard, but with the rope cutting into her wrists behind her back, she'd sink. Still, a watery death might be preferable. Who knew what the seven men on this boat—or the rest of the scoundrels on the ship they rowed toward—might have in mind. So she stared at the water sloshing at her feet, refusing to look forward or back.

Mr. Quail and his men did the rowing, and with each jerk of the boat through the surf, she cursed him for the villain he truly was. Alex had been right to distrust the man—and she never should've trusted Alex. A scream welled in her throat, already hoarse from pleading and bargaining. Why had she let either of those rogues stay at the inn on that ill-fated May day?

The rowing stopped. The boat bobbed. Johanna lifted her face, then was sorry for it, for a spray of salt water hit her in the eyes. She blinked, trying to work it away, the sting sprouting fresh tears.

"The woman were yer idea, Que." Mr. Cooper's voice rumbled from the bow like kicked gravel. He tossed something to Mr. Quail, or Que, or whoever he was. "Hoist her up and haul her below."

Rising, Mr. Quail held on to the thrown object, but did not pocket it. "I do the work, I expect a cut o' the profits."

"Oh? A businessman, are ye?" The red-headed Mr. Pickens glanced back at Mr. Cooper. "We know what to do with those, aye?"

Their laughter chilled Johanna more thoroughly than her damp gown and wet feet.

Without a word, Mr. Quail stuffed the item into his pocket. Then he grabbed her around the waist, lifted her up, and slung her over his shoulder like a sack of unwanted kittens to be thrown into the sea.

She squirmed, but his grip tightened as he straddled the center thwart.

Her face mashed into his broad back, his topcoat as wet as her gown.

"Be still," he warned. "Or we'll both take a dive."

She hung there, balanced between a grave of the deep and a ship full of miscreants, jostling on the shoulder of a man who smelled of sweat and danger. The rowboat bobbed smaller and smaller beneath her as Mr. Quail began climbing a rope ladder, rung by rung. She'd known fear, for Tanny had taught her well, but never anything like this. The shakes trembling through her were unstoppable. No one would help her—no one could. She was alone in this. Horribly, dreadfully deserted.

By the time Mr. Quail lugged her over the gunwale and stood her on her feet, even the afternoon sun abandoned her as it ducked behind a cloud. Men moved about like spiders, creeping in the sudden shade, setting sails and coiling ropes. The silence in which they all worked shivered down her back.

Mr. Quail grabbed her arm. "This way."

She wrenched from his grasp.

He yanked her back.

"I knew you were involved with smugglers." Her words came as fast as the trip of her feet. "I should've turned you in."

He dragged her toward a door. "Good thing for you that you didn't."

"No wonder your music was so awful." It was a churlish thing to say and wouldn't do her a bit of good, but it felt like a small victory.

Without a word, he dragged her down a set of narrow stairs to a corridor below. When her feet hit the bottom, he released her and swung about to face her.

Suddenly she wished for the brightness of the deck, for the lantern light down here emphasized the sharp angles on his face. Her throat closed. When had he grown to be so large? She'd always compared him to Alex, but here, standing solitary before him, he stood at least a head taller than her.

He advanced, and she pressed her back against the wall.

"Listen," he whispered.

She bit her lip to keep it from quivering. Why did he not shout? Or rage? She knew what to do with a man's anger, but this? All the unknowns twisted her belly as sickening as the sudden cant of the ship.

"I've not time to—"

"What's this?" A man stinking of ale and strong cheese stumbled off the last stair. "What ye got there, a little lacey?" He peered over Mr. Quail's shoulder, his black eyes fixed on her. "Oh, a dainty nibble, I'd say. You a mind to share?"

Quail wheeled about. His big back blocked her, and she was glad to not have to face the venom in his voice. "This one's mine. Shove off."

The man scuttled down the corridor like a rat.

Quail turned back to her. "Come on."

He didn't grab her this time, he just pivoted and strode down the narrow passage in the opposite direction of the other man. She stood for a moment, debating on making a run up the stairs and a dive overboard. But the thudding of her heart indicted her for a fool. She'd never make it across the deck—and the tromp of boots coming back down the corridor signaled the return of the other fellow.

She hurried after Mr. Quail.

He stopped in front of a door and swung it open, indicating for her to enter with the tip of his head.

She edged past him, expecting what, she had no idea—but not this. Something dark and furry whisked across the floor just ahead of her. She spun. Were her hands not tied behind her back, she'd drop to her knees and throw her arms around his legs. "Mr. Quail, don't do this. Please, let me go."

Thin light from the corridor lantern lit only half his face, moving over the strong lines of his jaw and straight edge of his nose. "This will soon be over. For your own sake, Miss Langley, stay quiet. I will return."

The door slammed. A key jiggled in a lock. Mr. Quail's footsteps faded.

Johanna stood still, too frightened to move or even think, for it would feed the panic begging release. Blackness so thick it breathed closed over her. So she counted. Numbers. One after the other. Anything to distract her from what she'd first seen when she'd entered the room. But time and again, the scratch of claws scurrying across wood forced her to start back at zero. When her skirt hem riffled from the nose of an inquisitive rat, she abandoned her counting as she'd been abandoned—

And screamed.

∞

Alex dove into the undergrowth at the side of the road, dropping the rest of the guns he'd picked up and loading his own. Better to face an enemy with an old friend in his grip. By the sound of it, two horses neared, so he kept the other guns within reach and flattened belly down in the grass. Timing was his truest asset.

He sweated at the approach and held his breath when the horse drew even. As soon as the second horse passed, he shot to his feet and aimed his muzzle at the back of—

"Lord Coburn?" He gaped.

Heart pounding, Alex released the hammer and lowered his pistol. The viscount had no idea how close he'd come to death at the hand of the man he'd brought along to protect him.

Coburn swung his horse around, Alex's mount following, tethered to his saddle. "Lose something?"

Alex heaved a sigh while retrieving the rest of his weapons and his horse. "I thought I told you to stay put."

"I did—until your mount barreled past me. I figured you'd be needing it." He nodded to where Alex shoved the guns into a pack lashed to his saddle. "Looks like you gained a few new trinkets."

"Found 'em lying on the road. Imagine that."

"And their owners?"

With a smirk, he hove into the saddle, eager to be on the move instead of sitting ducks. "It's a good afternoon for a swim, don't you think? And a ride. Shall we?"

Side by side, they rode the rest of the way to Ramsgate unmolested. He'd kept a vigilant eye the whole way, but didn't detect any more threats. It would be harder now, though. As they neared the harbour, night fell hard. A half-moon peeked out from clouds, shyly, sporadically, like a scullery maid sneaking glimpses of a stable hand out in the yard.

The viscount took the lead, and when he dismounted, Alex did as well. As Coburn swerved into a narrow lane, Alex took the opportunity to cock open one of his pistols, covering their rear. Years in London's rookeries had taught him well.

They walked the horses down a narrow passage between two buildings. The stink of waste—both of man and beast—hung thick and heavy. Good thing it was too dark to see what his boots strode through. Eventually they came to an opening, surrounded by broken crates and a few overturned barrels missing staves, all sitting on a stone walkway. Water lapped at the other side of it. Across the bay, moored at the nearest dock, was an East

Indiaman—but by the looks of it, it wouldn't be there for long. A towboat was even now being attached, readying to haul her out to sea.

Coburn shook his head. "Something's not right."

Alex clutched his gun grip tighter. "How do you know?"

"Captain Fielding was to meet me here." The viscount yanked out his pocket watch, scowled, then shoved it back. "We were to swap clothes, the men onboard that ship"—he aimed a finger across the bay—"being none the wiser."

Alex snorted. "Surely you don't sound the same as the captain."

"No need. Fielding gave the crew express orders the rest of the voyage was to be completely silent and dark. Once he returned—or rather I did—they were to set sail."

"Are we too early? Too late?"

"No." The viscount's voice tightened. "Right on time. I've made sure of it."

"Well," Alex blew out a breath. "The ship's obviously still there, but not for long."

"Then we board her before she sails." The viscount pulled out his gun.

Alex planted his feet on the slick stones. "I don't like it."

"There's nothing for it, man. We must. *I* must! It's of national importance."

"What—?"

"There's no time to explain." The viscount's gaze burned deep into Alex's eyes. "Are you the man I've credited you as, or not?"

Alex hesitated, as uneasy about accompanying Coburn into an unknown situation as he was about trying to haul the viscount against his will back to safety. Either way was a risk. . .but which stakes were the best bet?

"Give me a moment." He slipped back to remove the extra guns from the horse's pack and tucked them into his belt—a mite uncomfortable, but far better than taking a bullet for being unprepared.

He and the viscount secured the horses, then worked their way along the stone walkway and across the edge of the shingle to the jetty, where the ship was docked. Each step of the way ratcheted his heartbeat up a notch.

Before the viscount could set foot off the beach, Alex tugged him back by the sleeve. "Pocket your gun but keep it handy. Hide your face in the shadows as much as you can, but walk with a purpose. Sometimes swagger can save your life."

Just then the moon peered out, casting a milky light on Coburn's scowl.

"No wonder you took so much of my money at the table."

Alex bypassed the man and strode down the dock, gaze darting from the sailor untying mooring ropes, to another up near the gunwale, coiling them up. The gangplank remained against the dock for now, but once that sailor finished his task, it would be drawn up. Alex increased his pace.

The viscount's footsteps followed. The sailor looked them over as their feet hit the gangplank. Without slowing, Alex tipped his flat cap at him, and for a heartbeat, he held his breath. But thanks to Coburn's forethought, their longshoreman clothing made them blend in. They navigated the plank without a remark.

The deck was a ghost ship, with inky specters working in silence, save for the scraping of ropes and clanking of tackle as the men prepared to raise sails once the ship was towed out to sea. Danger lurked here, but where exactly? Alex exchanged a glance with the viscount. His face was unreadable in the dark. Well then, why not meet it head-on? Alex stalked toward the quarterdeck, where the captain was sure to be—until a woman's voice stopped him.

"Father?"

Alex turned. The viscount stood where he'd left him, facing a short man with curves like a lady—and the voice of Louisa. No wonder she'd blended in with the sailors, for she was dressed as one. Robbie was nowhere to be seen, and unless he was busy below deck, that left only one plausible conclusion. . .

Louisa was the traitor all along.

Alex crept to the mainmast, flattening against it not only to watch the spectacle, but also to gauge the precise moment to nab her. He shouldn't be surprised, really, that a shipment of rockets was to be offered over to England's arch enemy by the hand of a woman—for had not Eden fallen in the same manner? Suddenly Ford's directive to ally himself with Louisa via a betrothal made complete sense.

"Louisa!" Coburn's voice shook. "What are you doing here?"

Louisa pulled up in front of her father. "The real question is what are *you* doing here, Father? But no matter, not now at any rate. There's a scheme in motion that for once is not of your conniving—one you cannot control. In fact, it's too late for you to change anything. Far too late."

And it was. For all of them. The sailors had already heaved in the gangplank. The ship freed from the jetty, and the deck rocked beneath Alex's feet.

"For God's sake, Louisa," Coburn's voice roared. "What do you think you're about?"

Louisa fisted her hands on her hips, the stance of a gamecock set to kill. "You shouldn't have come. You will have to be put overboard."

"What on earth are you babbling about?"

"How does that feel, Father, to not know what shall happen next? To not comprehend the actions and commands of those around you." She stepped closer to the man, her words gaining in speed. "To have no say whatsoever in what your future might be."

If she meant to cow the man, she'd gone about it the wrong way, for he straightened to a ramrod. "I don't know how you found out I'd be here tonight, but I do know this—your little tantrum has gone beyond bounds, even for you. What was it you hoped to accomplish?"

"Ask all you like, but you will have no answers."

"Looks like I have mine, though." Pulling his gun, Alex strode from the shadow of the mast, aiming the muzzle at the viscount's daughter. "Louisa Coburn, I arrest you in the name of the Crown."

Coburn pivoted. "What's this?"

"I knew it!" Louisa growled, quite the brave act at the other end of a pistol. "I knew you weren't who you appeared to be, Mr. Morton. But there's no crime in elopement. On what charges could you possibly arrest me?"

A sickening feeling twisted his gut. Had he been wrong in his assessment?

But no. . .a woman like Louisa would say anything to gain the upper hand. He cocked open the hammer of his gun. No sense letting the little vixen try to slip her way past him. "You are charged with conspiracy. It took some untangling, but it looks like I've finally found the real traitor."

Another hammer clicked open, just behind his head.

"Are you sure about that, Alex, ol' boy?"

CHAPTER THIRTY-TWO

Alex froze, body stiff with a gun at his back, but his mind took off running. Robbie stood behind him—though he should've been in Dover loading frames. Judging by the wide eyes of the viscount in front of Alex, Coburn was just as surprised to see his nephew here. Only Louisa appeared at ease, gracefully balancing on the deck as the towboat began to row them out of the harbour. Robbie must've paid the captain well to dare such treachery.

"Drop the gun, Morton." Robbie's voice cut the air, a sharp contrast to the relative silence of the sailors scrambling up ratlines and securing ropes.

Releasing the hammer, Alex let the pistol fall to the deck, the clank of it as loud as a shot. No worry, though. Two more guns dug into the tender skin of his waist beneath his coat.

"Good chap. Now, turn slowly, hands in the air."

Alex pivoted. Robbie's smirk was that of a man holding a set of aces.

"Line up with the old man there." Robbie tipped his head, moonlight slicing his face in half. "But keep your distance. You two have held hands long enough."

"For pity's sake, Robert." Disgust coloured the viscount's tone to an ugly darkness. "Lower your weapon. As usual, you've fouled up everything."

"Shut up." Robbie pulled the trigger.

The bullet tore through the viscount's arm. He crashed to his knees, clutching the wound. He didn't howl, but his breathing chopped out in draws and huffs.

"Father!" Louisa dropped beside him. "Robbie, stop it! Are you mad? This ship is full of gunpowder. One wrong shot and we all go up in flames. Just put them overboard and be done with it."

He pulled out another gun. "It's not that easy, love."

Louisa couldn't see Robbie's face as she ripped the hem of her shirt to create a makeshift bandage. But Alex didn't miss the pleasure shining in the whites of the man's eyes.

"The way is never easy for a traitor," Alex murmured.

Robbie shook his head. "I'm no traitor, just an opportunist. As are you, Morton. What's the matter? Did I not supply a sufficient sum in that envelope I sent you? Or were you somehow angling to get more from the old man?"

"Dash it!" The viscount scowled up at Alex, the pain of his wound—or maybe the way Louisa held his arm out to bind it—evident in the stilted movement.

"Really, Uncle, Morton's not worth that much passion. He was merely a pawn in this game of mine, necessary for only a short while."

"You have no idea what you're doing." The viscount's words travelled thick and slow in a strained voice. "Because of you, England now faces an attack."

Robbie chuckled. "Calm down, old man. There's no real threat—not yet, anyway. That was merely a seed I planted in the head of Overtun during a rather exclusive round of cards."

"To what purpose?" The viscount strangled a cry as Louisa tucked in the ends of the bandage.

Alex watched Robbie with hawk-like intensity, looking for an opening. Any opening. But the man kept his gaze pinging between his uncle and Alex.

"Money." Robbie shrugged. "It's always about money, is it not?"

"You. . .you sold out. . .to whom?" It was hard to tell which robbed the viscount's breath more—Robbie's treachery or Louisa's somewhat rough handling to help him to his feet. He wobbled for a moment, then growled, "And why?"

"You should know, Uncle. You've chided me for it often enough. I have no loyalty to a country that saw fit to humiliate, brand, and rob me of everything."

"You deserved that cashiering." The viscount's indictment was as salty as the air.

"I don't deny I deserted, but it was quite by accident. An opportunity arose—it simply took more time than I thought it would to cut the deal." His eyes narrowed. "As you would've known if you'd ever taken the time to listen to me."

Alex studied Robbie's face by threadbare moonlight. Something wasn't right about his story. "There's more to it than that, isn't there?"

"See?" Robbie flashed him a grin, the whites of his teeth skeletal in the dark. "That's what I've liked about you from the start, ol' boy. Ever so keen. You're right, of course. There was also the trifling matter of disorderly conduct unbefitting an officer. Aah, but fleecing that colonel still makes me smile."

"I don't think you'll be smiling when you hang for this," Alex said. The eerie snap of a rising sail magnified his threat.

"They'll have to catch me first, and judging by the looks of things, that'll take quite some doing."

Alex's gaze drifted. He should've noticed before what a minimal crew ran this vessel. Were the viscount not wounded, they maybe would've had a chance at taking charge.

He flicked his stare back to Robbie. "And what of the viscount and me?"

"That is a problem." The moon disappeared, pulling all light from Robbie's face. "I suppose I shall leave you in the hands of my associates once we land."

Alex shook his head. "You know what Leaguers will do to us."

"A pity, that. Good faro players are so scarce."

The viscount swore. Beside him, Louisa didn't so much as gasp. Though why should she? Dressed in men's garments and no stranger to her father's outbursts, it should come as no surprise the lady didn't display ladylike sensibilities. She merely stood, propping up her father with a hold on his good arm.

"*La ligue la liberté!*" The viscount swore again. "You're selling out to the French?"

"The French will pay a premium for a shipment of rockets and frames," Robbie explained. "Enough to fund my travels around the world."

"You mean to India." Louisa let go of her father's arm and stepped toward Robbie.

"Eventually," he said.

"*Eventually?*" The word flamed out of her mouth like a cannonball. She stopped, halfway between her father and her lover. "That was not part of our deal."

Alex rocked back on his heels. Good. This he could use. If he could get Robbie to focus more on Louisa and less on him, he'd have the space of a breath to pull out one of the pistols beneath his coat.

"Tell her, Robbie. Tell her all. You have no intention of going to India and never did. Once a leaguer, a leaguer for life. You are no longer a free man, but a puppet, with failing revolutionaries holding the strings. Miss Coburn"—he shot her a half-smile—"how did you think Robbie, a court-martialed soldier living off his uncle's charity, managed to give you French perfume, that Cross of Lorraine pendant that is even now surely hot against your collarbone, or supply champagne to a viscount's entire household?"

She looked from him to Robbie, face pale in the night. "What does he mean?"

"Don't panic, love." Robbie spoke as to a child. Bad mistake. She'd pick up on it, and it would fuel her rage.

Alex stifled a grin.

"Just a few more obligations, Louisa, and then—"

"Your obligation is to me!"

"Of course, but—"

And there it was. Robbie turned his face toward Louisa.

Alex pulled a gun, cocking the hammer wide open. "Drop *your* weapon, Mr. Coburn."

Robbie jerked his gaze back to Alex.

And behind them all, the hammers of four more guns clicked, followed by a raspy voice. "Drop yours as well, Mr. Morton."

☙❧

Seven hundred twenty-nine. Seven hundred thirty. Seven hun—

Something warm probed Johanna's toes, just at the tips. But it would move from there. She'd learned the pattern, thanks to the wisdom she'd gained from Alex and a stubborn barn door.

"Assess the situation first. The easiest way to manage a difficulty is to think before acting."

Squeezing the fabric of the gown she bunched in her hands at her back—for she'd also learned the unpleasantness of having a rat trapped between her legs and skirt hem—she waited. Let the nose sniff, the tentative paw poke. Wait for curiosity to throw abandon to the wind, heft a furry body up onto the top of her foot, and—

She kicked with all her strength, then immediately started counting again. Better to focus on numbers than the thwack of the rat's body hitting a crate. Judging by how many times she'd done this, at least an hour, probably more, had passed. Curse that Mr. Quail!

Falling back into a rhythm, she escaped the dark hopelessness threatening to strangle her. There was comfort in counting. Soothing, predictable. . . she stiffened. An off-beat thud of boots scattered her numbers like blown dandelion seeds.

A key scraped in the lock, and the door swung inward. Light flooded inside, not brilliant, just a yellow glow slanting in from a lantern on the corridor wall. Even so, she blinked.

"Told you I'd be back. I. . ." Mr. Quail stopped just inside the threshold, eyes fixed on the floor. "What the devil?"

She followed his gaze. Three furry bodies lay unmoving, long tails a tangle. She frowned. Only three? Surely she'd kicked more rats than that—which meant they'd only return to torment her again.

She scowled up at Mr. Quail. "How dare you leave me in here."

Without a word, he set down the mug he carried and pulled a knife from a sheath strapped to his belt.

Johanna retreated until her back smacked up against a tower of crates. Hands yet lashed together, she'd be no match for the man—and likely wouldn't be even if she were free and held her own blade. "What do you intend? You won't get away with this. Please, Mr. Quail!"

Her breath came so fast, little sparkles dotted her vision.

He grabbed hold of her and spun her around. Two tugs and a yank later, the bindings on her wrists dropped to the floor. She whirled, ready to pummel him if he touched her.

"I am sorry for this, truly." Stepping back, Mr. Quail tucked away his knife and ran a hand through his hair, then breathed out a curse. "I will see you safely to shore."

She rubbed the ache in her arms, which helped some, though it did nothing to remove the pain of what was to come. "I suppose damaged goods will not draw as fair a price once we land in France."

"What?" His dark hair hung low over his eyes, yet no need to see, for the confusion in his voice spoke volumes.

But what did he not understand?

His chin lifted, and he shook his head. "No, Miss Langley. I will not see you sold. That was only an excuse to keep them from killing you."

Her hands fell to her sides, the urge to return to her counting strong.

Numbers made sense. Mr. Quail's words did not.

"Why spare me?" she asked—then wished she hadn't. The answer might be worse than rodents crawling over her feet.

He said nothing, just crossed back to the door and retrieved a cup. "Here, drink this."

Her throat tightened. Thirst waged war with her brain, telling her not to accept what might be poisoned. She tested the liquid with her tongue. Tepid. Smelling of nothing other than the damp wood of the mug.

She drained the cup dry. Better to die here than face a life of degradation at the hands of unknown men.

"Better?" Mr. Quail took the cup from her.

She peered at him, his dark curls framing an even darker face lost in the shadows. "Who are you? Really?"

"I suppose, circumstances considered, I owe you an explanation." He pivoted and, with some effort, turned two crates on their sides. He sat on one, and swept his hand over to the other. From this angle, light bathed him like an archangel. "My name is Clarkwell, Miss Langley. Henry Clarkwell. I am a revenue officer, as are the rest of the members of my band."

Slowly, she sank onto the crate. His information, while outlandish, rang true, somewhat. "I knew you weren't musicians," she murmured.

"And it was very gracious of you to allow us lodging despite our shortcomings. You will be compensated, but you must understand that while we were in Dover, we had to remain in character—as we must continue to do until we land."

"What is this all about, Mr. Quai—I mean, Mr. Clarkwell?" The name felt foreign on her tongue—but no more strange than conversing in a storage closet with rats at her feet.

Mr. Quail–Clarkwell leaned forward, dangling the empty cup between his knees. "I came to Dover to uncover and break up a guinea gang. Are you aware of such activity?"

"I know smuggling of all sorts is common."

"Well this sort is the very worst, other than wrecking, that is. It's no secret that gold is in short supply—and in great demand across the Channel. Opportunists ship our guineas over to the French, who pay a premium, trading in lace, silks, and other luxuries. I thought I'd embedded myself in with just such a gang." His words slowed, and for a moment he said nothing.

"Turns out, it's far more treacherous."

Something in his voice shivered—or maybe it was she who quivered. She folded her hands in her lap, gripping her own fingers for support. "What is it?"

Reaching for her, he patted her knotted fingers. "Don't worry yourself, Miss Langley. I sent for reinforcements yesterday. As I've said, this will all soon be over." He stood and offered his hand. "Come, let's find you a better place to hide and leave the rats to their foraging."

She stared at his outstretched fingers. Calloused. Nails bitten off. Strong and unflinching and determined. Should she trust this man? Was this a trick? She lowered her face, and her gaze landed on one of the rat carcasses splayed on the floor. Some choice.

She put her hand in his and allowed him to lead her out the door.

"Que!" His name was belted out from down the passage. "Where ye be?" Boots thudded closer.

"Blast!" Mr. Quail huffed out a curse and shoved her back into the storage room.

"No, not again." She tried to hold on to his hand, but his fingers wrenched from hers.

"Sorry." He slammed the door, leaving her in the dark.

Leaving her with the rats.

CHAPTER THIRTY-THREE

How many rats were on this ship? Closing the hammer, Alex dropped his gun to the deck, as bid by the growling voice at his back. Robbie did the same. Along with the viscount and Louisa, they all turned to face Major General William Overtun. Three soldiers stood at his side, aiming guns their way. So did the general. How many more layers of subterfuge could there possibly be?

"Overtun?" The viscount stepped toward him, relief bleeding from his voice as fluid as that from the wound on his arm. "Thank God for putting a stop to this. . ." His words dripped to a stop, and his feet froze. "But why are you here? What's gone wrong?"

Overtun shrugged, and Alex flinched. One wrong move with that loaded pistol in his hand could mean someone's corpse on the deck.

"Other than a few anomalies—namely the entourage you seem to be travelling with," the general swept out his free hand, "nothing is amiss. The plan is running along as expected."

Clutching his wounded arm, the viscount swayed. "But you were never to be connected in any way with this mission."

"I believe your nephew stated it more plainly than I ever could. What was it you said, Robbie? Aah, yes, you, and all of you now, I suppose, are 'merely pawns in this game of mine, necessary for only a short while.'" A full grin slashed across the general's face. "Tell me, Robbie, are you certain it was you who planted the seed of an impending invasion during that card game you and I played—or was it *I* who did the planting?" He shook his head, his upper lip curling. "You should've done as your uncle said and stayed with the frames in Dover, boy. But you were never one to follow an order, were you? Nor were you, Edward."

The major speared the viscount with a deadly stare, one that even in the dark gleamed with the threat of murder. "You should've finished the job the rajah sent you on, hmm?"

The viscount staggered back to Louisa's side. "Good heavens, Overtun! Surely you don't mean—"

"Of course I mean it! I've meant to do this since that day years ago when your treachery took the life of my sister and her family in Siswapur. I watched them die. I barely escaped!"

Alex sucked in a breath. The viscount had been right about his past sins, but had the man expected the incubus would manifest here? Tonight?

Overtun widened his stance. "I was merely waiting for the best opportunity to take your life *and* your honor forever. But apparently, I'll be taking your family as well. Goodbye, Edward."

A flash of spark, the sharp crack of a small explosion, and a bullet whizzed through the air. The viscount flew backward, his head split apart before he hit the deck.

Louisa screamed and dropped to his side.

Alex tensed, ready to drop when the soldiers decided to let loose their fire.

The general turned his face to his men, his thick lips opening to give the order—

"Stop!" Robbie shouted, his hands reaching for the sky. "We had nothing to do with the old man's treachery."

Overtun cut a glance to Robbie. "True, but you've seen me now. I can't very well lay the blame on your uncle for this stolen shipment of rockets with you three to say otherwise." He turned back to the soldiers. "On my mark—"

"I can get you more money than you can imagine!" Robbie's voice tightened to a shrewish tone, competing with the wailing of Louisa.

The general's big chest expanded, then he blew out a breath and held up his hand to his soldiers. "I'm listening."

"The frames for these rockets are no longer in Dover. I hired a crew to smuggle them off. That ship is to rendezvous here within the hour. My league contact is paying top dollar, likely more than yours, and expects both rockets *and* frames."

"I should've marked you as a leaguer." Overtun chuckled. "How much?"

"Two thousand guineas."

Alex's brows rose as high as Robbie's hands. That was quite a sum. No wonder the traitor had paid him such a whopping amount to keep the viscount distracted.

"Hmm." The general scratched his jaw. "All right. We'll see if your story is true and wait out the hour. But we won't be needing the others."

"Don't be so hasty, Overtun." Alex lifted his hands as well. "I can beat his deal." Sweat beaded on his brow. *Think! Think!* What could he possibly offer?

The moon broke out again, highlighting the general's thick lips. "You know, Morton, you've been a wild card since the day I met you. What's your bid?"

"Double that."

"How?"

He swallowed. How to make this plausible without being an outright lie? "It's true that France will pay a generous amount, but the Prussians will pay even more. I have connections—unless I'm dead."

"Well, well. . .quite the high-stakes game we've got going, eh? Just like old times."

Overtun turned to the soldier nearest him.

Alex froze, his heartbeat hinging on the general's next words. Around them, sailors crawled up and down the ratlines as if on deck men's lives were of no account. Louisa's sobbing added to the madness. Surely perdition could be no more horrific than this.

"Take them below, Jonesy. One wrong move, shoot them." Overtun pried a pocket watch from his waistcoat and snapped it open. "You've got an hour, Robbie. If those frames show up, we'll sell them to your accomplices. More poetic if the viscount is blamed with a sale to the French." He snapped the lid shut and stuffed it back. "But if not, I'll go with Mr. Morton's offer."

One of the soldiers stalked out from the rest, the muzzle of his gun urging them to move. The gawky man appeared to be sixteen or perhaps seventeen. A youth, at any rate—with hopefully not much fighting experience. That could be an asset, one Alex tucked away as securely as the last gun that yet remained beneath his coat.

Alex reached for Louisa's arm to haul her up.

"Not the woman," Overtun growled. "Louisa stays here."

She lifted her face to Alex, her wide eyes staring into his, helpless and pleading. "Help me."

"I'll come for you," he whispered.

"Move it!"

The cold jab of a pistol barrel stabbed him in the back. He stumbled forward, catching up to Robbie near the stairs. As they marched down, tripping in the only light from a lantern at the base of the hold, a gunshot rang out.

Alex's gut jerked. The villain! All of them! Coburn. Robbie. Overtun. As scheming as Louisa was, she'd not deserved such an end. He hesitated on the last stair, trying desperately to assess the situation.

But a kick to his backside sent him sprawling ahead.

"Have a seat, boys," Jonesy ordered.

Alex used the momentum of the kick to yank out his pistol and whip around.

The soldier's eyes widened. So did Robbie's.

"Think, Jonesy." Alex spoke low and calm. "Do you really want a gunfight down here, with a hold full of rockets and gunpowder? Put your weapon down."

Jonesy's jaw dropped. His gun didn't. Did the fellow know his threat was empty—that it would take more than a gunshot to fire off this load?

"If you shoot me, you'll have no time to reload before Robbie here takes you out." Alex tipped his head toward Robbie, who lowered into a crouch, ready to spring. "Let it go, Jonesy, nice and easy."

The young man's Adam's apple bobbed, a grotesque movement in the lantern light. But he did as bid, and squatted to lay down his gun.

The second his fingers let go, Alex lunged. He drove his gun grip into the man's skull. Now it was Jonesy's turn to sprawl. Alex scooped up the soldier's gun and swung around to face Robbie.

"Nice work, ol' boy!" Robbie flashed him a smile and held out his hand. "Give me one."

Alex grinned back. "Sure."

Once again he lunged, this time clouting Robbie in the head. Robbie hit the planks as hard as Jonesy.

Tucking the pistols back into his belt, Alex sidestepped the fallen men and reached for the lantern. The light hung over a barrel of water just in case the thing chanced a fall. Best to assess the situation first, then act, though he wouldn't have much time.

Above deck, a madman reigned with no compunction about shooting on a whim. And down here? Alex strode deeper into the hold, along the center aisle. Big bales wrapped in canvas lined both sides. He frowned. Rockets wouldn't be bundled in naught but fabric and rope.

He set down the lantern and slipped out his boot knife, then cut one of the bindings and sliced into the fabric. His blade dug deep and stuck into a bale of cotton.

Cotton?

What lunacy was this? Had the whole rocket scam been nothing but that—a scam? Had someone double-crossed the double-crosser, or was a triple-cross at play? He yanked out his knife, baffled. This was beyond his reckoning.

His gaze shot to the dark rafters above, and he prayed, for there was naught more to do. "So many lives are at risk, God. The stakes are too high, and I—I—"

His prayer juddered to a stop. So much anguish choked him he could hardly breathe—a feeling eerily like when he'd rotted in the gaol's hole...and yet God had been there, as He was now.

He gasped, lungs suddenly filling. What a thick-headed dolt. Had he not learned that already? "Of course, God." He smiled. "You are here, so help me. I cannot do this on my own."

Blowing out a long breath, he cracked his neck, waiting for some kind of wisdom. None came. Nothing but the purl of the water against the hull. The purl of the water. . . If rows of thick cotton lined this hold, he'd not be able to hear that so clearly.

He pulled down the bale he'd cut open, then hauled out the one below it, creating an opening. Retrieving the lantern, he held it aloft. Golden light landed on the slats of crates. Stacks of them, by the looks of it. Once again he set down the lantern, then worked to probe a crate between the slats. His blade tip first met straw, then snubbed onto metal. Rockets. He'd bet his life on it—and just might.

Backing out of the passage, he snagged his light along the way. Someone had gone to much trouble to hide the crates behind a wall of cotton, probably as a front on the off-chance of an impromptu dockside check. Not that it mattered now. He had to stop these rockets from landing in enemy hands— and the cotton was going to do just that.

Bale upon bale, slice upon slice, he yanked and grabbed and spread a trail of loose cotton from one end of the aisle to the other, the length of the hull. Sweat trickled between his shoulder blades. His hands cramped and his lungs labored. But he worked like a demon, unstoppable—until a grunt ended his crazed dance. Either Jonesy or Robbie would soon be sounding an alarm.

He snatched the lantern and lifted the glass, then touched a piece of cotton to the flame and threw it on the loosened tinder. He repeated the action, working his way back toward the stairs, toward the men. By the time he reached them, flames licked at the bales—and would soon hit the crates.

And the rockets.

Robbie sat up, dazed, moaning, holding his head.

"Time to go," Alex hauled him up.

"Wha. . . ?" It might've been a question. Or another moan. Hard to tell

Alex shoved him toward the stairs. "Move it, man!"

Robbie started stumbling upward. Alex grabbed a pail and dipped it into the bucket. Hefting the pail, he dumped the water on Jonesy, who immediately sputtered and choked, coming to with great gasps.

Alex threw the lantern toward the inferno then darted up the stairs after Robbie.

Up top, Robbie bent over the bodies on the deck. Louisa's crumpled form heaped atop her father, closer in death than they ever were in life. The sight twisted Alex's gut.

"Fire!" Sailors broke into a dead run toward them—toward the stairway.

Alex grabbed Robbie's arm and dragged him to the gunwale. They both peered over, Alex judging the best place to land. Black water licked up the sides far below them.

Robbie turned to him, the whites of his eyes wide. "I can't swim!"

Alex growled. Did no one consider swimming a skill to be learned?

"Over there!" Overtun's raspy voice hit him in the back.

Alex grabbed Robbie's arm. "There's no time. Hold on to me."

Without giving the man a moment to consider, Alex swung over the rail and tugged Robbie down into the sea.

The coldness sucked his breath.

The darkness was worse.

Alex kicked, struggling to break the surface. Robbie was a dead weight. *God, please!*

His head emerged from black into black, but at least there was air. He sucked in until his lungs burned. So did Robbie, every time he bobbed up long enough to snatch a breath.

"Kick your feet, man!"

An eternity later, they worked out a rhythm—though Robbie refused to let go of his stranglehold on Alex's arm. It was impossible to see the shore, despite the eerie light of spreading flames behind them. Hopefully Robbie was right about that rendezvousing ship of his and it would arrive soon. Alex strained all his muscles into plowing through the waves.

Putting as much distance as he could between themselves and the rockets that would soon explode.

∽

Forget the counting. It wasn't working anyway. Neither was fear or worrying about how Mam was suffering on her behalf—for surely Thomas had told her by now of how she'd gone to look for Mr. Nutbrown. Johanna curled her fingers into fists. There had to be a way to get off this ship of demons. She'd waited long enough for Mr. Quail-Clarkwell to rescue her—if he were even telling the truth.

But what to do? Maybe, if she were able to pry off a lid from one of the crates, or even a single slat, she could whack whoever next entered the door right in the head, then make a run for it. Jumping into the sea was a better option than wallowing in this dark hole.

Feeling about, she set to work. What seemed like hours later, she'd broken three fingernails, and so many splinters needled her flesh, she felt like a human pincushion. But the pain finally paid off, and she worked loose a piece of the wood.

There wasn't much room to practice swinging. More often than not, she smacked her elbow. One time her sleeve caught on a nail and ripped the fabric. Her hair stuck in her eyes and her stays chafed her skin. But she managed to figure out that a chopping motion, slicing downward from high over her head, was the most suitable action. Now, to judge how far to stand from the door.

She crept across the small space, taking care to avoid the earlier rats she'd downed, one hand out to feel for the wood—then stopped.

And listened.

One explosion. Two, three, four. Fives and tens and twenties. Popping, hammering, like the bang of fireworks she'd heard the one time she'd visited London. She clutched her slat, driving splinters deeper into her fingers. These were not fireworks, not on the sea, which could only mean one thing.

The ship was under attack.

Panic tasted like vinegar. No! She had to get out of here. Now.

She sprang ahead, dropping her pathetic weapon. With both hands, she beat against the wooden door. "Let me out—"

The door jiggled in the frame. She paused, hands yet upraised.

A locked door wouldn't jiggle.

She swung the door open wide. Light barreled in from the lantern in the corridor. For a heartbeat, she stood frozen.

Really God? All this time I could've walked free?

Stunning, truly, but no more than the inner voice that answered her back.

Is that not a picture of your life, child?

She gasped. God did have everything in hand—and always had, even when she ran ahead of Him or lagged behind, trying to do things her own way.

"Forgive me," she whispered, tucking the truth away to savor later—then snatched up her jagged piece of crate-wood. After all, if God went through the trouble of opening the door, she probably should go through it.

CHAPTER THIRTY-FOUR

S harp pain cut into Alex's arm, each tug on the rope agony, but he held. Thank God he held. Robbie clung to him like a woman. They both banged against the hull of the newly arrived ship. Just a few more pulls and they'd clear the gunwale—if his shoulder didn't dislocate before then.

The swim had been brutal, but a far cry better than remaining on the ship behind him. Or what was left of it. The last of the rockets exploded. An eerie orange light violated the darkness. Flashes of red shot out intermittently. How many men had made it off? How many hadn't?

Deliver them, God—and us as well.

A groan ripped out his throat as a last, mighty heave lugged them over the wooden rail. He and Robbie hit the deck like landed mackerels. Wincing, Alex stumbled to his feet. A hank of wet hair fell over his brow, dripping salt water into his eyes. The sting was terrific. Blinking, he shook his head like a dog.

"Well, this is a surprise."

He froze, then stared into a swarthy face, hellish in the fiery glow. Quail. The irony of being saved by a smuggler punched him in the gut, yet a half smile twitched his lips. "I knew you were scum from the moment I met you."

"What a coincidence. I thought as much of you. This is going to be a real pleasure." Quail nodded to his band—smugglers all—lining up beside him. Every one of them pulled a gun from inside their coats, yet none raised their muzzles. A quiet threat, but a threat nonetheless.

"Thanks, ol' boy." On the other side of Alex, Robbie staggered to his feet, then clouted him on the arm—his sore one. "We might be out a load of money, but we're safe."

He smirked. This was safe? Facing six men with guns at their sides?

"What'd ye haul up there, Que? Turn 'em around. Nice and slow."

Throbbing started behind Alex's eyes. The voice, altogether too familiar with its bass bluster, stabbed him in the back. There was *nothing* safe about this.

He and Robbie pivoted. Alex planted his feet.

But Robbie strode over to Blackie and Axe. "Good job, men. I'll take it from here."

Alex sucked in a breath. If luck smiled on him, the remnants of fire on the sinking ship behind him would be bright enough to blind Blackie from seeing his face.

But the villain stood there, leaning on his good leg, riding the canting deck like a sea monster come aboard—and the longer he stared, the wider his eyes opened. So did the red-headed scoundrel a head shorter next to him.

Blackie pulled a pistol. "Well, well, there is a God after all. Look what the deeps spit up." A chuckle rumbled in his throat, garbly and altogether mirthless.

"We been gunnin' fer you a while now." Charlie pulled the axe out of his belt. "But ne'er thought to look in the sea."

Robbie glowered at them both. "Put those weapons down. This man just saved my life."

"And he'll take it as fast." Charlie hefted his axe.

"I'm in charge here. Drop your weapons!" Robbie's voice bellowed, dark and deadly—a surprising tone, coming from the dandy of a man. . .or was he?

Alex scanned the immediate area, scrambling to find an out. Behind him was Quail and his men. That was a no go. In front, sure death. To his sides, cannons lined the decks. If he dove for the cover of one, who would shoot him first—Blackie or Quail?

Blackie belched out a curse at Robbie. "Idiot! You got no idea who you been keepin' company with." His black eyes shifted to Alex. "Tell him."

Despite the cold, wet clothing sticking to his body like a second skin, sweat beaded on his brow. Once his identity was revealed, there'd be no mercy. A lawman's blood was a prize. A trophy. A crown of glory to the criminal that drew it first.

He clamped his jaw shut.

Robbie swung his head toward him. "Do you know these men?"

He breathed in until his lungs burned. What a question. He'd been in sticky situations before, but this one? This just might be his last.

His gaze darted from Robbie to the gun in Blackie's hand, then on to the axe in Charlie's. A sour taste swelled at the back of his throat, one he knew too well. Regret. All his life he'd fought to be the best runner of the squad. To make Ford proud. And now? He swallowed hard. He'd end up the same as his father, gunned down by vermin.

Robbie angled his head in a jerky movement, grotesque actually, as if he were coming unhinged. "Answer me! Do you know these men?"

He sucked in a breath, desperately scrambling for a way to talk himself out of this. Absolutely nothing came to mind. . .except for four small words. *No risk, no gain.*

The sentiment he'd spoken forever ago to Johanna barreled back in his mind with startling clarity. Of course the biggest risk was telling the truth. It always was. His whole body pulsed with the rightness of it. He *would* take the biggest risk of all, and while he might still lose, he would not be gunned down without a fight. If this was his day to die, then so be it.

He threw back his shoulders. "Let's just say this is quite the reunion."

Blackie narrowed his eyes. "One I been waitin' on fer too long, Moore."

"Moore?" His name was a blasphemy on Robbie's lips.

"That there's Alexander Moore, Bow Street Runner." Charlie spit on the deck. "Liar. Scammer. And killer."

Despite the black of night, Robbie's face darkened. "Is that true?"

Alex grunted. "Some of it."

"Which part?" The tip of Quail's muzzle jabbed him in the back.

He threw back his shoulders. He might as well go out with bravado. "Axe is right. I am a Bow Street Runner, and you, gentlemen, are all under arrest."

Robbie swore.

Blackie laughed—then sighted along the barrel of his gun.

Charlie hefted his axe, poised to throw.

Behind Alex, the click of six guns was a sound eerily reminiscent of the last ship he'd been on—and that hadn't ended so well.

But then his entire world shifted onto its axis, draining his blood to his feet. Across the deck, a dark figure in a skirt scurried into his line of sight, face pale, hair loose, eyes cavernous.

God, no!

∞

Hiking her skirts, Johanna took the stairs two at a time, her prayers as fervent as her pace. Whatever was happening above deck couldn't be good. The popping explosions grew louder. Men's angry shouts interspersed between the blasts. She clutched her gown tight in one hand, and in her other, the crude club she'd wrested from the crate. If she could make it the short distance across deck to the railing without being accosted, she stood a good chance of jumping overboard—though her odds of swimming to shore were in God's hands. But then, hadn't He just shown her that was the best place to be? She ramped up her prayers and burst through the open door into night.

Or into hell, more like it.

Wicked red light bled onto a macabre scene. Beyond their ship, eruptions of fire shot into the sky from a vessel lying sideways, soon to be swallowed by the sea. Thank God it wasn't cannon fire she'd heard. But with or without artillery, that ship was going down and no doubt taking men with it. Her heart constricted at the thought of the sailors about to lose their lives, whoever they were.

No time to lament now, though. She darted onward, eyes straining to pick out the best route to the rail that would avoid the sight of the men on deck. And the guns. Sweet heavens! So many guns. Was every last man armed and ready to shoot? But why? They were clearly not under attack.

By some miracle, the route to the railing was clear. No one focused on her, for they were all too busy looking at a poor wretch who stood at the center of their attention. All muzzles aimed at the man's guts. But he didn't seem to care a fig. His broad shoulders were thrown back, feet wide, the stance of a warrior about to wage battle. Either he was addle-brained or beyond reason.

Paces from the railing, though, Johanna stopped. Freedom beckoned—but so did the niggling suspicion creeping from her head to heart. Surely, she was wrong.

But she had to be sure.

Slowly, she retreated, craning her neck for a better view of the man. When her gaze landed on him, an invisible tether lifted his face to hers.

Time stopped, as did life and breath. Men in back. Men in front. All hefted weapons. All aimed at Alex.

Her scalp prickled. Her arms. Her soul. Despite the way he'd taken her heart and thrown it back into her face, she couldn't stand here and watch him die, because she'd die too. Such was the love that throbbed in her veins.

"Alex!" It was more a scream than a name, one that competed with the boom of an explosion.

He didn't move, not even as the air vibrated with the last blast from the dying ship. But he saw her just the same. The dark of his eyes slipped ever so slowly to the left, back at her, then to the left again. Commanding. Pleading.

She bit her lip. Even without looking she knew exactly what he asked. The stairs. He wanted her below deck. It was a good idea, and she took a tentative step toward them—then stopped. Was this how it'd been for Mr. Nutbrown? Had he faced death alone, perhaps a needless death because of the inaction of a fearful bystander? How could she hide away and let Alex die without doing something?

Yet what could she—a simple girl with a stick—do against men with guns?

She clenched her piece of wood tighter, the rough grain cutting into the tender parts of her palm. *Assess. Assess.* Repeating the words in her head, she matched her breathing to the rhythm until her heart rate slowed.

Between Alex and the railing stood a line of men. Unruly hair curled out from beneath the hat of the central figure, tall of stature, less burly than Alex, but just as familiar. Mr. Quail-Clarkwell. If the man truly was a revenue officer, he wouldn't harm Alex. Unless he still believed Alex to be a smuggler. But being a lawman, as long as Alex didn't threaten him, the man wouldn't shoot him. . .would he?

She snapped her gaze to the men in front of Alex. There were only three. A dandy of a fellow, who appeared to be unarmed, the axe-wielding Mr. Pickens, and the gun-toting Mr. Cooper—and who knew when that villain would let loose. Behind those three, near the opposite railing, seven others stood with guns raised as well.

Her shoulders sank. The situation was beyond her salvation—but that didn't mean she couldn't try. Perhaps if she got Mr. Cooper's attention, for even the space of a breath, maybe Alex could use it to his advantage.

She crept forward.

Just as five more men emerged out of the hatch from below. She grit her teeth. Wonderful. More guns.

"Stop!" Mr. Quail-Clarkwell's command boomed.

Johanna froze. So did everyone else. Was he speaking to her or to the others?

"As the man said, you're all under arrest." Mr. Quail-Clarkwell and the rest of his men stepped abreast of Alex.

She blinked. Surely she wasn't seeing this, but. . . apparently she'd been wrong. Very wrong. Mr. Quail-Clarkwell and his men hadn't been aiming at Alex, but at the three others in front of him. No wonder Mr. Cooper hadn't pulled his trigger yet.

"If you're lying, Moore, you're a dead man." Mr. Quail-Clarkwell handed Alex one of his guns.

Moore? Johanna angled her head.

So did Alex—a movement she'd learned from living with him the past month that meant he was confused yet still determined to be in charge. He grabbed the pistol, his gaze once again meeting hers, this time with a visible twitch of his head toward the stairs.

Then he extended his arm and aimed the barrel at Mr. Cooper. "You should've shot me while you had the chance."

Grating laughter rumbled out the man's mouth. "Night's not over yet."

"It is for you. Drop your gun."

To her left, near the railing, a man crept toward her, closing in fast. Without thinking, she whaled the board at him.

And missed.

He roared.

A nightmare unleashed. Popping, smoking, curses and hollers exploded. Something hot whizzed past her cheek, grazing a line of fire across the skin.

Was it too late to reach the stairs?

CHAPTER THIRTY-FIVE

One bullet. Just one. Alex crouched behind a cannon, shots pinging off the metal. Smoky haze distorted the scene. Blasts of red dotted the night. Rising slightly, he waited, assessing, judging where best to place his one shot. Thank God Johanna had disappeared below deck. Beside him, Quail reloaded. Why the devil had the man jumped sides?

Burnt gunpowder stung his nose. So did the thick odor of spilled blood. Around the deck, men dropped like swatted blackflies. Except for one man, crouching low, who duck-walked his way toward the quarterdeck. Alex knew his short shape well. He aimed his gun at Robbie's lower half and fired, hoping for a wound, not a kill—just as a bullet whizzed past his own head. He dropped behind the cannon.

The popping died out. Quail and his men reloaded once again. Likely the other side did too. Alex used the lull to rise up and evaluate how many were left. Bodies were strewn about, not the one he'd shot at, but another snagged his attention at center deck. Blackie sprawled in a dark pool, his wooden leg splintered off mid-calf. He didn't move.

Next to Alex, Quail raised his gun.

Alex flung out his arm. "Hold. Look."

Across the deck, smugglers were in various stages of throwing down guns and flinging themselves overboard—and one of them had red hair.

"Grab some rope," Alex ordered, then bolted and grasped the man. Squeezing a mite tighter than necessary, he kept Axe in a chokehold until Quail brought the rope.

Breathing hard, he straightened. Charlie yet struggled at his feet, but he wouldn't be going anywhere—except to gaol.

Around him, Quail's men seized fleeing smugglers. Some slipped their clutches, but most they nabbed and tied up.

"You know your business." Quail clouted Alex on the back. "Looks like you really are a runner."

He snorted, swiping the sweat from his brow with his still-wet sleeve. "And you? Who are you, really?"

Quail's eyes found his, and for the first time, no hint of foolery or scheming glowed in their depths. "The name's Henry Clarkwell, revenue officer, sent to ferret out a guinea gang operating out of Dover." He scanned the deck. "Looks like I stumbled onto something bigger."

"That you did. Sedition, which is why I'm here, though I'm currently missing my traitor." Alex darted his gaze around the ship. No Robbie. Had he missed his mark?

"Come on." Alex sprinted over to where Robbie should've been, then followed a gruesome path. The bloody trail ended at the rear of the ship, portside gunwale, where a few men wrestled with ropes and a ferrying skiff, just about to lower it over the side. Only one man stood inactive, grasping on to the railing to keep from falling over. A dark stain spread from his knee to his foot.

Alex pulled his gun. "Stop right there. Step away from the boat."

A bluff, for he had no ammunition. Would Robbie and his few minions fold, or did they have a last ace to play?

No matter. Clarkwell and his men caught up, fanning out on both sides of him, weapons drawn. He'd never expected a miracle of such magnitude in the guise of bad musicians, and he stifled a laugh. Indeed, God surely did have a sense of humor.

"Deserting again, Robbie?" Alex smirked. Judging by the twitch on Robbie's jaw, the question struck sharper than a well-aimed right hook. "I'd have thought you'd learned your lesson by now."

Robbie unraveled quite a string of profanity as he sank to the deck.

For the first time in weeks, the tension in Alex's shoulders loosened. He lowered his pistol and glanced at Clarkwell. "Can you and your men manage these few without me?"

"I may not play the violin with finesse, Moore, but I do know my way around smugglers." Clarkwell flashed him a grin. "Go. Tend to Miss Langley, for I have no doubt you'll not rest easy until you do."

Shoving the gun in his waistband, Alex turned and sprinted back to the stairs. He took them two at a time, nearly missing the last, but landed on solid footing nonetheless. Lanterns lit a corridor, and halfway down one of them, a lone figure in a gown huddled on the planks.

His step faltered. As much as he wanted to gather her in his arms, she might not wish to be held. Not by him. Especially not when he told her all—for he must. He knew that now. It was time he revealed who he really was, laid bare his soul before her, and risked either her gain or loss, for such was the ultimate power of truth.

Oh, God, go before me. I cannot endure the thought of losing her.

He strode ahead, driven by grim determination, and gripped her by the shoulders, pulling her upward. "Johanna?"

She lifted her face to his, and he staggered back a step. She held a cloth to her cheek.

Soaked with blood.

∞

She'd lived a hundred years this day. Or more. By the looks of it, Alex had too. Silently, Johanna studied him in the dim light. His wet shirt clung to his muscles, alluring, but judging by the bend of his shoulders, he was worn as thin as her. Hair clung to half his face, darkened to burnt honey from seawater and sweat, all snarled and wild. Smoky residue smudged his jaw. Creases at the edges of his eyes disappeared as his gaze narrowed, focusing on her.

"You're hurt." Pain raged in his voice, as if he'd been the one grazed by a bullet.

Slowly, he pulled her hand from her cheek. With a touch infinitely tender, he angled her chin and bent to examine the wound. He smelled of the sea and gunpowder, of salt and man. An awful scent—yet marvelous, for it meant he lived. He breathed. He was here.

For a second, she closed her eyes and whispered, "Thank You, God."

"Indeed," Alex echoed, then he released her and ripped off a strip from the hem of his shirt.

She stood, dazed, too spent to move or even care.

"This is going to sting, but it will help in the long run." His eyes held her gentle, then his voice broke. "I'm sorry."

He pressed the cold, saltwater fabric to her face.

She sucked in air, fighting to shove down a scream. Her cheek burned like a thousand beestings. Tears bled from the sides of her eyes, and she clenched her hands to fists. Merciful stars! That hurt.

Through it all, he held on, applying firm pressure. He said nothing, but a strange, strangled groan rumbled in his throat.

Finally, the pain began to ebb. She unclenched her hands and breathed easier. Maybe—just maybe—this nightmare had come to an end.

"Is it over?" Her voice came out choppy. She cleared her throat and started again. "I mean up there." She lifted her gaze to the rafters, then back to his. "No one's trying to shoot you anymore?"

"No, leastwise not this bunch." His lips curved, a bitter smile, but a smile nonetheless. "What are you doing here? Why are you not safe at home?"

She blinked. How did one explain what'd happened over the space of a hundred years? So much. Too much. "Long story," she murmured. "The short of it is Mr. Cooper wanted to kill me, but Mr. Quail, er, Clarkwell talked him out of it."

Alex shook his head, the damp straggles of his hair brushing against his collar. "I really do owe that man a debt."

Despite the pull on her cheek, she frowned. Why would a gentleman of Alex's wealth and stature owe a revenue man anything? For that matter, what was he doing here instead of courting his betrothed? "I don't understand any of this. What have you to do with the law? Why are you even here?"

His breath huffed out, warm against her brow. "In your own words, it's a long story. The short of it is I'm not who you think I am. I am a Bow Street officer, a lawman, just like Clarkwell, though here for different purposes. I was sent to uncover a plot against the Crown." He tucked his chin, much the same as Thomas when caught in a mischief. "My true name is Alexander Moore."

"Moore?" She tasted the name, rolling it around in her mouth, unsure if she liked the flavor or ought to spit it out. "Not Morton."

"That's right."

The knowledge lodged in her mind like an unwanted guest—one she desperately wanted to evict. He'd lied. Alex had lied. To her. The realization pricked worse than her cheek.

She leaned back against the wall, grateful for the support. How many lies had her mother heard from her father's mouth? Memories surfaced, one after the other, as black as the water keeping them afloat. So many arguments. So many tears.

"Only going out for a bit, lovey. Back in a trice."

"I swear I don't know where the rent money could've gone, sweetling."

"No, of course I'd not gamble away our future, darlin'."

Johanna moaned as a horrid understanding spread from her heart to her head. She'd done exactly what she'd vowed never to do—fall in love with a deceiver. A beautiful, handsome deceiver. What a fool. Just like her mother. Bitterness nearly choked her.

She reached to pull his hand from her face. "Then you are not a wine merchant, either."

"No." His arm was steel. "Please, allow me to hold this a minute more."

She clawed at his sleeve, desperate to get away from his touch. "I suppose you're not a gambler, either, or a rake or a rogue?"

He held firm, but his voice softened. "To my shame, those things are true."

So, a gambler *and* a deceiver. She had almost reconciled herself to his gaming, but now lying, too? Her anger flared, and she scowled. "Who are you, really, Mr. Moore?"

A tremor travelled up his arm, trembling his fingers against her cheek. "I'm just a man, Johanna. A sinful man, but one who loves you very much."

He leaned close, closer, a breath away. Surely he didn't mean to—

His mouth claimed hers, and to her horror, she pressed against his wet, solid body. Traitor! She was the deceiver, telling herself she'd never love a man like. . .

Her thoughts, her anger, her everything drifted away on a rising swell of sweet warmth. An ache, not unpleasant and altogether enticing, settled low in her belly. His lips were a whisper, a balm, one with hers—and yet ought not be.

She pulled away, breathless, hating herself for having enjoyed such a forbidden fruit. What was she thinking? Even if he were who he said he was, that didn't change the fact of his engagement. She pushed his hand away, and this time he let her, his brow weighted with an unnamed sorrow.

"Johanna," his voice was a sea of pain. "I lied to you, and for that I am eternally sorry. I thought it necessary because of a sense of misplaced duty, but I know now that my one and only duty is to God first, man second. It is much to ask, but I do. . . I beg your forgiveness for my deception, for so it was. Even though I did so for the sake of an order, that doesn't change the fact that it was wrong. That *I* was wrong."

She froze, unable to move or breathe or think. What was she to do with an apology of such proportion? She'd been right all along, that he was like her father—but then again, not at all. Her father lied, too, but he'd never once admitted he was wrong or that what he did was wrong. He always had an excuse, a reason, a crutch. This level of integrity in a man was wholly unnerving—and completely irresistible.

"Johanna?"

Alex's voice pulled her to the present, and she stared at a face she'd never forget, even if she tried. "Though my pardon pales in light of God's, I freely give it, for how can I do any less?"

He pulled her close again. Aah, but she could live here, hearing his heart beat strong against her cheek, wrapped in his arms and—she pulled back. Those arms were not hers to claim. "We should not do this. You are to be married."

"No, I am not."

She frowned, the pull on her cheek a slicing burn. What was she to believe? A fine whine sounded in her head, so high-pitched she winced.

He sighed, and Atlas himself couldn't have sounded more burdened. "Forgive my bluntness, but Louisa is dead."

"What?" She gasped. Would the macabre surprises never stop? "Oh, Alex. I am so sorry for you. How you must feel."

Refolding the square of fabric, he pressed it into her hand. She stared at it, afraid to read the emotion, the grief, that surely must be weighting his brow.

"The truth is, Johanna, that I never had feelings for Miss Coburn, despite my pledge of troth. I tried several times to tell you I'd been ordered to marry her, but. . .well, the point is I overstepped the line. I gambled the one thing I couldn't afford to lose—you. And that is a risk I don't plan to ever take again. My heart has been yours since the day you fell into my arms. Whatever you believe of me, believe this. . ."

He grew silent, and she lifted her gaze to his. Such a burning fervency blazed in the blue of his eyes, a charge ran through her from head to toe.

"I will come for you once this situation is over. I vow it. Wait for me. Only me. Will you?" His fingers reached for her, but a whisper away from making contact, he pulled back, then retreated a step, giving her space. Giving her time, for he stood there, saying nothing more.

But every muscle beneath his wet clothes hardened to sharp edges.

If nothing else, she knew then she held his life in her hands. His heart. His happiness. And hers, depending upon what she said. She swallowed, afraid to speak. Afraid not to. Afraid of the wild beating of her heart and the thrumming in her temples. Had it been the same for Mam?

She bit her lip. First Alex had been a gentleman, too far above her station to notice her—but he wasn't, not really. Then he was engaged—but by compulsion.

And now? He pledged his love to her—a door opened by God alone, for she'd not done a thing to earn or encourage it. Should she risk walking through it? Was the gain, Alexander Moore, worth it despite his deceptive past?

She lifted the cloth to her cheek, the hurt as painful as the years her next words might employ, and met his gaze. "I will never stop waiting for you."

And she wouldn't. She would keep her word.

But would Alex?

CHAPTER THIRTY-SIX

Johanna leaned her head against the wall, eyes closed, where she sat in the public room of the Ramsgate Arms. This early in the morning, the inn was just beginning to stir. A pot banged in the kitchen. The stairs creaked with shuffled steps. She really ought to use this opportunity to study the workings of this inn to compare it to the Blue Hedge, see if there was anything she could improve upon, but she was beyond exhausted. After a night of danger and love, her priorities had focused to more important things. . .like simply breathing.

A small nudge to her shoulder popped her eyelids open.

"Excuse me, miss." Mr. Wigman, the Arms proprietor, stared at her with hound dog eyes and a snout as long as a beagle's. "I let you rest as long as possible, but the coach is ready to leave."

"Thank you, Mr. Wigman." She rose, fighting back a yawn. Her cheek ached enough as it was. "Has Mr. Moore arrived?"

Speaking Alex's true surname woke her more effectively than Mr. Wigman's earlier nudge. It felt strange to think of him so.

He shook his head. "Sorry, miss."

"Very well. Thank you for allowing me to wait here."

"Don't thank me, miss. Thank your Mr. Moore when next you see him. He paid more than a fair amount for you to wait here till the coach arrived and paid your fare to boot." Mr. Wigman dipped his head. "Safe travels, Miss Langley."

The innkeeper darted off to the kitchen, where another pot banged. A small smile quirked her lips, glad she didn't have to deal with the noise. Some poor cook would likely feel the wrath of Mr. Wigman this morning.

But her smile faded as she stepped out into the July sunshine and scouted the Arms' courtyard. At center stood a coach—dust-worn and as travel weary as surely she must look—with a coachman opening the door and lowering the stoop for a couple ready to board. But those were the only figures moving about. A blue-eyed, broad-shouldered Alex was nowhere to be seen.

Disappointment stole what little vigor Johanna had left, and her steps dragged over to the waiting coach. She'd wanted to hear his voice before parting, feel the strength of standing near him one more time, pretend her aching cheek and night of horror had never happened and this was just an outing to be enjoyed.

The coachman stood ready to assist her up the step, when a deep voice boomed behind her.

"Hold up!"

She turned. Alex trotted across the courtyard, bedraggled yet all the more handsome for it. She smiled in full, despite the stinging burn on her cheek.

He nodded at the coachman. "I'll help the lady."

"As you wish, but secure the door behind her. I'm running late enough as is." The coachman turned on his heel.

Yet Johanna couldn't manufacture any interest in the man's movements, for the only man she cared about stood real and warm in front of her. "I was hoping you'd come before I left," she breathed out.

"And I was hoping I'd make it. Arranging transport to London for a traitor and myself was harder than I thought it would be. Granted, the hour didn't make it any easier." He bent, studying her face. "How are you faring?"

"I'm fine. Some of Mam's famous salve and I'll be right as a thruppence in no time. Thank you for all you've done—"

The coachman blew his whistle, cutting off her last word.

Alex shoved back a wild fall of hair from his brow, taken in flight by a morning breeze. "I'll come for you as soon as I'm able. In the meantime, go to the Rose Inn. My belongings are still in room three. There's a wooden chair near the window. Turn it over and you'll find an envelope of money I secured to the bottom of the seat. Take it. It's yours, yours and your mother's, to pay off your debt."

She opened her mouth. "But you've already done so much, I can't—"

His finger pressed against her lips, warm and firm. "No buts, understood? Now off with you. I have a criminal to haul to London."

He grabbed hold of her hand and lent his strength as she mounted the stair.

She turned before he could leave, a sudden desire to leap out of the coach and into his arms rising up from her heart. Despite his promises of last night, what if she never saw him again? Transporting a criminal was no safe thing. "Please be careful."

His gaze held her for a moment—a beautiful, glorious moment. "You as well."

Then he tucked away the stair and shut the door, securing the latch.

Ignoring the other passengers, she sat and pressed her face to the window. The coach lumbered into motion, and she watched the retreating form of the lawman, the gambler, the man that she loved.

⚭

Alex counted each *tick* of the massive clock in the office corner, the fixture as dominating as the black-suited man behind the desk. The *tick-tock*s were the only thing left to count, for he'd tired of numbering the magistrate's fingertips drumming on the desk and the varied shouts and hoots outside on Bow Street. Every passing minute in London was one less spent with Johanna. It seemed a lifetime ago that he'd boarded her on that coach in Ramsgate and sent her away to the Blue Hedge, though in truth it'd been less than a week. Aah, but he couldn't wait to hold her in his arms again.

He shifted in his chair, the slight movement drawing the steel-grey eyes of Richard Ford.

Leaning forward, the magistrate planted his elbows on the desk and tented his fingers. "That's quite the tale. I suppose I shouldn't be surprised at the outcome, though I'd have bet my money on the traitor being Louisa Coburn, not Overtun."

"First bets are most often lost, until you learn the playing habits of your opponent." Alex shook his head. "I only wish I'd seen it sooner for the sake of the viscount and his daughter. It's a shame Overtun won't stand trial for their murders."

"He got what he deserved." Ford sniffed. "I'd say it was a very fitting end for him."

A bitter taste filled his mouth as he recalled Clarkwell's report from his revenue reinforcements. Quite a few bodies had washed ashore—leastwise those that had jumped ship, Major General Overtun's among them. The rest lay buried in Davy Jones' Locker, likely burned beyond recognition from the rocket explosions. Alex nodded absently. "At least Robbie shall receive his just reward."

"And likely already has. You know he won't last on a hulk, not with that deserter brand on his back. He'll be lucky to live until trial."

"No doubt." Deserter or not, few survived the horrors of a prison hulk, especially a military vessel. Alex rubbed the tightness at the back of his neck. If the other prisoners didn't get to Robbie, typhoid or some other disease likely would.

"Come now, so morose?" Ford slapped his hands on the mahogany, and Alex jumped. "It was a job well done. I knew you'd pull it off. Congratulations. What you did was no small thing. England is a safer place because of you, and you are a far sight richer."

"Thank you, sir." He sighed. "But it was by God's grace alone I managed it."

"What's this? A new humility in Alexander Moore?" Ford's brows jerked to nearly meet his shorn hairline. "This mission accomplished more than I'd hoped for."

In spite of himself, he chuckled. The magistrate could have no idea all that had changed inside of him.

"Now then, for your next assignment—"

Alex shot up his hand. "With all due respect, sir, there won't be a next."

He stood and reached inside his dress coat. His fingers wrapped around the worn handle of his tipstaff for the last time. For the space of a heartbeat, he memorized the feel of the wood against his skin. So many adventures. So much thrill and danger and justice he'd experienced with this tool. This bit of wood and metal had been an extension of his life and dreams. Was he truly ready to give it up? To cast aside his ambition of becoming the best Bow Street had to offer?

A small smile quirked his mouth. For Johanna, he'd give up the moon and stars were they his to give.

He pulled out the tipstaff and laid it on the magistrate's desk.

"Let me guess." Ford's gaze drifted from the tipstaff to him, a single grey brow arched. "Is this on account of a certain innkeeper's daughter?"

"It is." He smiled, a silly, sloppy grin but one that wouldn't be stopped. "Being the top officer no longer holds appeal. I leave on the morrow."

Ford leaned back in his chair and laced his fingers behind his head. "Hmm. That doesn't give me much time, but I suppose I can be packed by then."

Alex studied the man, but the magistrate's face could bluff even a faro champion—one as well practiced as himself. "What do you mean?"

"I should think it obvious. I'm going with you."

Ford was known for his grapeshot comments, but this one peppered him back a step. "Sir?"

"Oh, have a seat before you fall." His arms dropped to his sides, and he leaned forward in his chair. "I'm sure you have some idea as to my unfinished business in Dover. The question is *what* do you know?"

Alex sank into the chair. As much as he wanted to tie up the last of his London loose ends, this might be his opportunity for a glimpse into Ford's past life. "Mrs. Langley told me some of your story," he admitted. "But not all. I know you married another, a colonial, for the sake of duty."

"That I did. While it wasn't of my doing, nevertheless it was my fault Miss Harrington came to be with child." His right shoulder twitched slightly, the closest the man ever came to a shrug. "What else was there to do?"

The afternoon sun cut a swath of light through the Bow Street window, highlighting a faraway glaze in the magistrate's eyes. His voice lowered to a near whisper. "She died in labor. By the time I returned to England, Eliza had already married William Langley. Not that I blamed her, and I still don't. I'd always planned to rectify that situation, for I've never loved another like her. But the timing never seemed right."

Alex scratched his jaw. Each successive *tick-tock* clicked the assorted facts he'd gathered into place. "So that's why you placed me at the Blue Hedge."

A smile grew slowly, like the first sprig of grass shooting up from a wintery field, until it bloomed into a full grin. "I'd hoped it might get me a foot in the door, though I wouldn't swear to that under oath."

Alex smirked. It couldn't be helped—nor did such an insubordinate tic matter anymore, for he was no longer under the magistrate's rule.

The smirk quickly faded, though. If Ford left Bow Street, neither would the magistrate be beholden to enforcing the law, to mete out justice, to continue in a career he'd held dear above everything else. Alex swept out his hand. "You'll leave all this? Your respected position? Your cherished vocation? That's quite a risky bet for someone you've not seen in years, someone who may not have you. Mrs. Langley is not a woman easily swayed."

"True. She may not succumb to my charms. But what was it you said?" Ford sucked air in through his teeth. "Aah, yes, 'First bets are most often lost, until you learn the playing habits of your opponent.' If so, and I lose, well, then I'll just have to make a study of Eliza until I figure out a way to win her."

Alex laughed. That would be a game he'd love to watch play out. Rising from his seat, he offered his hand across the desk. "I wish you well, sir. Mrs. Langley will be a worthy opponent."

Ford gripped his hand. "Tomorrow, then."

"Yes." He turned and trotted to the door, then paused with his hand on the knob. "I leave at first light. Don't be late."

"I assure you," Ford lifted his chin, "this time nothing will keep me from Eliza."

Alex yanked open the door and stepped out into a firing line of three sets of eyeballs, all gunning for him. He eased the door shut behind him and planted his feet. "This can't be good."

"It could be, depending upon your answer." Nicholas Brentwood, the tallest of the trio, leaned back against the wall and folded his arms. His dark hair was shorter than the last time Alex had seen him, though the man's trademark shaggy ends would not be tamed even by pomade. His clean-shaven face had filled out a bit more, and his dress coat strained against his shoulders. Is this what marriage did to a man, fatten him up and style his hair?

Alex eyed him. "Good for whom?"

"Me!" Killian Flannery, the redheaded firecracker next to Brentwood, thumped a finger against his own chest. "I stand to make the most."

On the other side of Brentwood stood a dark shadow. Alex frowned at Thatcher and shook his head. "Don't tell me you're wagering with these two."

Thatcher's chin jutted out, yet he said nothing.

With a sigh, Alex turned back to Brentwood. "All right, what's the bet?"

"Thatcher here," he tipped his head toward the man, "has been telling me of a certain innkeeper's daughter down Dover way, one who can hold her own against the likes of you."

Alex hid a grin. Showing any kind of amusement would only spark a wildfire of teasing. "What of it?"

Brentwood laughed. "I say you'll be married with a babe on the way inside a year's time."

"Listen, Brentwood." Flannery pivoted to face the man. "Just because a bit o' skirt snagged you don't mean it's the same for ol' Moore. He's a man's man, he is. A sight too smart to get hooked fer life."

Brentwood snorted. "Admit it, Flannery. You're jealous. I see it every time you stop by and dandle my son on your knee or linger over dessert with me and Emily. The family life is what you want, what every man wants if he's brave enough to admit it."

"Bah!" Throwing out his hands, Flannery retreated over to Alex's side. "Tell 'em, guvner. Tell 'em you ain't about to fold."

Before Alex could speak, Brentwood's green gaze skewered him. "Am I correct? Did you give Ford your resignation?" Unfolding his arms, he stepped away from the wall and looked down his nose. "Are you not even now sweating about the collar to be off and racing back to Dover?"

Perspiration did dot his brow. Not that he'd admit it to this bunch. What on earth had Thatcher told them? He frowned at the man. "You know, for a man of few words, you certainly manage to utter the most revealing ones."

A slight smile curved Thatcher's lips, lightening the dark looks of him, yet he said nothing.

Alex turned to Flannery. "You best pay 'em up."

"Blast!" Flannery cursed his luck, his fellow officers, and something about a dog or maybe a potato—hard to tell when the passion lit up and his brogue took over. Even so, he jammed his hand into his pocket to pull out a handful of coins.

Brentwood reached out and squeezed Alex's shoulder. "Congratulations, my friend. You know you've a home whenever you're in town. Emily should be glad of a little female company for once." He frowned over at Flannery.

Alex chuckled. He'd miss this banter. He'd miss these men. "Bring your wife and boy down to Dover, Brentwood. Johanna and I shall run the finest inn in all of Kent. You're all welcome, any time."

"C'mon Flannery." Brentwood cuffed the man on the back, nudging him down the corridor. "I'll help you count out your pennies. Lord knows it'll take some muscle to pry them from your fingers."

Their voices faded down the stairs, until Alex and Thatcher stood in silence. What ought he say to the ghost in the night who'd always been there for him? For once, Alex couldn't put together two words if paid a king's ransom.

Slowly, Thatcher reached out and offered his hand. "Godspeed."

Alex gripped the man's hand, and for a moment, his throat closed. It was hard to let go, to leave behind all he'd known, especially this officer of shadow and dust. But what he was moving toward was even more alluring—something his friend here could have no understanding of. Riding the countryside was a godforsaken lonely job. Would that Thatcher might find a wife as perfect as he'd found.

"To you as well, my friend." He released his hold. "Your day will come, Thatcher. If it can happen to me, it can happen to anyone."

CHAPTER THIRTY-SEVEN

Johanna sat between Mam and Thomas, staring at the taproom door of the Blue Hedge Inn until her eyes burned. Salvation might yet waltz through it. A pack of hungry dockhands or a load of passengers from a late ferry could pile in with empty bellies and full purses. It wasn't wrong to yearn for redemption via a room full of hungry patrons. . .was it?

But all that filled the taproom was Thomas's consistent kicking of his good foot against the chair leg. Tap, tap. Tap, tap.

She sighed. Even so, it was a blessing to be alive. To hear her brother's taps instead of the awful sounds she yet heard in her dreams. Though it'd been little over a week, it seemed like forever ago when she'd been trapped inside the hold of that ship, an eternity since Alex's arms held her protected—and far too long since he'd kissed her. He said he'd come for her. But when? Oh, that it would be today. Staring at the front door, she willed a full-shouldered, tawny-headed man to cross the threshold

Tap, tap.

Pulling her gaze away, she picked at a thread on the hem of her sleeve, trying to push the thing back into the fabric with her nail. A futile endeavor, but it gave her fingers something to do. Drat the Rose Inn! Drat that Mrs. Neville, the innkeeper. The woman had been more stubborn than Tanny Needler about not letting Johanna into Alex's chambers without him being present. A good policy, laudable, even—but one that meant she'd not been able to retrieve the money Alex had hidden. Even after Mam gave Mrs. Neville a good earful, the inflexible innkeeper still wouldn't relent.

She picked more furiously. It was hard to sit here awaiting Mr. Spurge with their shortfall when the full amount was waiting in an unoccupied guest room at the Rose.

Mam reached over and laid her hand atop hers, quelling such industry.

Tap, tap.

The incessant rhythm crawled beneath her skin, and she shifted on her chair, pressing her lips shut. It wouldn't do any good to say anything. The boy was as tense as them all, waiting, wondering, wishing their entire future didn't teeter on a mere five shillings.

Then suddenly, for one blessed moment, the tapping stopped.

Thomas screwed his face up at Mam. "Tell me again why I have to sit here?"

"We will attend this meeting as a family. Your sister has shouldered the financial burden for too long, and for that I am sorry."

Mam's fingers squeezed hers before releasing her hold.

Tap, tap. Tap, ta—

She blinked. Was it her imagination, or had the door jiggled just the tiniest whit? Could just be a gust billowing in off the Channel. . .but no. The door edged open an inch now. A windy blast would've swung the wood wide, not teased it agape at such a steady pace.

"Do you see. . . ?" Her words died as a bloody, yellow-stockinged leg appeared, followed by another, both barely holding up a man who looked as if he'd fallen beneath a miller's grinding stone.

Mam gasped.

Thomas stopped tapping.

Johanna shot up and dashed over to the man. "Mr. Nutbrown?"

He collapsed against her, weighing hardly more than Thomas. Mam joined her and they both bore him up, drag-walking him over to a nearby bench.

"Thomas, bring a drink. Quickly," she called over her shoulder, then lifted the back of her hand to feel for Mr. Nutbrown's breath. Thankfully, warm air collected on her skin. "Mr. Nutbrown, can you hear me?"

His eyelids flickered open, and she drew back.

A world of pain and grief glazed his eyes. His lips moved, but no sound came out.

Her heart squeezed. No matter how eccentric the fellow was, he was still a man, one of God's creations—and a very broken one at that.

Thomas rushed in with a mug while Mam sank onto the bench next to Mr. Nutbrown and helped him guide the cup to his mouth.

While he drank, Mam eyed her. "What do you suppose happened?"

"I don't know. I'm not sure he can speak. . ."

She straightened. Of course. She'd never once heard him talk without Nixie. The smashed puppet was long gone, deposited in the dustbin over a week ago. But upstairs…

"Stay with him. I'll be right back."

She darted upstairs to Mr. Clarkwell's former chambers. Neither he nor his band had returned to claim their belongings. Perhaps he'd ride in with Alex? Hard to say. But it was a boon for now that his pile of puppeteering gear sat heaped in the corner. She snatched up the red-coated Punch and dashed back to the taproom.

Both Mam and Thomas's brows rose as she laid the puppet on Mr. Nutbrown's lap. His head dropped to his chest, gaze fixed on the offering. Slowly, carefully, he lifted one finger and stroked the length of the cape. A giant tear splashed against the felt, and he stroked that away too.

"Oh, Mr. Nutbrown." Johanna's throat closed, and she swallowed. "I am so sorry for whatever befell you."

His shimmery eyes lifted to hers. Mam patted his hand.

But he pulled away, and almost reverently, glided his bruised and scabby hand into the body of the puppet. Punch rose, not nearly as high or perky as his old friend, but enough that the little head bobbed once. "Mr. N–Nutbrown is t–tired."

The puppet flopped to his lap, and Mr. Nutbrown's head leaned back against the wall with a thump.

"Of course you are." Mam tucked her arm around him and hefted him to his feet. "You shall have a good lay down."

The puppet landed on the floor.

Mr. Nutbrown whimpered.

Snatching up Punch, Johanna offered it to him. "I think your new friend is in need of a rest as well."

A weak smile wavered on his lips. He clutched the red felt like a little boy holding on to his Mam's hand.

"I shall be right back." Mam nodded at her, then helped Mr. Nutbrown shuffle off to a room.

Before Thomas could scuttle away, Johanna wrapped her arm around his shoulders. "Come wait with me, Brother. We decided we'd face this as a family, remember?"

"Aww, Jo." Though he flapped a complaint, he allowed her to lead him back to the bench, where in no time Mam joined them once again.

"Did you find out any more?" Johanna asked.

"No. The poor man's eyes closed before his head hit the pillow."

Tap-tap. Tap-tap.

Johanna clenched her jaw to keep from reprimanding Thomas. After having witnessed Mr. Nutbrown's sorry state and with the sure-to-be drama coming from Mr. Spurge, in truth, she felt like kicking her own foot against the table leg.

Without warning, the front door banged open, and her heart sank. All the hoping and wishing for Alex to arrive had done no good. Mr. Spurge entered, reaching to remove a black top hat from his greying head. He paused and eyed them up for a moment from across the room. "The entire Langley clan? This *is* quite an event. Good morning to you all."

"Good morning, Mr. Spurge," Mam and Johanna said in unison.

Thomas tapped all the faster. "Ain't nothin' good about it."

"Thomas!" Johanna hissed.

Thankfully Mr. Spurge let the boy's remark go unanswered. He strode to their table, set his hat down, then as quickly yanked it back up. With his elbow, he bent and wiped off the area—though it was clearly spotless to begin with. Apparently satisfied, he once again set down his hat, then flipped out his coat tails and perched on a chair opposite them. "Shall we be about our business, then?"

Without a word, Mam pushed a pouch of money across the table.

Mr. Spurge's bushy brows hiked skyward. "Well, well. . .I must say I am surprised." He snatched up the bag like a dog might a shank of mutton. Hefting the pouch in one hand, he held it mid-air, jiggling it now and then.

Slowly, his brows lowered, as did the sides of his mouth. "Feels a bit light."

Thomas stopped kicking and leaned forward. "How the scag-nippity would you know that, you old spidery—"

Johanna shot out her arm and pulled Thomas to her side, crushing him against her with her hand over his mouth. "Please excuse my brother, Mr. Spurge. His leg has yet to fully heal and sometimes he's out of his head with pain."

Thomas squirmed. She held tight.

Mam leaned forward. "While the bulk of what we owe is in your hand,

Mr. Spurge, you'll find our payment short by five shillings, only five, which we will have to you by end of next week."

Mr. Spurge grunted. "Good."

Good?

Johanna's arm dropped. All the sleepless nights? The angst-filled days? She'd worn her nerves to frayed threads for nothing? Her shoulders wilted, as did Mam's. God had answered! Not as she'd expected, with the blessing of some extra coins, but with the mercy of a white-haired banker. Shame bowed her head.

Oh God, forgive me for not trusting You. Your ways are not my ways.

"Thank you, Mr. Spurge." Mam's voice floated to the heavens, and Johanna had no doubt her mother lifted her own silent prayers as well.

Mr. Spurge pushed back his chair and stood. In one hand he clutched the bag of money. With the other, he reached inside his coat and pulled out a folded document and handed it over to Mam. "You might want to reconsider that sentiment, Mrs. Langley."

Johanna stiffened.

Mam opened the paper, the crispness a brittle crack in the silence. Thomas didn't even tap as she read. Almost imperceptibly, the fine, white document started shaking.

"What is it?" Johanna's question hung like a black cloud.

Mam said nothing. She didn't have to. The creases puckering her face screamed a warning.

Johanna took the paper from her and scanned the contents. It was a legal document, dated and signed, with three names penned in impossibly perfect cursive.

Eliza Langley. Johanna Langley. Thomas Langley—

All due to report to St. Mary's by the end of the day.

Her blood turned to ice, and she shivered despite the warmth of the July morning. She dropped the awful paper and shot up from her chair, scowling into Mr. Spurge's face. "But you hold nearly the entire sum. You would send us to the workhouse over a mere five shillings?"

He clapped his hat back atop his head. "I would and I am."

"Please, Mr. Spurge, have mercy." The world turned watery, and she blinked. "Upon my word you shall have the rest of the payment by week's end. I vow it!"

"Your word, Miss Langley, while encased in very pretty housing, is null and void as far as I'm concerned. Today was the deadline. You have your papers. And I have just acquired a new property. I expect you gone within the hour."

"But we have a guest who is unable to be moved."

His brows pulled into a sharp, grey line. "Then your guest will have to find other accommodation, for this is no longer an inn." With a snap of his heels, he pivoted.

Beside her, Mam rose. "Have you no heart, sir?"

"None whatsoever, madam." His pace didn't so much as hitch.

Johanna reached for Mam, and they clung like two thin yew saplings, desperate for anchor in a storm. Thomas pushed back from his chair and plowed into them.

Mr. Spurge stopped at the open door, a black silhouette against the brilliance of day. "Oh, I forgot to mention. . .on the off-chance you were thinking of hooking up that decrepit pony cart, think again. Everything here is my property. If so much as a cracked mug is moved off-site, I'll see the three of you in Market Place Gaol instead of St. Mary's. It's a fair walk, should take you all day, so I suggest you start now." He tugged the brim of his hat. "Good day."

◌⃟

At last the road descended, leading to the town nestled between sea and land by great, white cliffs. Alex kicked his horse into a canter, zealous to reach Dover proper—until Ford caught up to him and forced him to slow.

"Ease up, man." The magistrate—*former* magistrate—frowned at him. "I'm as eager as you, but these horses are spent."

"My apologies." Alex squinted as he eyed the buildings hugging the harbor. Afternoon sun glinted bright off the bay. "We are so close."

It took all his strength to hold the reins loose, to not give in to urging his mount faster than a trot. But Ford was right. He had pushed their pace the past three days.

A fresh breeze rolled in off the Channel, carrying a fishy aroma. Likely ol' Slingsby and his crew were even now on the beach, cooking cod over a fire, plotting some new way to lighten a load of tea or rum from some poor vessel.

Alex loosened his collar, reminding himself it wasn't his job anymore to

309

hunt down criminals. Would he miss it? A definitive answer was as elusive as the thin clouds overhead, but he doubted it, not with a dark-haired, brown-eyed woman at his side. His chest squeezed. Aah, but it couldn't be soon enough until he reached Johanna.

He glanced over at Ford as they turned onto the High Street. How different it was to arrive in Dover this time, not moving fast enough to arrive at the Blue Hedge Inn. "So, what's your plan of attack with Mrs. Langley?"

"Nothing."

He arched a brow. "The great Bow Street magistrate has no strategy whatsoever?"

Ford glanced at him sideways. "I didn't say that."

Alex grunted. "You're not going to tell me."

"You never were a patient one." A chuckle shook the man's shoulders. "Oh, all right. If you must know, I intend to allow Eliza all the time she needs to pummel me, hence my doing *nothing*. But by the time I must return to London to finish up Bow Street business, I suspect my charms will have won her over." He faced Alex and winked. "We shall retire on my land up in Shropshire."

"You own land?" His brows shot skyward. "For as long as I've known you, you've lived in London."

"Never had a need for it—until now. As you know, I married an MP's daughter. Her father granted me a small piece of property in hopes we'd eventually settle there one day. Of course that never came to pass, but I still have it. Besides"—a slow grin eased the lines on Ford's face—"you don't really want me underfoot with your new bride, do you?"

"You know me far too well." And he did. Emotion clogged Alex's throat, and he faced forward. "Thank you. You didn't have to take on my provision when my father died, yet you did."

"Alex."

His name travelled on the air like an invitation, one he couldn't refuse. He turned his face back to Ford. Steely grey eyes met his.

"I'm only going to say this once, for we are not men given to sentiment. You were a fine lad and are an even finer man. Johanna Langley is a lucky woman to have you."

His eyes burned. His throat. His heart. He said nothing more, nor could he if a gun were held to the back of his head. They rode in silence the rest of the way until they finally rounded the corner to the Blue Hedge.

"Go on." Ford dipped his head. "I'll give you a moment."

Alex swung out of the saddle and sprinted to the door. "Johanna?"

Bolting inside, he looked for a blue skirt, longing for a flash of her smile. But the taproom was empty.

He dashed into the kitchen, expecting her sweet face might be bowed over a pot of stew. Yet the hearth was cold, and had been for quite some time. The first hint of alarm prickled at the nape of his neck.

"Johanna!" He strode out of the room, calling her name again and again as he pounded up the stairs. After a search of the guest rooms, he lunged up to second floor, a highly improper action but so be it. He punched open the doors of the women's chambers. All empty. Barren, even. Only the leftover scent of the rose soap he'd given Johanna lingered like a slap to his face.

He charged down the stairs and tore out the back door, rising dread pumping his legs faster with each step. Flinging the stable door aside, he stalked in. The decrepit pony cart languished all alone. The horse was gone.

Alex turned in a slow circle, concocting all sorts of explanations, but the only thing he knew for sure soured in his gut.

Something was wrong. Very, *very* wrong.

He sped back to Ford and vaulted into his own saddle. "They're gone."

Ford eyed him where he stood near the front of his horse, neither mounting nor moving. "What do you mean?"

"The inn is empty, and by the looks of it, they're not intending to return. The hearth is cold. There are no personal effects anywhere. It's not right. Something's happened." His voice shook, but it couldn't be helped. "Come on! We've got to find them."

Ford's hand snaked out and grabbed hold of the headstall on Alex's horse. "Think, man. Don't just act without evaluating. It will accomplish nothing and more than likely waste your time."

He grimaced. What a hypocrite. He'd told Johanna the very same thing that day she'd struggled with the stable door. "You're right." He sucked in a huge breath. Spurge was his first guess, but not the only one. For all he knew Tanny Needler could've had a hand in their disappearance. "Let us go to the local magistrate. Perhaps he might know something."

"Now you're talking sense." Ford released his hold of Alex's horse and grabbed his own mount. Together they trotted back to the High

Street—where a familiar figure strolled.

"Mrs. Scott," he called as he dismounted. "A word, please."

Johanna's friend, Maggie, turned toward him, a wriggling babe in her arms. Beneath her bonnet brim, her forehead puckered, then cleared. "Oh, it's you, Mr. Morton."

He let the name slide, unwilling to spend one second more than needed to find Johanna. Forcing a calm tone to his voice, he asked, "Where is Johanna? Where has she gone?"

A small cry garbled in her throat. "You don't know? She and her family are on their way to St. Mary's."

Calm be hanged. The workhouse? But Johanna ought to have had more than enough money to pay her debt—unless Spurge had upped his asking price. Rage lit a fire, painting everything red. "Why? How?" His voice thundered even in his own ears.

Eyes wide, Mrs. Scott retreated a step, clutching her babe tighter.

Behind him, Ford grumbled an admonishment.

"I'm sorry." Alex ran a hand over his face, praying for peace. "Forgive me, but I must know everything. Please, Mrs. Scott."

She blinked, then lifted her chin. "Mr. Spurge called in his loan this morning. To my regret, I hadn't the extra funds to lend them."

"But there was no need. They had more than enough to pay off Mr. Spurge. Unless. . ." his gut sank. Unless the money he'd taken such care to hide had been stolen.

"Surely you are mistaken, sir. My husband is even now driving them to the workhouse. Hopefully it won't take long for them to pay back their debt, though I don't know how they'll manage once they get out and—where are you going?"

"Excuse me, Mrs. Scott," he called over his shoulder as he swung back up into the saddle. "But I have a wagon to catch."

CHAPTER THIRTY-EIGHT

Johanna stared at the dark stain marring the July afternoon. Behind a fence of black iron, St. Mary's grew larger with each turn of the wagon wheels. Situated outside of town in the middle of nothingness, the workhouse hunched like a beast, ready to stretch out a paw and claw in anyone who ventured too close.

A faint smile traced a ghostly pattern on her lips, and she lifted her chin despite the monster ahead. Losing the inn had been hard, but it hadn't been the end—and this wouldn't be either. Now that her worst fear had come to pass, surprisingly she wasn't as crushed as she'd imagined. The sun still shone, the wind still blew, and God yet reigned in the heavens. She lifted her face to the sky, and a peculiar kind of lightness filled her soul.

Could it be that the real demon tormenting her had never been this ugly brick building but her desperate act of holding on to things too tightly, things she had no right to hold on to in the first place?

The wagon lurched over a rock in the road, and she grabbed the side. Mam sat between her and Mr. Scott, wedged in safely. Behind, in the wagon bed, Thomas bumped around. None of them spoke, except for Thomas, whenever he spied another traveller on the road. This far out, though, it wouldn't be likely they'd see anyone.

Johanna patted Mam's leg. "With God's help, we'll weather this, Mam. I feel sure of it."

Mam's hand closed over hers. "I was tired of being an innkeeper anyway."

Johanna gasped. Why had her mother never shared that with her before? "What—?"

"Caw! Look at that cloud o' dust snaking up. Someone's riding hard." Thomas scrambled as best he could to the gate at the back.

For a moment, Johanna was tempted to turn around and focus on the approaching traveller instead of on the open gates ahead. But no, better to face her future—even a challenging one—head on.

"It might be. . .yes!" Thomas shouted. "It's Alex!"

Alex?

Her heart flipped. She yanked her hand from Mam's and jerked forward. "Stop the wagon, Mr. Scott."

The wheels barely slowed before she scrambled down to the dirt. Clutching her skirts, she ran to Alex.

"Hah! Look at her go." Thomas laughed.

Or was that her laughing? Her cheek hurt from smiling, but it couldn't be helped, not when the man she loved hefted his leg over his saddle and his boots hit the ground. She launched into his arms, and the world spun. Her feet left the ground as he swung her around and around, and she buried her face in his shirt. He smelled of hard riding and smoke, all man and muscle and strength. He'd come. He'd really come, just as he'd said. He'd kept his word and for that she wept with joy.

Too soon, he set her down and cupped her face with his hands, brushing away her stray tears with his big thumbs.

"You're here," she said, breathless. She covered his hands with hers, touching his warmth to make sure he was real, that she hadn't been taken by madness. Was she even now dreaming and the next bump of the wagon would jar her awake? "You're well and truly here."

His gaze swept over the remaining scrape on her cheek, and for a moment, his brow furrowed. But then as suddenly, he flashed a smile, brilliant on his sun-kissed face. "I told you I'd come for you, and looks as if I'm just in time."

"I hardly know what to believe anymore," she murmured.

"Then believe this. . .I love you, Johanna. I love you more than life." He bent and for a glorious eternity, his mouth brushed against hers.

"Eew!" Thomas screeched behind them.

She pulled away, smiling, shaking, so wild with emotion she'd fly away were it not for his firm hold on her hand.

With a smirk, Alex led her to the wagon. "Turn this wagon around, Mr. Scott, if you please."

Up on the seat, Mr. Scott lifted his hat and scratched the shorn hair beneath. "Can't. If I don't deliver 'em here," he hitched a thumb at the workhouse, "it'll be the gaol. You an' I both know they'd not last a week in that hole."

Mam frowned, though hard to tell if it were from Mr. Scott's threat or Alex's inappropriate kiss. "He's right, son. We have an obligation, one you cannot change by a simple turn of the wagon."

"There is no more obligation, Mrs. Langley. Your debt is paid in full, leastwise it will be by the time we return to town." Alex looked from Mam to her. "You are free."

Johanna's heart fluttered with abrupt understanding. "You paid it."

"I did, or rather one of my friends is seeing to it now." His gaze slipped from hers and met her mother's—and a queer twinkle in her eye glimmered.

Johanna batted his arm. "I believe, sir, there is much more for you to tell me."

His big grin disarmed her. "Ask me anything, and I'll tell you."

She couldn't help but smile back, and they stood, silent, breathless, beaming at each other as if no one else in the world watched.

"Caw!" Thomas cried. "Yer not going to kiss again, are you?"

"Good idea." His lips warmed her brow like a sweet benediction.

"Eew!"

"Thomas, leave them be." Mam's voice grumbled along with the wooden wheels as Mr. Scott turned the wagon about.

"Tell me, my love." Alex's voice was soft and low, a caress of the most intimate kind. "Instead of being an innkeeper's daughter, how would you like to be an innkeeper's wife?"

Her heart skipped a beat, or maybe more. She wasn't counting—and never would again. As this man's wife, beneath that gaze of love, she wouldn't care if they lived as kings or paupers, innkeepers or—she bit her lip. What exactly was he saying?

"But you're a lawman. Aren't you?"

"Not anymore." He shook his head, the ends of his hair grazing his collar and shaking loose bits of dust from his fast ride. "Thanks to the Coburns, Robbie in particular, I have more than enough funds to buy back the Blue Hedge and make it the finest inn in all of Dover."

"You would do that?" Tears welled in her eyes. "You would sacrifice your career and your money to purchase a run-down hovel of a building?"

The grin on his face broke as large and warm as the afternoon sun. "I would buy the moon and stars if that's what made you happy. Besides, no risk, no gain, right?"

The wagon pulled up alongside them, and he lifted her back to her perch next to Mam—but he didn't let go of her hand.

"You still haven't given me an answer."

Bending, she pressed her lips to the back of his fingers, despite the accompanying "Eew" that was sure to follow from Thomas.

"I can think of nothing better than to be an innkeeper's wife." She met Alex's gaze and held it. "My answer is yes."

HISTORICAL NOTES

Oak Apple Day

Oak Apple Day (sometimes called Royal Oak Day) is an old holiday that is still celebrated in some parts of England every May 29. Its roots go back to the year 1651, when King Charles II escaped the Roundhead army by taking cover in an oak tree. In commemoration, traditional celebrations include parades and the pinning of an oak leaf or an "oak apple" to the lapel in order to avoid a pinch. An oak apple (also called an oak gall) is caused by the larvae of a cynipid wasp. The gall looks a bit like an apple. Nowadays it is also a tradition to drink beer and eat plum pudding.

Bow Street Runners

The Bow Street Runners were the first fledgling police force in London. Founded in 1749 by magistrate Henry Fielding, the original team of men numbered only six. The officers never called themselves "runners," and in fact, considered the term derogatory. At first the men did not patrol the streets but merely delivered writs and arrested offenders as charged by the magistrate. Eventually the force grew to great proportions by expanding into a horse patrol and stretching their jurisdiction to all of England. With the creation of the Metropolitan Police in 1829, the runners eventually became incorporated into their ranks and were completely disbanded by 1839.

Congreve Rockets and the Napoleonic Wars

Believe it or not, rockets were used way back in the early nineteenth century. The Congreve rocket was developed in 1804 by William Congreve and experimentally tried first against a French fleet at Boulogne, France, in 1805. These were the days of Napoleon's threat against England. The rockets were gunpowder-propelled and used incendiary warheads. Think of a giant bottle-rocket and you'll have a rough mental image of one. They were launched from tubes set on special ladder-like frames and could be shot from land or sea. And lest you gloss over this, thinking such information has nothing to do with America, think again. You know the line in the US national anthem: *"And the rocket's red glare, the bomb's bursting in air, gave proof through the night that our flag was still there"*? Yeah, those were Congreve rockets.

ACKNOWLEDGMENTS

I can only do what I do because of the sweet support of some awesome people. Here are a few (though I'm bound to forget somebody). . .

Julie Klassen, you keep me on the Regency straight and narrow, my friend, and for that I'm grateful.

Elizabeth Ludwig, despite your ridiculous writing schedule, I am grateful you take the time to polish my work.

Shannon McNear, I promise I will learn about horses one day so you don't always have to fix my horsey blunders.

Ane Mulligan, your brainstorming is a welcome kick in the pants to get me started every time.

Chawna Schroeder, your keen eye for plausibility and plot holes is second to none.

Annie Tipton, you believe in me and my writing, which is a tough job but somebody's got to do it.

MaryLu Tyndall, you always make me ask why—and that's a *very* good thing.

My cheerleading squad: Linda Ahlmann, Stephanie Gustafson, Cheryl & Grant Higgins, Lucie Payne. . .y'all look so cute in your mini-skirts.

And last but not least, I couldn't do this without Mark, my expert in blowing things up and my best friend.

ABOUT THE AUTHOR

Michelle Griep has been writing since she first discovered blank wall space and Crayolas. She seeks to glorify God in all that she writes—except for that graffiti phase she went through as a teenager. She resides in the frozen tundra of Minnesota, where she teaches history and writing classes for a local high school co-op. An Anglophile at heart, she runs off to England every chance she gets under the guise of research. Really, though, she's eating excessive amounts of scones and rambling through some castle. Keep up with her adventures at michellegriep.com. She loves to hear from readers, so go ahead and rattle her cage.